Praise for *K*

"With lyrical prose, sparkling banter, a̶
two beautifully imperfect leads, *Kilt Trip* is as enchanting a̶
itself."
—Jen Devon, author of *Bend Toward the Sun*

"Move over, Jamie Fraser, because there's a new hot Scot in town.
Kilt Trip is an utterly charming enemies-to-lovers romance that will
make you laugh, swoon, and want to book your next trip to Scotland."
—Erin La Rosa, author of *Plot Twist*

"*Kilt Trip* may begin in the Scottish Highlands, but it will end up in
your heart. I swooned and sighed with Addie and Logan each time
they bantered on the tour bus or locked eyes in an ancient castle,
and fanned myself every time they did so much as brush hands.
Alexandra Kiley is a master not just at creating chemistry between
her characters, but in crafting a world so lush and enchanting that it
made me immediately want to book a flight to Scotland. I laughed,
I cried, and I cheered Slainte!"
—Amanda Elliot, author of *Sadie on a Plate*

"Impossible not to get swept away. You'll lose your heart to
Alexandra Kiley's stunning prose, breathless banter, and atmospheric
descriptions just as readily as Addie and Logan lose their hearts to one
another."
—Jessica Joyce, *USA TODAY* bestselling author of *You, with a View*

"Enemies-to-lovers perfection in an expertly rendered, ultra-romantic
setting, Alexandra Kiley's *Kilt Trip* is one of my favorite books of the
year. This stunning debut left me with an incredible book hangover
and lots of internet searches for plane tickets to Scotland. An
absolutely gorgeous read I'll return to again and again."
—Sarah Adler, author of *Mrs. Nash's Ashes*

"A deeply romantic and breathtaking escape... Readers will be
swooning and flocking to Scotland long after they've turned the last
page."
—Livy Hart, author of *Planes, Trains, and All the Feels*

"A poignant debut novel with the perfect balance of delicious banter and emotional depth and steeped in Scottish charm, *Kilt Trip* was a thrill to read."
—K.A. Tucker, internationally bestselling author of *The Simple Wild*

"Alexandra Kiley's debut is an enchanting, immersive vacation in book form. Sure to cure your wanderlust, *Kilt Trip* boasts a rugged Scotsman to swoon over and a heroine you can't help but root for. This one hits every beat of an enemies-to-lovers romance to utter perfection."
—Amy Lea, internationally bestselling author of *Exes and O's*

"Passionate and playful, *Kilt Trip* brings all the swoony and steamy goodness that readers crave in an enemies-to-lovers romance. Alexandra Kiley's debut is an absolute delight."
—Sarah Smith, author of *Faker* and *Simmer Down*

"*Kilt Trip* is funny, warm, and sweet. A delightful read!"
—Trish Doller, author of *Float Plan* and *Off the Map*

"*Kilt Trip* is such a charming and sure-footed debut from a promising new voice in romance. I fell in love with Addie, a woman on her own personal journey, and Logan, a big-hearted tour guide who knows how to rock a kilt, set against the dreamy backdrop of Scotland. This book made me feel cozy and cared for in all the best ways."
—Alicia Thompson, *USA TODAY* bestselling author of *With Love, from Cold World*

KILT TRIP

ALEXANDRA KILEY

CANARY STREET PRESS

CANARY
STREET
PRESS™

Recycling programs
for this product may
not exist in your area.

ISBN-13: 978-1-335-00929-6

Kilt Trip

Canary Street Press
22 Adelaide St. West, 41st Floor
Toronto, Ontario M5H 4E3, Canada
CanaryStPress.com

Printed in U.S.A.

For my grandma,
who encouraged me to explore the world.

1

Addie Macrae's internal compass was irreparably dam-aged. For all the traveling she did, and the relative ease of navigating a city with English street signs, Edinburgh's jigsaw puzzle of gray-toned buildings and twisting streets left her head spinning.

Under different circumstances she might've been swept away by the city's lantern-topped streetlights and cobblestone roads, but not while the architecture and charm conspired against her. She'd missed a full thirty minutes of her newest client's city tour, the last one before their meeting tomorrow.

If she was going to turn The Heart of the Highlands around, revamp their tours, and pull them from the brink of financial ruin, she needed to know what she was walking into. The thrumming in her chest slipped into the realm of heart palpitations, one tier below racing for a connecting flight.

Which she'd already done today.

Striding along another street lined with red and teal storefronts, she tugged at her collar, letting the chilled air slice through the humidity inside her plasticky yellow raincoat. Nothing in sight resembled a *staircase at the bottom of Calton Hill*—the starting point mentioned on the website.

Gigi, the irritatingly sunny voice of Google Maps, shouted, "Turn left." She was hopelessly laggy, sending Addie in one direction, then two minutes later changing her mind.

Addie followed another skinny tunnel between buildings constructed long before the invention of motor vehicles. It deposited her into an unmarked courtyard, paths fanning out in all directions.

"Rerouting."

Grinding her teeth, Addie restarted Gigi, tripped over a cobblestone, and cursed.

Side-eyeing the red battery icon on her phone, she checked the time again. *Dammit*. At this rate, she'd miss the entire itinerary.

Cars rumbled by on the wrong side of the road as she wound through the bustling downtown and crossed the construction zone that was the North Bridge. A light drizzle began to fall, dripping from her hood and curling the end of her blond braid. *Great*.

A low brick wall to her left did nothing to contain the old-growth trees threatening to hop the street. She walked right past a staircase tucked between the disheveled, leafless forest before backing up.

Begging to be missed, a miniature blue sign attached to a lamppost pointed up the stairs to Calton Hill. Addie shook her head. *How were tourists expected to find this?*

Her annoyance drowned out any relief at finding the tour.

As she headed toward the steps, her phone rang. *Boss Babe* lit up the screen. Devika filled all the roles in Addie's life: best friend, coworker, mother hen.

They were kindred spirits—always stayed late, snuck champagne and slippers into the office to work through the holidays, and sent each other postcards from airports around the world. Every time one of them got to a new destination, they checked in. Like the lone-women-travelers' buddy system.

In the haze of lost luggage and misdirection, Addie had forgotten. She answered, "Sorry. I'm here safely, although sans suitcase." Her green hardside—scuffed, covered in stickers, and affectionately referred to as Frank—had taken an impromptu side trip without her permission.

"That blows. Do they know when it'll be back?"

Addie started up the stairs, dragging her fingers over the sculpted lion's head at the base of the shiny black handrail. A tower in the shape of an old-fashioned spyglass rose out of the knotted trees above her. "Hopefully tonight, or I'll be wearing my airport-acquired rain gear to my meeting."

Devika laughed. "What's on the books for today?"

The answer to their running joke was, of course, always, *work*. Six months ago, her mentor, Marc, started a new agency—Dawsey Travel Consulting—and took Devika and Addie with him. It could hardly be called *poaching* when she would follow them to the ends of the earth. Addie wanted to be them when she grew up.

Devika was a powerhouse karaoke song. She brought people to their feet with her magnetic presence and got shit done like a boss.

Marc was quieter, more serious, but in an industry full of power-hungry men, he always listened, remembered vegetarian *and* gluten-free options, and cut off interrupters with a stern "Addie wasn't done talking." He was the one person who'd taken a chance on her when she'd been at her lowest, who'd taught her how to keep moving when she wanted to give up.

They were in a million different time zones right now, hustling to build a name for themselves in the competitive world of travel consulting. With ironclad non-competes from their old firm, their client roster currently consisted of Marc's friends and whatever referrals their favorite clients could muster.

Every project had to go perfectly to make their new business turn a profit. The future of their venture depended on it. And as the junior partner—the first one to be cut if things went sideways—Addie's job did, too.

She scanned the spiderweb of paths at the top of the hill.

A random cannon sat in the median. This had to be the right spot. "Research," Addie said. "I'm already docking them three points for starting the tour in an obscure location."

There. A group of ten or so people carrying colorful umbrellas huddled around a man in a kilt. *Bingo.*

"Are you *spying*?"

Her stomach clenched at the censure in Devika's voice. "I've got this." Maybe it was the jet lag making her a bit desperate, or the fear of what would happen if she failed, but she'd take whatever edge she could get. "Besides, gathering intel isn't illegal," Addie defended, even though Devika was right to worry.

Rebuilding trust with the client took time she didn't have, but this was a calculated risk. As a rule, executives didn't take kindly to corporate espionage in any form. However, executives were also rarely objective about their own tours. They chalked lagging sales up to *uninspired marketing* or *internet algorithms*, never to generic itineraries, up-charging for headphones on an audio tour, or rambling guides.

Metrics on destination costs and ticket prices were important, but the way people responded to their guides told an indisputable story. One day trip could show her more about a company's weak spots than five board meetings combined.

"You better hope you blend in."

Addie bit her lip as she looked down at her attire. Between the yellow raincoat and poppy-splashed wellies, she looked about as unobtrusive as a knockoff Paddington Bear waving a sign that read *I'm crashing your tour.* But it was fine, she could totally pass as a tourist. "You're not helping at all. I have to go be sneaky."

Devika laughed and made the word *bye* last for three syllables.

Addie moved to the back of the group where two people speaking Japanese, having clearly forgotten their raincoats, wore see-through Heart of the Highlands–branded ponchos.

Practical and effective swag, 1 point.

Gigi shouted, "Keep right at the fork!"

All eyes swung to Addie and heat flooded her cheeks as she struggled to turn off the speaker. "Is this the Hidden Gems tour?" she asked the approaching guide. "I got lost..." Addie looked up into crinkling gray eyes.

Whoa.

Curls fell over his forehead, a wavy sea of honey and bronze. On anyone else, she'd have said he was in dire need of a haircut, but it worked for him—matched the close-trimmed beard and the power of his shoulders.

He would be intimidatingly rugged if he wasn't draped in clear plastic.

"Aye. Welcome. Are you Heather Munro?"

Her gaze slipped down to his navy blue and forest green kilt... *Damn.*

She'd never considered herself one to swoon over a kilt, but his work boots and rounded calves were doing something to her stomach she couldn't feasibly attribute to her bumpy flight. The navy cable-knit sweater, too—much better than the frilly pirate shirt that usually accompanied this getup.

Although, it did little to set their guides apart.

Gimmicky uniform, minus 2 points...on anyone else.

The last words he said filtered back to her, and heat crept up her neck. *Shit.*

"Oh, yes. Hi. That's me." Addie was more accustomed to sleeping on planes than in her own bed, but she was clearly more jet-lagged than she'd realized if she couldn't remember her own fake name.

The guide's lips curved into an amused smile. "I'm Logan."

She could tell a lot from a handshake.

Crushing: domineering and a pain in the ass to work with.

Limp: kind but required vast emotional resources to make decisions.

Wet-fish: well...that was never a good sign.

But Logan's firm handshake was warm. It said: *I know what I want. I'm not afraid to ask for help or entertain new ideas.*

Not that it mattered. She'd be working with the owner and his son, not the guides.

His grin sent tingles whispering over her skin as he dropped her hand and turned back to the group. "This way to the National Monument of Scotland, built to commemorate those who fought in the Napoleonic Wars." Logan gestured to the Parthenon-style structure missing two and a half sides of pillars. "Or, as it's affectionately called, Scotland's Shame. As you can see, funding ran out rather quickly." A few snickers and an abundance of smiles followed his remarks.

"Edinburgh is nicknamed the Athens of the North, and these buildings celebrate our architectural feats and enlightenment. But long before the monuments were constructed, Calton Hill was a site for many pagan rituals. My favorite is Beltane, the Celtic festival hailing the reappearance of summer and the fertility of the land. Fire represents the return of the light, and revelers celebrate in its glow."

Logan could have described the architecture, the historical figures, or the politics at the time of construction. Addie had been on that kind of tour in the real Athens and knew firsthand how hard it was to keep guests' interest with dry facts. Instead, Logan's tales of rejoicing and fire, spirits and drums, enthralled the tourists. The group huddled around him, his voice low and soothing like it'd wrapped around everyone and pulled them in.

If all the guides were this good, Addie wouldn't need to bring in a story-crafting coach; Logan would make a dishwasher manual sound interesting.

Engaging the guests, 3 points.

"If you fancy a more strenuous walk, you can try Arthur's Seat." Logan gestured to the hill in the distance rising as if the earth had pushed it up in three slanted tiers. "Holyrood Palace is down below."

"Is that where the Queen used to stay?" a pink-haired, twentysomething asked.

"Aye, it's the royal Scottish residence."

"Is it on the tour?"

From Addie's research, The Heart of the Highlands tours didn't stop at the palace, Edinburgh Castle, or the Royal Mile connecting the two. All missed opportunities.

The way their outdated website—the first thing getting an overhaul—boasted about hidden gems was almost haughty, like the major attractions were beneath them. Logan appeared to be of the same mind as he brushed off the bid. "It's a fifteen-minute walk if you're interested," he said, releasing the group to climb on the National Monument.

Skipping major attractions, minus 5 points.

There was definitely a market for off-the-beaten-path tours… but it wasn't usually profitable.

Highlights of every country had the broadest market appeal, which meant the highest chance of success for their clients and Addie's company. She needed a portfolio project to win new business. Itineraries with easily recognizable destinations to show the value Dawsey Travel Consulting brought to the table.

She'd recommend scrapping this tour in favor of the city-center hot spots. Who came to Edinburgh and didn't want to visit the castle?

Addie wandered to the gravel path at the edge of the site, rubbing her frozen hands together. The smell of autumn's leftover leaves hung heavy in the chilled, December air.

Below her, the hill tumbled down to sandstone buildings pressed together all the way to the silver coast as the last rays of light settled on slate-peaked roofs.

Logan stopped beside her, his hands clasped behind his back. Their eyes met, but instead of the reflex smile that accompanied accidental eye contact with strangers, a tiny jolt of electricity zipped from him to her, supercharging her nervous system. Logan's eyebrows lifted as if he felt it, too.

Addie scuffed her boot over a clump of grass. "You can see all the way to the ocean," she said, blaming the panoramic view for stealing all her insightful commentary.

"The Firth of Forth. It's an estuary that meets the North Sea," he said, like he truly cared that she understood the difference.

Her lips twitched to hold back a smile. "Is that like a fjord?"

"Similar…" He turned and narrowed his eyes. "You're taking the piss, aren't you?"

Addie grinned, and the reappearance of Logan's dimple stirred up some fluttery nonsense in her chest.

Small talk came easily to her—a helpful by-product of traveling so frequently for her job—but Logan's intense eye contact and stubbled jawline knocked her off-kilter. She rolled the nylon strap of her shoulder bag between her fingers and kept her attention resolutely on the estuary.

Logan collected the group, walking backward on the path. As they passed the newly renovated observatory, Logan chronicled its two-hundred-year history.

Detailed commentary on historical buildings no one really cares about, minus 2 points.

"The proper, professional photos from Calton Hill are taken from right over here. Now, I want you to watch your shoes as we walk this way. Don't spoil the big reveal."

Logan's face held the suppressed excitement of someone leading a friend into a surprise party. "Throughout our history, Calton Hill has been the location of our most important festivals. This place ties us to our past, to the mystical beauty our land is known for, to the medieval city that has changed over time but still bears marks of our history and achievements. It's a reminder of our roots, of where we come from."

Addie swallowed past the dryness in her throat. She couldn't remember having roots. They grew shallow in the desert.

When Logan talked about community and history, though, she could almost remember the allure, that longing she'd doused years ago.

"A bit farther." Logan stepped back with wide arms as if hosting his own HGTV show. "Okay, now look."

Gasps erupted from the group like drunk people watching fireworks. They scrambled to grab phones and cameras.

Addie gazed out at the view. The Dugald Stewart Monument dominated the foreground, like a tall and skinny stone carousel. Nestled between hills and water, the city spread out below them. A pink-lit Ferris wheel spun at the base of a blackened spire, and a clock tower's pearl face glowed in the distance.

"We call this the gloaming, where time is suspended between day and night."

Addie closed her eyes and breathed in, a hint of salt lingering in the humid air. An undercurrent buzzed lightly in the breeze, a glimmer of mysticism, like the leftover magic of standing stones and faeries.

Edinburgh Castle ruled the skyline—a silhouette against the golden light hanging on the horizon, balancing the purple sky above. The blush of the waning light echoed those early mornings in the desert, so far away, and so long ago.

Once every fall, Addie's mom had climbed into her bed before dawn and whispered, "Rise and shine, baby."

Her dad made hot chocolate in the light of the range hood, while Addie dressed in layers of winter coats. They squished into the front seat of their beat-up pickup truck and drove into the desert. The headlights shone on worn-down center lines, the stars a twinkling map, as they searched for wonder, their wheels kicking up red dirt in billowing shadows behind them.

They stepped into the cold morning air, and Addie's mom wrapped a black-and-white plaid blanket around her shoulders as her dad handed her a thermos. They made their way past boulders and scrubby bushes, only the sound of their footsteps filling the air, as if the dawn held too much power and they'd wreck it with words.

With mittened hands curled around cocoa cups, they settled on rocky seats.

Off in the distance, in the bowl of the valley, hot-air balloons filled, glowing like rainbow bubbles expanding in the night.

Only when all the balloons hung in the sky, embracing the pink clouds of morning, did they speak.

Her dad wanted to explain the physics of flight, but her mom shushed him. Eyes shining, she said, "Watching them rise, one after another, it feels like magic. Like anything is possible."

After Addie's mom died, when her dad had shut himself away and that feeling was nowhere to be found, Addie would drive their white pickup into the desert. The patchwork of rough cracks on the leather seats scraped her bare legs, and she had to pound the radio to keep the static down, but anything was better than the crushing silence of the house. She drove those same back roads, the ones the desert might reclaim at any moment, the pavement rippling with summer heat, searching for the wonder she was terrified she'd never find again.

Addie pressed the heel of her hand hard against the twisting ache under her breastbone.

The brush of plastic against her arm startled her, and she took half a step back, blinking fast.

Logan tipped his head, a curl falling to the side. His eyes held a quiet earnestness, soft around the edges, like he could see the memories splashed all over her face. Like he was giving her permission, somehow, to give in to the pull.

She drew in a deep breath, the cold snagging deep in her lungs.

The woman next to Addie whispered to her partner, "Let's go to the castle tomorrow."

Addie cleared her throat and refocused on the tourists who'd started to mill about.

Edinburgh was full of stray reminders waiting to jump out and snatch her back into that old grief. But she wasn't here searching for Scotland's magic or the disarming beauty in her mom's old stories.

She was here to work.

And while this was a nice photo op, these people would share a selfie at the castle with turrets and ramparts—or whatever they were called—in the background.

Ninety percent ranked the Royal Mile favorably on TripAdvisor. She couldn't in good conscience give Logan full marks for a tour that barely broke Edinburgh's Top 25 Attractions, while he dangled the top destination in front of them.

As they headed back down the hill, Addie compiled a mental report card.

Way off the beaten path, minus 5 points.

Appealing to a wide range of ages and nationalities, not only young Australian backpackers, 2 points.

No stops at a gift shop, minus 2 points.

"I hope you enjoyed our time together. If you have any more questions, you're welcome to join me for a dram at my favorite pub down the road. Enjoy Scotland."

Recommending local restaurants near the end of the trip, 1 point.

Addie had never heard of a guide socializing after the tour. He might be highly incentivized, but she got the distinct impression he simply appreciated the company.

Whatever the reason, it was a genius sales strategy. It might be difficult convincing other clients to pay guides for additional tour time, but there was no doubt about the effect on this group. They followed Logan down the hill like ducklings—six, seven, eight, yes, all nine of them. She'd bet her wellies they would recommend this company to everyone they knew.

Making guests feel like friends, 10 points.

She shifted her weight. She shouldn't follow. Didn't need to stand out to Logan in case he told his boss she'd been there.

But it was in her best interest to be curious about Logan—professionally, of course. The promise of whisky and a warm pub after a hectic travel day was simply a bonus. Besides, what was the harm in one drink?

She joined the end of the line in her rubber-duck raincoat. Logan wouldn't even notice her.

2

Logan ranked the success of his trips by the tourists'
faces. Glassy-eyed from Scotch whisky—at least a six. Smiling at their own Scottish-folklore jokes—a sure eight. He lived for the groups that came for immersion in his land and history.

The tour today was a solid ten, due to one woman in particular.

Heather sat on the far end of the community table, her blond hair curling around her temples and backlit by the hearth. She chatted with the mother and daughter from Spain, all big hand gestures and bright laughter that continued to snag his attention from Ling asking the most direct route to Skye.

As Logan detailed the complicated public transport to the remote island, he sank into the comforting bustle around him. Nothing about this pub had changed in the ten years since he and his brother Jack had known exactly how many drunken, shuffling steps it took from the brass-plated front door to the university residence halls. His old friend, Gavin, tended bar like always. The scent of stale beer greeted him at every visit, the shelf of books ringing the perimeter of the room remained un-dusted, and the same tweed-outfitted men congregated in front of the footie match.

Logan had brought thousands of tourists through this pub over the years—they'd end up at The White Hart if left to their own guidebook-influenced devices—but he'd never been quite so pleased to see someone settle in here as he was watching Heather unwind her scarf and roll her shoulders against the heat of the fire.

His favorite tourists were the ones who came here for an experience and a connection instead of rushing to cram in the sites. There was no greater joy than knowing someone carried a piece of his world in their hearts when they returned home.

Heather understood the beauty of living in the moment, forgoing the distraction of a camera, and gazing out at the city as if his stories had moved her. When she'd pressed her hand against her chest, taking in the skyline, the same thrill had pulsed through him as the first time his dad had taken him up Calton Hill.

She undid her braid and the firelight sifted through the blond strands, damp from the rain. Her dark, wistful eyes conjured to his mind a selkie—the seal folk—a beautiful creature of an-cient legend rising from the sea.

She wasn't alluring, she was fucking ethereal.

A glass shattering across the room and the subsequent "Ooh" from the patrons dragged him from his musings, and Logan re-focused on the tourists gathered round him. He wasn't one to cheat his guests from the sights and stories they might otherwise miss. "Have you heard the selkie's tale?" he asked the group.

Met with interested expressions and elbows placed on the worn wooden table, he began. "These mythological beings, who transform from seal to human and back again, are said to be graceful and enchanting. Legend has it, a lonely man, tired of returning every night to a house that was never a home, came upon an astonishingly beautiful selkie sunbathing on a rocky shore."

Heather watched him, amusement dancing in her eyes. And maybe something heavier, like interest. She dragged her thumbnail across her bottom lip in a particularly distracting manner.

"He stole her sealskin, and because each skin is unique and irreplaceable, the selkie was forced to stay with him. She made a fine wife, but she longed for the ocean. Whenever the man was away, she searched the house for her skin and, one day, found it hidden in the rafters. She disappeared forever, and the man lived out his days with a broken heart. A selkie will always return to the sea."

While the woman across from him cooed over the sad story, Heather looked at him from underneath her lashes as she sipped her drink. Her tongue teased the corner of her lip to catch a drop of whisky, and his blood pounded in his veins.

There was a reason they called whisky the *water of life* in Gaelic.

For the next hour, Logan shared stories and answered travel questions, unsuccessfully keeping his gaze off Heather. By the time the last tourist clapped him on the shoulder in parting, she was still at the far end of the table, flipping through a stack of postcards.

It was his duty as the guide to check in with all guests before they left, but the excuse sounded flimsy at best as he slid down the bench. He couldn't help imagining his knees brushing hers under the table or stop himself from leaning in on his elbows and closing the space between them.

"Can I help you with anything before you leave?"

"I'm waiting for my suitcase. It took a side trip to Berlin."

"Mind if I join you? I'm sticking around a bit." He tipped his head toward his mate sliding open a keyboard stand on the makeshift stage. "My friend's in the band."

"I take it you come here a lot?"

He nodded, raising his hands to encompass the room. "Best pub in Edinburgh."

"And best kickbacks?" Heather quirked an eyebrow.

"No. But they do appreciate the business. Tourists spend more on drinks than these chaps—" he jerked a thumb at the driving-capped group currently pounding their fists on the tables to punctuate the Hibernian FC fight song "—cheering for whoever's playing against Manchester United."

Heather's smile lit up her face, as blinding as the first clear day of spring.

Logan gestured to the russet-haired barkeep. "The pub's been in Gavin's family for generations. I'm happy to help in whatever small way I can."

Jack and Logan had met him the first time they'd come in. They knew all about the anxiety Gavin dealt with keeping his family business afloat while supporting his ailing father living upstairs.

Heather settled her chin on her fist and studied him. "How long have you been guiding?" she asked.

"Och, it feels like forever."

Since the early days on their dad's tours, when they could barely see out the window of the coach, he and his brothers had planned to run The Heart of the Highlands together. Carry on the family legacy. Logan never questioned their future.

But Jack and Reid had.

If Logan hadn't wanted to leave his mark on the family business, if he hadn't pushed them to invest in whisky tours, if he hadn't stepped out of line… He scrubbed a hand over his face. Stewing over his mistakes and why his brothers left him to fail alone got him nowhere.

"Did you grow up around here?" she asked.

He didn't quite know what to make of the interview questions. From someone else, he'd assume she was a bit nervous, but that didn't fit the woman in front of him. Her posture exuded confidence, her bright eyes discerning.

"Born and raised in Edinburgh. My family's all here." But he didn't want to talk about the lot of them at the moment. Logan lifted his chin to the pile of postcards she'd been shuffling. "What have you got there?"

"I send my best friend postcards from every place I visit." Her eyes glimmered with humor as she turned the stack toward Logan. "What do you think?"

The plaid-printed card read *Kilt: It's what happened to the last bloke who called it a skirt.*

Logan narrowed his eyes at the card and then at her. "Clever," he said dryly, playing her game, and the corners of her lips tipped up.

She flipped to the next card featuring a cartoon bagpiper captioned *Pack Yer Bags.*

"A highly overrated instrument, if I'm being honest."

"Mr. Scotland himself doesn't like bagpipes," she said, shaking her head and tsking.

He bit the inside of his cheek to keep from smiling as she slid the card behind the rest. *"The haggis is offal good?"* he read, furrowing his eyebrows just to see her grin. He couldn't deny the warmth spreading through him was from more than the whisky.

"It sounds even better when you say it."

With an amused grunt, Logan swiped the stack of postcards from Heather's grasp. "Give me those." He turned the card so she could see the two kilted men tossing bread in a lake for Nessie and leveled her with a mock-chastening scowl.

"What, they have it all wrong? She only eats canned shrimp?"

"And irreverent tourists who wander too close to the water."

Heather's cheeks pulled up into a hidden smile, and perfectly straight teeth pressed down into the curve of her full bottom lip. A primal urge to do the same coursed through him. Logan pushed the irrational desire away, focusing all his attention on thumbing through the remaining cards.

He Frisbeed one across the table with a huff, and she caught the paper-doll Scotsman before it slipped to the floor. Naked but for a fig leaf and two socks, the card provided punch-out clothes and accessories including a pint, a tam-o'-shanter, and a black Scottie dog.

"I agree. It's the clear winner."

"That's a fine representation of Scotland you have there, lass." Logan tapped the cards into a stack against the table and slid them to her. "You can send these, but the Royal Mail will most likely destroy them. Might as well use them as fuel," he teased.

Waving the paper doll, she said, "Maybe I'll keep it. I always was partial to a man with a sporran."

The wooden bench creaked as Logan shifted to ease the expansiveness ballooning in his chest. He'd been initiated in the ways of flirtatious travelers ages ago. It came with the territory and the kilt. Starring in some American girl's *Outlander* fantasy imploded when she inevitably went back home—he'd learned that the hard way at nineteen and hadn't dallied with a guest since—and yet there was something different about Heather that made him linger.

She made him feel light. Reminded him why he loved this job when most days it felt like the weight of the business on his shoulders might crush him.

Between her raincoat and her smile, she was sunshine. And sunshine never went unnoticed in Scotland.

"Can I buy you a drink?" He wouldn't get carried away, but he was undeniably intrigued.

3

The dim light in the pub cast a cozy, intimate glow over the room. The TVs—tellies, Addie corrected herself—blared in the background with the clipped tones of soccer—er, *football*—announcers, and rowdy patrons yelled at the screens. Even the chairs were upholstered in red-and-green plaid as if to say *Welcome to Scotland.*

Relinquishing their hold on the community table, she and Logan settled on stools at the bar. Her brain whirred with all the reasons this was a bad idea. Definitely no way to stay inconspicuous. But maybe it was too late, anyway. It was also a drink, not an invitation back to his place—which, under different circumstances, she might consider.

They were simply two people used to meeting strangers, well-matched in harmless flirting.

Addie let herself sink into the buoying force of a new connection. Exploring, seeking, meeting new people, it kept at bay the deep sadness that had filled so many years. She frequented enough bars and restaurants that the prickly awareness of eating alone didn't bother her anymore, but she wasn't wasting a chance to chat and share a drink.

Especially with someone so damn charming.

"What are you having?" He pushed the hair out of his face with a sweep of his fingers. His bicep flexed, even under the bulkiness of his sweater.

Good thing her contract didn't have a clause against ogling the tour guides.

"Benromach, please."

Logan's eyebrows arched. "An American who knows her whisky."

"I know what I like." Before she got swept away by this man's accent and the warmth in his gaze and this drink turned into something it couldn't, she refocused. "So do you tour all year round?"

"Aye. Winter's the best time to visit Scotland. We have it all to ourselves." Logan's lazy smile curled around her like cocoa steam in predawn air.

He turned in his seat to face her more fully, their knees interlocking. His kilt bowed between his legs, bunching slightly where her knee pushed against it, exposing a sliver of muscle. She should've twisted away, but too much of her brain was distracted calculating the exact distance between their thighs. Centimeters was a good metric. They were in the UK, after all.

The bartender set their drinks in front of them, the tap of the glass against the polished wood startling her. She tore her gaze away from where Logan's kilt rode up.

He raised his drink to Addie. *"Then catch the moments as they fly, and use them as ye ought, man: Believe me, happiness is shy, and comes not ay when sought, man."* He leaned in conspiratorially. "That's Robbie Burns for you."

Trying to drown the lightness blooming in her stomach, she clinked her glass against his and sipped her favorite Scotch whisky. The smoky flavor tasted even better in Scotland.

In a life of busy airports and high-stakes board meetings, where so much was a blur of stress hormones or first-day-of-school jitters, it was rare to have an encounter like this, where time seemed to slow and stretch. Logan didn't look at his phone or check his watch. She could bask in his attention. Settle in and stay a while.

"Are you here for business or pleasure?"

The way the last word rolled off his tongue, that lilting brogue…

Oh, shit.

Wait.

Panic tingled through her limbs. She couldn't tell him she was here for work.

"Uh, a heritage trip…in part. This used to be my mom's favorite place." Her stomach curled around the impulsive answer.

Addie had resolutely avoided Scotland. She didn't want to think about the graduation trip they didn't get to take or find the untamed wilderness was little more than a folktale that didn't live up to the magical stories her mom had woven.

"*Used to be?* What kind of place could knock Scotland from the podium?" Logan asked.

Addie looked down at her clasped hands. "She passed away." More than ten years later, and the words still scraped her throat on their way out.

For someone who traveled light, Addie carried a hell of a lot of baggage.

Logan's large hand, calloused and comforting, covered hers. "I'm so sorry." His eyes were as warm and calming as a full glass of whisky, lowering her inhibitions enough that she wanted to tell him all her sad stories.

But if Addie had learned anything, it was that no one liked the Sad Girl. People withdrew when she talked about her past, and she didn't need to burden this handsome stranger. She pulled away, forcing her mouth into a semblance of a smile and spun the cardboard coaster on the shiny bar top. "It was a long time ago."

The arrival of an oversize plate of nachos interrupted whatever Logan was going to say.

When Gavin turned to the next waiting patron, Addie spread her hands in a gesture of outrage. "What kind of pub is this? Where's the haggis? The fish 'n' chips?" she asked, steering them back to lighthearted fun.

"There's a nice minced pie, if you're not interested." Logan tugged the plate closer to himself.

"Oh, no, I'm interested," Addie said, letting the double meaning hang in the air and appreciating the slight pink flush creeping up Logan's neck. "But I'm a tough crowd. I grew up in New Mexico. It's in the southwest—"

"Near Mexico?"

"Smart-ass." She scooped a chip out from the bottom of the pile, careful not to notice Logan's lips quirk or the reappearance of that smile line. She bit into the tortilla chip with perfectly melted cheese and groaned. When was the last time she'd had anything resembling Mexican food?

"Is New Mexico home for you, then?"

She wiped salt from her bottom lip. "Boston, but I'm hardly ever there." Addie's apartment was basically a personal laundromat with a bonus bedroom.

"Ah, a free spirit, then?"

More like a restless, wandering soul. But that wasn't something to bring up on a first date—not that this was a first date. *Work function, Macrae.* "Something like that."

Logan's eyes bored into hers, like he was trying to piece her together, to understand what would make someone that way.

Before she could stop this promising beginning of an inquisition in its tracks, Logan tilted his head and said, "Sounds a bit lonely."

Addie's pulse beat too fast and too loud. This light flirtation had veered way off course.

She wasn't *lonely*. She chose this life.

"I've been to seventy countries. And I meet amazing people all over the world. I love traveling," she said defensively.

Logan held her gaze for a full scrape of a barstool against the hardwood floor, as if deciding whether to press further. Then his hands moved to the edge of his seat, and he leaned back, physically giving her space. "Aye, we have that in common."

Relief loosened her shoulders, and she dragged a chip through the heap of sour cream.

"Tell me this. What's your favorite city with a castle, historic university, and a scenic old town, all surrounded by stunning hills?" He arched his hand through the air as if painting a picture of Edinburgh.

Addie grinned at the obvious maneuver to steer the conversation away from a topic she didn't want to discuss. "Heidelberg."

Logan dropped his arm on the back of Addie's chair and hung his head. "Och, lass." Her body flushed the second he moved into her space. Made her feel day-drunk-at-a-baseball-game buzzy.

She liked the way he called her *lass*. A smart guiding move for a man who looked like a modern-day Highlander—she knew that was all it was. But it felt like they'd leapfrogged ahead in a friendship, straight to the nicknaming stage. It made her feel like more than a passing acquaintance. Like she might be someone he remembered past this afternoon.

She would certainly remember him.

When he straightened, shifting closer, she caught a faint trace of his cologne—pine and leather—and her breath hitched. Their gazes tangled up, but her phone buzzing on the bar top distracted them both.

The message she'd waited for all afternoon didn't give her quite the satisfaction it should've. "My luggage is back at the airport. I should get going."

Logan tilted his head as if deciding something, then reached behind the bar to grab a pen. He scribbled on the back of a coaster and slid it across the sticky bar. "Call me if you get lost again," he said with a wink that flipped her stomach.

She huffed out a laugh at his teasing.

He gestured for the bill to the bartender who shook his mop of auburn curls, and Logan bowed his head in thanks. She imagined that quiet communication happened every time Logan came in.

He stood up and pulled the strap of his bag over his head, his shoulder muscles rolling and the hem of his shirt riding up. "Enjoy the sights."

She absolutely was.

Addie watched his hips sway as he wove through the haphazardly placed tables to the exit, raising a hand to the old men taking a break from shouting at the TV to bid him farewell.

She grabbed the paper-doll Scotsman and wrote Devika a note on the back: *Can't confirm the real-life likeness, but sure wouldn't mind finding out. Xoxo*

It was nice to have someone to bail her out from a city that might swallow her whole, but even as she added his number to her Contacts under *Logan Hot Scottish Tour Guide*, she knew she wouldn't use it.

She didn't need a distraction while she was here. There was too much riding on this project. Marc trusted her with a personal contact, not just a referral. Addie wouldn't let him think for a second he'd made a mistake.

She tucked away her phone and threw back the rest of her drink, hoping the father-son duo she'd meet tonight would be one-fifth as charming as Logan.

4

With Frank in tow, Addie hailed a cab from the airport.
The jet lag that had mysteriously vanished in the pub settled in
Addie's bones in the back seat of the too-hot car.

Marc and Neil—the owner of The Heart of the Highlands—
went way back, and Neil had offered Addie his son's spare room,
insisting she live like a local. Since that might be nice—sometimes
hotel rooms had all the appeal of five-day-old Chinese food—
Addie had agreed.

But she also wasn't clueless. The last thing she wanted to do
was extend this endless day, but if she got even a single iota of
that empty-parking-lot-at-night feeling from Jack, she'd check
into a hotel. Marc would understand.

The cab stopped in front of a block of row houses Addie could
barely make out through the raindrops streaking down the window. Reddish bricks Tetrised their way up to the gray shingled
roofline. Four steps bracketed by wrought iron handrails led to
the door of each unit from the tiny hedgerow-bordered lawns.
The stacked bay windows capped off the charm.

She thanked the driver and opened the cab door into a blast of rain, her red umbrella ready to open like a shield.

As she tugged Frank out of the cab, the wind grabbed and ripped at the umbrella, flipping the whole thing inside out until it resembled a palm tree in the middle of a hurricane. The rain stung Addie's cheeks, and the broken umbrella knocked her off balance with every gust of wind, dragging what little energy she still possessed from her muscles.

Frank scuffled with the cobblestones and Addie yanked the handle like the leash of an ill-disciplined Rottweiler. Addie's hood blew off, icy rain streaming down her neck.

She fought the impulse to tip her head back and scream into the deluge.

Tussling with the metal arms of the umbrella, she made it into the refuge of the building. When she finally restrained it with an aggressive Velcro maneuver, she made the mistake of looking up the steep stairs that disappeared around the corner.

Addie slumped back against the door.

This day.

By the time she stood in front of flat 206, she was red-faced and panting.

Addie's knock was answered by who she assumed was Jack, a man about her age with dark hair wearing a sky blue button-up and thick-framed glasses. He gaped at her as if she'd crawled up from the depths of the sea before rearranging his features into a friendly smile. "You must be Addie."

"Yes. Thank you for letting me stay with you." Her attempt at shaking off the rain in the stairwell was useless. A lake-size puddle came in with her.

"You're more than welcome," Jack said.

A woman in a plum-colored fisherman sweater bustled to the door, a look of deep concern etched around her soft eyes. "Oh, you poor dear. Jack, fetch her a towel. There are clean ones on the rack."

"It's my flat, Mum. I know where the towels are."

Addie suppressed a grin at Jack's eye roll.

"I'm Gemma, and this is my husband, Neil." She gestured to the man with a push-broom mustache, Argyle sweater vest, and kind smile currently crowding Jack out as he pushed past to get the towel.

"Nice to meet you." Addie smiled too wide to cover up her racing pulse. She didn't look or feel presentable in the least, and she needed to impress these people.

Gemma clucked over the broken umbrella while Neil said, "Let me get that," taking her yellow jacket and hanging it on a wobbly wooden rack. He ushered her deeper into the warm space. "We're delighted you're here. Marc had such wonderful things to say, and well…we've gotten into a bit of a bind. I've been running this business for thirty-five years, and money's always been tight but manageable—"

Jack returned and handed her a white towel. "Dad, she's been traveling all day." His tortoiseshell glasses glinted with the motion of his exasperated headshake. Addie gave him an appreciative smile. As excited as she was to get to work, she needed a shower and a solid night's sleep first.

"Of course, of course." Neil took a step back with a self-deprecating smile at his overeagerness.

Addie dabbed her face and wound the towel around the bottom of her hair. "Sorry for the monsoon I brought in with me." She wasn't sure if using the towel on the floor would be polite or frowned upon.

"Och, the weather's just faffing around. Wait until February," Neil said.

She'd better be long gone by then.

Gemma placed a hand on Addie's shoulder. "Let's get you settled."

"Yes. I'll give you the quick tour," Jack said. "Here's the living room." He gestured to the leather couch hugging the back wall and the love seat framing the fireplace. An overstuffed bookshelf stood in the corner. "You're welcome to anything in the lending library." Addie immediately imagined curling up in the oversize reading chair tucked into the alcove of the bay window.

Just not tonight or she'd end up sleeping there.

Gemma straightened Jack's collar as he moved past her, and he swatted her away. "Mum," he pleaded. "Through there's the kitchen." He pointed to the open doorway and picked Frank up, dripping water down the hall. "And here's your room."

Addie studied him while he dug in his pocket and handed her a set of keys. "That's for the flat, and this one for your room locks from the inside." Jack wasn't giving Addie any bad vibes with his brotherly demeanor, especially with his parents fluttering around, but the extra safety measure settled any reservations she had about this setup.

Gemma brushed past Jack into the bedroom, tweaking his collar again on the way and earning a heavy sigh. She waved Addie in. "We have three boys, and I always wanted to decorate a room with flowers."

"Oy, are you giving this tour of *my* flat, or am I?"

Neil's mustache snuffled as he tried unsuccessfully to hide a smile from his wife.

"You didn't need to go to all this trouble on my account," Addie said.

"Jack rents this room. It was a perfect excuse for some updating." Gemma linked arms with Neil. "You're helping my boys make changes around here already."

Floor-to-ceiling gray curtains lent the room some grandeur. Sprigs of lavender stood in a brown-bottle vase on the nightstand. The cushy bed beckoned Addie. She wanted to face-plant into those pillows and not move until morning. She could already feel her weight sinking into the mattress and the lilac duvet, soft against her cheek.

Gemma pulled her attention to the three watercolors of Scottish thistles hanging above the headboard. "These are Scotland's national flower—a native plant both bold and beautiful."

The only things Addie had any attachment to in her Boston apartment were the blackout curtains she'd purchased in a jet-lag-induced haze. Gemma had created a sanctuary for her.

Despite the cold drenching from the weather and the water droplets that now stuck her shirt to her shoulder blades, Addie felt warm all over. The maximum effort clients typically expended on her account was offering a cup of coffee. She wasn't used to people fussing over her.

It was nice, if a tad overwhelming.

"The thistle symbolizes courage and bravery," Neil added with gusto, and Gemma beamed at him. "Legend has it that during an invasion, the Vikings planned to sneak up on the Scots and overcome them in their sleep. Only, as they crept in barefoot, a Norseman's foot came down hard on one of these wee prickly flowers and he cried out, alerting the Scots, who charged into battle. The rest, as they say, is history."

Addie's gaze landed on Jack as he lifted his glasses to rub between his eyes, and she almost barked out a laugh. She felt some immediate kinship with Jack, both of them at the mercy of Neil and Gemma's excitement.

Gemma gestured her over to a framed picture of a fairy-tale castle nestled on a tiny island surrounded by rolling hills. "Our Jack took this photo."

"Wow. You're very talented."

"I appreciate it. Wish the galleries thought so, too."

"That's a tough business."

Neil interrupted. "One of the most revered castles in all of Scotland. Eilean Donan."

Addie's heart pinched. She remembered the name from her mom's stories, the ones Addie told herself over and over. *Scotland is a magical place. Full of kelpies and shaggy Highland cows and*

*the Loch Ness Monster. Fairy wells, standing stones, emerald hills.
And the castles, Addie. You'll love the castles.*

"It's the clan seat of the Macraes, so I thought you'd like it,"
Gemma said proudly.

Addie swallowed past a lump in her throat as she nodded.

Her mom used to imitate the Macrae battle cry and tickle
Addie until she couldn't breathe. Every once in a while, Addie
listened to the war cry on YouTube to make sure she wouldn't
forget.

But the sound of her mom's echoing laughter had faded into
the unreachable part of her subconscious. Even her expressions
had narrowed in Addie's memory to match still-frame photos.

She had so little of her mom left.

"It's gorgeous," Addie choked out.

"Aye. And it's been an important stronghold since the thirteenth century." Neil puffed up like he was about to embark
on a story.

Jack leaned across Neil with arched eyebrows. "I can call security on them, if you'd like."

"Oh, posh," Neil said with a dismissive wrist flick.

Addie pasted a smile on her face. She should be laughing at
their easy banter and appreciating their generosity, but she was
bone weary and out of her depth. Maybe this was why she always stayed in hotels.

Gemma moved to the picture of purple flowers across the rolling hills. "Heather in bloom, my favorite part of late summer."

Addie's mom's name was Heather.

She blinked back the weepiness that was surely the sleep dep-
rivation getting to her. If she calculated how many hours she'd
been awake, the number might break her.

This city had apparently given her memories a get-out-of-
jail-free card, and she needed some space to pull herself together. "This is so thoughtful. And I don't mean to be rude,
but I'm exhausted."

"Of course, hen. There's soup on the stove for you before you turn in." Gemma bundled Addie in a hug wrapped in the scent of cloves and cranberries. Addie stiffened. The embrace was too comforting, reaching a part of her heart that barely remembered being mothered. Addie was spent and overwhelmed by a prickling of homesickness for a family that didn't exist anymore. She pulled back.

"Soup sounds wonderful, and I'll see you two tomorrow at the office," she said to Neil and Jack. She wasn't here to be fussed over. Or for castles or lochs or silly traditions. She had a job to do.

"Oh, not me. My brother. A right bawbag," Jack said, like it was an endearment. "You've been warned."

"Jack!" Gemma admonished.

Addie and Jack shared a smile, and he pushed his hands together, elbows out. "Right, then. Off with you two, and, Addie, let me know if you need anything."

"Thank you."

Jack forcibly removed his parents from the flat, and Addie sat down in the kitchen with drooping eyelids, the warm soup pulling her into an all-out delirium.

When she finished, she unpacked Frank in less than four minutes, climbed into the soft bed, and texted Devika.

Addie: All settled.

Devika: Get out and explore while you're there.

Addie: Rich coming from you.

Devika: I mean it. You're finally in Scotland.

After so many years.

Devika: And you're not going back anytime soon. Next three va-
cays are beachy!! No take-backs.

Addie grinned. Iceland had lived up to its name, and Devika
still hadn't forgiven her.

But Devika was right. Addie's next project could be in Thai-
land or Morocco or Edinburg, Texas. There was no reason she'd
be back.

She pulled her shoulder bag onto the bed and took out the
Polaroids of her parents' honeymoon in Scotland.

Her family had never captured the big moments. She didn't
have the quintessential pictures of the first day of school or crying with a mall Santa or blowing out birthday candles. The
pictures she had were quiet. Holding a ladybug, pointing to a
double rainbow. Resting an arm out the driver's-side window
with impatient teenage surliness while her mom leaned against
the dusty pickup truck, Tevas on her feet, a flowy hippie skirt
ballooning in the breeze.

Pictures of landscapes lost their power when time had stripped
away the magnitude of the mountains, the grit of the sand, or
the humid scent of flowers clinging to salt-curled hair.

Only pictures of people could hold those emotions, ready
to resurface with one look, like the ones her dad had taken of
her mom all those years ago.

Addie drew a finger along the worn edges of her mom's pictures. They were their very own love language, their very own
vow.

They said, *I will bear witness to your joy as well as your anguish.
I'll cradle the snapshots of your life as if they were my own. I'll hold
your hand. I'll love you forever.*

Back when her dad still believed he had a forever.

Before he abandoned Addie in his grief.

She breathed past the ice crystals filling her chest, cutting
and scraping with the reminder of all she'd lost.

In quiet moments, she could admit she wanted to find where the pictures were taken. Yearned to drive up to Macrae lands and walk around the castle staring back at her from across the room… but the photos in her hands could've been taken anywhere.

One of the Sutherlands might recognize the backgrounds. It was a better prospect than asking her dad, who shut down—shut Addie out—every time she brought up her mom. But it wasn't only her aversion to Brian's stilted phone calls holding her back. It wasn't like she'd never tried to recapture her mom.

Addie had driven out to the desert once after college, bought gas-station hot cocoa and sat alone on the rock her mom used to claim. She watched the hot-air balloons rise in the distance, the glow in the light of daybreak, but she'd felt nothing.

Like they'd used up all the magic.

If she ventured out onto the Scottish moors, stood where her mom had stood, and it was windy and cold…and empty? No. Addie would rather leave the possibility lingering out in the universe. She couldn't handle a confirmation that her mom was well and truly gone from her.

5

Logan took the office stairs two at a time. The weak, wintery sunlight filtered through the arched windows and turned the strung-up tour photos along the back wall to silver. Over the forest of potted ferns, he could barely see the few early-to-work employees. They looked up, and Logan raised a hand in greeting, finding that the smile sat more easily on his face today.

He wove through the desks set off at random angles, the printer chugging in the background, and strode into his dad's office.

Neil wore his checkered jacket usually reserved for special occasions. His mustache twitched as he collected pens and shuffled papers as if he was...organizing. Unease prickled across the back of Logan's neck. "Morning—"

"Morning, lad. Meet me in the conference room?" His dad's voice was too bright, and he blustered past Logan, not meeting his eye.

"What's going on?" Logan asked as soon as they turned the corner.

The caterpillar mustache stretched into a guilty stripe. "I've hired the travel consultant."

Heat flared through Logan's body before he fully processed the news. "The American consultant you said we'd continue to discuss before bringing on?"

"Well…yes." Neil pursed his lips, smartly retreating behind the protection of a leather-backed chair. "In my defense, you haven't entertained a discussion. You've been banging on for weeks about not wanting her help. It's doing my head in."

After all these years of working side by side, of learning everything his dad could teach him, Neil still didn't believe Logan could do this alone. And now he entrusted the company's future to some Yankee they'd never even met? Without Logan's buy-in?

He clenched his teeth. "We *don't*—"

"The Heart needs modernizing. It's years overdue."

Logan shook his head at the familiar argument. They already knew what happened when they strayed from their vision: their business fell apart. His thoughtless risk had resulted in canceled tours that nearly cratered their finances. Logan couldn't understand why his dad believed another shake-up would fix it. The only path forward was to refocus on the tours that had worked for thirty years and market them to a broader audience to fill their buses.

There was tradition to uphold.

Elyse walked in carrying two steaming mugs, one the size of a cereal bowl with the word *AunTea* scrolling around the side. As if sensing the tension in the room, she skirted the conference table and leaned against the exposed brick wall, the same copper and cinnamon as her hair. "Mornin'."

She set one mug down and sipped her tea, eyes darting between Logan and Neil, and arched an eyebrow with the same nosy interest as the day they'd moved in across the hall from each other at uni. Somewhere between toilet-papering every nook of Logan's room and competing with him and Jack to place traffic cones on Edinburgh's most prestigious statues, Elyse had become family.

"A couple from yesterday plans to join Big Mac's next tour. Have you heard from them yet?" he asked her.

"They left a message last night. I have them all signed up."

Neil rocked back on his heels and studied the ceiling as if willing it to swallow him whole. Logan knew the maneuver well and braced himself for what was surely more dire news. "What else?"

"While you're ruffled…she's staying in Jack's spare room."

Logan threw his hands in the air. "She's here already?" Neil's averted gaze confirmed there was no way to stop this. Logan had been punishing himself enough already—surely this was excessive?

Elyse said, "And she just texted. She'll be arriving any minute."

"You knew about this, too?"

"He asked me to keep quiet." Her droll look asked *Who do you think organized it?* Elyse was much more than their office manager. Without her, the entire company would crumble. Of course she already knew. He just never expected her to cross enemy lines.

There was a lot of that going around. Apparently, Jack's line in the sand over discussing work extended as far as not mentioning a new flatmate. Logan had been there two nights ago playing video games and ignoring Jack's mild harassment, same as most nights. He'd had plenty of opportunity to fill Logan in while they indulged in his superior whisky collection.

Now, it appeared, Logan would be relegated to his own empty flat for the foreseeable future. He grunted. This consultant had managed to disrupt his professional *and* personal life. And they hadn't even met yet.

He moved to the window overlooking Edinburgh's Old Town, pressing his forehead against the cool glass in a vain attempt to gather his thoughts. The blowing rain picked up forgotten leaves and hurled them all around, one splatting on the pane like a starfish.

Jerking back, he changed tactics. "How much is this going to cost?"

Neil licked his thumb and rubbed an old coffee ring on the table. "You spend money to make money. That's the first thing you would've learned in business school." He raised an eyebrow, as if Logan hadn't heard it enough. "And I thought you didn't care how much money we made."

"I don't. I didn't get into guiding to make millions."

Elyse laughed. "And you won't, at this rate."

Logan leveled her with a glare that said *Too soon*, and she hid her grin inside her teacup.

"But I won't leave you a pauper, either," Neil said. "She's an expert in efficient itinerary planning—"

"People leave our tours with full hearts and rave reviews. Why would we change that?"

"It's a necessary—"

"We don't need some outsider coming in here telling us what's special about Scotland," Logan said, gesturing to the door—

That suddenly contained Heather.

His heart kicked out of his ribs like an old cartoon. *Buhboom buh-boom.*

But the look on her face was all wrong. Brows raised. Eyes wide.

His stomach clenched. He felt out of his depth, like being on the outside of a secret everyone else knew. Something darker than confusion slithered through his mind before the bricks of understanding fell into place.

American. *Clunk.*

Travels the world. *Clunk.*

The way she'd flinched when he asked, "business or pleasure?" *Clunk.*

Heather was the travel consultant come to destroy his business.

6

Logan's knees nearly gave out as Neil bounded across the room, hand outstretched, the caterpillar mustache about to crawl off his face. "Come in, come in. This is Logan, my son and business partner."

His dad and Heather had met already…because she was living with Jack… Logan's thoughts were like forgotten porridge, sticky and caked to the sides of his mind. He shook his head to jump-start his brain.

Heather mouthed the word *son* before swallowing hard and extending her hand to him.

She hadn't been drawn into his stories about Scotland, hanging on his every word, soaking up his knowledge about Edinburgh. She hadn't been reveling in the magic of the city skyline.

She'd been *assessing* him.

Logan's stomach churned, and he gripped her hand a little tighter than necessary, but he couldn't rein himself in. The woman in front of him now was nothing like last night. Her golden hair was tied up in a knot at the back of her head. Her slacks and blouse were impeccable, her handshake firm, her eye contact intentional. A vision of corporate America here to capsize his business.

Albeit a beautiful one.

It wasn't just his family conspiring against him. The universe was in on it, too.

"Hi. I'm... Addie Macrae."

His breath came out in a gut-punching rush. A fake name to boot. What an utter arse she'd made of him.

Her eyes pleaded with him to keep her secret. It would serve her right if he exposed her and told his dad what kind of *trustworthy* adviser he'd hired. Logan wanted to, just to see her as twisted up as he was, but if she mentioned how he'd chatted her up... Well, he wasn't planning to call Neil's attention to that error in judgment.

"Addie," he ground out.

Her eyes spewed confetti *thank you*s, and he pictured snatching them out of the air and lighting the sentiment on fire. At this rate, the whole company was going up in flames, regardless.

If she hadn't stuck around for a dram, maybe he wouldn't be so worked up. But she had, enchanting him and fabricating a connection he thought was genuine and rare when she was only sniffing out information.

"And this is Elyse," Neil said.

"Nice to meet you in person. And thanks for all the coordinating you've done."

Elyse handed her the other cup of tea with a bright smile. "Happy to help." Next thing he knew, she'd be giving Addie a fern in lieu of a friendship bracelet.

"Are you settled in?" Neil asked, beaming as if Addie was the patron saint of aging tour guides and flustered fathers.

"Yes. All unpacked. Will you thank Gemma again for the soup?"

Logan's pulse thrummed in his neck. If his mum was making her supper, *she* was a lost cause, but he wasn't about to give Addie any opportunity to pull his dad into her charade. "Shall we get started, then?" Logan asked, ignoring the disapproving look his father had perfected over a lifetime of raising three boys.

Addie gave him a thin-lipped smile, her shoulders thrown back in a confident stance as if she could force this to be their first meeting by pretending hard enough. "Of course." She slipped into a chair at the other end of the table and opened a leather folio.

Neil sat and gripped the edge of the table, rolling his chair closer. "Well, now. I'm nearing retirement—"

Logan snorted. *Sure, he was.* He'd have to believe in Logan for that to ever happen.

Neil didn't disguise his stern face. *Choppy seas ahead*, his eyes warned. "And I've been delinquent in changing itineraries—"

"Marketing is our highest priority," Logan cut in, redirecting. Changing the tours was nonnegotiable. These trips were a map of his childhood. Summer days spent climbing the wild hills, the smell of the lochs, the purple heather blooming in the valleys.

"The website *definitely* needs an overhaul," Addie said.

Logan cracked his neck. He'd spent three months teaching himself HTML.

"I've wanted to add more pictures for ages," Neil said, as if he simply hadn't gotten around to it. His father still hunt-and-peck typed, for Christ's sake.

"Absolutely. And with a family-owned business, we can sell your story and make the site a great representation of your brand." Addie spoke with graceful hand gestures like she was casting a spell on his father, and if the happy caterpillar was any indication, it was working.

"Yes. We wouldn't want to give the wrong impression," Logan said. "About our tours."

Addie stiffened. He gave her a decidedly insincere smile and reveled in the pink splotches blooming on her chest. Not that he was looking.

Elyse moved to the cloudy whiteboard and wrote *Website* followed by *Reservation System*. "I field far too many calls supporting the booking process."

Addie took notes as she talked. "I know a number of vendors that could work well."

"Wonderful. We need all the help we can get," Neil said, leaning back in his chair. Logan fought the desire to throw a dry-erase marker at his head. He and Elyse were discussing The Heart as if none of them had any business sense at all.

"Our social-media communities are highly engaged and growing quickly," Logan said. If they could better convert their followers into bookings, they'd be set.

"You know they're not coming for Folklore Friday, right? The millennials fancy the beard and kilt," Elyse said with a smirk which morphed into a you're-no-fun look when she took in his scowl.

"Social media can be a smart place to direct resources, especially in an industry with compelling content. And you're a natural-born storyteller..." Addie's eyes went wide. "I'm assuming...since you're related to Neil."

The buttons on Neil's jacket were nearly popping off, he was so chuffed. At this rate, he'd be adopting Addie by the end of the meeting.

"But marketing won't save you if your product isn't what people want. From what I've seen, I recommend a complete overhaul of your tours."

Logan's pulse pounded in his temples. *She can't do that.*

"I agree," Neil said. "Most of our trips haven't changed since Logan and his brothers were coming with me on school holidays." The caterpillar straightened over Neil's teeth in confession like it was a bad thing. Only the whisky tours were brand-new, and they all knew how that ended.

Logan tried to force some calm into his voice. "I won't let The

Heart become one of a hundred other tour providers with gimmicks and lackluster destinations. A hairy-coo logo is no victory. We know the land, the history, the secret places that leave a lasting memory, and it gives our tours a richness and complexity."

"These two talk about Scotland as if it's a single malt," Elyse said, writing *Itineraries* on the board, as Neil chuckled. Logan glared at the back of her head.

"I love the sentiment, but this is business." Addie's soft and conciliatory tone didn't disguise her true implication that his memories with his dad and brothers were wistful and had no place in her world.

Logan couldn't think of an appropriate retort through all the red in his brain. "The castles and cities don't change much around here."

"But the interest in them does. You have something like *Outlander* come out and people want to say they went to Castle Leoch."

"Same set as Winterfell in *Game of Thrones*, by the way," Elyse added.

"Those aren't *real*," he bit out.

Neil turned a sit-down-and-stay-quiet look on Logan that was remarkably similar to his mum's. He repressed the impulse to swing his feet like an admonished child.

"People want a connection to their interests, and regardless of how inauthentic that is to you, it holds marketing weight." Addie pinned him with a hard stare. "That's your goal, right? Marketing?"

Her eyes held a challenge, more of an order, really, to back down. But Logan couldn't heed that warning. Not when her changes threatened to destroy what was special about their tours. Loathing welled up inside him.

Her gaze shifted past him, and she rolled her lips inward.

Logan turned to find Elyse adding the final touches on a hairy-coo cartoon that took up three-quarters of the whiteboard. The Highland cow's tongue reached up to its snout, and orange hair covered its eyes. She wrote *Moo* with a flourish and stepped back to beam at him, then winked at Addie.

Neil straightened the lapels of his jacket. "We have to adapt, lad."

Logan swallowed down a tsunami of resentment. Everyone was abandoning him.

He ignored his dad and that damn smirking coo and turned to Addie. "How much time have you spent in Scotland?"

Her cheeks flushed at his barely veiled implication of incompetence. "I know what clients want out of their vaca—"

"Do you, now?" Logan stood, bracing his hands on the table. "Have you ever seen Ben Nevis when the rising sun paints the snowcap pink? Or felt the world fade away when the mist settles in a glen? There's magic in this country, and it's to be found in all manner of places, whether it ranks in your spreadsheets or not."

Addie rose to her feet and tipped her chin up to meet his eyes. "If only painted-pink snowcaps paid the bills."

Neil stood and gripped Logan's shoulder, pressing him back in his seat. "We'll defer to the expert. Addie, Elyse can get you settled. Logan's guiding most days, so you can share his desk—"

"My de—" Was nothing sacred around here?

"Please don't hesitate to ask for anything you need. We'll look forward to your recommendations."

Logan rolled his shoulders and pushed out a slow breath through his nose. Addie may have come here expecting the Highland games, but this meant all-out war.

Logan scowled at Addie where she sat across *his* desk, looking particularly comfortable in *his* chair, while he had to twist sideways to work on his computer, his thigh pressed against the wooden back panel.

Granted, he shouldn't have been in the office this week, but Harris had been more than happy to take Logan's four-night

Orkney tour so he could stay here and fight the good fight. Unfortunately, Logan's plan to hinder Addie's every move was not without its flaws. Namely that he had grossly underestimated not only her tenacity in acquiring details about their tours but also her ability to charm his employees.

That first day, Agnes, their one-woman HR department, had pulled Addie into her office—cordoned off by the potted plants Elyse filled the office with—and immediately started in on stories from her thirty-year tenure at The Heart, the most prominent featuring Logan as an overeager lad.

Keith, who stopped by everyone's desk before taking the wheel on his day trips out of Edinburgh, had included Addie in his morning rounds each of the last four days, as if she fit seamlessly into this office.

Logan could have anticipated Harris and Brandon—two of his newer guides—falling all over themselves around Addie, desperate to tell her about their favorite trips and bits of Scotland, if only to steal a minute of her attention. He couldn't blame them. He'd felt the same pull, after all. But Big Mac and Margaret going out of their way to make her feel welcome? That stung.

Elyse crossed the room with her dueling teacups and sat in the tattered emerald chair, the wheels whooshing along the carpet as she rolled up to Addie's side of his desk and peeked at her computer. "Golly gee," Elyse said, drawing out the vowels as only Americans do.

Addie laughed. "No one says that, Elyse."

Ignoring her, Elyse set the mugs down and turned Addie's computer toward him. "Logan, take a look at this."

A video of a redheaded yak snorting and waving its horns around played on Addie's computer with the caption Fancy mooooves #hairycoo #highlandcow #visitscotland #tourism.

Addie's vexing eyes sparkled. "In case you needed inspiration."

He cracked the knuckles on his index and middle fingers

to release the frustration he hadn't been able to grind out between his teeth.

"This is for you," Elyse said, handing the tea to Addie who discreetly slid her coffee cup to the other side of the desk.

She took a sip and grimaced before giving Elyse a weak thumbs-up. "Delicious."

"Throw it in the harbor and we're done," Elyse teased, launching into the morning report on the office gossip as if Addie was their long-lost friend from uni.

Traitors, the lot of them.

"Hey, can you hear me?" a tinny voice whispered—the miniature recording device Logan had stuck on the metal trash bin at Addie's feet. It'd been murmuring the same phrase at random intervals all morning.

It was proving to be less distracting than he'd hoped, but the way Addie's eye twitched every time the bug went off lightened his mood dramatically.

The prank was juvenile, to be sure, but he hadn't even bought it specifically for Addie. His initial target had been Big Mac—to retaliate for the dead fish, filed under *F* in Logan's filing cabinet, which went undetected until the entire office reeked to high heaven—but desperate times, and all.

"Did you hear that?" Elyse asked, looking around the desk and lifting the branches of the potted fern.

Addie leveled Logan with a cold stare. "Nope." She'd caught on to the owner of the bug, then.

Logan braced his hands behind his head and crossed an ankle over his knee, not bothering to disguise his smirk.

"I heard it," Big Mac called. "And it's driving me up the bloody wall."

"Huh," Elyse said and launched back into her storytelling until the ringing phone pulled her away.

Without missing a beat, Addie turned to him. "I need the

itineraries for each of your multiday tours as well as the Edinburgh city tours," she said.

"They're on the website."

"Yes, but those don't list specific restaurants or accommodations. And I need the timetables for each destination and the routes between them."

"I don't adhere to a strict schedule. It really takes the authenticity out of the experience, don't you think?"

"Hey, can you hear me?"

Big Mac whirled around in his chair. "Where the *fuck* is that coming from?" he shouted and started ripping open drawers in his desk, rattling the picture frames on top.

Addie's eyelids fluttered closed, and she pulled in a long breath through her nose. Logan bit the inside of his cheek to keep back a smile.

"You heard it, didn't you, Margaret?" Big Mac asked, lifting up stacks of papers and his computer keyboard.

Margaret looked over the heavily padded shoulder of her red blazer. "Maybe it's bees."

Laughter bubbled up inside Logan at the outrageous hypothesis, his ribs creaking with the restraint to hold it in. None of his guides would've agreed to this prank if he'd asked them, but they were playing the part beautifully.

Addie placed an open palm in the middle of the desk, clearly not letting this go. "You do follow a specific itinerary, though. You're only going to locations communicated to the customers prior to leaving, right?"

Logan tipped back in his chair, balancing himself with one foot on the desk. "Och, Scotland is a wild country meant to get lost in."

She narrowed her eyes. "Would you say the other guides follow a similar philosophy?"

"Everyone has their own methods. You'd have to ask them."

Her lips tipped up in a menacing smile. "Fine."

Chair legs hit the floor with a thud, and his stomach mirrored the plummeting sensation. Speaking to his guides was the absolute last thing Logan wanted her to do.

Addie descended upon the newest member of the team. Brandon had all of Logan's detailed notes on each trip in his possession. Essentially a filing cabinet filled with information Addie would love to get ahold of and run through the shredder. Logan's fingers twitched with the need to interfere, but he couldn't think of a plausible reason to interrupt. He gnawed on the end of a pen cap.

"Hey, Brandon." She drew out his name, and his head of shaggy black curls bounced up, delight in his eye at her attention. "Do you have your training documents handy?" She cast a quick look over her shoulder at Logan, and his blood heated.

"Sure."

The plastic cap snapped between Logan's teeth. He had to do *something*. "Could bees be in the printer, do you think?"

Big Mac jumped at the suggestion, storming to the corner of the room by Brandon's desk to investigate while Addie rubbed her temple. Logan moved closer to hear their conversation better, picking up a fern in a red pot to bring to the window as an excuse if anyone asked.

"What are you looking for?" Brandon still vibrated with the urgent energy of an intern.

"Information on where we stay, stops for food…?"

Don't look in her eyes.

"Hey, can you hear me?"

"That's it!" Big Mac roared, climbing onto Margaret's desk. She scooped up a lit scented candle to keep it from being knocked to the floor while Big Mac popped up the square ceiling panel.

Logan couldn't even appreciate the mayhem while Addie interrogated Brandon. How was she so singularly focused?

"Logan's so overwhelmed right now, I don't want to bother him," Addie said, clearly trying to recapture Brandon's attention.

"Oh, sure. Let me see…" While he rummaged through stacks of paper, Big Mac stepped one foot onto Brandon's desk to reach the next tile. Logan willed Brandon to come up empty-handed. To slip the training materials to the bottom of the pile, or better yet, into the bin. They'd be safer there.

Hold it together, mate.

"Here they are." Brandon pulled out a handful of folders and handed over the gold.

Logan threw one hand in the air. What a blundering fool.

Addie turned into the full force of Logan's glare, but instead of shrinking back she swished the folder like a red matador cape. She gave him the first genuine smile he'd seen from her since the pub and flipped through the pages with delight. Logan's pulse roared in his ears.

Elyse cleared her throat, and Logan whipped around to find her lips puckered and one eyebrow raised. Never a good sign. "Can I offer you a piece of advice?"

Logan squinted at the ceiling. "No."

She took the fern and balanced it on her hip like a baby. "Getting your way is an art form, and spitting soor plooms across the room isn't it. She's going to make changes around here, and right now, you're the only one withholding input. You might mention your ideas unless you can live with Brandon's vision for The Heart."

Logan's muscles tightened like his body was ready to enter the boxing ring with that particular idea. The only vision that mattered was the one his dad had built this company on thirty years ago.

Big Mac popped another ceiling panel out and swiped his hand along the opening. White dust cascaded like a chalky flash flood directly onto Addie's head, debris pinging off her shoulders, powder ballooning into the air.

Logan barked out a laugh before slapping a hand over his mouth.

Addie turned, her back ramrod straight, her hair and suit jacket painted an ashy gray. The fire in her eyes clearly communicated that the professional veneer he'd been chipping away at was well and truly gone, and he was about to suffer.

Big Mac voiced Logan's thoughts. "Well, shit."

Tempting Tattie smelled of burnt potato skins in the best possible way. Potatoes hung in wire baskets on the wood-paneled walls of the tiny shop that two and a half people could fit comfortably inside. Addie and Elyse stood in line along the skinny display case while a man in a black beret and rainbow scarf plopped into their baskets whatever unlabeled toppings they pointed to.

But even the decadence of a shop that sold nothing but baked potatoes wasn't enough to redeem this shitty day.

Addie grabbed an orange drink that Elyse bullied her into choosing and paid. While she waited, she snagged the stools by the floor-to-ceiling window and checked her email.

From: Marc Dawsey
To: Addie Macrae; Devika Shah
Talking with Amsterdam City Tours about Phase 2 this morning and three other prospective calls this week. Buckle up, we're about to get busy! Send an update when you have a minute.

The sick feeling was back, twisting in Addie's stomach. She couldn't very well write:

Dear Marc,

Things are off to a promising start. Neil speaks of his latest fishing achievements, and I ask insightful questions based on that one time I watched *Salmon Fishing in the Yemen*. If he's in a sparky mood, he explains some random bit of folklore on his mind due to the upcoming equinox or a particularly windy day. Maybe he has a bad case of senioritis or some misplaced faith that Logan will take the reins on this one. Either way, the place runs on fairy tales instead of data.

As for Logan, he dumped his trips on another guide for the express purpose of getting in my way. He's been sitting on reservation-system options for four days and would rather drown in the North Sea than be of any help at all.

I have a sneaking suspicion all their vendors are old family friends and their attractions hold personal sentimental value, because I can't understand the appeal otherwise. As far as I can tell, The Heart of the Highlands is afloat by some miracle of god, also known as great word-of-mouth references, which, as you know, Marc, cannot be counted toward the bottom line.

Love,
Addie

She smoothed a wrinkle in her skirt that was probably permanent from all the hours she'd spent hunched over this disaster of a business.

All the prospective calls were great for their company, of course—much needed reassurance they could make this work. But it put the pressure directly on Addie like thumbs pushing too hard into the soft flesh under her shoulder blades. She needed to wrap this up and be ready for the next project the minute Marc signed a new contract, and she'd accomplished next to nothing. She couldn't be the reason their business didn't pull in enough revenue because she was stuck here with Logan blocking her at every turn.

Elyse slid onto the stool next to her, sunning herself in the window like a sleepy cat. "You have to admit, the prank was a belter."

Addie raised a skeptical eyebrow. "Maybe for someone who won't be finding bits of ceiling in their hair for the next week."

A grin spread across Elyse's face. "Logan's been waiting to retaliate against Margaret for the time she switched his background to a screenshot of the log-in screen and he couldn't figure out how to get into his computer for an entire afternoon. It probably wasn't even meant for you."

"Uh-huh," Addie said dryly, but a smile fought its way past her foul mood. Lunch with Elyse had that effect.

Fork halfway to her mouth, Addie paused, stomach dipping. "What are you eating right now?"

Elyse gave her a questioning look. "Tuna."

"On a baked potato?"

"Mmm-hmm." She dug in. "It's my favorite."

Trying to stifle her disgust, Addie took a hearty swig of Irn-Bru, coughing from the flavor: fizzy Hi-C mixed with bowling alley. She struggled to keep it in her mouth.

"Fond of haggis? Could try blood sausage next."

"If you promise to hold my hair."

Elyse had jumped in like they'd been friends for years, not an acquaintance who'd set up Addie's computer and apologized for the reprehensible desk arrangement.

In all her travels, she met plenty of genuine, friendly people, but Elyse was different. For one, she was deeply invested in the tea thing, convinced Addie would come to enjoy it after enough forced attempts, as if Addie wouldn't be drinking Frappuccinos in the Frankfurt airport in a handful of weeks.

She acted like Addie was staying and made her feel included

or, at the very least, enjoyed making fun of her accent. Whatever her reasons, Addie appreciated her company every morning and her insistence on eating exclusively baked potatoes for lunch.

Elyse had quickly become more than someone who cured afternoon boredom with office gossip. She'd bypassed the introductory conversations Addie was used to, that only ramped up when it was time for her to move on.

Elyse shifted on the stool, adjusting her tartan wool vest that might or might not have been ironic. "Alright, you need to know the goss if you're going to make it here. Big Mac and his wife got in a row last night, and she was so steamed she slipped a raw fish in his rucksack. Steer clear of his desk. It reeks."

Addie laughed and took another tentative sip. "What were they fighting over?"

"Oh, most likely it was nothing. They love the making-up part, if you ken my meaning." Elyse waggled her eyebrows.

"Sounds healthy." Addie had never heard of retaliation being the key to a relationship. Then again, she wasn't exactly an expert.

"But never dull. Come on, then. Tell me you don't want a man who gets your insides so minced you can't sleep."

"Or so strung out you can't resist burning their clothes?" she said jokingly, to cover her terror at the thought of getting that close to someone. She'd seen firsthand the kind of destruction love could wreak. You never knew when someone would leave you, whether they meant to or not. It wasn't worth the damage when they did.

Elyse laughed. "It's nice having someone my own age to talk to for a change." The way she smiled made her words sound like *It's nice having a friend*.

Addie didn't make many of those. Full-time traveling wasn't conducive to relationships. She'd eaten cake at one too many going-away parties to think she'd hear from her old coworkers ever again, let alone clients.

Devika was the exception. After her husband died in a car

accident three years ago, the office had filled with flowers and well-wishes. But shock wears off pretty quickly when the grief isn't yours to bear. The sting of loneliness Addie felt for Devika brought with it the ghost of people pulling away, of her high-school boyfriend breaking up with her saying, "You're so fucking *sad* all the time," like there was some alternative she refused to consider.

Late one night, on a project in Monaco, she'd knocked on Devika's hotel-room door. Addie held out a bag of peppermint chocolates. "They don't help, but they do taste good. Do you want to talk?"

Devika hiccuped out a laugh, invited her in, and told her about Samir. Addie talked about her mom for the first time in years. It turned out, ordering takeout and working long hours with a friend helped dull the ache as much as jet-setting.

Elyse's animated hand gestures and lively stories had that effect on her, too.

"Really nice," Addie agreed.

Elyse pressed the prongs of her fork against her lips like she was thinking. "You're right, though. I don't need a frustrating man in my life. I already have one of those. Logan's been all over me with the social-media plans. He'd still have a flip phone if it hadn't broken, and now he's over here telling me about filters."

Addie rubbed her eyes. "Tell me about it. He can't find time to pull together costs for the trips, and yet he had me swapping out fourteen different versions of Scottish-thistle pictures on the home page yesterday." It was unprofessional to complain to a client's employee, but the executive team who hired her didn't usually include a giant Highland boulder intent on obstructing her path.

Elyse chuckled. "He's a tosser. But I'm happy to help wherever I can."

"Like getting me cost breakdowns?"

"Consider it done."

"Seriously?" Relief flooded through Addie, and she took an oversize bite of bacony potato. "Thank you."

Elyse shrugged. "I love this place. It's like family, but without all the complicated bits... Or maybe that's just mine."

"Mine, too." *Wait.* Elyse's welcoming nature overrode Addie's instinct to deflect, to the point where she almost *wanted* to commiserate. But she knew better.

"I told them I took this job, and my mum said, 'How nice, a secretary.'"

"That's shitty. An office manager is an important job. This place would be a wreck without you."

Elyse flicked her hair over her shoulder in a move that was definitely meant to be ironic. "Doesn't matter what they think. I love it."

"I can see why." Addie worked in a lot of offices every year. There was definitely something special here. The new trainee wore only Heart of the Highlands hoodies, and the drivers always came in to chat before their trips. The HR lady left flattering notes on pink Post-its at random, including for Addie.

"I want to take on more, but it's hard at a family business. I'm not sure it's my place."

Addie knew exactly how that felt. "I get it, but there's certainly enough work and they adore you. I say go for it."

"Maybe. Don't say anything to Logan, alright?"

"We're not currently speaking, so all good there." If it wasn't for him, this place would be a dream.

The afternoon light was gloomy by the time Addie and Elyse strolled back from the potato shop and crested the stairs into the noisy office. No sleek lines or skyscraper views here. The Heart of the Highlands's office resembled a pub more than a workplace, with dark timber desks, thick-paned windows, and ferns on every available surface. They parted ways, Elyse to her desk along an exposed brick wall, and Addie to the hooks holding the office's various keys near the door.

From her bag, she pulled out silver bagpipe keychains she'd found in a tourist shop on the way back. The little yellow bag crinkled and Addie crumpled it up to stop the noise. Slipping the metal loops over her thumb, she grabbed the first set of van keys, slid her nail between the split ring, and twisted.

Attaching trinkets to all the keys was childish and also deeply satisfying. Logan would despise it. When she was done, Addie stepped back to admire the miniature bagpipes swaying and coming to rest against the wall.

That bit of revenge enacted, she headed to the desk she shared with Logan. Any levity she'd recaptured at lunch evaporated when she spotted the dartboard Logan had hung earlier in the week, directly behind her chair. The bull's-eye lined up with her nose when she was sitting.

A yellow jar of assorted pushpins and other office supplies sat on Logan's side of the desk, and feeling immature and adamant about it, Addie tipped it over. With one finger, she rearranged the paper clips to spell out *bawbag*. The Scots slang Jack had taught her was really coming in handy.

Locally inspired insult—Addie, 1 point.

She settled on her side of the desk—in the ergonomic chair—and opened her laptop to send Marc an update. Even though she'd already read his email, her heart kicked a wild beat at the sight of his name. Addie shoved a pencil a little farther into the bun that had turned messy with the stress of the day.

She was flying blind on a project that determined her firm's entire future. As a brand-new consultancy, their every client needed to have profitable tours—for their own cash flow and to keep Dawsey's reputation intact. She couldn't fight the thickening unease that even the smallest setback could wreck Marc's faith in her. He was counting on her, the one person who'd always cheered her on. He'd pulled her out of an absolute nose dive the night of her college graduation, when her life could've spiraled in a completely different direction.

That day, her dad had flown in for a celebratory dinner. Maybe she'd hung too many hopes on that gesture, forgetting how this always went.

Common sense had abandoned her on the first glass of wine. "Do you think Mom would be proud of me?" she asked.

Brian sank back into his chair, into himself, his voice whisper-soft and haunted. "I don't want to talk about Heather."

Mechanically, he ate the rest of his rigatoni. Addie, the waitress, the room full of people, none of them existed. He might not have noticed when she paid the bill, when she got up and left.

In that moment, she'd stopped holding out hope for the apology she wanted, the overture she craved, the return to the family they'd once been.

With nowhere else to go—pitiful as that was—Addie had swiped her newly minted employee badge at the office where she'd interned—the only place she felt any claim to. She stopped before each shiny, framed print of faraway destinations. Imagined floating in the aquamarine waters of Tahiti and swinging along a rainforest canopy in Costa Rica. By the end of the hall, the pain in her heart had scabbed over.

Marc had been at his desk, tie discarded. "Shouldn't you be rip-roaring drunk by now?" When he noticed her raccoon eyes and the red cap and gown slung over her arm, his gaze softened. "Want to talk?"

"My dad—" Addie croaked. Cleared her throat. Tried again. "My… Nope. No, actually, I don't."

"When life feels like too much, Damien and I get on a plane." He pushed his glasses up his nose. "You know what you need? The French Riviera. Devika starts a new project in Cannes next week. Join her. She can teach you everything you need to know. For people like us, life can be one big adventure."

Addie had taken his advice—worked her ass off to prove he

hadn't made a mistake entrusting literally anything to a twenty-two-year-old. She was *still* hustling, making sure he never regretted including her in his new venture—*their* new venture.

She wouldn't let him down or watch Marc and Devika turn into the kind of ex-coworkers she never saw again. Logan wasn't going to derail the dream team over some childhood nostalgia bullshit.

Addie heard a snort, and then a box landed with a crash on the desk, sending the shiny metal paper clips flying like shrapnel. She jolted back. "Hey!"

"How was lunch?" Logan asked, resting his arms on the top of the cardboard filing box. "Have you tried The Abbey yet? *Great* nachos."

So she didn't announce her presence on that tour. *Get over it.*

He tapped the top of the box with papers haphazardly sticking out the sides. "I heard you needed cost breakdowns. These invoices should help."

As much as she appreciated Elyse's intervention, the idea of piecing together costs from literal scraps of paper sent a wave of panic through her belly like a Category 5 hurricane heading straight for their fledgling business. She didn't have time for this.

Most clients revolved around analytics. At best, someone handed her a flash drive of everything she needed. Even the Atlantic City Scavenger Tours had more documentation than here—and it was run out of some guy's basement.

Logan crossed his arms on top of the box and gave her a gloating smile. She fantasized about hurling ninja stars into his thick forehead.

Knowing a more hygienic way to draw blood, Addie picked up the phone receiver and dialed. The smug curl of Logan's lips slipped as the ringing sound trilled in her ear. "Hello, Alasdair?" The color drained from Logan's face. Addie couldn't hide her grin. "This is Addie Macrae. I'm a consultant with The Heart of the Highlands Tours, and I'm conducting satisfaction surveys of The Heart's preferred vendors."

Logan glowered at her from his chair, his stare burning a hole in the center of her forehead.

"Do you have a moment to chat with me?...Great!" Addie locked eyes with Logan. "To start off, on a scale from one to five, how would you rate their level of professionalism?"

She held up three fingers and overexaggerated a wince.

Logan leaned across the desk on his forearms. "He's an old fishing friend of my dad's. There's hardly a need for formality," he hissed.

Addie dismissed him with a wave of her hand as she asked the next question. Logan turned the spray bottle Elyse had given her for the fern until the nozzle pointed directly at Addie.

She picked up a dart and spun it like a top, glee a giddy sparkler in her chest. She could almost hear his teeth grinding.

Addie, 1 point.

"And what about their expertise?" She held up five fingers and nodded to Logan, giving him a thumbs-up. He flipped her off.

"Ease of communication?" She wrapped the curly phone cord around her finger. Logan could take it as a metaphor for Alasdair, who was happily reporting every detail of their partnership.

She straightened. "Sorry, did you say they *fax* you reservations? I will make that my number-one priority." She was shocked Elyse hadn't mentioned it already.

A dial tone blared in her ear, and she pulled the receiver away, staring at it, until she noticed Logan's pointer finger pressing down the switch hook.

"You have *no* right calling our vendors," Logan growled.

"I thought you'd approve of me getting to know the locals," she said with mock innocence.

"Let's get something straight."

"Please." She steepled her fingers under her chin.

Riling him up past cold disdain—Addie, 1 point.

Logan braced his hands on the desk and leaned over the small surface. "This is my company. My tours. My vendors. If you need something, come and talk to me first."

"Because that's been going so well."

He winced like he realized how ridiculous he sounded after his elaborate attempts to derail her.

Comeuppance had never tasted so sweet. Addie crossed her legs and leaned back in her chair. "I'd love your itineraries."

The muscle in Logan's jaw jumped. He stalked to her side of the desk, pressing into her personal space as he dropped into a crouch.

"What are you—" Her attention snagged on his thick thighs, the way his fingers splayed across jeans that were three seconds from busting the seams. The leather band wrapped twice around his wrist lent him an air of rebelliousness like vacation crushes and swimming in the ocean at night.

She looked into stormy eyes rimmed with dark lashes. Even if she'd wanted to look away—which she didn't, she wouldn't give him the satisfaction—she was trapped in his gaze, in the heat, in the flicker of longing hiding in the depths.

Her heartbeat settled between her collarbones.

In quick succession, his eyebrow rose, a half smile formed, and a dimple appeared off the coast of his full lips. "Do you mind?" He gestured to the drawer she was blocking with her foot.

Her cheeks turned molten, and she tore her gaze away from his arrogant like-what-you-see? look, searching desperately for something else to focus on or, at the very least, a stack of manila folders to build a barricade around herself.

She pushed back in the rolling chair as he rummaged around in the drawer for half a century while she drowned in his pine and leather scent wafting her way.

How was she still affected by this?

Probably because that damn dimple reminded her of the real smile he had turned on her at the pub. It would be much easier to hate Logan if her mind would stop pulling up *Exhibit A: Grin-*

ning in the Firelight over a Drink as proof that he had once been genuine and earnest and not a complete dickwad. Shouldn't there be an off switch for any lingering attraction she still felt for him?

She was a professional, dammit.

Logan unfurled to his full height, his eyes gleaming, as he handed her a stack of maps printed from MapQuest, the routes hand-drawn in red marker.

Unbelievable. He was truly planning to block her at every step. Children running down a hotel hallway at two in the morning were less infuriating. "Sorry, is this a crayon drawing of the Hundred Acre Wood?"

Logan only smirked, crossing his arms like a self-satisfied bodyguard knowing Addie couldn't get past him.

She looked away from his chest muscles, irritatingly sculpted in that pose, and turned her attention to the top map and a dot way out of alignment with the rest of the loop. Addie stood and pointed to it. "Here's a great example. Castle Storn? No one's ever heard of it. The draw has to warrant the drive time, and this is wildly out of the way."

Logan's itineraries were a huge liability. Tourists might visit this random castle and—like in the desert—feel nothing. Hot spots fostered connections and never failed to disappoint.

The corners of Logan's lips tipped down. "You write off these places you deem too insignificant to warrant a visit, but you haven't mentioned joining a tour to see for yourself. Are you so good at your job you don't even need to see the sights?"

Addie swept up the maps, tapping them together on the desk. "I've already seen you work. And I'm not here on vacation."

"Take a lot of those?"

Her blood simmered. "I don't have time to go to a thousand castles next week, so we can have this conversation. I know you think you can convince anyone of the magic of Scotland once they're on your tour, but if they've never heard of these sites, they're not booking. Let me help you get the numbers on your bus."

"I want *people* to see how they fit in the fabric of Scotland. To come away from their experience with more than an overpriced bottle of Johnnie Walker. This isn't a job for me, it's a way of life." He raised his eyebrows accusingly. "You wouldn't get it."

"Why not?"

"You're a Macrae. You came all the way to Scotland, and instead of trying to connect with your heritage, you're in the office around the clock."

Addie stiffened. "I'll connect on the weekend." With a bottle of Scotch and a book, tucked in by the bay window.

Logan's eyebrows rose. "Will you? Where are you headed, then?" He sat on the edge of the desk like he was settling in to hear a delightful tall tale.

Addie bristled at his clear disbelief. There was no backing down now and only one place she knew by name. "Eilean Donan."

"Ah, the clan seat of the Macraes." Logan pushed his sleeves up to reveal muscular forearms dusted with dark hair. Not that Addie was looking, but her brain wouldn't let her forget. He rested his elbow on one knee, rubbing his knuckles under his chin. "Gorgeous castle. Need any recommendations for the trip?"

"I have it all planned. Lonely Planet, you know."

"Little light on the history, last time I checked." His jaw clenched, and she reveled in the tell.

"That's what Wikipedia's for."

"Might want to leave the laptop at home, if you can manage."

She narrowed her eyes, refusing to blink first. "Maybe you can make me a map with red markers so I won't get lost."

His face brightened, and it undermined the point she thought she'd just won. "I'll do you one better. I'll lend you a van."

Addie's stomach swooped, and Logan must have heard the sputter of her heart, because victory shone in his eyes. "Unless you don't think you can handle it?"

"I can handle it," she assured him.

"You're all sorted, then."

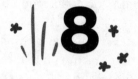

Addie kicked a stray rock across The Heart of the High-
lands parking lot. One push from Logan and she'd bluffed her
way into a heritage trip. But it was fine. She was ninety-eight
percent sure she held keys to a tour bus, at which point she could
turn down this ludicrous idea and cry foul play.

She pressed the key fob Logan had bestowed upon her last
night, his smug smile still burned onto her retinas.

The headlights of a navy Sprinter van blinked in the misty
morning light as if to say *Gotcha*.

Addie's stomach shriveled and her lungs restricted airflow
in protest. She forced out a breath.

It wasn't like she *had* to go.

She could claim the weather was shit, which—being December in Scotland—it was. Or fabricate the entire trip...but that
asshat probably checked the mileage.

He *would*.

Addie could say she changed her mind, but her shoulders

pinched at the thought of surrendering. She could just *see* Logan's glee.

No, she wouldn't give him the satisfaction.

Besides, she was here already. In the parking lot, keys in hand. In Scotland after all this time.

Devika would tell her to go forth and conquer. Marc would give her an overly enthusiastic double thumbs-up. Addie could do this.

She swallowed whatever self-preservation instincts she still possessed, tucked her mom's pictures into the passenger seat, and inserted the keys into the ignition.

It immediately became clear that after a decade of taking public transportation, Addie's overconfidence in her driving ability was laughable. Not only was she driving on the wrong side of the road, but the steering wheel was on the wrong side of the van.

It took four excruciating minutes to locate the correct lever for the windshield wipers by a blind-groping technique and she wasn't positive any driver's-ed advice she could still summon was even relevant in this country.

How was Gigi so eternally calm? *Stay in the center lane. Turn west in ten meters.* As if any of that was helpful when confronted with forty-five fucking roundabouts.

What Gigi should say was *Look right for oncoming traffic. No, not left. Pull to the far lane. Look how brave you are. You can do this.* That's the kind of encouragement Addie needed right now.

And she *could* do this herself. She'd done much harder things on her own. Granted, she couldn't think of anything specific at the moment, but that was simply because cars kept zipping past from all sorts of unexpected places as she navigated the cobbled streets leaving the city.

She successfully managed to enter the motorway, but if the speed didn't kill her, the weather certainly planned to. The menacing sky opened into a full-on downpour. *Dammit.*

The road narrowed with every streak of the wiper across the

windshield. The roll of the hills and bare-leafed trees blurred on either side of her. Every bump of the patchy asphalt ratcheted up her blood pressure, and the stitching of the steering wheel bit into her palms. Was she more likely to hydroplane in a van?

Fantastically unprepared for this drive, Addie couldn't ignore the voice in her mind chanting *How will you get home?*

"Rerouting," Gigi announced and directed her to an exit for an A road that sounded familiar from Addie's very brief perusal of a map last night. She maneuvered off the highway with only one car honking and congratulated herself on her impeccable driving skills.

The center line was more or less washed away, and Addie prayed there wouldn't be a semi taking up both their lanes around each turn, but she couldn't deny the smaller street was a vast improvement.

After twenty minutes of empty road, lulled by the pattering rain and the sweep of the wipers, Addie began to relax. The warmth from the vent cascaded over her and pushed the adrenaline from her muscles with every mile.

She'd show Logan. Everything was fine.

A meadow opened up ahead of her, the edges lined by old-growth forests and, beyond them, the shady outline of distant hills.

Addie took her first deep breath of the day.

If her mom was here—riding shotgun instead of printed onto photo paper—the floral scent of her Clinique Happy perfume would disguise what should have been a diesel smell in the van and better not have been Logan's cologne.

Heather's voice, loud and boisterous, would ring out with bits of trivia from a library guidebook. The second-grade teacher in her required it.

Seventeen-year-old Addie would've rolled her eyes.

But now… She'd memorize every fact, peel her eyes off the road long enough to find the crease that appeared between her mom's

brows when she was really concentrating. Wait for Heather's re-
sulting car sickness to set in, when she would suddenly crank the
dial on the air-conditioning and jolt the vents to blow directly
in her face, then cling to the handgrip with eyes pinched tight.

And when it finally passed, she'd turn on Van Morrison, settle
her feet on the dashboard despite Addie's dad's swatting attempts
to remove her, and pull out the gigantic bag of Twizzlers.

That first bite of sticky, artificial strawberry marked the beginning of summer for Addie. The last weeks of school were
always a frenzy. Her mom came home tired from picnics and
field trips, the graduation parties of past students. She belonged
to everyone else.

But once the Twizzlers came out, Mom was all hers.

On that last trip, they'd followed roads with street names like
Rio Vista and Narrow Gauge. Took exits for point-of-interest
signs to Camel Rock and Buffalo Bill's grave on Lookout Mountain. Searched for wonder in the Rocky Mountains.

They'd camped beneath the stars and ate gas-station hot
dogs and relied on Brian's exceptional sense of direction to get
them home again.

The lush land around Addie, so different from that trip,
hummed with secrets. Each fork of the road—dotted with croft
houses, ancient trees, or expansive meadows—beckoned the
explorer in her.

"Into the Mystic" came on the van's speakers, and she turned
the volume up. Heather used to belt out the chorus in the way
that made Addie whine *Mommm* when her friends were in the
car. Before she knew how much she'd miss it.

Addie ripped the bag of Strawberry Laces with her teeth,
not daring to take both hands off the wheel. She'd seen the
British equivalent of red licorice in the store the night before
and bought their customary road-trip snack on a whim. The
sweet, artificial flavor was almost the same, and the reminder
warmed her heart.

While Addie meandered down a back country lane, she smiled, realizing her pulse had returned to normal.

Some people found their mother's spirit in butterflies or wildflowers. No matter how much Addie willed it, she never got that tearing-up jolt of recognition. But the clouds broke up and the sun streaked down across the fields, and Addie thought she felt something close.

She skirted the mossy rock wall along a sharp turn. Down the road, white puffs littered the fields, spilling onto the pavement—

Sheep!

Addie slammed on the brakes, heart in her throat, as the van skidded toward the open field.

The van lurched to a stop, and the seat belt caught her forward momentum, slamming her back in her seat.

Her breath came out in short, sharp gasps, hysteria threatening to overtake her, while the offending sheep chewed grass and looked at her with all the haughty disdain they could muster.

Which was a lot.

They didn't even bother moving off the road when she blared the horn in three long blasts. After a minute of catching her breath, Addie locked eyes with herself in the rearview mirror. "You can do this," she encouraged herself. She attempted to reverse the van but cringed at the dreaded combination of revving engine and slipping tires.

She opened the door and stepped into ankle-deep mud. It took less than a minute of shoving against the bumper before she remembered that in the movies, there was always a driver to hit the gas. And bodybuilder extras to do the heavy lifting.

She opened the door to the van and climbed back in, attempting to kick off as much mud as she could. Her wellies wore brown boots of their own.

Addie sighed. "I'm sorry, beautiful shoes."

Slouched over the steering wheel, chilled and overheated at the same time, Addie twisted her now-frizzy hair away from her face.

How could she get out of this mess without Logan finding out?

The last thing she needed was an I-told-you-so from *him*.

If she sat here too long, the rain would soak the earth until it swallowed the van whole. She'd be forced to abandon it and start a new life in the nearest village. And Addie would not cohabitate with sheep that snooty.

Maybe they had AAA here.

Already knowing the state of the internet connection, she fished out her phone and prayed for divine intervention, but she must have used up all her celestial favors for the day pleading for empty roads.

Not a soul drove by.

She was going to get hungry in about thirteen minutes.

Addie glared at the pretentious tail-twitching outside. She couldn't say she'd ever been judged by a sheep, but it felt about as bad as the thought of calling Logan to tell him she'd sunk his van.

She considered dialing Elyse instead, but honestly, the two of them would end up initiated into the flock. And it wasn't like she could legitimately hide this from Logan.

Summoning her remaining courage, Addie searched for his number. *Logan Hot Scottish Tour Guide* stared back at her mockingly. She cracked her neck, then updated his contact info.

Satisfied, Addie tapped *Logan NOT Hot Scottish Tour Guide* and brought the phone to her ear.

"Enjoying all the beauty our country has to offer?" he asked in lieu of a greeting.

"No tourist wants to spend two hours driving these hellish roads just to get stuck in a herd of seriously jaded sheep. Ask me how I know."

"Are you alright?" Logan sounded genuinely concerned.

"Oh, I'm fine. And the van's fine," Addie rushed to add, a bit surprised he hadn't asked about that first. "But I'm stuck in the mud and need a tow. Is there a specific place I should call? I'm on the A84, past Strathyre, I think?"

"That'll take ages up there. I'll come."

"I can handle this." Under no circumstances did she want him to come up there.

"What are you doing out there, anyway?"

"Gigi. My GPS," she clarified. "She hates Scotland."

His full-throated chuckle would have captured her attention the first time they met, but now she ground her teeth in response. "Could have used my map after all."

Hot coals burned under her skin. The audacity of this man. "Go ahead. Gloat."

"I'll wait to do it in person. I'm on my way…any second."

He'd probably leave her for hours. Addie tossed her phone into the passenger seat where it landed with a thud on top of her pictures.

She hadn't even wanted to go to Macrae lands. Drafty European castles were indistinguishable from one another. It wasn't like she'd feel her mom's spirit inside a centuries-old rock wall or standing in front of a random mountain. She'd been lulled into some kind of stupor by thoughts of a trip that never happened.

Addie was all alone in a van she didn't know how to drive, in a country she'd resolutely avoided, dreaming of the one life she could never have again.

No amount of pretending would bring Heather back.

Apparently Addie had to learn that one last time.

She bit and yanked a wannabe Twizzler with a satisfying snap. Damn Logan for pushing her into this. She never should've told him about her past. So what if she wasn't spending every free moment tracking down her ancestors? What did he know about it, anyway? He had the perfect family.

He didn't know how much it hurt to go chasing down ghosts.

9

When Logan told Addie that day in the pub to call if she got lost again, he hadn't pictured his dad being with them. Or quite so much accusation lurking in her selkie eyes—even diluted through the van's windshield.

His feet squelched in the mud as he shooed the sheep. They bleated in response and carried on with their lunch.

Addie rolled down the window. "If the horn didn't work, you swatting at them certainly won't."

"What about the glare?" Logan twirled a finger to encompass Addie's narrowing eyes. "Aye, that's the one," he said, resting his arm on the open window.

Her lips pursed into her typical unimpressed frown. At a minimum, Logan wanted to grin in the face of her misfortune. Preferably dance a Highland jig around the van. Only…her eyes were a tad watery, and her hair curled wildly around her face.

She looked downright ruffled.

A tiny seed of guilt unfurled inside him. He'd taunted her into this drive, thinking she'd be more open to his ideas if she left the office and saw the land for herself. And…a bit to torture her. But he hadn't accounted for the sheep. *Arseholes, the lot of them.*

If Addie gave up now and headed straight back to Edinburgh, he knew how this would play out. She would write off the whole country and recommend he invest in a fifty-passenger bus and only allow them to stop at Stirling Castle and Loch Ness.

The Heart bore a responsibility to the community they supported—the quiet bits of land they returned to, the friends who welcomed them into their restaurants and B and Bs, tour after tour. They would suffer if The Heart went elsewhere.

Logan couldn't bear to be the reason for that kind of hardship for someone else. He carried the suffocating weight of it himself.

He had no other choice but to show Addie the colors and beauty she was intent on missing. Why these places she deemed obscure mattered for their tours. Why they set them apart.

Logan could salvage this. He tapped the inside of the car door twice. "I'll get you hooked up, and we'll be on our way in no time."

She handed him her floor mat when he asked, and he grabbed the one from the passenger side, sliding them under the wheels. His boots sank into the mud as he connected the cars, but at least the rain had slowed to a quiet mist. He gave Neil a thumbs-up and told Addie to accelerate. The van groaned before lurching onto the shoulder.

Logan collected the chain and sloppy mats and tossed them into the back of the truck, waving his dad off.

Addie leaned halfway out the window. "Who was that?"

"My dad."

She made a grumbly whine in the back of her throat. "He knows, too? Wait. Why is he leaving?" Neil's car pulled past them, heading back to Edinburgh.

Convincing a Disillusioned Addie to accept his tours would be an even bigger challenge than convincing Obstinate Addie. "I'll come with you and show you some sights."

She jerked back. "Um, no, thanks! I've had enough adventure for one day."

"I can drive us back, then."

"I'm perfectly capable."

Logan shrugged and tipped one hand out. "You just crashed into a flock of sheep."

"I swerved." The fire in her eyes made it clear he wouldn't win this one.

"Right, then." Logan made his way around the front of the van to the passenger seat. He climbed in, scooping up a handful of photographs and sweets before sitting down.

Addie snatched the pictures back. "Don't touch those."

"Are these fair game?" he asked, biting off a piece of Strawberry Laces that tasted like childhood.

A mutinous look passed across her features before she tucked the pictures into her bag like they were nuclear codes.

Logan made a show of fastening his seat belt, tugging on the chest restraint to confirm it was in working order.

Addie rolled her window up in deliberate, aggressive cranks. She was so unbearably stubborn, acting like accepting his help might literally kill her.

"Try to keep the tires on the road. The shoulder may look flat, but I assure you it's not."

"Yes, it occurred to me." She enunciated each word but put the car in gear.

"Alright, let's go. Turn on your indicator to the left."

She scowled in his direction but the blinking arrow appeared.

"Check your blind spot."

"Logan, so help me god."

He didn't disguise his grin. Getting under her skin was better than his footie team bringing home the Scottish League Cup. "You'll need to accelerate quickly into traffic."

"Maybe I'll crash on purpose." She spared a quick glare for him. "I'll make sure you see it coming."

A surprised laugh escaped him as she pulled onto the road. He'd nearly forgotten she had a sense of humor.

After Addie turned the van around, she asked, "How can I make this up to your dad? Whisky?"

"Loads of whisky."

"And what about you? How will I pay off my debts?"

"Watching you drive this slowly is surely payment enough."

He half expected her to swerve, causing his head to crack against the window and claiming it was the shit road—Jack would've—but all she did was huff.

They drove without speaking, the smell of her floral perfume and the tension rolling off her making him claustrophobic.

It was of utterly no consequence, but in the office, she chatted easily with his employees, asking about their lives, making them laugh. But she didn't share anything of herself. If someone was looking closely, she was guarded and controlled—worse when she was with him.

It wasn't as if he wanted to break through her walls or get to know her, but he couldn't stand the awkward silence for another minute. "Who's in the photos?" he asked.

"Mind your own business."

Christ. Did everything have to be such a goddamn battle?

Addie blinked too fast and swallowed hard, sparking the realization he'd blundered into something heavy and painful he knew nothing about.

He'd barely gotten a glimpse, but the woman in the picture looked an awful lot like a dark-haired Addie.

Her mum.

Guilt bloomed in Logan's stomach. The strawberry flavor on his tongue turned tangy and sharp.

Without thinking, he reached to comfort her, squeezing her forearm, and Addie nearly incinerated his hand with her eyes.

Right. He yanked his hand back. He shouldn't be surprised and certainly not hurt—they didn't have that kind of relationship.

And he knew deep in his soul that Addie wouldn't welcome his questions or condolences.

"I'm sorry about the van," he said, apologizing for the only thing he thought she'd accept. "That was a dick move."

She tilted her head for a split second as if trying to discern the sincerity of Logan's words, and the gesture tweaked his heart. What was wrong with him to have let things get to this point? "My dad let me drive it once before I got my license, and we nearly ended up in a loch."

The puff of air she released was the saddest excuse for a laugh he'd ever heard. Her chest was nearly pressed against the steering wheel, which was quite a feat in the spacious van, and her fingers were curled so tightly her knuckles stood out in solid white. Of course she was missing the beauty all around her.

He wouldn't offer to drive in her stead again—he wasn't looking to get decapitated—so he tried to calm her in the only way he knew how. "Have you ever heard the story of the Piper of Clanyard Bay?"

"Is that the one that starts with *Once upon a time*?"

Logan grunted. "*In days gone by*, a dark network of tunnels was said to extend from the cove to the cliffs of Clanyard Bay. Locals believed that faeries lived in these caves, and no one dared to disturb them. But one day, accompanied by his faithful dog, a foolhardy piper entered the tunnels, brazenly playing his pipes. Now, the music droned on for hours, slowly fading away until it could no longer be heard. Suddenly, the dog dashed out of the cave, barking its head off, without any of its hair!"

Addie's lips tipped up in the smallest of smiles. But it was something. She rolled her shoulders, loosening her arms.

"The piper was never seen again. Although the caves are long gone now, on summer nights, locals have heard the distant sound of bagpipes coming from deep under the ground. Perhaps it's the wind whistling through the old underground caves or a trick of the mind, but maybe it's the spirit of the piper, playing his haunted melodies forevermore."

"Moral of the story, don't go wandering around with strange men? Clearly a lesson I haven't learned." She tossed him a look, and he grinned. She irked him to no end, but he couldn't deny sparring with her gave him a heady rush.

They drove for another hour in a silence that wasn't companionable but wasn't excruciating either, and Logan took the opportunity to watch her while she wasn't shooting daggers at him.

Freckles he hadn't noticed in the dim light of the pub dusted her nose. Her blond hair was half-dried and wild instead of perfectly tied back. She looked a bit undone, like a warrior without her armor, although Logan knew better than to assume she was unarmed.

She was quite lovely when she wasn't interrogating his guides and shredding the integrity of his company.

The drone of the tires was oddly soothing and stirred up some fanciful musings like what would've happened if she'd simply been a tourist.

Not that he should still be looking for that woman from the first day.

They passed through pockets of leafless forests and empty farmland. "Right through the trees there—" he pointed over the dash "—you may be able to make out Linlithgow Palace. The birthplace of Mary, Queen of Scots."

"You packed the kilt, didn't you?"

"Och, ye best watch yerself, lass," he said with a grin.

Eyes she hadn't managed to peel from the road flashed to him in surprise, and he realized his misstep—the familiarity they could no longer claim. His chest flooded with heat, and he cleared his throat. "We're a ways from Macrae lands, but there's a historic battlefield nearby. You'll have heard of Robert the Bruce?"

Addie lifted her hand off the steering wheel for a brief second.

"What am I supposed to get out of standing where some dead guy stood five hundred years ago?"

Logan saw firsthand how impactful that could be on a regular basis, but he'd go out on a limb and wager she wouldn't appreciate an answer. "Seven hundred," he corrected under his breath.

"I'm not here to sightsee."

"That's the beauty of this job. It can be work *and* play."

Addie's words from earlier flickered in Logan's mind. He *could* convince anyone of the magic of Scotland. How had he not thought of it before?

She wasn't going away, and she certainly wasn't backing down. Logan needed to change her mind. The constant whir of anxiety receded for the first time in months.

Their unique itineraries left a lasting impression on their guests. All he had to do was let her experience it for herself. "Come on a tour with me."

A surprised huff escaped her lungs and a crease between her brows appeared, but he couldn't decipher her silence. She might have been intent on his directions as they navigated the streets of Edinburgh back to the office or not planning to answer at all.

She parked the van behind the building and turned in her seat. "You have a financial deficit that, in my professional opinion, cannot be rectified with a pretty website."

Logan's chest pinched at the reminder of their money problem. The one he'd caused.

"And I have explicit instructions from my boss to design *profitable* tourist-trap extravaganzas. Grandpa McHann's Shetland Pony Stable may be an absolute delight, but it doesn't instill confidence in prospective clients that I have any idea what I'm doing. If I don't recommend golf trips, I better have good reason and sound numbers to back me up."

Despite the dismissive way she talked about an imaginary tour stop that *did* sound like a delight, it somehow made him feel better knowing she had a stake in this, too. That this stubbornness came from loyalty to her boss, not that her mind couldn't be changed.

"Give me a chance to convince you to keep the tours the way they are. If you don't fall in love with Scotland, if you still think we should add tourist attractions, I'll take them sailing to find Nessie myself."

"If I agree and get swept away by your tour—" her tone made it clear how unlikely that would be "—then we have two people placing bets on a sinking ship."

"No, then we use your expertise to market the tours better."

"You're not going to let this go, are you?" she muttered to the windshield and rolled her neck, finally turning to him. "Fine."

"That's it?" He'd mentally cleared his schedule to debate this until sunset.

"I'll go on your tour. If you come on mine."

"Ah, there it is." *Never easy with this one.* "Just one small detail." He held up his thumb and pointer finger pressed together. "You don't have a tour."

"I can build one. *You* could, too." She arched an eyebrow. "The possibilities are endless."

His heart kicked with a twinge of longing he didn't recognize. But she was goading him, and he wasn't taking those kinds of risks anymore. He had a business to save and a legacy to protect. "You'll give it a fair chance?" he asked.

"As long as you will."

Logan nodded.

"I'll go first, then. We can start after Christmas."

He held out his hand. "Deal?"

Still holding the van keys, Addie gripped his hand, and the pipes of the abhorrent keychain dug into his palm. He fought back a wince and didn't miss the glint in her eye.

"Deal."

10

Logan had avoided the Torchlight Procession his entire
life. People only *thought* they liked parades. If he wanted to aimlessly walk the Royal Mile until he made it to Holyrood Park,
he would do it on a day without so many people.

And in better weather.

He stuffed his hands farther into the pockets of his green
puffer jacket, bunching his shoulders against the frigid night air.
Elyse shook a cowbell directly in Logan's ear, and he clamped
his hand over the broken eardrum. As if he needed more misery tonight. She grinned before raising the bell to torment Jack.

Most of the shops and restaurants along High Street were
closed for the night, the buildings hidden in shadows. The
crowd, maybe twenty people across between the barricades,
shifted and stamped against the cold.

"Ready for the itinerary?" Addie asked, the red pom-pom
on her hat bouncing. Her face was flushed, maybe from the
cold, but he'd put his money on revelry. The smirk she sent
him seemed to hold in the word *checkmate*. His jaw clenched at

her bold assumption that she would win him over. She was so confident in her abilities to design a tour from scratch, so relentless in pursuing what she wanted.

He chased away the flutter of admiration in his chest that he refused to recognize.

Elyse blew into her gloved hands. "Gee whiz, that sounds boring."

Addie laughed. "Nobody says *gee whiz*, Elyse."

"American movies beg to differ." She hooked her fist like a line dancer. "Darn tootin'."

Addie shook her head, but the smile didn't fall from her face. "Night one—" she waved wide hands like a magician "—the Torchlight Procession. We take to the streets with ten thousand of our closest friends."

Logan scoffed. These were strangers walking the world's slowest footrace and freezing their arses off together. Using the same hashtag didn't forge a kinship.

He could meet most people where they were at, and he didn't look down on an overindulgent celebration, but these kinds of tourists, running around with Scottish flags draped across their shoulders like capes, in Edinburgh for the sole purpose of drinking blended whisky and checking under Scotsmen's kilts, made his skin crawl.

A deal was a deal, but there was no possible way Addie would convince him a city-sponsored event was more magical than what he had in store for her.

Jack swished the end of his black scarf over one shoulder. "We Scots love Hogmanay so much, we celebrate New Year's Eve *Eve*." He overemphasized his accent, like he was stepping into the louder, more animated version of himself—the way he used to when he was guiding.

At the reminder of this severed connection between them, Logan's heart buckled. He pushed down the bitterness that, even in jest, Jack would engage in this charade with Addie. That he could slip into that guiding persona for fun but not for real. Not to uphold their legacy, not to work alongside his brother.

It wasn't enough that Jack left, he had to consort with the enemy, too.

Addie leaned on her unlit torch, completely untroubled. "Tomorrow night you have a couple of options before the fireworks. The Street Party—"

"Or the Ceilidh," Jack said, pulling up the collar of his peacoat against the cold, "if you fancy a wee bit of traditional dancing. The Concert, too—"

Logan clenched his fists inside his pockets. Jack was tossing out ideas now? He'd thrown up some serious boundaries on his way out, wanting a clean break or some shite and wouldn't entertain simple questions about payroll, let alone discuss real solutions. He'd thrown Logan in the deep end, acting like it was for his own good, and completely ignored the possibility that he—and their business alongside him—might simply drown.

"No one needs a guide to get sloshed in Princes Street Gardens," Logan said. The price of drinks was pure extortion. The bands who headlined the show were wankers who appealed to the masses. And the queues for the toilet…

God, it sounded bloody awful.

He ignored the way Jack's lips pressed together into a hard, disappointed line, as if he would ever tolerate these options. He knew Jack was trying to help, in this roundabout and completely perverse way, but the resentment simmering under the surface was hard to tamp down. Logan scrubbed his hat over his forehead where the wool had started to itch.

Above them, spectators lined the windows, beer bottles dangling negligently from their grips. He shuffled closer to Addie to protect her from a concussion. The last thing he needed was for her to file a claim against his liability insurance.

"Then we'll kick off the New Year with the Loony Dook, dressing in costumes and throwing ourselves in the Firth of Forth. An unforgettable experience. Submerge yourself in Scottish culture…" Addie waggled her eyebrows. "See what I did there?"

"The Firth connects to the North Sea. Even in the peak of summer it's nowhere close to warm."

They made their way slowly past St. Giles' Cathedral where floodlights cast the arches, windows, and spires in forlorn grays and blacks. Addie bumped against his arm as if fueled by his misery and coming back for another hit.

"If you don't like this idea, I'm also considering ghost tours in the city center. Zombie makeup could lend some real authenticity." The deadpan look she gave him was feigned, he was nearly positive.

He gripped the back of his neck like he could hold himself back from taking her bait, but his restraint was nonexistent around this woman. "Hogmanay is a time for the community to gather and share a dram before the winter sets in, not parade around in fancy dress."

"Logan," she pleaded, "seventy-five *thousand* tartan-drunk people attended this festival last year. You have a captive audience ready to spend money." Before he could argue that he didn't want splashy, she smacked him on the shoulder with the back of her hand. "Ooh. You can bring them to the fun drinking parts *and* to the plaid-sock-weaver *and* the Nessie-ladle-maker."

Despite the egregious made-up companies, which he would not deign to react to, she wasn't wrong. An interesting opportunity to support local businesses, certainly. And a new tour during the slow season wouldn't sacrifice their current itineraries or hurt their vendors.

But Addie didn't need to know that. She could wipe that self-satisfied smirk off her face.

"You know, it's not *that* historic. The procession only started a couple hundred years ago," Logan said.

Addie rolled her eyes. "It's a reimagining of the old ways. Nothing stays the same forever."

The barb hit him straight in the chest. Wasn't that the truth.

"For fuck's sake, you two." Jack locked Logan in a choke hold, or his best attempt while wielding a fire stick.

"Really, it's quite enough. I was promised a bit of messing about, not a workday," Elyse said.

Logan took a step back. Up ahead, a definitive line separated the relative darkness from the buildings aglow in the pinks, purples, and oranges of bonfire light. Lined up on the other side of the barricades, mobile phones lit bystanders' faces, recording the procession.

As they drew nearer to the lighting stations, shouts rang out in the night, and drumming from the marching band resonated in the air. The crowd rippled at the threshold, a full line of people turning round and touching their lit torches to the dry burlap of their neighbors behind them.

Logan shared a smile with a man in a gray knit hat and bonfire sparks in his eyes. Logan's torch caught, red and orange flames flickering and popping, and he turned to light the torch of the woman behind him.

The connection *was* a bit lovely.

They wove into the thousands of golden lights bobbing in all directions, and Jack waved his torch, a blaze trailing behind like a flag.

Elyse clamped a hand on his arm. "That'll do, ya chancer."

Thank god it wasn't windy. One wrong move and he'd end up with a singed eyebrow. Logan stepped closer to Addie.

Her eyes followed the orange embers floating in the air. The tangle of waves tumbling from her hat turned a gleaming copper in the firelight. She looked bonnie, painted in rose gold. And so like that first day: present, curious, enraptured.

Maybe it hadn't been an act after all.

A couple in front of them stopped to take a selfie, and the crowd bunched around the rapid they'd created.

Logan's body unintentionally curled around Addie's from the

push and shove of strangers, and he held his breath as his hips pressed against her arse, his chest flush with her back. His hand caught her waist to prevent them from pitching forward, and she looked back at him, lips parting, probably to yell at him—only she didn't. Their eyes locked, and his heart sputtered like his torch.

A heat he surely couldn't feel through the layers of their clothes burned between them, nonetheless.

Addie stepped around the couple and back into their line, but the distance did nothing to dull his pulse flickering in unwanted places.

"Do you want to say a few words?" she asked Logan.

"About what?"

The twinkle in her eye undermined her neutral expression by about a million percent. "The ancient traditions. Fire as a symbol of new beginnings..." She twirled her hand in a motion for him to continue.

Elyse and Jack burst into laughter, Logan's glare not diminishing their mirth.

"That's fine. I can show you how it's done." She turned to walk backward, gesturing to the crowd. "I'm Logan Sutherland. Welcome to The Heart of the Highlands Tours—"

Jack interrupted. "That accent may very well be a human-rights violation."

Truly abysmal, but the overblown outrage on her face made him grin. Long gone was the poised woman from the office, and in her place stood a playful version of Addie he hadn't realized he missed.

"Ahem," she said with an exaggerated hand on her hip. "Tonight, we'll recreate the ancient Hogmanay customs from a thousand years ago. Our ancestors lit bonfires—"

"I do love a good bonfire. Really any excuse will do," Elyse said—the poster child for Guy Fawkes Night. She thrust her torch into Logan's face. "Hold this, will you?" She bit the finger of her glove and pulled it off to better retrieve Goldbears from their crinkly plastic bag, dropping the sweets into Logan's outstretched hand.

"You've lost complete control of this tour already," Logan said around a mouthful of gummy sweets. It was a spot of fun to tease Addie. To be lighthearted with Jack and Elyse.

It felt like the old days when they'd wander down to High Street looking for traffic cones to steal and red phone booths to take drunken photos inside. Before everything was complicated.

Addie was different around them, too. More carefree. Less like she was seconds away from stabbing him with the blunt end of a pen.

Jack swiped Elyse's Goldbears, and Addie cleared her throat dramatically, ignoring their interruptions. "They'd light bonfires and roll fiery tar barrels down the hills. The roots of these festivities can be traced back even further to the Norse pagan festivals. Your torches—not to be confused with the British word for *flashlight*—aren't wrapped in animal hide luckily, but we'll assume the modern-day smoke will still ward off evil spirits. Now, have fun and don't light anyone on fire."

The history and symbolism did lend itself to a good tour. Community. Being a part of something bigger.

He was begrudgingly impressed by how much she'd prepared for this tour over the Christmas holiday. She was dedicated, he'd give her that.

A small part of him wondered what they could do if she worked with him, not against him. He was irrationally warm all over at the thought.

"Logan would have droned on for ages longer," Jack said, and Logan stuck out a foot, tripping him.

Following the crowd, they walked to the beat of the marching band. The bagpipers were too far ahead to see, but their shrieking version of "Auld Lang Syne" resonated in the frigid air.

Whooping punctuated the deafening chatter of the crowd, and

a smile split Logan's face. He couldn't help it. The revelry was contagious.

As much as he'd planned to loathe every minute of this high-liability event, now that they were there, under the cover of darkness and surrounded by people hollering into the night, he could see the appeal. *A bit.*

The river of fire wound its way through the heart of Old Town, transforming High Street into a world all its own, a sliver of the sleeping city come to life. With each step, he waited for the swish of Addie's jacket brushing against his. The motion sent tingles up his arm.

Once the procession emptied into Holyrood Park, the crowd thickened and jostled as they wound through a fenced course and came to a stop. When enough of the torchbearers filled in, from above they formed the shape of two people shaking hands.

A symbol of togetherness in a time of division. Light in the darkness.

There *was* something special about this tradition. Certainly, it was a once-in-a-lifetime experience for many people. Running a group through here would be challenging, but if he started at the pub to share some history before they set out, created a buddy system…perhaps it could work.

And Addie was right: there was a captive audience. Nearly guaranteed income that meant he wouldn't have to worry quite so much about where his employees' next paycheck was coming from.

The crowd migrated to the stage in the middle of the park, waving their burned-down torches in the air like gigantic lighters encouraging the band. Blue lights flashed and scanned through the crowd, and the bass line reverberated in Logan's chest.

When the band finished their set, fireworks burst into streaks of color above the monuments on Calton Hill. The silvers, reds, and violets couldn't compete with the awe splashed on Addie's face.

She turned and caught him staring, and his breath stalled. The swell of the bodies around them, the sounds of yelling, all faded, as if they were alone in a sea of upturned faces. He watched the sky explode in sparkles, twinkling and blinking out as another set of colors took their places in the reflection of Addie's eyes.

She lit up with a triumphant smile and stuck a finger in his face. "I can see you're swept away."

What he'd thought were fireworks booming in his chest were actually distress flares. He'd been a bit swept away by *her*, which was completely unacceptable.

"No one's leaving this event saying it wasn't authentic enough. It has history, community, fire, *and* its own hashtag."

She was right. The faces of the people around him were euphoric.

But it wasn't quite the same as *moved*.

He wanted his tours to be engaging and fun, yes, but also personal and meaningful.

Jack crashed into his back, and Logan turned to holler at him, but a bloke in a tam-o'-shanter and a pool towel printed like a kilt wrapped around his waist pushed past shouting, "Sorry! My bad!"

"Look. He's having the time of his life," Addie said with a knowing tilt of her head, like tourists bumbling around piss-drunk was some measure of success.

Foreboding inched up Logan's spine. She couldn't even see what she was missing.

Taunting had been the only way to get her out of the office, and she'd come right back to Edinburgh after those damn sheep wrecked her plans. He couldn't imagine where else she might have gone and connected in any meaningful way. "You're going to reject my tours outright, aren't you?"

She flinched like he'd hit the mark before a defensiveness stole over her features. "Like you're doing with mine, complaining this whole night? Of course not."

If she didn't get to know the country and the people before

she stepped on his bus, he didn't stand a chance. And what better way than a party? "Hogmanay is meant to be celebrated at home with family and neighbors. Come to my parents' tomorrow. I'll show you."

Addie's eyes narrowed suspiciously.

"My mum insisted," he said to sway her. Gemma wouldn't mind another guest. To guilt Addie further, he hastily added, "She felt bad you turned down her Christmas invitation."

His confidence in this ill-conceived proposition eroded in direct proportion to the wily smile spreading over her face. "I do love your mom's cooking."

It was perhaps the first time she hadn't lined her boots up with his, ready to argue until the bitter end. With her easy acceptance came a thick knot in his stomach like he'd fallen directly into a trap.

Gemma and Neil lived on the outskirts of the city in a
brick house easily classified as a cottage. A row of shrubs lined
the front yard, their orange leaves still holding on, as dormant
ivy snuck up to the chimney pipes.

Jack walked through the red front door and hollered, "Mum,
I'm home!" while taking Addie's coat and hanging it on the
rack. Addie didn't even have a key to her dad's house anymore.
She couldn't imagine walking in without knocking.

The noise of banging pans and creaking floorboards tumbled down the hall. Pictures lined the walls of their entryway
and evergreen garlands still wrapped the banister. The scent of
rosemary and onions hung in the air.

The only thing more quaint than this house was a Hall-
mark movie.

"Jack, is that you?" Gemma called.

"Aye, and Addie's here, as well."

As much as she was looking forward to Gemma's cooking,
Addie's motives for joining the Sutherlands tonight weren't ex-

actly pure. Jack coming early to help Neil with supposed computer viruses and suspicious emails was the perfect opening to
talk to Neil about new itineraries without Logan sabotaging her.

In the downtime between Christmas and New Year's, Addie
had filled every minute designing the Hogmanay tour and other
hot-spot itineraries—hoping all that progress would feel like
an accomplishment, like she wasn't so unreasonably behind
schedule. But the sickening dread in her stomach every time
her email dinged said otherwise. Marc was going to need answers, and soon.

She'd been naive to think all it would take to change Logan's
mind was a unique *and lucrative* tour suggestion in the middle of
their slow season, since he was clearly allergic to profit and determined to cling to the past to the detriment of all their futures.

But he wasn't the only one in charge of decisions at The
Heart.

If she could get a few minutes of Neil's time to plead her
case, she could finish this project before another contract came
up. So she'd be ready to hop on the next plane out of here, to
keep growing a business—a future—with the people she loved
most in this world. She wouldn't let Devika and Marc down.

Addie pushed away the niggling guilt tweaking her conscience that Logan had mostly given her first stop a fair chance
and she was going above his head.

But she couldn't afford to sit on her hands any longer. And
neither could The Heart.

While Addie slipped out of her shoes, Neil appeared, wearing his outrageously checkered jacket she recognized from their
first meeting. He wrapped her up in a quick hug with a pat on
the back. "Haud Hogmanay, my dear."

"Haud Hogmanay," Addie repeated.

Gemma barreled into the foyer, apron tied around her waist
and tendrils of graying hair escaping her messy twist, a testimony
to a morning of cooking.

Neil inched closer to the open kitchen doorway. "It smells lovely in there. Maybe I'll take a wee taste—"

"Oh, no you don't," Gemma said, swatting at him with the dish towel while he hopped away. It was the most charmingly domestic scene Addie had been privy to since her mom had passed.

Gemma enveloped Jack in a hug he barely tolerated and proceeded to adjust his collar. She was ready to go in for his hair when he swatted her away.

If Addie didn't miss having a mom who fussed over her, maybe she'd be annoyed, too, but she couldn't help feeling Jack was ungrateful and didn't even know it. She swallowed down the twinge of resentment. She wasn't wrecking a festive party by feeling sorry for herself.

"Happy New Year, Addie." Gemma pulled her in for a quick squeeze. "Don't you look nice," she said, clasping Addie's shoulders to get a good look at her. "We're so pleased you could join us."

"Thanks for having me." Addie smiled and glanced back at Neil, but he and Jack had somehow disappeared before she could preempt the computer mission.

The ticking of the grandfather clock mocked her. Neil did nothing in a timely manner. At the thought of Logan's impending arrival, a lead ball the exact weight of a tour bus she had no intention of getting on settled on her stomach. "Maybe I'll wait with them…" And make sure they didn't go off the rails the way Neil's vendor calls did, dissolving into bragging about fishing conquests within three minutes.

"Nonsense. We'll have a cup of tea and a blether," Gemma said, guiding her down the other hall.

Jack and Neil were already gone, and she didn't want to be rude. "That would be wonderful, thank you." Addie pushed aside her mounting anxiety and let Gemma lead her into the kitchen to wait. She'd make an excuse and check on them in twenty minutes.

Walnut cabinets lined the walls, copper pots hung above a stove that might have been from the Bonnie Prince Charlie era, and soft light filtered in through the bay window.

"What am I smelling? It's heavenly."

"The turkey. I like to get it going nice and early."

"What can I help with?"

"Och, you settle in and keep me company. I'm not putting you to work," Gemma said.

Addie wasn't offering to be polite. She'd been too much of a typical teenager to care about preparing a holiday meal the last time she had a chance. "I'd love to learn a family recipe."

Gemma's eyes crinkled with an affectionate smile. "Come over, then." She pulled an apron from a drawer and slipped it over Addie's head, tying it in the back. The motherly gesture made her eyes prickle, and she blinked back the emotion. Must've been all the onion in the air. "You can help me make a clootie dumpling."

"A what?"

Gemma gave Addie's shoulder a playful nudge. "A cloot is how we say *cloth*. We'll make the dough and wrap it up in a cloot before boiling it. It's a dessert."

Gemma unrolled a large tan cloth—the same texture as an old pillow case—before pulling out the flour, sugar, and spices. "The recipe has stayed the same for hundreds of years. I like to think you couldn't improve the clootie dumpling."

Gemma set her to mixing.

"My mum passed away when I was young, but I remember cooking all these recipes with her. They're in her handwriting so it feels like she's still here with me in a small way." She handed Addie a yellowed card bordered with roses and elegant writing from another time.

Blood roared in Addie's ears. "I lost my mom, too."

Gemma was so welcoming and maternal, the words slipped out like an admission of guilt. She clasped Addie's hand, understanding shining in her bright eyes. "There's a loneliness you carry deep in your bones when you've lost a mother, and I find the only way to soothe it is to share her with others."

Addie wasn't confident in this theory. Dredging up memories of Heather risked opening a floodgate she couldn't close, but it was too late.

Addie could see her mom in the kitchen at the first snow of the season, surrounded by a cookie explosion of flour and sprinkles. Making popcorn and apples on lazy autumn evenings. Reading poetry by Carl Sandburg in the heat of the summer, legs kicked up on the side of the couch.

"Will you tell me about her?" Gemma asked softly, pouring a small cup of milk into the mixing bowl.

Addie focused all her attention on whisking. "Umm… She was a school teacher. Always planned to get an MFA one day." One of a thousand things she never got to do. "She loved gardening and hiking. Really anything outside."

Gemma's warm smile encouraged her to keep going.

"In high school, when I went out, she'd always wait up for me." Addie could still feel the comfort of sliding under the black-and-white plaid throw blanket, tucking under Heather's arm. "She'd say, 'Tell me everything,' like she genuinely couldn't wait until morning to hear about the boy I had a crush on." Listening to that level of hormone-induced pining had to be the definition of true love.

Addie's heart ached for the ghost of the tether that had once bound them. She tugged on her mom's gold necklace, the chain biting into her skin. "I'm not really doing her justice."

This random list didn't touch the person Heather had been—how her excitement, her curiosity, had been irresistibly contagious. She'd been infinitely patient and caring and bright. But Addie had no idea how to put any of that into words, especially to someone she barely knew, no matter how kind.

"She sounds lovely."

Addie tried to return Gemma's smile around the tears stinging the backs of her eyes. "She was." She cleared her throat twice. "Sorry. I don't talk about her much." Unable to take a deep breath through the tightness in her chest, she turned to the window. Her watery gaze anchored to the lone, leafless tree in the yard.

Gemma came around the island, drying her hands on her apron. "And your dad?"

Addie blew out a tattered breath. He'd fallen apart on her. "He was grieving, too."

After her mom died, the first day back at school had been brutal. Her stoic facade crumbled at the muttered apologies, at the slightest touch. She'd left early, retreating to the safety of home, where she never had to pretend.

The house had been dark when she walked in the door, groceries still in bags scattered around the kitchen, ice cream melted through the carton in a pink puddle. Fear seized her, and she ran through the house, throwing open doors, convinced she'd find Brian collapsed.

He had collapsed—in his bed, surrounded by a mountain of tissues. He got up when she shook him. Walked to the kitchen. Put away groceries and microwaved SpaghettiOs, every movement robotic, silent.

She hadn't known it yet, but she'd felt it.

She'd lost him, too, and grief had tightened around her heart and doubled, forming a wall she hadn't let many people through.

Gemma was an accidental exception and a stinging reminder of why she didn't talk about this. It hurt too much.

"How long has it been?"

An eternity and only yesterday all wrapped into one. "Thirteen years." Quickly approaching the moment when she'd lived longer without Heather than with her. Addie swallowed past the burning in the back of her throat. The heaviness in the air threatened to drag her back to the chest-crushing intensity of the first days without her mom.

"I'm sorry she didn't get to see you grown. For all that she'll miss. But I know without a doubt she'd be proud of the woman you are."

Addie pulled her sweater over her knuckles and dabbed at the corner of her eyes. It was something a mother would say. Addie nodded in response because her throat was all choked up with tears.

Gemma squeezed her shoulder and, as if sensing Addie's need for space, crossed the kitchen to the kettle and poured boiling water over the cloot in the sink.

While Gemma's unfazed acceptance of Addie's tears was surprising and comforting, Addie didn't want to spend another second in that fragile state, powerless against the swirling memories ready to burst from her tightly held dam and sweep her away.

This was more than enough emotion for one day. In fact, she'd used up her quota for the next three years.

Taking a deep breath, Addie packaged up all those feelings with no intention to return to them, like a dusty memory box she couldn't quite part with, tucked away in an unused closet.

As Gemma wrung out the cloth, laid it on a wooden cutting board, and sprinkled it with flour, she gave Addie a running commentary on Hogmanays past. "When the boys were little, Logan would follow me around the kitchen begging to help. I'd pop him up on a chair and give him little jobs. Reid and Neil would spend hours on puzzles. And Jack always wandered off and got into one kind of mischief or another."

"That tracks with what I know of Logan and Jack."

Gemma smiled. "Those two have always been the best of friends. I worry about them now, if we pushed them down paths they didn't want to take."

"What do you mean?" Addie asked.

Gemma wrapped the dough and cloth into a dumpling-shaped ball, securing it with butcher twine. "Jack seems to only be finding himself now. And Logan puts so much pressure on himself. He's so afraid to disappoint Neil, even though he never could."

Addie wished Gemma hadn't mentioned Logan and his fears. She couldn't unsee that glimmer that he might be a bit scared of everything she represented and not thwarting her in the name of immaturity. He was simply fighting like hell to keep his business—that was also family—safe.

Wasn't she doing the exact same thing?

Without permission, her mind cast him in a light which was entirely too warm and golden for comfort. As much as she cringed at that damsel-in-distress moment last week, he'd rescued her from sheep on a moment's notice. She'd seen the joy in his eyes at the Torchlight Procession, the lightness in him around Jack and Elyse.

It couldn't change anything—she had a job to do and people who depended on her to do it—but Logan cared deeply about his business, and she couldn't help but respect that.

"We only want what's best for them." Gemma gestured to bring the clootie dumpling, and Addie lowered it onto a down-turned saucer in the middle of the pot.

"They're lucky to have you. Not everyone has such caring parents." She smiled, trying to cover up the revealing implication about her dad.

Gemma patted Addie's arm and said, "As parents, we do the best for our kids, but we're human, too." The way she tipped her head made it clear she wasn't only talking about her and Neil. A flicker of something akin to guilt settled low in Addie's stomach. Brian had always been larger-than-life to her, but maybe that was an unfair standard to hold him to.

The front door banged, and Logan called out a hello in his deep brogue. Addie's heartbeat perked up. She wiped under her eyes and smoothed her hair back.

Another voice rang out. "Don't start without us." A young man blew into the kitchen like a winter storm, tugging off his hat and combing his fingers through his sandy blond hair. The family resemblance between the brothers was strong, but where Logan gave off *pro rugby player* vibes, Reid could only be described as *dapper* in his dove-gray vest.

He bent down to kiss Gemma on the cheek and then moved toward Addie, hand outstretched. "You must be Addie."

"Nice to meet you," she said, shaking his hand, but her attention snagged on Logan's appearance in the doorway. He came in wearing the hell out of a black sweater and jeans. But she was immune to him. Absolutely.

"Mum, you put her to work? She's our guest." Logan set a bouquet of red berries and eucalyptus on the counter, and as he stepped into Gemma's embrace, he studied Addie. If she didn't know him so well, she'd swear there was concern etched around his eyes. Then all at once, suspicion took over his features. "What are you doing here so early?"

Addie's heart lurched, and she wiped her hands on her apron. *Dammit.* She'd gotten so caught up in the past, she'd forgotten all about Neil.

After Gemma shooed Addie from the kitchen—at Logan's insistence that she come enjoy herself—he swept out his arm for her to precede him into the living room. His smile said *Aren't I a doting host?* but his eyes said *I'm watching you.*

Gemma handed Logan a charcuterie platter. "Help me set the food out, will you?"

Gemma for the win. Addie headed straight for Neil who was mixing drinks behind a wooden bar cart in the corner, rattling the cocktail shaker like a kid with a snow globe. It'd been a long time since she went to a party that wasn't a mingler, but she had a sense that conducting business tonight would be a faux pas. Especially after their guests arrived. She was running out of time.

"Can we talk a minute?"

"Of course, of course." Neil poured amber liquid into a cut-crystal tumbler, dropped in a sprig of rosemary, and handed it to Addie with a stately bow. His gaze cut to something behind her. "Oh, Reid, you're here, too. How're the repairs coming, son?"

Addie stifled a groan as Neil's attention was pulled away.

Reid plunked down a whisky bottle on the bar cart. "I reckon I'll have everything up and running by the time I'm a hundred and fifty or so. But a man can dream." He flashed her a charming grin and began rolling up the sleeves on his button-up shirt.

Neil poured another concoction into the silver cup and shook it wildly above his head. "Reid's renovating a distillery," he said, filling Addie in.

"Wow." Addie opened the black hangtag looped around the neck of the bottle. "Is this yours?"

"Och, no. He's selling you a lemon. The place is a bit of a rubbish heap. Has been for about forty years now. How are the changes coming at The Heart?"

Perfect segue. *Thank you, Reid.* Clearly the helpful Sutherland brother.

Logan reappeared from the kitchen and something fluttered under Addie's breastbone that was probably panic over a potential interruption but also might've been guilt. "Good." She lowered her voice. "Actually, Neil, I've been meaning to ask you—"

"Dad," Logan called. "Addie hadn't heard of Hogmanay before. Can you believe it?"

Her heart kicked an angry rhythm against her sternum and she glared at Logan. Turning Neil's storytelling on her was low, even for him. "I'd heard of it—"

Neil clasped his hands, eyes dancing with excitement and ushered them to the sitting area where Jack reclined on the sofa. His feet were propped on the edge, arm thrown over his face, as if he'd just returned from a three-day mountaineering expedition instead of a micro stint in tech support. He dropped his arm and caught sight of Reid. "Aren't we looking posh?"

"Someone's got to keep up with Pops, here," Reid said, patting Neil on his checkered lapel.

"Did you know Scotland had a ban on Christmas until the '50s?" Neil asked Addie, not deterred by his son's teasing.

"The 1950s," Logan clarified, setting a plate of shortbread cookies on the coffee table.

Reid and Neil pulled up folding chairs, and Addie took a seat on the stone hearth, picking at her cuticle. Neil might as well have been on a different continent for how accessible he was to her now.

The heat from the fire licked its way up Addie's back, but when Logan settled next to her, a shiver spread through her, defying the logic of thermodynamics.

He leaned to the side and braced an elbow on his knee. His storytelling posture. "Scots didn't celebrate Christmas for nearly four hundred years. The official ban was lifted long before, but everyone worked over Christmas so Hogmanay became the primary celebration in the winter."

"I had no idea," Addie said. She couldn't tell if he was on to her and purposely keeping her from Neil or if Logan was really this interested in sharing holiday factoids.

"Hogmanay is meant to see out the old year and welcome the new with a fresh start. Our traditions stretch back to when pagans and Druids walked our bonnie land. We don't know all of their rituals and the meaning behind them, but it's reasonable to believe the winter solstice was a way to ask the gods for a return of the sun in the deep, dark nights of winter."

That twinkle was back in Logan's eye, the one she recognized from the Edinburgh tour, and so was the flutter in her stomach. It was hard to suppress when his brogue was dialed up to ten.

Jack groaned, mumbling, "'Sake," and pressed a pillow over his face.

Addie swallowed her laugh when Neil sniffed, push broom twitching. "One of my favorite customs to welcome the New Year is the First Footing. To ensure good luck for the household, the first person through the door after midnight should be a handsome, dark-haired man."

Logan leaned in like he was sharing a secret, and it sent an unwanted tingle up her spine. "That bit goes back to the Vikings. If a blond bloke showed up at yer door, ye wouldn't be in for a good year, ye ken?"

While she could feel herself settling into the way his rich voice pitched low—just like how he'd sounded in that unwieldy van—her drink would probably have the same calming effect without all the conflicting data points about where she and Logan stood.

Because people didn't invite enemies into their childhood homes, no matter how dedicated they were to their jobs.

And they didn't tell themselves they *had* to sit this close, touching shoulder to hip to knee, or risk knocking into the stand of fire pokers—even though the curved edges were covered in soot and would definitely wreck her white sweater.

"Otherwise, I'd clearly be the first-foot," Reid said.

Logan shoved his brother's shoulder, and Neil tutted. There was an easiness between this family she envied.

"Jack and Logan tussle over the honor every year," Neil explained.

"We have an impartial judge. What do you say, Addie?" Jack asked.

She held her hands up, staying out of it, but her gaze inadvertently collided with Logan's, and her traitorous heart fluttered, enjoying being in his sights even when she was trying so hard to stay out of them.

The doorbell rang, and Neil stood, flattening his already flat lapels. "Gemma, they're here!"

"Answer the door, then!" she called back.

Addie's heart sank. *Dammit.* How did she always get so sucked into their stories? She could only assume Neil's stamina for hosting guests was on par with sharing traditions and folklore.

He wasn't approving new tour ideas tonight.

Addie rubbed her temples.

The clatter of ice in the cocktail shaker startled her, and she looked up to Logan's irritatingly victorious smirk. He tilted the silver canister, offering it to her. "My dad turns into an absolute minstrel on Hogmanay."

Especially with a little encouragement.

Logan, 1 point.

She bit the inside of her cheek and held out her glass, ignoring the lack of righteous indignation that should've been pulsing through her veins. When the hell had the challenge Logan presented turned from infinitely infuriating to…a bit exciting? That spark she'd been trying to smother since she'd first set foot in the office was looking for any opportunity to catch.

She downed the old-fashioned, attempting to douse those feelings fizzing in her chest.

Neighbors arrived, and Gemma introduced Addie around. She briefly considered calling an Uber, but she hadn't been to a party like this in a long time. She might as well enjoy herself.

Over the next three hours, the noise level in the room rose in direct proportion to the alcohol consumption. Neil clapped his friends on the back as he laughed at their jokes, and Gemma sparkled, insisting everyone eat a bit more. The Sutherland brothers tried to trip each other every time one of them went to refill a drink.

Addie ate foods she didn't know the names of, and Logan swiped a biscuit from her fingers with a mumbled, "Trust me," before disappearing into the kitchen.

She had dinners with Devika and Marc—strategy sessions where Marc would cook elaborate Italian meals and they'd drink and dream about their business. The nights would end with laughter over insufferable clients and outlandish travel stories from their favorite places around the world.

But it wasn't quite this loud and boisterous and warm.

Addie got involved in a competitive game of Sticker Stalker with the lady who lived next door. Even with her back turned,

she could feel Logan's eyes on her, could pick out the low timbre of his voice, the way it rose and fell in deep waves. Her
temperature ticked up with each glance she met, until heat radiated from her cheeks.

He was so different around his family than he was in the
office; she'd noticed the change at the Procession, too. Those
smile lines were on full display, and he seemed relaxed and content in a way she remembered from their first meeting. She'd
assumed it was his guiding persona—the way she'd learned to
master moving with calm assurance, how to command a room
of predominantly men who weren't going to like what she had
to say.

But the way he carried himself was genuine.

She didn't hate this version of him at all.

Neil and his rosy-cheeked friends started up a drinking song,
taking turns spontaneously rhyming, which quickly devolved
into creative insults and rowdy laughter.

Logan was right about Hogmanay. If a shared drink at an
airport bar was a spark, this was a raging bonfire in her heart.
The simple act of a drink shared between friends was powerful and intimate.

She could see why the tradition had stuck around for a thousand years.

He appeared next to her, leaning back against the sideboard,
feet crossed at the ankle, black sweater stretching across his broad
shoulders. He stood close enough to touch, close enough to notice
the faint flush on his cheeks, the curve of his bottom lip.

She rarely had chances to let loose. It wasn't smart to drink
so much in a city not her own. But she felt safe here, buzzy
and light.

But not nearly drunk enough to justify the urge to trace the
edge of his jaw, the line where his stubble ended and smooth
skin emerged.

When she realized neither of them had said a word, she

cleared her throat and scrambled to pick up a picture from the sideboard of a teenaged Logan midjump in a green jersey. "Soccer star, huh?"

Logan smirked and pulled a forgotten sticker from the game off her shoulder, the subtle brush of his fingers sending lightning through her veins. It did nothing to help her regain her composure. "In school, we took pictures with the footie team out in Rabbie McMillan's pasture. I'm not sure why, come to think of it. But I'm standing there, one foot propped on the ball, arms crossed—" Logan demonstrated, tilting his head "—looking very braw."

Addie rolled her lips between her teeth and nodded in exaggerated agreement.

"I hear a snuffling sound, maybe a bit of pawing, and suddenly my heart is beating wildly. Then I'm running, a hair's breadth away from a hairy coo's lowered horns."

"Did it spear you?" She laced her voice with hope, but she secretly enjoyed the way he lit up when he told stories.

Logan snorted. "I took cover behind a gorse, which is really no match for an angry coo, until Rabbie's da distracted it."

She remembered that look he'd given Elyse when she drew the hairy-coo cartoon on the whiteboard. "And you've been a sworn enemy of the Highland cow ever since?"

"Nah. Look at the photo. Very fierce, indeed." When he looked back up, that curl hung over his forehead. She clasped her hands behind her back and dug her fingernails into her palms to keep from sweeping it back.

They couldn't go there. *She* couldn't go there.

A guide—maybe. Someone on the executive team who had no stake in her changes—she never ruled it out entirely. But Logan was so far out-of-bounds she shouldn't even imagine it.

He didn't even like her.

"It's almost time." His hand slipped to the small of her back, and her heart stuttered as he led her to one end of the room. There was no explaining the way her body lingered in the curve of his arm, static electricity dancing across her skin where she brushed against soft wool. Logan slid the windows open. "To let the old year out," he explained, and a smile spread across her face.

Cold air danced along Addie's flushed skin as a countdown to midnight started in a raucous chant.

Ten... Nine...

She never put too much stock into New Year's Eve or resolutions. The turning of the calendar was arbitrary, but tonight... anticipation hung in the air like something magical was afoot.

Logan perched on the windowsill, his hand gripping the open window, bicep flexing. Her breath stalled in her chest.

Eight... Seven...

His cologne washed over her, blown by the breeze, the heady scent leaving her dizzy. Whatever barriers her mind had been tossing up against Logan's dimples and relentless sweaters exploded into smithereens the second he leaned into her space. His eyes darkened and his lips parted, and Addie's stomach flipped with the irrational thought that he might kiss her when the clock struck twelve.

Then his eyes cut to the other side of the room and back to her. He winked, swung his feet over the sill, and dropped out the window.

13

Logan and Jack jostled on the doorstep. A playful breeze spun fat snowflakes as they made their lazy way to the ground, but the night air was biting cold.

Two… One…

The cheers for a happy New Year were muffled through the door, though Neil's deafening "Haud Hogmanay!" reached them quite clearly. Then a rousing rendition of "Auld Lang Syne" started up. Logan wrapped his arms around himself against a fit of shivers.

"Forget something?" Jack asked, clapping Logan's back, intentionally trying to knock him into the bushes.

"Addie distracted me."

Jack flashed him a cheeky grin. "It's like that, is it?"

A tingling swept over Logan's neck, the heat an unsettling contrast to the frigid air. "It most certainly is not."

He was having a hell of a time sorting through this highly inconvenient attraction. She was impossible—what with going behind his back to win over his dad.

And also captivating.

He'd nearly kissed her—quite by accident—pulled by some magnetic force he couldn't resist.

The way her selkie eyes had gone wide, full of wariness and yearning all mixed together, made him think she might have welcomed it.

Not that it mattered. Addie quite clearly communicated a *No attachments* vibe, and Logan simply wasn't built for a fling.

He stepped forward, sending Jack lurching to the side, and knocked on the door first.

"Ye wee daftie." Jack shoved back and did his own knocking.

Logan dusted snow from his shoulder as Gemma opened the door, Addie in tow. Addie's hair curled over one shoulder of her white knit jumper, making her look relaxed and casual. Homey.

"White rabbits, white rabbits, white rabbits," Logan and Jack shouted. Addie took a half step back, but a smile spread across her face. The heat of her attention warmed him from the outside in.

"We come bearing gifts to welcome the New Year." Jack bowed dramatically.

Their mum beamed. "We return the welcome and hospitality."

"Bread so ye always have food in yer home." Jack handed over the plate of shortbread his mum wrapped expressly for this purpose.

"Coal for warmth." Logan held up the black rock in demonstration before handing it to Gemma, his gaze on Addie. Her eyes danced with excitement, a sure sign she felt what he wanted her to experience. As much as his family was completely preposterous, it pleased him to no end to see Addie enjoying herself.

"Salt for flavor." Jack placed a white salt shaker in the shape of a sheep in Gemma's pile.

Logan pulled a coin from his pocket. "For prosperity." He was hypnotized by the light pink staining Addie's cheeks—the same color as fireweed when it first bloomed across the hills.

Jack set a small evergreen branch on top of the rest. "For a long life. And don't forget the whisky for cheer and toasting." Jack raised the bottle above his head, and Logan pulled a flask from his pocket which he raised in the air.

Glasses clinked, and voices shouted *"Slàinte mhath!"*

Addie looked behind her, grinning wide before mimicking the toast. He offered her his flask and held on when she took it, just to see her eyes narrow.

He wasn't disappointed.

She never backed down, even from the smallest challenge.

A thought hit him full in the chest, stronger than any shove from Jack. Logan liked her—everywhere but his office.

She took a drink as they closed the door behind them. The neighbors made their way back to the living room, chattering and stumbling into one another.

"I could have sworn 'And crown thy good with brotherhood' was in 'Auld Lang Syne,'" she said with a cheeky grin, handing back his flask.

Logan snorted. "Och, no one really knows the words."

Reid adjusted his vest. "No one but Dad," he said, moving to the threshold of the entryway in a blur. His constant motion always made Logan think he was trying to make up for being born five years behind.

Maybe he didn't grasp it, but Reid was the counterbalance that rounded out their family. Affable to Jack's brooding. Daring to Logan's caution. The linchpin that held them all together.

And a better lookout than he or Jack would've made. "All clear," Reid said without taking his eyes off the living room.

Logan retrieved a stack of napkins from where he'd stashed them earlier as Jack pulled the plastic wrap off the shortbread. They haphazardly wrapped the cookies in the unfolded paper and stuffed them into Jack's coat pockets, darting looks to where Reid scanned the gathering in the other room.

"What's going on?" Addie asked.

Jack shushed her. "Want to get caught?"

"D'you have it?" Reid whispered.

"Of course I do." Jack reached into a bag sitting at the foot of the coat rack.

Addie pulled the bag from his grasp. "Umm, can I help you?"

"Well…" Jack grimaced with drunken exaggeration as he retrieved a red box. "I needed something big enough to hide it." He tapped twice on the shrink-wrapped box of Walkers shortbread complete with plaid background and a Scottie dog.

Addie gasped. "You used my bag! To smuggle shortbread into *Gemma's house.*"

"She's a great cook but can't bake for shit." He pointed at the bulges in his peacoat.

Reid pulled out a pocketknife and sliced through the plastic wrap before Jack swiped the freed tin, stuffing cookies in his mouth and batting away Addie's attempts to get any.

She somehow enhanced this night. Broke the tension that had settled between his family these past months. She brought a lot of chaos into his life, but also a lot of light.

He'd feel her absence long after she'd gone.

Logan pushed the irrational thought away, chalking it up to the whisky and the magic of the night.

In a daring maneuver, Reid managed to pull the shortbread away and offered it to Addie.

"I could murder a curry right now," Jack said absentmindedly and wandered back to the party, still buttoned into his peacoat.

"The nerve of that guy. Using *my* purse." Addie chewed a cookie on the side of her mouth.

"He's a right bawbag," Logan said, the glow of the whisky traveling through his limbs.

She tipped her head, amusement splashed on her face. "Funny. Some people say that about you."

Reid's booming laugh, so similar to their dad's, abruptly stopped short, and a warning whistle took its place.

Logan's heart sped up. He scooped up the shortbread and took Addie by the wrist, towing her up the stairs.

"Mum!" Reid's voice was unreasonably loud. "Can I get you another drink?"

"What an eejit," Logan mumbled, his heart racing from adrenaline and the feel of Addie's pulse flickering under his fingertips. He released her, slumping against the wall.

She clamped a hand over her mouth, eyes crinkling in the corners. With shaking shoulders, she slid down the wall until she landed on the step.

Logan mirrored her movement and settled on the stair below hers, their bent knees brushing. The smell of her perfume—flowers and sunshine—diminished the space between them, and he couldn't pretend a race up half a flight of stairs was to blame for this out-of-breath feeling.

"Admit it. You're having fun."

Addie nodded. "Tonight was perfect."

He'd meant to tease her, expected an elaborate eye roll, but she sounded so sincere, Logan studied the wistful look on her face.

"I didn't know parties like this still existed," she said, arms wrapping around her middle. "Last year, I was with Devika in the office. We bought very expensive champagne and ate ourselves sick on those Lindt peppermint chocolates." She turned and searched his eyes. Logan wanted to give it to her...whatever it was she wanted. "This was nicer than you know."

The way she said it, like she was all alone in the world, made him want to offer her something to make it better.

Addie straightened as if this was some sort of horrible admission and tugged at her ear. The emotion brimming in her eyes disappeared, a steel door clanging shut between them. "But," she said with a wave of her hand, "this proves nothing. Bringing tourists home with you isn't an option."

A wave of frustration rolled through him. He'd thought he'd broken through the stronghold wall she so diligently guarded. "You're missing the point."

"Why are you so unwilling to make changes?"

"Because the last time I tried, I lost everything." Logan's heart beat hard against his ribs, not dissimilar to the coo chase. He hadn't meant to say the words so forcefully—or at all, truthfully.

Addie leaned back against the wall, two fingers pushing into her bottom lip as she studied him.

Logan blew out a breath and gripped the railing above him, clenching tight. "Reid, Jack, and I grew up planning to run this business together. To build a legacy. We spent every summer and holiday as kids on tours with my dad." And yes, maybe Logan had wanted to leave his own mark. But more than that, Reid had started to get restless. Logan felt him pulling away. "I suggested branching into whisky tours—"

"That's a good idea…" Addie's eyes darted between two cracks on the ceiling as if mentally scanning financial statements and competitor reports.

"I thought so, too. Well, it's Reid's passion, really, but—" Logan waved away the explanation. It didn't matter if he had done it to keep Reid engaged. He'd believed in it, and it hadn't worked out. "We brought a group out, and I…convinced a lad I knew to bring us into the distillery after hours."

Logan had wanted to impress their group, to set The Heart above the thousand other whisky-tour providers out there, to give the tourists a behind-the-scenes peek. "One of the tourists posted it to TripAdvisor. We were banned from touring there again. The industry may be competitive, but it's surprisingly tight-knit. Word got round, and soon we weren't welcome at any of the big distilleries. And my mate got sacked."

Guilt still churned in Logan's gut when he thought about it. He'd been so reckless, so unconcerned with the risk.

"Oh, no."

"I had to cancel the upcoming tours. We lost loads of money. Hence…" Logan gestured to Addie and everything she represented, although he couldn't summon the same ire he once harbored.

Instead of getting defensive, she looked thoughtful. "You didn't give it a fair chance."

Logan clenched his teeth. "Someone lost their job. Because of me."

She held her hands up, palms out. "And I'm sure that weighed on you—"

"It still does. It's not easy to design new tours. Our guides don't have a background in whisky—aside from personal experience—and bussing to Islay is expensive. It was all very complicated."

"I could help you. Negotiate rates with distilleries. Orchestrate kickbacks—"

"I hate kickbacks."

"Of course you do. Look, whisky is an enormous industry here. This is a great idea."

"No."

Addie lowered her voice like she was talking to a scared child. "It was one risk that didn't pan out."

"And cost me everything." Logan pressed the heels of his hands into his eyes.

"That's a tad dramatic."

"Jack and Reid left the business after that."

"Oh," she whispered.

"Reid realized how much he wanted to work in the whisky industry—he's in a master's program in Edinburgh right now and fixing up a distillery our grandfather inherited somewhere along the way. If I'd tried harder or known more…he would've loved running those tours. And we'd still be together like we're supposed to be."

"Would he have left eventually?" Addie spoke the question that snaked through Logan's mind on quiet nights. *Maybe.*

Reid had spent his summers tinkering in the dilapidated distillery on the coast, only joining them on the tours after their grandfather passed. Even before he was old enough to drink, whisky had been in his blood.

Maybe there was nothing Logan could have done to make him stay. "I don't know."

He stared at the dim stairway light, hand gripping the rough edge of the carpeted stair. He'd never questioned if Jack and Reid wanted this as much as he did. Their future had always felt certain to him.

"And Jack?"

Jack. His leaving hurt even more. He had no burning desire to do something else, just a desire to *not* work with Logan. "It must have been the out he was waiting for. He said he couldn't stand being on the road so much, and even though he'd taken on more of the business side, he never loved it."

"It's hard traveling for work. I have *one* close friend in Boston, and we get along because we both travel all the time. She gets the lifestyle. It's not for everyone."

Logan twisted the leather band around his wrist.

Addie sat up, reaching for him. She rested her hand lightly on his arm, her light pink fingernails curving toward his skin. Her thumb tracked slowly back and forth over the sensitive crook of his elbow, sending his pulse skittering. "I know what it's like when someone who's supposed to be there for you isn't."

When he met her gaze, her eyes were soft, but he could tell by the set of her jaw, the tightness in her shoulders, that while she empathized with him, she wasn't giving him an invitation to dive into her past.

"It wasn't your fault. You couldn't have made them stay—*shouldn't* have made them stay—if that's not what they wanted." She squeezed his forearm, not letting go. Addie was the last person he expected to comfort him, and also the only person who'd lightened this weight he carried. A glimmer of truth rang out in her words, and some of the tightness in his chest receded.

But he still couldn't forgive himself for wrecking their family business. He couldn't afford to branch out, to risk what was still intact. "I can't live with myself if I destroy what we've built. Please don't go to my dad. My tour is this week. Give it a fair shot."

Addie twisted her necklace around a finger, lips pressed to one side. "Okay."

14

Addie dragged Frank over the uneven sidewalks on the way to Logan's tour and checked her text from Marc. *Any updates?*

A chill settled on her like the numbness of a foot asleep, promising the sting of pins and needles. For so few words, there sure were a lot of lines to read between.

She hated when he skirted the periphery of micromanaging, even if she should have sent a progress report by now. Should have *made* progress by now.

The wind pulled a strand of hair from her braid, snapping it across her face so it stuck to the corner of her mouth. Addie yanked it away and blew out a breath.

She'd told Logan she'd give his tour a chance, like he'd done for her. After Hogmanay at Gemma and Neil's, Logan had joined her at the Loony Dook. She'd borrowed a flamingo floaty Elyse inexplicably had lying around, and Logan had surprised Addie by showing up in a costume. Granted, he'd dressed in a sheep onesie—complete with a bell around his neck—just to taunt her, but he'd still jumped into the freezing Firth of Forth with her and come up whooping like the rest of the Dookers.

She'd even snuck in a ghost tour after all. Since Logan only corrected the guide twice when the stories got sensational, Addie considered it a win. There was really no way she could skip out on his tour now, especially after he'd shared his family's traditions and the reasons Jack had left the business. The way Logan's shoulders had curled in, his voice turning raspy when he'd talked about Jack damn near broke her heart.

But she couldn't mend the brothers' relationship or change the past. Her job was the only thing she had control over. Sentimental stuff was very moving—but in this case, it was moving money out of the corporate bank account. The Heart couldn't go on much longer with half-filled tours.

She wouldn't jeopardize either of their company's futures, and she sure as hell wouldn't disappoint Marc. These tours were unsustainable, and she'd document every long drive time between sites, heinously outdated accommodation, and obscure destination.

Logan didn't like the idea of reimagining the tours, but he couldn't argue with cold, hard facts.

Addie turned the corner, and heat rolled through her. She'd braced herself for the impact of Logan in a kilt, she really had, but her memory was faulty.

He leaned against the blue bus leafing through the contents of a manila folder, one leg crossed in front of the other, the smooth curve of his sizable calves exposed for all to see. The pushed-up sleeves of his cable-knit sweater made him look equally ready to throw logs or snuggle up for a movie.

Since New Year's, her mind had returned to that almost-kiss on a well-worn cul-de-sac she couldn't find her way out of, but if it'd been more than disappointment coursing through her when he'd jumped out the window, she wasn't going to analyze it.

The breeze toyed with his hair, and he pushed it out of his

face in slow motion, his eyes coming up to meet hers on the glide. Addie tripped on a cobblestone, catching herself on the handle of her suitcase.

A slow smirk spread across his face like he was awarding himself the first point of the day.

If they were at war—and she was pretty sure they still were—Logan's strategy appeared to be waiting her out. Unnerving her with his watchful eyes, letting her anticipate when his next attack might come.

But he shouldn't turn his back on her, either.

"We're only off for three days," he said, tipping his chin toward her oversize suitcase.

She clapped her hands over the sides of the stickered hardshell. "Don't listen to him, Frank."

"Frank?" Logan's lips pinched at the corners like he was holding back a smile before his gaze cut to her feet. "Are you planning to hill-walk in those wellies?"

She let the ridiculous name for hiking slide and rushed to defend her flowery boots. "In a country this gray, I need all the color I can get."

Amusement and maybe something more potent lit his eyes. "We'll see if you're a match for the Highlands, lass."

A drawl called out, "Howdy. Is this where the tour starts?"

Logan leaned close to Addie's ear instead of pulling back like she expected. "Your people are here," he whispered. He winked before turning around, leaving a charge in the air.

A wink.

How they'd gone from wanting to push each other down the office stairwell to winking was a mystery the stutter of her heart didn't know how to solve.

"Welcome. I'm Logan." He and the new arrivals fell into a conversation about the trip across the Atlantic while Addie dug into her cross-body bag for her notebook, needing a reminder of what this trip was about.

Logan was on his game today, but she was, too.

An eclectic group of twelve people gathered on the sidewalk in front of the navy bus sporting a Scottish thistle and The Heart of the Highlands's logo splashed on the side.

Cowboy Hat and his wife climbed aboard behind another couple with oversize backpacks. A middle-aged brown man in shiny aviators chatted with a family of three while they waited in line. The teenager in baggy black jeans and a studded belt glared at them through the sweep of his black-and-red bangs. Emo Boy was perfection. Logan already looked put out by his disinterest.

Addie followed them onto the bus, noting the empty seats.

The bus smelled better than its American counterparts—used for shuttling drunk guests around wedding weekends.

No underlying vomit smells, 1 point.

Keith sat in the driver's seat wearing a shirt and tie covered by a windbreaker. Balding and friendly, he was her favorite driver and always made a point to greet everyone in the office when he came in.

"Morning, Keith," Addie said. "Can I just say, I have the utmost respect for your ability to drive this thing." She shuddered at the memory of getting behind the wheel of a much smaller vehicle.

Keith chuckled and raised his coffee mug. "There's a good lass. I liked ye straight off."

Addie tried to walk past Logan in the front row, but he reached an arm out to physically block her path. "I saved you the best seat in the house. Here, let me get that." He reached for her shoulder bag. "Does this one have a name, too?" he asked, while lifting it into the overhead rack.

The movement brought him into her space, and the smell of a forest after a spring rain washed over her. What was he, a freaking lumberjack? His navy blue sweater stretched over the expanse of his chest, his biceps forming a cage around her face before his arms fell away. Her body tensed, anticipating his hands falling to literally any part of her on their descent.

Which they didn't. Of course they didn't.

She let out a shaky and hopefully inconspicuous breath. "Don't be ridiculous," she said to herself as much as him.

Logan gestured for her to sit in the window seat. He turned to the passengers, leaning casually against the back of Keith's seat, and Addie mimicked his pose, her heart rate refusing to chill out. "Welcome to The Heart of the Highlands Tours. We're happy to be sharing our bonnie country with you. You've picked the only sunny day of the year, so someone must be a good-luck charm among you brave people visiting Scotland in January."

The group chuckled, and Logan fell into the easy banter of a seasoned guide, asking everyone's name and bestowing compliments on the two gray-haired white ladies who whispered and giggled, clearly jazzed for this trip.

As soon as Sofia and Carlos introduced themselves, they turned inward. She brushed her thumb along the light brown skin of his jaw before curling her fingers into his dark hair. His hand slid up her thigh as he tipped his nose against the curve of her shoulder. *Honeymooners*, Addie decided, looking away.

She didn't need any additional ideas of what this kind of forced-proximity might do to someone.

She sat down, but Logan's hips, clad in blue-and-green tartan, rested four inches from her face. Gripping the spiky wool of the seat, she counted cobblestones on the deserted street.

They set off with a rock of the bus, and Logan launched into a full-fledged history lesson, pointing out gray stone buildings that all looked alike, but his deep voice and exaggerated accent kept everyone entranced.

That's what was going on here: his lighthearted mood plus the kilt effect reminded her too much of that first day and brought all the fluttery feelings rushing back. This reaction was simple muscle memory.

And she needed to lock that shit down.

Once they picked up speed, Logan settled in his seat, his shoulder brushing Addie's and his legs spread wide under the hunter green kilt. He couldn't have taken up more space if he tried.

Minimal leg room, minus 3 points.

Addie bumped her knee into him. "Not cool, manspreading."

"What is that?"

She spread her legs in imitation of his stance, and his eyes hung at the junction of her thighs before snapping to the windshield. Warmth suddenly washed through her chest, and Addie shifted away from the pressure of his leg, slipping off her jacket. But she could still feel the heat lingering between them. This bus needed better air-conditioning.

Poor climate control, minus 3 points.

She half-listened while Logan answered questions and told stories as the land stretched out flat and windswept in every direction under the washed-out blue of the winter sky.

Addie scribbled, *Filling drive time with engaging stories, 1 point.*

"What are you writing in your wee diary there? How braw I look in my kilt?"

Startled by Logan's attention, she clutched the notebook against her flushed chest. "A tally. Plus one for the accent. Plus two for flirting with the old women. Minus three for not introducing the driver." Addie raised her eyebrows. "Keith deserves better."

Keith chuckled in front of them.

Logan jumped up, bracing his arms on top of the seat. That was definitely a sigh behind her.

"Ladies and gentlemen, it's been brought to my attention I forgot to introduce my dear friend, our driver, Keith. He plays a mean bagpipe and grew up in the Highlands so he knows his way around a winding back road, never you fear. You're safe in his hands."

Keith waved over his shoulder to the polite applause behind him, which Addie only noticed because she was trying her hardest not to check out Logan's ass.

"And up front with me is Addie Macrae. She may be a selkie—half woman, half seal—who dooms men to a life of pining for her love. So have a care." Logan's wink started a wave of laughter, and Addie's cheeks burned at the same time her stomach exploded into pink butterflies. He slipped back into his seat and glanced her way with a perfectly neutral face.

"Logan." She hit him with her notebook.

"How many points did that cost me?" he asked with a teasing glint in his eye.

"Seven hundred."

"Worth it."

Despite her embarrassment, she barely suppressed her body's reaction to his lopsided smile. It seemed wildly unfair for him to have a dimple.

They were hardly out of Edinburgh, but she could tell Logan had this in hand. He had a way with people.

Introducing her as part of the team, not the scapegoat to blame if things went wrong, made her feel included and special. Like that first day. It was far too easy to get swept away by that feeling.

Addie crossed her arms and looked out the window.

After another half hour of their legs brushing together, she was ready to crawl out of her skin. Buses with armrests would be at the top of her recommendation list.

Logan turned to catch her looking at him. "Thinking about improvements and revenue? Shall I pass around merchandise for sale?"

"How can I focus with you in a kilt?" The words slipped out with an edge of annoyance he hopefully interpreted as sarcasm instead of the truth. He was goddamn distracting.

Logan smirked and raised the hem an inch. A measly inch.

Her stomach dipped as if they'd plowed over a pothole. Addie mouthed *Oh my god* and wrote *Consider audio tour* in sprawling letters to throw him off. And to keep her eyes off the curve of his muscular thigh.

Logan snorted and grabbed his water bottle.

She needed to get a grip. On herself *and* the situation. "I'm too preoccupied with your impressive *shtick*."

Water flew out of Logan's mouth, and Keith thumped the steering wheel with mirth.

"Watch the road, man," Logan choked out. He shot her a dirty look before standing in the aisle to address the group. Addie bit her knuckle to keep from yelling, *Ha! I'm not the only one affected here.* She marked down *Flouting safety precautions, minus 2 points,* but Logan staunchly ignored her.

"Ye know the saying *armed to the teeth*? The expression means to be loaded up with weapons, but it originated in the Highlands. After Culloden, all weapons were banned for the Scottish people. But there are laws, and then there are *laws*. In the Highlands, many people still carried weapons despite the risks, but farther south the risk of jail became much too dangerous. The area where the patrolmen enforced the laws more stringently was near the River Teith. Hence, *armed to the Teith*. It's been translated into many languages, but most people don't know it originated here."

The passengers behind them murmured with interest and delight like his story stirred up their memory-making-fervor. Addie could *feel* them trying to remember those details to tell their friends.

Sharing local history in a unique way, 1 point.

"I'll let you get on with your view. We'll be to the Ewes and Coos Farm in another hour or so." Logan turned back around and gave Keith's shoulder a squeeze before lounging in his seat, kicking a booted foot into the aisle. They carried on in silence, the bright landscape no competition for Logan's body shifting next to her.

There was no way she was going to make it through the rest of the day this close to him.

15

"Fàilte don Gàidhealtachd," Logan said, his eyes on Addie. The Gaelic words rolling off his tongue broke her points system. "Welcome to the Highlands."

He ushered them off the bus. Outside, he stopped Addie with a hand to her arm. "Would you mind taking photos today?"

"Trying to keep me distracted?" He shouldn't have bothered; Addie was nothing if not an excellent multitasker.

"Whatever gave you that idea?" he asked, handing her a Nikon camera and looping the strap around her neck, the brush of his fingers against her skin buzzing like live wires.

"Let me get a picture for social media. Really sell the experience." She waved a hand in front of his body.

"You're very much missing the point."

"Ooh," she said, playing dumb. "So we can sell copies to the tourists? Great idea."

Logan's eyebrows pitched down.

"Does fifteen pounds seem fair?"

"Give it back." He held out his hand.

Addie clutched the camera to her chest, and Logan shook his head, turning away and striding to where the group lined up against a wood-and-wire fence.

Highland cows nuzzled hands and snorted puffs of steam into the chilly air. Their horns curved out and upwards in a perfect imitation of a shrugging emoji and red hair dangled way past their eyes.

"Aww now, you rushed right past Duncan and straight for his coos!" Logan said in a mock-scolding voice. The tourists laughed, turning their attention to the middle-aged man in a green windbreaker and baseball cap embroidered with fluffy sheep and the word *meh*.

"Welcome to the Ewes and Coos Farm. As you can see, we raise these sociable beasts, as well as a large flock of sheep, following the old ways of sustainable land stewardship. Now, once these mongrels realize you haven't any food for them, they'll wander away, and Logan will want to bring you out to the old croft house." Duncan tussled Logan's hair, and Logan smoothed it down like a disgruntled child, much to the amusement of the group.

While Emo Boy's mom tried to work up the nerve to pet a coo's pink nose with the encouragement of the boisterous Australian couple, Addie sidled up next to Duncan. "So...what kind of kickbacks do you give other tours?"

"Och, we like to think of it as a partnership." He zipped his jacket a bit higher. "Logan brings the groups, and we give them a memorable experience."

A diplomatic answer if ever she'd heard one.

Logan gripped the crook of her elbow and dragged her away from Duncan. "Come meet Hamish."

Reaching his hand out, Logan waited for Hamish's lick. The coo was sort of adorable, like a redheaded yak in desperate need of a haircut. "Go on, introduce yourself."

As soon as Addie reached for him, Hamish about-faced—

quite gracefully for weighing two thousand pounds—and shook his hairy rear end back and forth in a perfect cow rendition of *neener neener neener.*

She stepped back, mouth falling open in shock, a prickle of indignation spreading over her neck.

Birdie and Gertie, the octogenarians whose excitement had not dimmed, clung to each other, cackling. Emo Boy hadn't looked up from whatever replaced her generation's version of a Game Boy but somehow already had his phone out, recording this embarrassing moment.

"You trained him to do this, didn't you?" Addie asked Logan, whose full-blown smirk made him look exceedingly culpable.

"I swear *I* didn't," Duncan said, hands held up in surrender, tears leaking out of his eyes.

"What is it with livestock in this country?" she grumbled. Logan did nothing to restrain his smile.

As Duncan predicted, the coos eventually tired of taunting the group and headed farther into the pasture.

"I know a bonnie wee trail we can take to get a real sense for the land and see a restored nineteenth-century cottage."

They followed Logan onto a graveled track while he answered questions about thistles, birds, and the weather. His description of the crisp air and chilling wind was spot-on. The land was beautiful in a haunting kind of way. Windblown grasses, bent and rusting, filled the valley. Snow powdered the rounded peaks in the distance, without a tree in sight.

A place untouched by time.

It called to Addie in its unyielding wildness.

Logan made his way up and down the line of travelers, chatting and probably making sure Cowboy Hat and his wife weren't going to expire from the exertion.

Addie turned on a switchback, and the pebbled spot slipped out from under her. Her weight shifted too far onto her heel to recover her balance. Her arms flailed out to no avail. She was going down, shutting her eyes against the impact of hard ground when strong arms grabbed ahold of her.

Logan.

His big hands gripped her waist, steadying her. She might've lingered a moment too long when his chest met her back. "You're doing brilliantly. I knew those wellies would come in handy," he whispered in her ear and patted her hip.

Not an ass slap. That would have been completely inappropriate. But it was close enough that all her hormones rose to the challenge.

"Shut up." Addie regained her footing and ignored his chuckle, suddenly hyperaware of her own movements. The irrational desire to adjust her hair flitted through her mind before she tamped it down. She wasn't fourteen, for Christ's sake.

And she definitely didn't watch him walk away.

They reached the end of the path, and Logan held out his arms to a dilapidated shack. "Welcome to the cottage."

Addie snorted. *Hut* would be a generous term for the low stone roundhouse with an unruly mop of thatch on top.

"This cottage allows us to step back in time and imagine life in the Highlands in the 1800s. Come in, come in."

Addie ducked down low as they all crowded inside. Who knew what was living in the roof.

"A whole family would dwell in this one room," Logan said. "They farmed the land and raised cattle and chickens, but this was a hard life, only for the most resilient of people." After a detailed explanation of life in that period, Logan released them from the damp, earthen house.

"After the fall of the Bonnie Prince and the Highland clans in 1746, many Scots dispersed across the globe. Who here has Scottish lineage?"

Addie and half the group raised their hands.

"We can trace our lineage back to a hamlet not far from here," Emo Boy said.

Logan glowed brighter than ever. "Your ancestors may have walked this land, raised their livestock in a similar manner to Duncan and Peggy, and lived in a home like this one," he said with animated hand gestures. "You come from hearty stock—hardworking, dedicated people who forged a living for themselves against the odds."

Emo Boy looked like a graduate after a particularly rousing commencement address. Addie had not seen that coming.

Building a personal connection with a tough guest, 5 points.

"Every family has their own story to tell, and each clan has a deep and varied history. My family name is Sutherland, and this is my clan's tartan." He gestured to his kilt. "The pattern is unique and identifiable, a way to show where we belong."

Addie's initial assumption had been wrong. He wore the kilt, not as a gimmick for the tourists, but because of his pride in his heritage.

"You have a connection here, a place in the fabric of Scotland." Logan looked directly at Addie, and she held her breath as her gaze was pulled to the mountain behind him.

She couldn't help mentally comparing it to the one in her mom's picture, even though she knew the chances of it being the same were essentially zero. It wasn't quite as jagged, even though the surrounding valley was similar.

Disappointment hit her bloodstream, fizzing and wearing her down. It was easy to ignore the pull of the pictures when she was a million miles away, but standing here—under the same sky, next to a mountain that *could* be the same—ignited some gravity that tugged harder on her heart the closer she got.

As Logan herded everyone into a semblance of two rows for a group picture, he said something that had Cowboy Hat slapping his back in amusement.

Without thinking, Addie lifted the camera to capture the laughter in Logan's eyes. At the click of the lens, he met her gaze, and the moment was charged like the flash had gone off and forged an electric current between them. There was only her and Logan, the chill of the wind and the heat in her chest, and suddenly her heart felt a little less empty.

Cowboy Hat recaptured Logan's attention while the group rearranged for a silly photo.

To keep her hands busy, she fiddled with the lens like she had even the faintest idea what she was doing. After a few more pictures, Addie had herself under control.

She might have gotten swept away for a minute, but she needed to remember what she was doing here.

Logan ushered them back onto the path. He brushed past her, as if there wasn't an entire valley's worth of space to get by, and her pulse picked up.

She fell into step with Birdie and Gertie.

Logan's kilt swished above his bulging calf muscles, and Addie tore her eyes away. Attempting to regain some equal footing, she said, "Gosh, I could go for a spa at the end of this. A hot tub or a massage..."

He spun around at her words, and she returned his glare with a completely innocent smile.

"Oh, that would be delightful," Birdie said, touching her purple perm. "What I wouldn't pay for one of those heated-stone treatments."

"Same. It's too bad the hotel doesn't have one." Addie held Logan's gaze and lifted her hand to him as if to say *See? I told you so.*

He stomped up to Cowboy Hat.

"Look at that man. I could listen to his accent all day," Birdie sighed.

"Does he read poetry, do you think?" Gertie asked, sounding hopeful.

"I seem to remember one about painted-pink snowcaps..."

Logan whipped his head around, and Addie rolled her lips between her teeth. His onward march slowed considerably.

"Ahh...tell us what's it like being with a man so...*virile.*"

Birdie waggled her eyebrows. Addie wasn't sure if she should laugh or crawl in a hole and die. Logan—walking backward—spread his arms as if to say *Yes, do tell.*

She hoped he tripped.

Birdie and Gertie wore matching expectant expressions, and Addie deeply regretted including those two in her battle plans.

"Oh, no. No. We work together." Addie leaned in so they'd catch her meaning. "He's *completely* available."

They dissolved into a fit of giggles, clinging to each other's shoulders and wiping away imaginary tears. "If I was forty years younger..." Birdie growled like she might pounce.

Addie clamped her lips together at the direction of this conversation and how far back Logan strayed from Cowboy Hat.

Gertie settled her hands on her waist, thrusting her chest out. "If I was *twenty* years younger!"

Their hooting laughter drew out the questioning glances of the rest of the group. Logan put his hands over his ears, and Addie's heart expanded into her lungs. She hadn't had so much fun since she and Devika went ATVing in Morocco.

Back at the farm, Duncan and Peggy invited the group into their kitchen. They took seats at the enormous farmhouse table while Peggy passed around scones, clotted cream, and jam, telling stories of the farmers who provided the local ingredients.

She was as warm and welcoming as Gemma. And just as encouraging to eat a wee bit more.

Logan sat with Duncan, arm tossed over his shoulder. He made it look spectacularly easy to maintain friendships while being on the road all the time. It wasn't nostalgia driving these tours, it was Logan's deep sense of community. He was at home on the road, and it made everyone else feel like they were, too. A part of something special.

His stories, the sound of his deep voice, made people not only listen but care. But he was more than an entertainer.

He formed connections.

By tomorrow, the group would be swapping email addresses to keep in touch, she was sure of it.

Logan caught her look and raised a shortbread cookie, giving her a quick endorsing nod. She huffed out a laugh. The inside joke warmed her insides more than the tea.

The group interacted with a comfort she'd never seen established so quickly. They raved about the coos and the cottage, buzzed with excitement over unpronounceable shared dishes and unique flavors.

Addie pulled out her phone.

Addie: Blood sausage is as revolting as the name suggests.

Elyse: What do your people eat, again?

Elyse: Oh, right. Corn dogs.

Addie grinned.

"See," Logan said, pulling up a chair and whispering over her shoulder, sending a shiver rippling across her neck. "You *can* bring tourists into your home."

She rolled her eyes but didn't have a retort. She'd been on tours all over the world. Meeting the locals gave a sense of attachment, a claim to this place she didn't usually feel.

Addie hadn't traveled like this since she was a kid. Heather used to say she didn't need to see the whole world, she only wanted to soak up the place she was in.

Addie had forgotten that somewhere along the way.

When they'd finished eating and said goodbye to their hosts, Addie followed Birdie and Gertie onto the bus. They strutted down the aisle like they were on a runway, their attention trained on Logan and their shoulders shimmying as they passed.

He flashed Addie a look of pure horror, and she hid a smile

behind her fist. On second thought, including those two had turned out to be the best decision she'd made all year.

"You're enjoying this, aren't you?" he asked with a nod toward Birdie and Gertie.

"So much."

Logan stood to make room for her to pass, and she accidentally brushed against his chest. Looking up was a mistake. The wind had mussed his hair and flushed his cheeks. His eyes darkened to the same shade as a gathering storm, and it sent a primal thrill of anticipation through her. Logan blinked first and stepped farther into the aisle, gesturing for her to move past.

She sat and tucked her hands into her lap to keep from checking if his five-o'clock shadow was as rough as it looked.

They headed north again, the engine humming, and the roads twisting. Logan's leg rubbed against hers as the bus turned on the corners. A fluttery feeling reminiscent of high-school field trips stirred in her chest. Now all they needed was to share a pair of headphones and make gaga eyes at each other.

Turning so her back was to the window, Addie struck up a conversation with Carlos and Sofia behind her, if only for some space. "What would you say is the big draw of Scotland? Edinburgh?"

Logan's eyes rolled up to the curls hanging over his forehead.

"Don't hurt yourself," Addie whispered.

The grin spreading across his face lit an ember in her chest.

"We're mostly interested in getting out of the cities," Carlos said.

"To see the castles?"

Logan turned in his seat, his knee resting against the outside of Addie's thigh, sending fire across her skin. "What she means is, what brings you two to Scotland?"

Sofia perked up, leaning forward, her dark eyes turning wistful. "I went to uni in Edinburgh. I've been dreaming of coming back ever since."

"Is it everything you remembered?" Logan asked.

"Even better. I was only interested in pubs and boys back then."

Carlos pulled her in for a teasing squeeze, and Addie returned her smile through the gap in the seats.

"But it feels the same. Like coming home," Sofia said.

Addie got a familiar feeling being here, too. But at the moment, a swell of motion sickness surged up in her, and she spun around, her body suddenly overheated.

Karma in its purest form.

She retied her ponytail, probably whipping Logan in her rush to get some heat off her neck.

"You're looking peely-wally."

"Whatever that means," she grumbled.

"Pale. Little travel sick?"

"A. Wee. Bit." Addie tried to hold her breath as if it would help keep back the contents of her stomach.

Logan's grunt could've been in annoyance or sympathy. "Switch seats with me."

When she stood, he gripped her waist to keep her from falling into him as he moved her to his seat, her jeans uncomfortably hot and scratchy.

Keith gave a definitively annoyed grunt. "Ye boak, and I'll take back every nice thing I ever said about ye."

"Leave her be," Logan snapped. Rushing to Addie's defense was almost enough of a distraction to make a full recovery.

"I'll make sure to aim for Logan's lap," she managed to get out, to the detriment of her stomach. Bile crept up her throat.

"Keep your eyes open, lass. Look out the front." The only thing orienting her was Logan's deep voice. The land whipping past the bus made it worse, and her skin broke out in a sweat as she battled the churning. She made a whining noise.

"Not working?"

She could only shake her head, consumed by the sound of her

rough breathing. Logan gently eased her forward so her arms rested on her knees, and he rubbed slow circles on her back.

"Close your eyes, then," he whispered close to her ear. "Listen to my voice. Picture sitting on the beach, a cool, salty breeze blowing off the ocean. Sink your hands into the sand, the cold granules slipping between your fingers, while a gentle wave reaches your toes. Take deep breaths. Follow mine." He took deliberately slow breaths, and Addie matched the pace, focusing on the slow movement of his palm as it trailed over her spine, intimate and comforting.

He blew against her neck to cool her down, and the sensation overwhelmed her. Like she couldn't be turned on and nauseous at the same time, so her body sputtered out.

"Here." Logan pressed his water bottle into her hands and she took small sips.

The second they pulled off the road and the whooshing of the breaks ceased, Addie dashed down the stairs. She squatted against the side of the bus, gulping down the crisp air like it was Dramamine.

The rest of the guests filed off the bus, and Logan held his arms out, directing them away from her. She studied Logan's profile, trying and failing to fit the nurturing man standing in front of her together with the arrogant man she'd first met. No one—outside of his family—had tried to take care of her in a very long time.

His boots crunched in the gravel as he made his way to her and crouched down. "Would you rather stay on the bus?"

Addie's heart gave an erratic thud like it'd frozen and keeled over from shock.

Logan genuinely wanted her to believe in the way he ran these tours. The fact he was willing to let her skip it spoke volumes about his character.

It said he cared more about her than winning.

He was a dangerous combination of sensitive and challenging, and Addie was having a hell of a time feigning disinterest. She kept discovering more and more to like about him.

She might intend to tear his tour to shreds, but she'd at least give him the decency of a fair fight.

"Wouldn't miss it." Addie accepted his outstretched hand, warm and calloused, even though she was perfectly capable of standing by herself.

Addie followed Logan as he led the group into the trees with the steady assurance of a man who grew up scrambling over rocky hills. Her nausea evaporated with every step anchoring her to the hard ground under her feet.

They followed what was essentially a deer path through the woods, and bare trees scratched the sky, clawlike in the fading golden light. The gloaming.

Logan pointed into the branches. "When no one is around, the trees tell stories of people who have walked below them," he said, his voice muted in the dense forest. "Over that rise is a sacred pool. There are many in the Highlands, all thought to bring magical healing. The folklore is very old, dating back to the time when the Druids walked these hills. People would travel farther than they ever had in their lives to find these pools, or clootie wells. The ailing person would soak a wee scrap of cloth in the well and hang it on a nearby branch as an offering to the healing spirits. Once the fabric disintegrated, they'd be cured."

If Neil had told her this in the office, Addie would have commended him on an excellent marketing ploy. But the woods were silent except for the sounds of their footfalls, and the power of this place settled around her shoulders.

A rust-orange blanket of leaves muffled their steps as the group followed behind. "I always thought the rain smelled like wet pavement, but it's pine needles and something else here."

"Peat," Logan said, his breath coming out in puffs in the cold air. "It's an ancient moss."

A smile broke out on Addie's face. "Ah, so the rain gives it that earthy perfume? That beguiling—"

Logan gripped her shoulders and gently shook. "That's enough out of you."

As they came to the top of the hill, the trees changed, their branches dense at the bottom, ominous in the fading light. "What is that?"

On closer inspection, fat ribbons dangled from the lowest branches like a shredded clothesline, swishing in the breeze.

Logan grabbed a handful of fabric strips from his shoulder bag and pulled one loose, handing it to Addie. "Go ahead and leave a healing wish—although you look hearty and hale to me now." Logan's words were light and playful, but his gaze sweeping over her body was anything but.

Addie snatched the floral-print material from his hand, ignoring the fluttering in her chest. "Prefrayed and everything. So where's the well?"

"I'll show you." Over his shoulder, he called to the group, "This way."

Winding through the trees behind Logan, Addie looked for a wishing well with a rope pull and wooden bucket but should have known it would be more archaic. Logan knelt down on the flat stones lining a miniature pond, moss threatening to overtake them. Addie followed suit, bumps of lichen under her palm. "I just dunk this in here?"

"Have some reverence about it, lass."

Biting back a smile, Addie gently laid the soft cotton on the shiny surface of the water and waited for it to be pulled under before lifting it out, dripping onto the rocks. "Now what?"

"Circle the well sunwise three times."

"Is that like counterclockwise?"

Logan's eyebrows drew together, and he stood, pointing. Addie tiptoed around the pool. When she finished her third lap, she went looking for an empty branch within reach, while Logan repeated the tradition for the others.

Including guests in ancient superstitions, 10 points.

Now, what healing to wish for?

The darkening sky and the eerie calm of that place collided with the answer and made it altogether serious and heavy.

Addie walked farther into the trees, her heartbeat in her ears. The wet ribbon chilled her fingers as she traced over the purple-flowered print of thistles, asters, lilacs, and lavender.

That summer, her dad never forgot to water her mom's lavender plants. Addie cut the blooms, sticking them in vases around the house as if their perfume could fill in the gaping cracks in their family. In some ways it had, giving them a shared way to remember Heather when they couldn't manage to speak her name out loud.

Addie wondered sometimes if he'd kept them alive after all this time. If she went back in the late summer, whether the yard would be blanketed in purple swaying in the breeze. If there was still some ritual, some connection, he sustained from so far away.

Addie tied the scrap on a branch with a silent wish for her relationship with her dad, her fingers lingering on the cracked bark. That he would heal enough from losing her mom to love Addie again, too.

The wish was childish, naive, and…surprising. Maybe there was magic in that well, after all.

But she wouldn't hold her breath waiting.

Even prefrayed, it would take a long time for that ribbon to disintegrate. Longer still for Addie to forgive her father.

"We should go. It's getting dark to be in these woods." Imbued with intentional spookiness, Logan's voice pulled Addie from the thoughts she usually kept buried. With a deep inhale, she squashed them back down with the ease that came from years of practice.

She'd gotten caught up in the moment was all. And Logan was a ridiculously gifted storyteller.

As if summoned, he appeared by her side. The short hair by his ear lifted into a soft curl from the misty air. "What did you wish for?"

Sharing about her mom when Addie didn't think she'd see him again had been an anomaly, but she wasn't telling Logan about Brian. "A wish won't come true if you tell it to someone."

"I never put much stock in that one."

"Not what I'd expect from you. What was *your* wish?"

"For a certain American lass to tell me how wrong she is." Logan winked. "Admit it, I'm winning." With a smirk, he turned on his heel, leaving Addie to stare after him.

In her head, she *could* admit it. The tour had charm that came from experience and talent—not something that could be taught. But magnetism wasn't money and The Heart was failing.

Addie scrubbed a hand over her face and rushed to catch up with Logan. "None of these stops would make it into a guide-book, you know."

He ran his knuckles over the stubble on his chin. "And yet, the guests don't mind."

They didn't. In fact, it gave them an exhilarated swagger, like following an underground band who would one day make it big.

Her strategy was a guaranteed success, and Logan's was a co-lossal risk. But so far, his tour had been undeniably magical, and that counted for a hell of a lot in this industry. Stellar reviews and personal referrals were worth Big Mac's weight in gold.

She'd never admit it to Logan, but her job had just gotten a lot harder.

16

They gathered around the banquet table at Carbisdale Castle, the retrofitted medieval chandelier casting a low light over the chattering group. Usually, dinners were Logan's favorite part of any trip. These strangers—bonded by a day he hopefully solidified in their memories as magical and unique— shared their life stories without reservation. But tonight, his attention strayed.

He should have sat anywhere but next to Addie. They had barely stopped touching today, and he couldn't focus on anything besides the way she tucked a rogue curl behind her ear and smiled at the other guests.

Her laughter overrode the music in the background and the story from the already-inebriated Australian couple. She raised her glass of whisky back at Ravi, the American bloke who might well have been Sendhil Ramamurthy's older brother. Logan scowled across the table.

"The temperature dropped overnight, and we woke up to iguanas falling—"

Evelyn grabbed her husband's arm, cutting in. "They literally fell from the trees, the poor dears. They couldn't move from the cold, and the maintenance men picked them up by their tails to get them off the sidewalks. It was quite distressing to the guests."

Addie looked at Logan and raised her eyebrows, like they both knew exactly who had been distressed. He couldn't deny the tiny thrill he got from her secret look. As she held his gaze, the rumble of conversation faded and the sound of his breathing rose, her look turning from playful to heated as the seconds ticked by.

"I travel because it costs the same as therapy but it's much more enjoyable." Sofia's loud voice reinstated reality, and the table erupted in laughter and clinking glasses.

Logan tipped back his whisky. His curiosity overruled his rational brain. He wanted to know everything about Addie's watchful green eyes, the stories she didn't share tonight, and what her lips would taste like. Between the warmth of the whisky and the memory of her perfume, he couldn't resist. He leaned in and whispered in her ear, "Come on, lass, what's your story?"

She fixed him with a willful stare, but her eyes twinkled. "Not a chance."

And maybe there wasn't, but he wanted it all the same. He was undeniably drawn to the parts of her she kept hidden.

Craig, the owner of the hotel, pounded on the opposite end of the worn wooden table, stealing her attention. "Thank ye for joinin' us tonight. We're delighted to welcome you to Carbisdale Castle. Now for a bit of history. This part of the building was erected in 1907 for the Duchess of Sutherland…" Craig launched into a full history of the castle and accompanying lands, but Logan tuned it out—he'd heard it too many times to count.

Addie watched Craig, her elbow on the table and hand cupping her chin, like she couldn't get enough of this tale. Logan had a flash of her joining these trips, rolling her eyes at the same old stories and whispering to him about the guests the way his parents had done.

All in all, dangerous thoughts to be having about a colleague he had more than a professional interest in. Someone who would undoubtedly be getting on a plane in a matter of weeks.

Logan lifted his glass to find it already empty.

"Our resident ghost Betty—the White Lady—appears from time to time, dressed all in white, in various places around the castle. But her favorite is room 206. Which of you lucky guests is sleeping in the Spook Room?"

Addie's spine stiffened. She whipped her head to Logan, the look of panic quickly replaced with a stiff smile at the good-natured ribbing from the other guests.

"I'm in 201 if you need protecting," Ravi offered.

The wastrel.

She flashed him such a look of gratitude Logan's insides churned. If anyone was going to protect her from a made-up ghost, it was going to be him.

Craig waved away the ruckus. "Och, lass. She won't bother ye. She only wants for a bit of company now and again." Addie's wide eyes darted to Craig before a light flush stained her cheeks. She twirled her fork around her plate.

In a hushed voice, she said to Logan, "You know, guests should pick their own level of accommodation. Some people want luxury, some people want hostels. Debatable if *anyone* wants a Spook Room."

"But who doesn't want a castle?" Logan asked.

She pursed her lips. "There should be a cash bar, at least." She was clearly poking at him for the sake of it.

"We could stop off at Tesco to pick up alcohol on the way. Give them the full range of choice."

"You're impossible," she said, stuffing a forkful of neeps in her mouth, presumably to avoid admitting defeat.

As the meal wound down, the group began to disperse to bed. Sofia and Carlos had disappeared an hour before. Addie remained at the table, running her finger around the rim of her glass and looking out into the room as if it was a museum. Craig pulled up the empty chair on Logan's other side. "I saved the Glenfarclas for you after everyone retires."

Keith materialized at the mention of whisky. Apparently taking their appearance as a signal for the end of the night, Addie stood and gave them a smile. "Nice to meet you, Craig. Night," she said to Keith.

Her eyes lingered on Logan's, and his muscles tensed under her perusal. On every trip, he and Craig reminisced after dinner about summers spent down on the riverbank. But tonight, he wanted to skip out on his old friend and follow Addie's retreating form up the stairs.

Logan rubbed the back of his neck. *That's not going to end well, mate.* He clapped Craig on the back instead. "Good to see you, man."

They shared a dram in the empty and echoing dining hall, but Logan's thoughts returned to Addie. When most people took in the hills, they stared with awe or reflection, but earlier her face had filled with something like the ache of longing.

Perhaps his tour was affecting her a bit, if only she'd let herself feel it.

She'd been lighthearted the rest of the day. Not that he minded the teasing—never that—but she kept herself detached. He had to convince her why they should keep these trips intact, not just show her a good time. He chewed on the inside of his cheek. The rest of the itinerary was comparable to today's. If the tour didn't move her, this wouldn't work.

He rolled his knuckles back and forth on the wooden table.

Addie needed something to connect with. Something personal. But he hardly knew anything about her, besides how to push her buttons. He knew about her mum and her family name, but she practically radiated *off-limits* when it came to her personal life.

Maybe he needed to show her what these places meant to *him*. The feeling was completely unhinged, but he wanted her to know his stories, too.

That was it. His lips curved into a smile, and he jumped from his chair, tossing "I'll be right back" over his shoulder.

The air in the stairwell held traces of stale smoke from the hearth. He took the steps two at a time, hoping to catch Addie before she went to sleep.

The bathroom door at the top of the stairs swung open.

Logan's breath caught a split second before she crashed into him—steam and lavender.

A too-small towel. A creamy expanse of skin.

He reached out to steady her before they both ended up horizontal. Her hair was a wild tangle of gold and butterscotch twisting over her shoulders. She seemed delicate and vulnerable like this, enhanced by the freckles dusting her nose.

Heat radiated from her palm spread in the middle of his chest, washing over him as if he stood in front of a fire.

A water droplet rolled down the hollow of Addie's collarbones and between her breasts.

His eyes snapped back to hers—mossy green and searching—and her lips parted slowly, her breath coming out in a rush.

She leaned into his hands, the pressure subtle but unmistakable. Kissing her might not be a battle like everything else with them. She might melt into him, soft and sweet.

As if sensing his thoughts, she gripped her towel harder.

Logan snatched his hands back from her arms, suddenly aware of how long they'd been standing there and how deranged a path his mind had wandered down.

They both moved at once, trying to make up for the misstep, and bumped into each other again. Logan flattened his back against the wall, jarred by his body's reaction to her. His mind stalled out with thoughts of how much he wanted her. Not only dripping wet and unbearably sexy but challenging and comforting and *his*.

"What are you doing?" Her voice came out breathy.

The white terry cloth did little to distract him from the fact she was *naked*. And not a divert-your-eyes kind of naked, either.

"Er, I..." Logan fumbled around like a lad speaking to a lass for the first time as she pulled the knot of her towel higher on her chest. *Don't look at her legs*.

He snapped his eyes back to hers. "I want to show you something in the morning."

"Okay." She gestured in the direction of her room. Minimally, as to not upset the towel.

The washrag of a towel.

"I'm gonna..."

Logan swallowed. Nodded.

Her hips swayed as she moved down the hall, an extra half centimeter of bare leg revealed with each step.

He prayed for a hale wind.

Addie turned at the door, catching his look. The one he was sure wasn't hard to interpret.

And then he stood staring at a closed door, sucking in oxygen, feet growing roots in the floor, on the off chance she came back.

Christ.

He was never going to sleep tonight.

17

Someone tugged on the blanket covering Addie, startling her from sleep. "I knew you wanted under my kilt."

She blinked up at Logan's blurry form.

"It's the Sutherland tartan," he explained, and she looked down at the forest green, navy blue, and red plaid blanket draped over her on the lumpy lobby couch.

Her brain was fuzzy with sleep and the aftereffects of hiding out from ghosts. Fragments of unexplainable drafts, creaking floors, and tapping on her window flickered in her mind, and she repressed a shudder.

Around three in the morning, she'd swallowed her pride and curled up on the couch in front of the hearth as if she actually believed in ghosts or the old Scottish superstitions Craig had shared the night before about warding off evil spirits with fire.

"What are you doing down here?"

She shoved her hair out of her eyes and stuck a finger in his face. "You put me in the ghost room."

Laughter danced in Logan's eyes. "Turnabout's fair play."

Understanding dawned, slow like a winter morning. The haunted room was payback for the Edinburgh ghost tour she'd forced him on. He'd probably been planning this since that night. A burning sensation flared through her chest. "You have got to be kidding me."

Logan grinned in the face of her fury. "I was about to wake you. Come on. Let's go."

"As if I'd trust you now."

"I'll tattle to my dad if you don't."

The last thing she needed was for Neil to think she wasn't taking this seriously.

She marched up the stairs and as she dressed in warmer clothes, her brain came fully back online. Before the ghosts had started up the night before, the Towel Incident had played on a relentless loop in her mind.

Logan's eyes refusing to peruse her body felt more intimate than if they'd raked over her curves. He wasn't immune to her, but the confirmation only fanned flames that would surely burn her.

She considered hiding out in her room until the official tour started just so she wouldn't have to face him, but the truth was she couldn't resist a chance to be alone with him.

When she met Logan in the lobby, bundled into her yellow raincoat that was no match for a Highland morning, he stood with hands clasped behind his back, rocking on his heels. He cleared his throat, not meeting her eye, like he'd been having the same thoughts. A high-strung awkwardness descended on the room. "This way."

She followed him through the stone-floor lobby, twisting the ends of her scarf around her hands.

Outside, daylight broke in purples and blues, and Addie followed him into the trees, boughs woven together over their heads. Their breath came out in puffs, the tang of peat sharp in her nose.

She grabbed the branch Logan held back for her. "Gosh, if I'd known we'd be bushwhacking on this trip..."

"Then what, you'd have worn your purple wellies?"

She snorted in amusement, thankful he'd followed her lead, allowing them back to familiar ground.

They fumbled through the frosted grasses until the forest deposited them on the banks of a sleepy river.

"This is the Kyle of Sutherland." The sun rose above the horizon, turning the rolling hills in front of them to a golden pink casting deeper with each passing moment. The flat gray of the water waited to catch the dusty rays and reflect the mirror of the sky. "When I tell you of the magic in Scotland that you scoff at, this is what I mean. You have to know the right places to look for color."

Logan pulled her in front of him, resting his hands on her shoulders a beat too long. She told herself to move, but she didn't, and he didn't, either. Her breathing turned shallow, as if the slightest movement might make him step away. If she leaned back against him, rested her head in the hollow of his shoulder, would he let her? Would he wrap his arms around her waist and tug her close?

She imagined turning in his arms, running her thumb along his full bottom lip, dragging her fingers across his stubble. A moment where they stopped backing away, where they gave in to this pull between them.

But she could sense the danger in this attraction, the impulsiveness, the desire to let him in and make it count, no matter the risk.

She wanted him in her bed, but she knew in her bones that giving her body would require giving some piece of her heart. And she'd seen what love could do to someone. How much power it had to destroy a person. She wasn't going anywhere near that.

But when he broke away to stand beside her, a strand of her

hair caught in his stubble just to make a liar out of her, like she couldn't stop reaching for his heat and his touch.

"The people that've come before us have walked through these glens and touched these trees and witnessed the sun greeting the mountains. Others will do the same after we're gone. This place matters to me. It's a site of my people. They walked here a hundred years ago, sure…"

Addie turned at the echo of her earlier protests.

"But even though no one lives here anymore, I feel an old and deep connection. Sometimes we find a place we've never been before, but it feels like coming home. That's what I hope people experience on my tours." His eyes, sincere and unguarded, urged her to understand what he described, that anchor to the land, to the past.

Her heart fluttered underneath her breastbone, remembering the red dirt of New Mexico, the way it got on everything, laying claim.

The untamed bend of the river and the swaying grasses on the bank called to her in the same way. She hadn't felt that tug of possession since she left behind the name that bound her to a man who no longer cared and took the name of a woman who was no longer there.

"There's a peace in the permanence of the hills. A reminder that all will go on with the world. To appreciate the beauty of the moment we're in, no matter how long we get to enjoy it."

Addie's heart swelled. Her mom used to say the same thing. That life was a collection of small moments. That she should never stop searching for the ones that took her breath away.

An unbridled desire raced through Addie like the sparkling river catching morning's first rays. If this mix of peace and longing in a land that held no significance for her could settle in her soul, she wouldn't feel empty if she found the places in Heather's Polaroids.

Gemma's words came back to her, about soothing the ache she

carried by sharing her stories. At the time, crying in Gemma's kitchen had felt horrible, but with some distance, Addie could admit how cathartic it had been, too.

Maybe there was some truth to Gemma's theory.

The times Addie chanced talking about her past, Logan always listened and held space for her. He never retreated. And if anyone could help her find the pictures, it would be him.

She breathed in deeply, drawing on the courage that seemed to gather around her. She swallowed against the thickness in her throat. "My mom's name was Heather. Heather Macrae."

"You took her surname?"

She'd expected him to make a comment about the fake name and the way they'd met, but of course he latched onto the second name. She shot him a look, and he raised his hands, letting it drop.

Asking Logan for help was hard enough without delving into all that. She brushed her booted foot back and forth over a clump of grass.

"I have four pictures of her in Scotland." Her pulse in her ears drowned out the birds' twittering morning song. "Would you help me find where they were taken?"

She pulled her phone from her pocket with shaky hands. Devika was the only other person in the world who'd seen them. Addie flipped to a picture, holding it out to him.

"Ah, yes, I recognize this look well. Snarly."

A surprised laugh escaped her lungs.

"She's bonnie. You have the same eyes." Logan met Addie's gaze, and her breath caught. He tapped the picture of her mom in front of a lake. "I think I know where this one is."

"Where?" Addie's voice raised an octave, and her heart didn't beat so much as vibrate. She'd carried these pictures for so long, and now she had a real chance to visit these spots, to stand where Heather had stood. Hope spread in her chest like wings.

Logan's eyes and voice turned soft. "Let me surprise you."

Addie smiled at the memory of him showing off the Edinburgh skyline on that first tour. She'd give anything to have a wonderstruck moment like that again. "Thank you."

"Of course," he said without hesitation. "Can I send these to myself?"

She nodded, and his fingers typed on the screen.

Logan's lips tipped up. "Oh, I'm in here already," he said, amusement heavy in his voice.

Remembering too late how she'd entered him in her Contacts, Addie's face flushed with an impossible warmth for the chill of the morning. She snatched the phone back.

He studied her, his eyes asking for confirmation that she'd felt that initial attraction, too, as if *Logan NOT Hot Scottish Tour Guide* wasn't a dead giveaway.

She considered maintaining that the moniker was accurate. But he was helping her. These past few days he was so much like the man she first met—endearing, soft, earnest—and she couldn't quite bring herself to shunt them back to the place where they poked and prodded each other.

"Don't let it go to your head. It's bound to explode from all the fawning everyone's doing over you." She rolled her eyes at his playful grin.

"Speaking of, we should get back."

"Lead the way, Tour Guide."

18

The ruins of Urquhart Castle tumbled down to the banks of Loch Ness. The walls of the castle dove below the surface of the lush grass carpeting the floor of ancient rooms as if the uneven earth was reclaiming its old belongings. Across the water, a hill caught a low-hanging wisp of a cloud.

The group crossed a footbridge Addie prayed wasn't the original and peered over the thankfully empty streambed below.

Logan had memorized the last eight centuries of the castle's bloody past, and he shared his infinite wisdom with the group huddled around him.

"For nearly a millennium this castle passed hands between the English, Scots, and the Lord of the Isles…" He led them through the ruins, painting a picture of what kinds of rooms these rock borders might have been.

Any malevolent spirits who must have lurked these halls were long gone…but Addie wouldn't set foot there in the dark, not after the night she'd had.

The group ascended an altogether too-creaky ladder to the

top of a tower Addie wasn't sure could hold their weight. Scaffolding supported the other side, but the view from the top—high above the crinkle of the water meeting the sheer, rocky bank—was worth the danger.

Safely back on land, Logan told the tourists to enjoy exploring the rest of the site, dip their hands in the frigid water, and make sure they didn't get nipped by Nessie. Then his fingers were a soft pressure on Addie's elbow, turning her from the group. "I have something to show you."

"Are you, Logan Sutherland, deviating from the script?"

He probably had stories to fill another few hours about clan chieftains, Nessie sightings, and prehistoric building techniques.

"I can be spontaneous."

"I'll bet."

Logan narrowed his eyes at her sarcasm.

Addie followed him past the tower and over a rolling slope of green grass facing the banks of Loch Ness. The leafless trees stood guard over the water, lined up in ascending height like the kids in *The Sound of Music*.

"What are we looking at? Is that Nessie?" Streaks of sunlight glinted across the ripples of the lake, enough to trick her eyes into a sighting.

"It's her photo."

Addie's heart gave a one-two punch against her rib cage. She'd been so focused on teasing him, she hadn't realized where he was taking her.

Loch Ness would never make it on his itinerary. He'd done this just for her.

Logan pulled his phone from his sporran, swiped to the summer version of this scene, and held it up to the lake.

She wouldn't have recognized the similarity without the full-leafed trees, but the lake was the same gray-blue. The same shadowy hills rose out of the water along the horizon to touch the sullen expanse of the sky.

Addie's limbs tingled, her nerve endings flooding with excitement or grief—either way, rushing too quickly to spread the news, *she was here.*

Heather had probably touched that water, those tree trunks.

Before Addie knew what she was doing, she stood on the bank, ran her hand down the smooth, light bark of the towering trees and scooped the water, so cold it burned her fingers.

She was here.

Addie's heart beat unsteadily, off-center and jerky.

The air felt colder. Maybe it was simply being close to the water.

Or maybe some lingering whisper of a ghost hovered around her. Not a haunting presence, a soothing one. A stroke over hair. A cup of a cheek. She closed her eyes and leaned into it.

Mom.

Addie's throat thickened as the lake and sky blurred together. Tears fell on the pebbled bank. She committed to memory the sound of the tiny waves lapping at her wellies, the heaviness of the clouds above her, the murky smell of this legendary lake.

A place that tied her to her mom through time.

Addie could see Heather sitting cross-legged on the shore, ponytail pushed through her baseball hat, her binoculars pressed to her eyes—the ones she bought for birding and football games but almost always forgot at home. Could picture her gasping and grabbing Brian's arm every time she saw a ripple.

For hours.

God, Addie would give anything for just one of those endless afternoons she hadn't appreciated at all.

A twig snapped, and Logan crouched beside her, running his hand gently up and down her back. She stood and stepped away, flushing, and wiped tears with the heel of her hand.

Addie blinked quickly. "Sorry." Her voice broke on the word. It'd been a long time since she'd missed her mom quite so physically.

Logan was probably inching backward in a silent retreat, deeply regretting bringing her here.

She rubbed her throat, trying to soothe the emotion buzzing under her skin, to keep from having a total meltdown in front of him. "We can head back." The forced smile didn't sit right on her face.

As she turned up the hill, Logan reached for her. She stared at his fingers forming a bracelet around her wrist, not tight enough to keep her if she wanted to pull away.

"You don't have to be strong on my account."

She looked up into eyes that held no pity, only compassion. He gave her the tiniest of smiles. Encouraging. Supportive. And it slowed the whirring in her veins. He wasn't running from the Sad Girl.

Logan turned and gazed out at the water like he had nowhere else to be. Like he wouldn't leave her here alone.

Addie didn't have any words. Not yet.

His grip on her wrist loosened. The pads of his fingertips tracked tiny sparks across her palm until they slipped between her fingers.

It has been so long since someone stood beside her. She squeezed his hand.

A tiny indulgence. Just for a second.

They took in the view as far-off voices brought on the wind harmonized with the steady rhythm of the water and her own deep breathing. Logan smelled like camping trips—pine needles and big sky, tranquil and freeing. Her pulse—or his—beat between their entwined fingers.

The breeze settled around her like a familiar plaid blanket. She curved her shoulders in, holding on to the fleeting feeling, while a silent tear made its way down her cheek.

Slowly, the magic slipped away. She breathed deeply against the sting of loss…only, it never came. Her heart felt light for the first time in years.

"Thank you. You don't know how special this was."

"It's my pleasure." The earnest timbre of his voice sparked the sensation of tripping down the stairs, the world tilting for a moment before abruptly righting itself. When she had her feet back under her, she met his gaze—a warmth there to soothe the iciness in her chest, a balm to all her raw emotions.

It scared her how easily he comforted her, how she handed over pieces of herself without meaning to.

She preferred how they'd been yesterday—fun and light. "We'd better get back. Who knows what trouble Birdie and Gertie have gotten into, unattended."

Logan shifted his weight, a crease appearing between his eyebrows as if deciding whether or not to allow this shift back to normalcy.

She smiled and tipped her head in a gesture that said *Let's go*. When he hesitated, she said, "They might be in the gift shop."

Relenting, he followed her back up the hill.

Needing a minute to herself, she tucked back into her window seat while Logan wrangled the tourists.

Addie had spent years designing tours to give people a sense of wonder, a connection to a greater community of people who walked the same path. But somewhere along the way, she'd forgotten the reason she'd started this job. To feel close to her mom and the way they used to travel. To search for magic in the desert or a strawberry field or on their own back stoop watching the sandhill crane migration.

And to seek a connection to the people who held her hand and shouldered her grief and shifted the axis of her compass back to true north.

Logan had reminded her that the true wonder was to be found in small moments. Yesterday, she'd seen how he made these tours personal, how the guests relaxed into a sense of camaraderie he built for them. They'd formed strong bonds with the locals and deep ties to the country. She'd felt the power of the land and the spirit of her mother.

The world deserved Logan Sutherland's tours.

Addie could no longer sanction steamrolling him with tourist attractions. If she was being honest with herself, that wasn't the way she liked to travel, either.

Picturing him guiding some huge castle where he didn't know anyone, had no personal anecdotes to share, killed her. But so did the idea of this company going belly-up and hers along with it.

There had to be some solution to accomplish what they both wanted.

As the guests found their way back onto the bus, they tittered over their purchases and the beauty of the ruins.

Once everyone was settled and Keith started driving, Logan slid back into his seat. He dug in his sporran and handed her a blue sticker in the shape of Scotland, the world *Alba* in white across the middle. "For Frank. He needs to represent."

The world shrank to their shared seat. The curve of his thumbnail holding out the glossy sticker. The heat of his leg against hers. The dimple peeking out from behind his stubble, his smile a mix of earnest and unsure.

Addie's chest filled like a hot-air balloon.

There was something about standing in Logan's glow. Being a part of his circle—huddled around him on a tour, or surrounded by his friends and family—wasn't simply a rush that came from being with the in-crowd. It gave her the sense that she was exactly where she should be, like all the excitement, all the laughter, was happening right here, right now, and she got to be a part of it.

It made her want to believe in fairy tales, if only for a moment.

19

Logan sat next to Addie at the dining table of Castle Storn.
He couldn't keep his eyes off her. The way she cupped her chin
when she was interested in someone's story. The way she looked
freer, her shoulders loose and relaxed, her smile easy. So far from
the polished consultant he knew in the office.

Nothing brought him more satisfaction than connecting
people with their histories. Any time he witnessed someone
finding a piece of their past, it was profound and hopeful. But
watching Addie today had been *more*.

Maybe because she seemed so unsure of her connection and
wary to explore it, where everything else he'd seen of her was
bold and determined.

Or maybe it had to do with the sadness he sometimes caught
lurking in her eyes.

He wouldn't pretend he understood anything about the grief
she carried, but she'd let him ease the pain for a moment there,
and it felt like a bestowing of a trust he desperately wanted.
He'd never felt so close to someone.

Oddly, her trust in him made him feel supported, too. Like his desire to seek out destinations that would give someone a deeper bond to his land wasn't frivolous or something he could walk away from.

It mattered.

For the first time, he wondered if there was an outcome where changing his tours wouldn't diminish their spirit but could turn them into something even more meaningful, more personal.

"We've got a wee surprise in store for ye." Malcolm, the owner of the hotel and Neil's favorite fishing competitor, interrupted Logan's thoughts. "Allow me to introduce our entertainment for the evening." He gestured to two lads holding their respective fiddle and accordion, as if they'd heard all the noise, grabbed their kilts, and come running.

"If ye haven't been to a ceilidh before, you're in for a treat. It's a traditional Scottish reel, and we'll be callin' out the steps so you can join in the dance."

Nervous laughter overtook the room, louder than the scraping of the chair legs.

A Riverside Jig started up, and Logan clapped above his head, herding everyone out. Malcom's voice boomed without the aid of a microphone. "Everyone pick a partner, and we'll start with a simple dance."

Logan looped his fingers around Addie's wrist. "Dance with me."

She stepped into his space and looked up at him with a grin. "Not a chance."

"Dance with me."

Addie narrowed her eyes, but she never backed down from a challenge. He held out his arm to escort her into the hall, and she curled her hand around his forearm.

The group broke into two parallel lines, the excitement palpable in the air.

The ceilidh was another highlight of the tour. No one was

particularly accomplished at this dance, always lagging behind the caller, but huge smiles lit their faces, nonetheless.

They held hands in their line and moved together and away again while Malcolm shouted, "*One*, two, three, jump. *Back*, two, three, jump. Right-hand side!"

Logan, Addie, Carlos, and Sofia placed their hands into the middle of the circle, pinwheeling about. As Addie spun, Logan caught sight of the open back of her black sleeveless shirt and his breath got lost on its way out, causing a gridlock and stressing his heart. The fabric draped in a thick X across her upper back, and the triangular cutout below revealed the curve of her spine. He wanted to tug the sashes tied together in a loopy bow at her waist more than he'd wanted a driving license.

"Left-hand side!"

Logan turned to whirl the other way, forcibly dragging his mind away from the burning desire to feel Addie's soft skin.

"Do-si-do your partner."

He crossed his arms out in front of him, stepping in a square around Addie, his skin tingling in every place they touched.

"Swing your partner, do-si-do," she called over the fiddle and the stomping.

"You sound like Elyse."

"No, Elyse sounds like me. Or a caricature of me. Shut up." The flush on her cheeks was probably from the dancing, but it warmed his chest either way.

Malcolm shouted, "Now your side partner!" and Logan repeated the box step with Ravi.

"And down the line!"

The four people at the ends linked hands up and over the two lines while everyone crouched down, clapping and laughing.

They repeated the steps until the song changed, and they fell back into their parallel lines. The people at the far end hooked elbows and spun like cogs twisting down the line.

The utter mayhem that was Birdie and Gertie barreled toward them, and Logan pulled Addie out of the crosshairs. She stumbled and fell against his chest. Her face glowed, framed by the light curls at her temples. One glittery smile and he wanted to bury his hands in her hair, push her against the castle wall and claim her mouth, the tourists be damned.

He reluctantly released her. In true ceilidh fashion, the fiddlers picked up the tempo, and the group devolved into absolute chaos, a flurry of shoulder bumps, sweaty palms, and beaming faces.

By the end of the song, Addie was on the other side of the room. She locked eyes with him and tilted her head out the door. He followed as if attached with a string.

Laughable, really, that he'd once thought he wanted to avoid this woman.

"I want to show you something," she said when he reached her.

"Trying to get me alone?" His heart beat in time with the lively music, anticipation pulsing in his veins.

"I don't *actually* want to see what's under your kilt, Logan."

A laugh burst from his chest, and he followed Addie into a room full of marble busts on pedestals. Lanterns hung from the ceiling, so dim they might have housed real fire.

"I found a Macrae in here earlier."

"Look at you, connecting with your heritage."

Her hips swayed as she wound through the room, and she tossed a dirty look over her shoulder. "Here he is." She gestured to the grizzled bust before bending to inspect the plaque, and Logan kept his eyes resolutely off her arse.

He leaned in closer, if only to take a deep breath of her perfume, like late-summer flowers, and to have a better view of the subtle curve of her lips. "Handsome bloke."

Addie tilted her head toward him, eyes twinkling. She picked at the inscription and the bust wobbled. As she steadied the column, she gave Logan a wide-eyed look that turned his insides to mush. She was downright addicting.

A part of his brain urged him to at least have a bit of fun before she left—no matter how irresponsible it might be. To pull her in closer. To cross his self-imposed barriers.

It was becoming impossible to resist her.

"Loch Lomond" started playing in the dance hall. "Oh, this is the one Scottish song I know." The excitement in Addie's voice nipped at his heart.

Against his better judgment, he started singing. Addie giggled, and he took her hand, twirling her. She came in strong for the chorus with a blundering accent and ended her spin in his arms.

Logan's muscles tensed, his fingers tingling with the urge to sink into her hair or her hips. Preferably both. He settled for spreading his hand over her jeans at the curve of her lower back, his thumb flirting dangerously with the tie of her open-backed shirt.

He leaned into the light pressure of her fingers on his chest, and the heat from her body singed him through the cotton of his button-up.

He'd forgotten how small she was. She was always such a formidable opponent.

They moved in a tight circle, their legs brushing with each turn. They were dangerously close to a tented-tartan situation he wasn't one hundred percent certain she'd appreciate. His mind prickled with the need for familiar ground. "What do you have to say for yourself, sabotaging my tour yesterday?"

She staged a gasp, complete with a fluttering hand to her chest. "I did no such thing."

It took everything in him not to smile at her. Or lean down and claim her lips. "Yes, you did. *The drive is so long. I want a massage. The rugs need upgrading.*"

Addie smirked up at him. "It was only a little to prove a point. And only because it makes you so surly."

"Surly? I am ever polite and mild-mannered," Logan said.

A wicked challenge lit her green eyes. "You're a delight to

rile up." Her fingers trailed up the curve of his neck and slipped into his hair. Heat bloomed in his chest, unfurling in dizzying waves at the clear invitation in her touch.

"If you think I'm delightful when I'm mad, you should see me when I'm not." He tugged her closer, his fingers slipping below the soft black bow.

Her soft intake of breath sent fire through his veins. She stilled in his arms, wet her lips, and looked up at him through her lashes. "Then, let's stop fighting."

Her eyes darkened, and his defenses crumbled like centuries-old castle walls, broken-down and useless. His skin burned with the thought of laying down their weapons. Of giving in to this woman. "Are you suggesting a truce?" he asked, barely holding on to the thread of conversation.

"A compromise."

The word was loaded, but for now he couldn't consider the two dozen pages of fine print that surely accompanied this offer. Whatever working together looked like tomorrow, tonight it meant Addie had let her guard down.

She'd seen the land, the traditions, the stories, that made up the very fiber of his being. She saw *him*, and it was enough to change her mind.

"You were impressed, then?" he asked. Sparring with Addie, the challenges she issued, made him feel out of control and also daring. But the quiet side of her that revealed her heart so carefully called to him in a way he had no choice but to answer.

"Birdie and Gertie sure were."

He searched her eyes for some assurance she felt the same, but he wanted to hear her say it. "And you?"

She slid her hand down the curve of his neck, past his shoulder, and gripped his bicep. Logan's heartbeat picked up speed like an accelerating train.

"I didn't know this about myself, but I'm a big fan of the Scottish accent." She caught her lip between her teeth.

He wanted *his* teeth on her lips. *His* hands in her hair. He was playing with fire but too mesmerized by the shimmering heat to step back.

"And the guide…" Her hand came to Logan's hip.

He struggled to pull in enough oxygen as Addie's head shifted closer to his. Blood rushed through his veins as if they'd been empty before. Powerless to stop his movement, he bent toward her.

"Sauntering around in a kilt all day…" Addie said, so close her breath warmed his lips. Her fingers splayed across his thigh, fissures of lightning spreading in five directions.

And then her fist closed, hiking the material of his kilt and shattering his resolve.

20

Addie simply couldn't summon all the reasons this was a bad idea. The need to know how Logan's chest would feel and if his mouth would taste like whisky consumed her mind.

His hand settled on her waist, and the other clamped around hers where it twisted in his kilt. But not to stop her—to spin them. He moved her backward, the space between their bodies holding steady like the opposing sides of magnets. She bumped against the cold surface of the old stone wall, and the resistance disintegrated.

In the slowest motion, Logan's legs pressed against hers, then his hips, then his chest. With one hand braced by her head, he pinned her against the hard wall. Not forcefully, but so every inch of him pressed up against every inch of her.

He threaded his hand into her hair, tipping her face up to him, and closed the gap between them. Soft. Light. Hesitant. His tongue reached out to meet hers. A quiet stroke. An invitation. "Is this alright?" he asked against her lips, the vibration of his words turning her needy, the shadows making it more illicit.

"Yes." *Very much, yes.*

Tugging her closer, Logan deepened the kiss, the brush of his stubble a tingly afterthought. Melting into him, Addie gave in to the sensation of his mouth and his hands and his body.

His fingertips slipped from her hair to the curve of her cheek and held her like she was something precious.

Logan's mouth moved slowly over hers, and she burned where he touched her. No one had ever kissed her like he did. Maybe rushed or sloppy, confident or demanding, but never sweet. Never *savoring*. Like he could do this for as long as she'd let him.

His lips and the confident hold he had on her were powerful and heady. And it felt like a connection and an understanding and maybe even a promise.

A quiet buzz of alarm mixed with the desire bubbling in Addie's veins. She was in too deep here. What had started out as an attempt to rile him up—fun and easy—had turned into a jump into the deep end.

Addie bunched up his shirt in her fist, trying to tug some of the intimacy out of the moment. She'd expected their kiss to be sizzling—how could it not be?—but she wasn't prepared for the heaviness, for the feel of his body sweeping her away.

Slipping her tongue into his mouth transformed all that tenderness into need, and his lips slanted against hers, turning into a battle.

Much safer ground.

She reached up on tiptoes to get closer. His fingertips slid over the waistband of her jeans. His thumb skimmed under the bow tied at her back.

He pulled her roughly against him, and the pressure of his hardness, not even having the decency to be restrained by pants, made Addie's brain fuzzy.

When they were both gasping for air, Logan's lips found a new combat zone on her neck, and she made embarrassing mewling noises at the heat and stubble rasping her skin.

Logan correctly interpreted the sounds as *Please, yes, more,* and his hands moved to her ass, lifting her up to wrap her legs around him, a low groan rumbling in his chest.

His hair was as soft as she'd imagined, and she'd been imagining it all day as he traipsed around looking like a Highlander she hoped would crush her against a wall. Or something in a more horizontal position.

Weren't castles full of settees, or something comparably Victorian, to be ravished on?

He set her on the deep windowsill, the chill of the stone a startling contrast to how she burned for him. Every nerve ending in her body urged her closer. Logan's hands wound into her hair, and hers gripped his shirt. His lips found the pulse at the base of her neck, and his tongue came out to meet it. The throbbing between Addie's legs was all-consuming.

Clapping erupted from the other room, and they both froze as if they'd been caught instead of secreted away in the dark. Her heart beat loudly in her ears as they balanced on a precipice.

They could let the group in the other room break this spell. Chalk it up to an emotional day and too much time spent touching on the bus. An inevitable outcome to the pent-up frustration over the past few weeks.

But every ounce of her attention focused on the hot look in his eyes, the slight part in his lips, his quick breathing. And she couldn't walk away.

The heaviness between them was more than long-denied desire. The intensity more than she'd bargained for. But she'd shown him her broken pieces and her sharp edges, and maybe that was enough. They could give in, and it wouldn't pull her under.

"I don't want to look back and regret not taking a risk," she whispered. "Come upstairs with me?"

21

Logan and Addie stumbled across the room and up the stairs, arms tangling, stealing kisses. Midway up, Addie pinned him against the wall. Their lips clashed, and her tongue stole into his mouth. He slid his hands over her bonnie backside, pulling her in closer.

Sparks of arousal shot through him as she ran her palms up his stomach and across his chest.

At this point, he didn't give a toss about decorum, but he probably should. "How many points if they catch us in the stairwell?"

She laughed breathlessly against his mouth and bit his lip. What little blood was still left in his head took a holiday to the south. Raking her fingers through his hair, she said, "I like it when you talk dirty."

Then her hands moved on to bigger and better things, namely, stroking him through his kilt.

Logan's knees threatened to give out.

"I'm going to last ten seconds if you keep that up," he said through gritted teeth.

She raised an eyebrow. "As long as you make it count." Her husky voice sent another jolt through his system, turning him reckless. She'd awakened something impulsive and greedy within him.

"You. Upstairs. Now." Apparently, she'd reduced his coherence to one-word sentences, too. Addie's throaty laugh furthered his impatience. Why had he resisted this moment? How had he even managed?

She'd captured his attention from the very first moment, clad in a yellow raincoat, when time had stretched around them. He wanted her.

But more than that, his heart recognized something in her. A reminder to see the world with fresh eyes. She made him feel adventurous.

When she asked him to take a risk, for once he didn't want to do the safe thing.

He needed to get her out of those clothes. He needed to feel her skin against his. Right the fuck now.

While Logan struggled with the key and the lock, Addie undid the buttons of his shirt. She pushed the material off the curve of his shoulders, her mouth following, sending shock waves rippling through him.

When she slid her hands along his thighs and under his kilt, she stilled and a smile stole across her face. "Seriously? Boxer briefs? Isn't this an affront to Scotsmen everywhere?"

He sank his mouth against her neck, breathing in lavender, while turning the doorknob and spinning them into the room. "Professional-hazard insurance," he said as he backed her against the door, the latch clicking into place.

Reaching behind her, he tugged the black sash at the small of her back. Addie's laugh transformed into a gasp as the knot popped and he ran his hands along her skin.

He pulled the top over her head, her mermaid hair resetting

over her shoulders and teasing the pink tips of her perfect breasts. His mouth watered with the need to taste her.

Letting out a shaky breath, he willed his body to slow down and savor this moment.

Addie gripped his shoulders. "Touch me," she said, her voice low and commanding. Her confidence in demanding exactly what she wanted drove him wild. But he wanted her as out of control as he felt.

Pretending he didn't understand, Logan brushed the pad of his thumb over her full bottom lip. He felt her tongue flick against the underside of his thumb all the way down to his cock.

Pulling back, he trailed the wet finger down her chest, between her breasts, and over her belly button.

"Logan."

His name was a warning—but he'd take whatever punishment she wanted to dole out. A featherlight sweep over the band of her jeans earned him a frustrated growl. Her fingernails dug into his biceps.

Logan brushed his fingertips across the dip of her waist, past her ribs, and over the curve of her breasts. Chills popped up on her skin, and he reveled in her whimper as she arched toward him. "Like this, lass?" His voice came out on an unreliable breath.

"No. Like this." Addie ran her hands over her breasts, cupping them together before pinching her nipples, her eyes full of fire. Logan had every intention of teasing, of driving her to the edge until she begged, but she stroked herself and the thread of his self-control that had been snagging and fraying since they first met finally snapped.

There was no holding back now.

He wrapped his arm around her waist and captured her nipple in his mouth, sucking hard.

"*Yes.*" She wound her fingers in his hair, pulling him closer, and her sexy moan had his body screaming to be inside her.

Addie moved to unfasten her jeans, but he batted her hands away. He unhooked the button and pulled the zipper down, the teeth parting one by one. Her hand wrapped around his wrist, guiding him downward. He loved how bold she was, how she gave him the confidence to be bold, too. The needy sound she made unraveled him.

"Logan." His name was a plea on her lips.

"I know, lass. I'm hurrying."

He helped peel off her jeans and panties, better than any present he'd ever unwrapped. Kneeling in front of her, he skimmed his hands up her soft skin before hooking one leg over his shoulder. She shivered as Logan kissed his way up her inner thigh.

Addie watched, her lips parted, her chest pink, her hair wild. The vision above him seeped under his skin.

She sucked in a gasp when he slid two fingers into her heat. He buried his face between her legs and ran his tongue over her as she clenched around him, rising on tiptoes. Her head fell back against the door with a thump. "Fuck," she whispered.

Thank god Logan was already on his knees or he would've hit the ground, hard.

He kissed and licked while Addie's hips tipped up to meet the next stroke of his tongue, her hands gripping his hair to the point of pain. Not that he minded. Nothing was getting through to his brain except the noises Addie was making.

He swirled his tongue and drove his fingers into her faster, discovering all the places that made her squirm. He committed her to memory so he could do this a million times more.

She tightened around his fingers and rocked against his mouth, taking what she needed and nearly sending him over the brink just from watching.

A hard shudder rippled through her body, and she looked him in the eye, the moment binding them together. Something unguarded and raw flashed in her eyes before they turned dreamy.

He'd never seen a more beautiful sight than Addie, cheeks

flushed under the light dusting of freckles, her lips falling open, her breath coming in waves. He held on to her shaky legs as the last of her orgasm fluttered through her.

Then her hands were on his shoulders, guiding him up. He trailed his hand up her thigh, along her belly, over her breast, and into her unruly mess of curls, usually so neatly tied back.

The little glimpses when Addie wasn't in control and put together were perfection. Even better when she let the mask slip enough to show him her vulnerable side. But watching her completely undone, head tipped back and eyes hooded, threatened to undo *him*, too.

He kissed along the column of her neck, tipping her head back to reach the soft spot below her ear. Arrows of desire ripped through his body as her hands explored his back, as her breasts pressed against his chest.

She kissed him, tongue sliding against his, and whispered, "I want you, Logan."

"I've wanted you since that first day." He hadn't meant for the truth to slip past his lips so easily, to throw out how serious this was to him, despite all his best intentions to keep his distance. Intentions that had become more and more lenient every time he saw her. Now he'd touched her, there was no going back. There was no way he could let her go.

Addie pulled back, and his heart dropped. She was always quick to push his buttons or toss out a sarcastic comment. Anything to avoid getting in too deep.

He braced himself for the impact.

She raked her fingers down his back and grabbed his arse, dragging his hips roughly against her. "And I've never wanted anything more than I want this right now."

Logan's heart echoed her words, hammering in his chest so he couldn't hear anything over its beating.

Shaking from the yearning coursing through his veins, he crashed his lips against hers, unable to resist her pull for another second, needing to be physically fused to her more than he needed to breathe. Addie's admission that she felt as strongly as he did was better than the feel of her body, and the feel of her body was a thousand times better than anything he'd imagined.

And he'd pictured this. Taking her for the first time in a tangle of sheets, her hair spilling over his pillows.

His movements stilled.

He was a damn fool.

He wanted to show her how deeply he cared. To learn her body and the taste of her skin. To hear her fall apart again when he was deep inside her. To hold her through the free fall.

Not have a quick fuck in a castle.

Logan braced his hands on the door behind her. Dropped his head to her shoulder. Breathed through his nose. It was too difficult to fight her riptide. He wanted to let go and drown in not only her body, but *her*, not concerned with coming back up for air. He was barely holding on to his self-control, his vision blurring at the edges.

Addie's hands cupped his jaw and tilted his face up, her eyes full of confusion.

"Hold on. No. Not like this," he said, panting. "Let's do this right."

22

Addie stepped out of the cage of Logan's arms, pulse skittering in her veins. She wasn't sure why she wasn't pressed up against the door calling out his name right now, but she had a pretty good idea.

For him, this would never be a night of screwing to get it out of their systems.

Sure, maybe for a second there, she'd fallen into him, into the way he looked at her, his eyes beckoning, like the sound of waves lapping a distant shore.

But Addie didn't want anything tender or slow or *candlelit*. She wanted his body on hers. Right. Now.

She turned away from the low bed covered in white down blankets and the floor-to-ceiling walnut wainscoting behind it.

Logan leaned back against the door, foot propped behind him, and slipped his thumbs into the top of the blue-and-green kilt hanging low on his hips. His chest rose and fell like he could strip away the urgency from before simply by slowing his breathing.

The light and shadows played over the waves of his abs, the dip in the muscles of his arms, the bulge under his kilt. A chill hung in the air, but inside, she burned for him like the embers in a campfire.

The span of four heartbeats passed as she stared him down from across their battle lines, drawn once again. "Need a minute?" she asked, pushing.

He swallowed hard. "Yeah, I fucking need a minute," he said, his voice gravelly.

Addie's breathing went sideways when he didn't immediately rush to her, when he held his ground. Crossing one arm over her chest, she gripped her shoulder.

This was no anonymous hookup in a pitch-black hotel room. Logan could see every detail of her in the bronze lamplight coming from the nightstand. She wasn't self-conscious, but the light combined with Logan's searching eyes stripped her down. Exposed her.

This was supposed to be fun.

Finally, he pushed off the door and crowded her without bringing their bodies together. His finger twisted in a curl and he pulled it straight, the back of his hand skimming over the slope of her breast.

The taut skin of his abs brushed against her belly and she gasped. He pulled back, cupping her face, gently tracing her cheekbone.

Making this heavy. Romantic. *Intimate.*

His eyebrows pulled together, his gaze dark, like he yearned for her. Like it physically hurt to stand there and not touch her. While her body could relate, she didn't want all this *pining.*

"Strip," she said.

Logan's dimple appeared from a lopsided smile, and he stepped back, undoing the buckles on each side of the kilt.

Addie held her breath, staring at him, hard and at attention.

The angular cut of his hips. The hair dusting his chest.

He was the sunset over a lake, mountains scraping the sky, uncharted territory, an endless expanse of wonder.

Logan tossed the rest of his clothes to the side, and they landed with a muffled thump on the wood floor, snapping her out of her reverie.

She traced the shadowed rift starting at his collarbone, and he shuddered under her touch, cursing softly. The tension in his body was palpable, his movements deliberate, as if trying to slow himself down instead of running away with this moment.

She placed her hand in the middle of Logan's chest and walked him backward. Pushed him into the chair and straddled him. His coarse hair rasped the back of her legs, his dick hard between them.

He made a deep rumbling sound in the back of his throat and trailed openmouthed kisses down her neck, hot and wet. Holding him close, she kept his lips pressed to her sensitive skin, tingling from the graze of his stubble. When she rocked against him, he groaned and flicked his tongue against her earlobe. Bit down. A surge of heat bloomed between her legs.

This was what she wanted.

Logan's hand skimmed down her thigh, and the other tangled in her hair as he claimed her mouth. Licking and nipping, he kissed her like he was starved, and she met every caress of his tongue with her own hunger.

The pads of his fingertips brushed the curve of her breasts and she arched into him, craving the friction of rough hands on soft skin, seeking the pressure he withheld.

His touch danced away and skated down her sides.

She was over his teasing. The torchlit laughter, long glances, and almost-kisses had been torture enough. "Logan."

When she bucked against him, he stilled her movements with strong hands on her hips. His fingers dug into her skin hard enough to make her gasp. Their gazes locked, his eyes invading hers. "I plan to take my time, lass."

The challenge in Logan's voice surged through her, and the power that had been entirely Addie's crossed enemy lines. The loss left her shaky, but she wasn't backing down. She dragged her fingers over the ridges of his ribs. "I'm sure you do."

With a low growl, Logan leaned forward, lifting her to wrap her legs around him, and resettled them with a sensual roll of his hips.

Holy fuck. He lifted her like it was nothing, moved her body like he controlled it.

"Look at me." His hands moved to the sides of her face and his eyes searched hers as if he could see into all the dark places she kept hidden from the light. He wasn't giving in to the passion between them. He was right there, demanding all of her. "Let go."

Addie pulled in a ragged breath. She didn't know if she could.

Panic rolled through her like a threatening summer storm sweeping across the desert. Three freckles dusted Logan's shoulder, and she pressed her lips onto each of them, buying herself time to calm her racing heart.

Her rib cage was no longer any protection, her skin too thin, her heart trying to burst out to meet his. Logan always broke through her defenses.

This was no different.

He cupped her cheek and brought her face back to his. Rested his forehead against hers. "Let go," he whispered again.

Logan knew about her past. He never retreated when she needed him. He was intentional and thoughtful. Someone she could count on.

She touched the tip of her nose to his. Closed her eyes. Brushed a kiss across his lips.

"Okay," she said softly, letting herself get swept away by whatever magic rippled in the air around them.

Logan carried her to the bed. Laying her down, he hovered over her on his elbows, not touching, just caressing her swells and dips with his eyes. He watched her like she might disappear if he blinked.

Then his mouth was on hers, fusing their lips with his heat.

She felt out of control, like a car skidding on ice, powerless to stop the inevitable crash. And also alarmingly confident Logan would be there to save her from the impact. She trusted him.

He pulled back, rummaged in his bag, and returned, rolling on a condom. When he moved between her legs, his thumb brushed her bottom lip. "Addie." The sound of her name in Logan's melodic accent reached her like a breathless whisper on the wind.

He slid into her, and she cried out, twisted her fingers into the curls at the nape of his neck.

Logan's breath came in short bursts, stirring the hair by her ear. She trailed her fingertips over each bump on his spine.

All the wanderlust she'd ever felt distilled into a singular desire to explore him.

Map him.

Claim him.

Addie's hands moved across the smooth skin of his back, the slope of his shoulders, the coarse hair on his chest, and she looked up into eyes as deep as the ocean.

They rocked together, moving to a slow rhythm.

His soft exhale warmed her lips. He cradled her face. Kissed her eyelids. Her nose. Her mouth.

Slowing down. Always slowing down.

His weight pinned her to the bed, but the lightness gathering inside her rushed up to meet him as if there was no distinction between his body and hers.

Everything in her was coiled too tight, demanding release. His heartbeat inside her body couldn't be ignored, and she rolled her hips, pulling him closer as she tried to prove all the words she didn't know how to say.

Finally giving in to the fire burning between them, he

crushed his mouth against her swollen lips, alternating between nipping and soothing.

He pulled her knee up to his side to move deeper inside her, and she whimpered. His hand skated up her thigh before reaching between them to stroke her. She shattered around him in a sea of electric sparks, the moment unexpected in its certainty.

He followed her over the edge and they lay panting, breathing in each other's air. His lips found hers again, soft and tender, as if, even now, he couldn't get enough.

Then he rolled away from her to clean up, taking the heat and security with him.

Addie pulled the comforter up to her chin. She wanted to close in on herself, but also to pull Logan around her and never let him leave this room.

She wanted to kiss him.

She maybe wanted to cry.

Logan reappeared at the edge of the bed, his muscles flexing as he stretched his arms above his head, every inch the Highland-laird fantasy come to life. He looked sleepy and sated, while Addie felt split-open, some baser instinct urging her to find shelter, to hide.

Usually, this would be the time she'd collect her clothes and hightail it back to her hotel. But she didn't want to do that with Logan.

He looked down at her and smiled, barely an upturn at the corners of his mouth, but she bathed in it. The heat and promise curled around her and soothed the cold panic clawing up her spine.

He climbed into bed, sliding his arm under her and pulling the blankets up and over them. He rolled them so his weight was half on top of her, pinning her to the bed, anchoring her.

Cuddling was a sentimental extravagance she'd convinced herself she didn't need. Yet here, in Logan's arms, as his warmth slipped beneath her skin, she could admit she needed this very much. She tucked her nose against his neck, her arm banded across his middle, and clung to him.

His breath filtered through her, same as the train whistle in the distance, swelling, receding, returning again. The skim of his fingertips was light across her collarbone, teasing at the hollow of her shoulder, the press of his lips following. He kissed her jaw, her cheek, her hair.

Slow. Deliberate.

So fucking earnest.

Addie's heart beat like the rain—too fast and too shallow. She wasn't sure she could reciprocate a declaration out loud, but she craved the reassurance that she wasn't alone in feeling stripped-down and raw, like she'd given some vital part of her that left her defenseless.

"Is it always like that for you?" she whispered, her voice muffled against his skin.

Logan slid onto one elbow, that sweep of hair falling over his eye, the pad of his thumb trailing across her cheekbone. "Never."

Addie was so shaken, she could only curl into him, needing the reassurance of his hard body and heartbeat, heavy under her hand.

23

They woke in the darkness, Logan's body curling around Addie's, his hands tucked against her heart. When she turned to face him, she buried her face against his neck and slipped her leg between his. His pulse started buzzing.

He expected her to roll her hips, to push the tempo, to force them back to something physical after the intensity of last night. Instead, she wound her fingers in his hair and held him.

The embrace—with seemingly no underlying motives—felt more intimate than what they'd shared earlier.

His hand stroked down her back, committing to memory the rhythm of her breathing, the softness of her skin, the flower-petal smell of her hair. He basked in the way her tidal restlessness, those unseen currents, stilled like glassy waters in the circle of his arms.

His alarm blared on the nightstand, shattering the quiet. As he rolled to shut it off, Addie asked, "What time is it?"

"Seven," he said, reaching for her, but she was already halfway out of bed, hunting for her clothes.

"Shit." She grabbed her shirt and yanked it on. "People will be up by now."

His chest tightened at the guarded look in her eyes. She was leaving.

If she walked out right now, there was a very real chance she would only come back in the dark. Or worse, pretend it never happened at all.

He wasn't oblivious to Addie's aversion to vulnerability. *Light and casual* seemed to be her motto, and he'd upended it before they'd even made it to bed. He'd known what he was doing. He wanted more of her. Always.

He wanted more of the stories she shared in the night about the cities that held a piece of her heart. Cenotes in Mexico, Japanese cherry blossoms, Saint Petersburg, sailing down the Ganges. He wanted to peel back the layers and understand what made her curious and adventurous.

But he may have made a grave tactical error. Logan knew how precarious his position was. She wanted a physical relationship. She'd made that clear. From what he gathered, she had a lot of practice running from the wounds of her past. If he pushed too hard, too fast, she might run from him, too.

All he could do was wait for her, find ways to give her all the love and connection she deserved.

Logan put on his briefs and moved to her, trying to soothe her skittish energy. "It's okay," he said, but she brushed off his touch, yanking her jeans on.

"No one can know."

The chill of the morning settled in his bones. He knew it shouldn't hurt. Just because he wanted to shout it across the bus's loudspeaker didn't mean it was smart. Of course they weren't walking into breakfast holding hands.

But he was so afraid the magic between them would burn off like the mists, leaving an emptiness he could never fill.

Maybe it was juvenile—certainly desperate—but sometimes

the only way to get Addie out of her head was to poke at her. Ignoring the quivering in his stomach, he touched the pale skin on the curve of her neck with his thumb. "It might be a wee bit late, with this hickey."

Her eyes flared, and she grabbed her neck. She spun to the gilded mirror to examine the column of her throat. Finding nothing, she dropped her palms to the dresser and heaved out a breath. Before she could turn and fight him, he wrapped his arms around her waist and met her eyes in the mirror.

She shook her head and muttered, "Bawbag," but a grin tugged at her lips.

This was better. He could keep it light for now if that's what she needed. Hell, he'd tell her every bad joke from every Christmas cracker he'd ever opened so long as she didn't shut him out. "I'll be your lookout, alright?"

The hall was empty as Addie made for her door, but watching her walk away from him sent icicles through his heart. He whistled the same tune he and his brothers used and she stiffened, glancing discreetly over her shoulder. When the only person she saw was him, she turned to walk backward and flipped him off with both hands. Her smile lit up the stone hallway, and all the warmth and connection he'd felt the night before stole through him.

After Addie had made it safely to her room, Logan packed his bag and made his way downstairs. Out at the bus, he helped the guests load suitcases and climb aboard while Birdie and Gertie giggled behind their hands, shooting him suggestive glances. His tsking only drew out their laughter, and he failed to hide his smile. It was a good day.

Addie came down the stairs in her yellow mac and his breath caught. She dragged Frank over the bumpy cobblestones—a surefire way to break a wheel—and Logan reached for the handle. "Let me take care of it." *Of you.*

She held his gaze for a long moment, like she understood what he meant. Like she might argue.

"Okay."

Heat flared in his chest at her easy acceptance. He followed her up the stairs and into the bus, congratulating himself on keeping his hands in his own seat. Mostly.

At Inverness Cathedral, they failed miserably to avoid eye contact. Along the river walk, they couldn't keep from brushing past one another. And when the group huddled around Logan at Clava Cairns and he pointed out features of the Bronze Age cemetery and standing stones, Addie only had eyes for him.

By the time they settled onto the bus for the long ride back to Edinburgh, Logan could barely see straight from wanting her. The hum of the engine and the high-backed seats created a bubble just for them. Relief coursed through him to finally have her to himself.

He twisted one of Addie's curls around his finger and tipped his head against hers, his mouth by her ear. "Did you know how much I wanted you that first night? With your selkie hair wild like this, like you'd wandered out of the sea to ensnare me."

Addie nodded definitively. "Handing me your phone number kind of gave you away."

"And what about you? That pretty blush spreading over your skin…"

"Such an overactive imagination. I was only there for the nachos."

He harrumphed and pulled her legs over his, settling her in next to him.

"Logan." She pushed back, disentangling herself.

"No one's paying us any attention."

She glanced up at Keith whose eyes were on the road, and then over her shoulder to the empty seats across from them. "Okay, but we're not doing this at the office. And this will cost you hundreds of points if anyone catches us," she said as she leaned against him, tucking her feet up like she was settling in on a friend's couch. His heart swelled at the familiarity.

"It's always worth it," he whispered.

Her knees rested against his thigh, and they watched as he drew lazy circles on the inseam of her jeans. He'd spent weeks dying to touch her. It felt so good to let himself reach for her now, without reservation.

As his hand roamed higher, a tiny whimper hit his ears and Addie bit the cotton seam on his shoulder. The look she gave him heated his blood.

He pressed his lips to the hollow below her ear. Then took her earlobe gently in his teeth. He was addicted to the breathy sounds she made. The rumble of the bus and the chatter of the guests faded away when Addie's fingers locked into his hair, tugging at his scalp.

His breathing was erratic at best, his vision distorting everything around them to a dull blur.

"Sound sure carries in stone hallways," Gertie said in an overly loud voice.

Addie straightened, her feet slipping back to the floor, and whispered "Oh my god," into the palms of her hands.

Panic hit Logan's bloodstream that this small remark would send Addie retreating.

He didn't want to lose her. Not now, not ever.

"It was just like that with my Arthur..." Birdie said wistfully.

When Addie turned to look at him, her cheeks were stained a bright pink. Logan smiled to reassure her. He reached his hand out, palm up, in a silent question he desperately needed the answer to. *If I take a risk, will you take a risk?* His heart collided with his rib cage like a hailstorm.

She met his gaze, her lips pressing to the side like it was a harder decision than inviting him to bed last night. Her pause was heavy like the space between lightning and thunder. Waiting. Counting. Anticipating the boom.

She slipped her fingers through his and brought their locked hands to her lips. Relief cascaded through him in hopeful waves, and he exhaled quietly. She rested their hands on her leg, and while they kept their attention out the windows, he was aware of every single breath.

An hour later, Addie's blond head tipped onto his shoulder. He tossed his coat over her, and her eyelashes fluttered where they rested on her cheeks. A tiny smile tugged at her lips. She burrowed into the fabric, and Logan's heart pinched with longing.

He could picture Addie here, joining him on the tours. Coming with him to every holiday and birthday and impromptu family gathering. Cooking with his mother, indulging his father, taking the piss out of his brothers. He wanted to take all her lonely memories and replace them with his loud family.

Her presence would fill his empty flat with a warmth like his parents' house, the kind that stemmed from the history of shared laughter. He could see them teasing, poking, but from love instead of fear.

When he returned from a tour, wired from the constant company, he'd find her curled in a reading chair waiting up for him. Winding him down. Settling him.

He could even hear the bump and scuff as she dragged Frank up the front steps, feel the rush of dashing down to meet her and sweeping her up in his arms. Giving her a place to call home.

It was so easy to imagine that life. To want.

His stomach clenched around the realization that her desire to keep things light between them might have been for his sake, too. Logan wanted forever, and all she had was now. He might have blown past the last barrier he had against losing his heart.

Now, it felt far too late.

24

Back in Edinburgh, Addie waited for Logan while the guests swarmed him in a flurry of backslaps, handshakes, and bright smiles.

Birdie proposed to Logan, clinging to him as he helped her off one knee, and when he turned her down, his eyes danced to meet Addie's. Some people would be absolutely drained by being *on* for so long, but it clearly fueled him.

Logan doled out the last suitcase and, after a parting wave, came to stand in front of Addie. The way he touched her stirred something she hadn't known existed and made her feel jump-on-the-next-plane-level exposed. They were dangerously far away from the fun she'd signed up for. But today, he was light-hearted and teasing, as if he sensed his playfulness would keep her instinct to run in check.

Addie slipped her finger into the belt buckle of his kilt and towed him toward her. He kissed her hard and then asked, "Want to grab food and bring it back to my place?"

She nodded and reached for Logan's hand. They wandered

down onto the High Street, the smell of hops hanging in the air as if trapped by the low clouds. Boston was full of old buildings, marbled and historic, but not this historic. Not blackened at the top from centuries of smoke historic.

Logan's presence allowed her the freedom to explore Edinburgh's layers of winding streets, bridges, and steps, without the fear of getting swallowed whole.

And his low voice was much more appealing than Gigi's.

He stopped in front of a passageway that felt like an entrance into a secret realm. "This is one of my favorite places in Edinburgh." *Advocate's Close* was stamped into the brick at their feet and on the gold-and-black placard hanging above the archway.

The tunnel framed a black lantern bolted to the wall, straight from Peter Pan's London, and behind it, the Scott Monument.

If the Eiffel Tower had been built with the intention to intimidate, compacted by rigid lines and left unwashed for a couple hundred years, it would be the Scott Monument. What it lacked in elegance, it made up for with jagged spikes pointing eight stories in the air.

"Wow." The possibility of surprise was around every corner in this city. "It's like there's a whole world hidden under the surface."

"Edinburgh has a way of slowly revealing her secrets. Like someone else I know." Logan's eyes lingered on hers and warmed her through before he turned and led the way back onto the Royal Mile.

Out in the street, a little girl, maybe six, swung her father's hand between them, pointing at people and buildings and pigeons.

Addie froze.

The scene could have been one of her family's long-lost snapshots.

The girl's golden hair curled into ringlets under a driving cap the same color as Scotland's greenery. She wore a matching kilt and sash—the full Highland regalia—a clear symbol of an indulged child.

The father was handsome and smiling, with unruly surfer-blond hair. Like old photos of Brian. Addie's mom used to joke that she only married him because he looked like a young Robert Redford.

The man gestured to St. Giles' Cathedral, probably explaining the stained-glass windows and the history and the Gothic rib vault while the girl scratched at the seaweed-green moss covering the bottom four feet of the church as if surveying severe flood damage.

Addie smiled at the innocence of the exploration—of how tiny details could hold a child's attention if they felt included in the important world of adults. Her dad hadn't taken her so far from home, but she still remembered the excitement in his voice as he hustled them toward the cathedral in Santa Fe, babbling on about the rose window and the architecture, while she dragged a string of dried chilies through the dust.

She was attributing grown-up words to the feeling now, but threaded through the memory was the sense of knowing exactly her place in the world—right next to the person so thrilled to share his passion with his daughter. Whose love was permanent.

The dad in the street scooped the little girl onto his shoulder, and she rested her head against him, looking back with a smile and a tiny wave.

The chill of the stone wall against Addie's shoulder did nothing to dampen the old resentment that sometimes bubbled up without warning or remedy. Her heart wedged so far into her ribs, she'd need pliers to get it out. She rubbed at the ache in her chest.

"What is it?" Logan's eyes followed the father and daughter.

Addie wrapped her arms around herself. "They…reminded me of me and my dad."

The rain picked up, pitter-pattering against the cobblestones and turning them glossy. With moisture dancing in the air, the small tunnel morphed into a refuge.

"You don't talk about him much."

That was an understatement. She wasn't sure she'd said a single word to Logan about Brian. "I don't talk *to* him much, either." She hadn't even answered his phone call at Christmas. Being in Scotland, inundated with thoughts of her mom, was overwhelming enough without the tangle of emotions that came from the sound of his voice.

Logan laced his fingers through hers. "Want to tell me about it?"

She took a constricted breath. He looked at her like he understood how much barbed wire was tangled up with these memories, and he'd do whatever it took to ease the pain. That somehow made it easier, even as her eyes began to water.

"He'd tuck me in every night and let me ask one question about anything in the world. He was a scientist, so he'd explain thermodynamics or the planets or whatever complicated thing I came up with to delay bedtime." People said their dads knew everything, but hers really did. "When I got older, he'd tell stories about marrying my mom under a red arch in the desert or the time I cut a triangle into my bangs when I was three."

Logan toyed with the end of her hair, a smile on his lips and softness around his eyes Addie wanted to curl into, like a buffer from the sting of her memories.

Her dad had driven her to school on cold days so she didn't have to wait for the bus and had taken her to minor-league baseball games on firework nights. That a foundation like that could be ripped away had been inconceivable.

"Then my mom died... It was so sudden, you know? One minute we were living this perfect life—one we completely took for granted—and the next, everything crumbled." Addie searched for words on the slope of the stone archway. "He retreated so far into himself, he stopped living. And he shut me out. He should have gone to therapy—he should have put *me* in therapy…" Addie picked at her cuticle in a spot close to bleeding. The biting sting hurt. She should stop, but this heartache needed somewhere to go. "He chose his grief over me."

She resented him for letting her stand in the middle of that field in her cleats and soccer jersey with no one to clap for her but her friends' parents. For the weighty feeling of fumbling with a self-timer in a prom dress because there wasn't anyone to take a picture of her and her date. For the emptiness of looking into a sea of people while moving a tassel from one side to the other, knowing no one would remember that moment but her.

Forgotten.

A resounding answer to the question *Do we still fit together without her here, our two irreparably broken pieces?*

Addie tried to flash a reassuring smile, to prove she wouldn't cry. Not that Logan would react the way most people did—stumbling through uncomfortable apologies, eyes darting around frantically looking for a distraction. Instead, Logan's wide stance bracketed her, creating a safe little bubble.

She swallowed past the dryness in her throat. "He missed every important moment back then. The one person who should have been there for me wasn't, you know? I needed him."

"Addie." Logan's voice broke low on her name, and she looked up at the emotion on his face, the hurt he felt for her. Pressing a rough kiss against her temple, he pulled her into his arms. She tucked her face into the hollow between his shoulder and neck, focusing on his hand skimming up and down her arms instead of the bile creeping up her throat.

Tears slipped down Addie's cheeks. For a mother's enveloping hug she could no longer curl into. The questions she could no longer ask. *What's your peach crisp recipe? Would I look good with pink hair? How was your day?*

For her dad, lost to her in grief and then in miles. For how deeply he'd hurt her with his silence, his retreat, his absence.

She cried for herself, too—the naive child who hadn't seen it coming. Who'd been too angry to reach out.

Too angry to go home.

Too angry to forgive.

For everything that had been snatched away from her that day. For the growing up she'd had to do all at once. The family she was no longer a part of.

The home she could no longer claim.

Suddenly, Logan's body encircling hers was too intimate, her heart too exposed. She stiffened and pulled back. He now knew more about her past than anyone besides Devika; the significance was not lost on Addie. The panic of this admission, this slip in her otherwise solitary existence, rose up in her, leaving her disoriented and wrung-out like she'd been tossed around by the sea.

Logan moved beside her and leaned back against the rough rock wall, respecting her need for space. "I'm sorry for everything you've lost. For how strong you've had to be on your own. But the way he handled things—that's not a reflection on you. It's his great loss."

Sometimes, she thought she should go back there and demand answers or accept that her dad dealt with his grief the only way he knew how. That it wasn't personal and forgive him. But it was much easier to be hostile and bitter.

Logan hooked his pinkie finger through hers. "I'm here for you."

The sensation of plunging through open air was worse than any turbulent flight she'd ever been on—one gust away from a crash landing. Relying on Logan was more terrifying than the prospect of reaching out to her dad.

"Enough of this." She waved at her surely puffy and splotchy face. "Didn't you promise me dinner?"

"Aye." He placed one last, lingering kiss on her forehead. "Besides, a dreich evening in moody Edinburgh calls for sheltering inside," he said and pulled her back into the rain.

★ ★ ★

While Logan bought food, Addie shut herself into a red phone box. Closing the door dulled the outside street noise, but not the blood pounding in her ears. The lingering smell of urine hung in the air and did nothing to slow Addie's quick breathing; even if she'd been able to draw in a deep breath, now she really didn't want to.

Breathing through her mouth, she called Devika on her cell, toying with the damp end of her braid.

"Hey, Ads."

"I slept with Logan." Addie's voice was about three octaves higher than normal. She winced at the panic in her voice. Having sex with him wasn't concerning. Inevitable, really. But *sleeping* with him? Staying the night? Telling him about her dad?

She didn't do that.

"That bad?" Of course, Devika would think this was an SOS cry. A call-me-in-ten-and-yell-emergency plea. Addie sounded hysterical.

"No, it was great. *So great*. I mean…" Addie whistled. "But it's like… He's just…"

"You *like* him." Devika would have made an exceptionally obnoxious big sister. Addie felt like an eighth grader freaking out over a crush.

"I do." She could admit that much to herself. The other words that came to mind—*craved, needed*—she pushed away. "But he takes everything so much *deeper*—"

"*Ooh.*"

"Stop it. That's not what I meant. He… I don't know. He's helping me find the places in my mom's pictures."

"That's big."

"Yeah." Addie cupped her hand around the bottom of the phone. "And I told him about my dad."

"Why are you whispering? Where are you right now?"

Addie ran her hand along the ribbed metal phone cord bolted

to the booth and then yanked her hand back. That couldn't be clean. She wiped her hand on her pants. "In a phone booth while Logan grabs dinner..."

Devika had the gall to laugh. "Very reasonable of you."

"I'm in way over my head here." She should eat something. This gnawing in her stomach was probably hunger, and she was overreacting.

In the loud intake of breath, Addie could picture Devika's face—changing from amused eye roll to concerned eyebrows. "It's okay to care about him and let him know you."

Addie closed her eyes and rubbed the bridge of her nose. The rumbling of a truck outside reached her through the thick glass of the phone booth. She scanned the concert flyers and advertisements for Tesco taped to the back wall above the pay phone.

"Look, if you're calling to tell me you have another friend in the world besides me, I swear I'm not jealous."

Addie huffed out a laugh. Devika always had a way to brighten her mood, to keep her from the darkness.

Maybe it was okay to let people know her. People like Elyse. But letting Logan in was like standing on a crumbling cliff above a very deep canyon. "I should call the whole thing off, though, right?"

"Do you remember how hard amazing sex is to come by? Why would you throw that away?"

"Because it's too serious."

They'd woken up spooning, hands twined together and tucked under Addie's chin like she could pin him there and keep him forever. Dread at the thought of leaving overshadowed her wanderlust like a solar eclipse, and it was unacceptable.

She didn't do hard goodbyes. Not anymore.

Addie looked down and realized she'd wound her navy scarf around her wrists and clutched it to her chest like she had with Logan's hands. She immediately dropped the material and flattened it against her jacket.

"You're only there for a couple more weeks. There isn't time for it to get serious."

Addie blew out a breath, telling her heart to stop being so dramatic. "You're right." This was fine. She was completely in control of the situation. Even though her chest went all warm and fuzzy when she looked at Logan, it wasn't *love*. It was simply because no one had ever *made love* to her before. This was what anyone could expect to feel after so many orgasms in one night.

She and Logan could keep getting to know each other, keep working together, keep sleeping together. In the end, she would go like she always did, and she'd be fine.

She always was.

"Get out of the phone booth and drag that man back to bed."

"Thanks, Devika."

"Call me with the details," she yelled as Addie hung up.

25

Addie was having a hard time letting go of a perfect weekend tucked away in Logan's flat, incapable of keeping her feet to herself under their shared desk. His lopsided smile would be obvious to anyone watching—and Elyse was most certainly on high alert after catching them springing apart in the stairwell this morning—but Addie couldn't bring herself to stop. Not when he leaned in on crossed forearms, dark eyes smoldering from behind the fern.

She slipped a finger under the collar of her shirt—an absent-minded scratch of a nonexistent itch—and Logan tilted his head up to the ceiling like she was killing him.

His Adam's apple bobbed before his heavy gaze settled on her again, and her stomach flipped at the desire reflected there. She could almost sense the air ripple with his low growl like far-off thunder in the mountains.

A smile broke out on her face. A devious, lust-filled smile. She couldn't get enough of being the center of Logan's attention. When he looked at her like that she floated, as if she hadn't fully returned from the haze of dreamy satisfaction she'd been living in since climbing on that bus.

Addie's phone vibrated across her notebook, snapping reality back into place.

As if she'd conjured Marc by absolutely, decidedly not thinking about him, his name glowed on the screen. Her heart thumped, and her hand twitched like an indecisive squirrel darting back and forth in front of oncoming traffic. As much as she wanted to retreat to the relative safety of the Decline Call button, she couldn't avoid him forever.

"I've got to take this," she said, gathering up her laptop and notebook, already on her way to the conference room. "Hi, Marc."

"Damien got me a new backpack for Christmas. You should see the number of pockets on this thing…" Marc raved about the many features of his work-of-art bag for so long, Addie dared to hope he was simply bored in the airport, killing time. "What's the latest at The Heart?" he said, segueing to the real reason for his call, and Addie's stomach cramped.

Basically nothing. She'd been so swept up in Logan, none of this had seemed to matter. How had she gotten so distracted?

She slipped into a leather chair and opened her laptop like it would shield the rest of the office from this conversation. "The bones of the reservation system and website are all in place."

"That's been done for a while. What about the tours?"

She didn't want Marc losing faith in her, but she couldn't straight up lie to him, either. "They're struggling with the big attractions since they have so many community ties and off-the-beaten-path destinations. I know they're places that don't usually show up in guidebooks, but the local flavor adds something unique—"

"Neil has always been a dreamer. It's part of their problem. Above all, they want a viable company, and they may have to make some sacrifices. You bring practicality and objectivity to the table. I've got deals in the pipeline that could come through any time. You know how fast things move when clients' budgets get approved for the new year. I need *something* here, Addie."

She bit the inside of her cheek. She'd been shuffling through potential solutions commercial enough for Marc, authentic enough for Logan, and lucrative enough for The Heart.

The competing requirements left her stranded in the impending doom of headlights barreling toward her from both sides.

God, the pressure really *was* getting to her. She was feeling for this imaginary squirrel.

Addie rubbed circles into her temples. When Logan had been blocking her at every turn, the hot-spot tours she'd designed were a necessity. She wouldn't send them to Marc as-is, but she could add destinations she now understood were important and meaningful, that kept the spirit of Logan's vision intact.

Her heart kicked back at the thought of Logan's reaction. She wasn't delusional enough to think the tours she had in mind would feel like a compromise to him.

But the trips might tide Marc over while she and Logan found something better, something that lit him up the way the Highland tour had.

"I have tentative itineraries designed, but I haven't shared them with Neil." Or Logan. "They're not finalized, but they'll give you an idea of what we're thinking."

"Thank you," Marc singsonged, but it didn't unwind the knot in Addie's stomach like she'd thought it would.

"I can have them to you by the end of the week."

26

Logan watched as Addie returned from the conference room with Elyse in tow. "Let's have a quick meeting about tour destinations," she said, not quite meeting Logan's eye.

They needed to figure out the main tours, the lifeblood of this company, before Logan had to make decisions he wasn't prepared to make. He knew that.

Keeping the steady hum of anxiety bottled up wasn't going to work much longer. Add to that his and Addie's uncertain future—which he was trying to ignore for a bit longer—and he was near to bursting.

But it didn't mean he relished this conversation.

Addie flipped her leather folio to an open page. She didn't so much as glance at him.

Elyse, however, had all the attention in the world to spare. She settled in the fraying emerald rolling chair, resting her elbows on the tabletop, chin in her hands, gaze bouncing between them.

He nudged Addie with his foot, but instead of green eyes

coming up to meet his, Elyse's eyebrows rose, and a cheeky smile filled her face. *Dammit.*

"Sorry," he mumbled and pulled his foot back. He couldn't even risk catching Addie's eye now without confirming Elyse's suspicions.

He'd told himself it would be like this. Addie had boundaries for the office he wouldn't cross. But it didn't dull the ache, the longing for her to be right there with him.

"The local spots are effective for day trips, but more Edinburgh tours could be a great way to fill guides' time between bigger trips," she said.

As if to answer the subtle criticism that they didn't have enough work for everyone, Big Mac's drone flew over their heads, propellers whirring. His boisterous narration of the flora inside The Heart of the Highlands—as if it was a remote jungle being explored by BBC Earth—entertained the rest of the office, but the hard press of Addie's lips as she tracked its flight felt like a judgment. A needling, sweat-inducing judgment.

"What about a museum tour?" she asked.

Unease pricked Logan's skin at the direction of her suggestions. At the sound of Harris's booming laugh, Logan looked up. Harris would be wasted leading hushed groups through marbled halls. Big Mac would most likely destroy some priceless relic. "Not what I had in mind. No."

She wound her hair into a bun, shoved a pencil to hold it in place, and blew a stray curl out of her face. Logan's heart withered as he watched Weekend Addie transform into Office Addie right before his eyes. She wasn't here as a confidante or collaborator, looking for middle ground.

She was a competitor, cool and distant.

Whatever had happened on that phone call had pulled Addie out of his reach, and a cold twinge of panic filled the cracks between his ribs.

While Elyse scribbled ideas, or perhaps hairy-coo logos, in a notebook, Addie said, "We could add a Royal Mile tour—"

"What?" His heart pounded in his chest. This wasn't a compromise. It was an ambush.

She held up a hand to stop his objection. "You don't have to spend the whole day at The Scotch Whisky Experience, but St. Giles'? The Mercat Cross? There are hidden gems galore."

When he shook his head, one part confusion, one part disbelief, Addie glanced up at the ceiling, frustration and annoyance barely concealed on her face.

Here was the fine print of their compromise ready to tangle him up and knock him down.

Elyse pressed holes in the dirt of Addie's potted fern. "Melrose Abbey could be interesting."

A whiff of relief settled near Logan's sternum at the intervention, if only to give himself a moment to catch his breath. "Aye, there's a good one," Logan said, impressed. Famous, but historically significant. If Addie would think more along those lines, they might get somewhere.

"Have I ever led you astray?" Elyse asked in a lighthearted tone, but the hint of seriousness in her eyes caught him off guard. He was probably imagining it. Everything around here felt heavy today.

"Only the time you convinced me to make homemade fireworks for Guy Fawkes Night."

Elyse's smirk was interrupted by the phone ringing. "It'll probably be Alasdair again. He's thrilled to death about the new booking reports. I told you vendors would like electronic copies." She shot Logan a smug look.

Even these simple changes made him seasick.

"Toodle-oo," Addie called as Elyse headed to her desk.

"No one says tha—" Elyse broke into a full-throated laugh when she caught on to Addie's teasing. "Well done, then."

They were reframing their entire future, and no one was taking this seriously or giving the tours the attention they deserved.

The drone whizzed close enough to trim Logan's hair and he shot Big Mac a look that went ignored. *Christ.* He couldn't focus in the office. He needed big skies, fresh air, and inspiration.

"What about The Kelpies?" Addie asked.

Logan grimaced, his pulse picking back up at the decidedly wrong direction she was pushing this conversation. Pushing *him.* "They're enormous horsehead sculptures."

"Have you even been there?"

"It opened in 2014. Not a lot of history."

"Stirling Castle, then. Built in *1014,*" she said facetiously.

"My business is failing. You're not the only one stressed here," he bit out, tugging on the leather band around his wrist at the reminder of what could happen when the sand ran out in the hourglass.

He'd have to sack Agnes, who'd snuck him lemon drops when he came into the office as a child and to this day gifted him a bag tied with red ribbon each Christmas. Or Brandon, who embodied exuberance and dedication.

The thought of calling Alasdair, or Gavin, or Malcolm and telling them they wouldn't be coming through anymore made him physically ill.

"Hey." She ran her hand over his forearm. "I'm sorry."

Her touch—breaking her rule in order to comfort him—soothed the tension threading through his limbs. He hung his head. She had people depending on her, too. "No, I'm sorry, lass. I shouldn't have snapped." He placed his hand over Addie's and squeezed, wishing they were somewhere besides the office so he could reach for her. "It's hard to reimagine what's felt like second nature for so long."

She stole her hand away, but before he could miss the touch, her foot slid between his, curling round his ankle, comforting. "I've seen how you are on tours. You know amazing places, and you care so much about giving people an unforgettable experience. These itineraries could be award-winning if we anchored them with famous places. I might have said it sarcastically before, but you *can* convince anyone of the magic of Scotland."

He lifted his eyes to hers, and a wry smile tugged at her lips.

"And I also believe you can tailor any experience—even Loch Ness—to make it personal and meaningful. You can do this. I believe in you."

"Thank you," he said, his voice low and scratchy. That faith in him made him want to take risks, to be bold. And to make her feel cared for and supported like she did for him.

He wanted to show her a place she might love if she gave it a chance. To push further than the murky stipulations of their fling. All she needed was a little encouragement to feel comfortable and safe and wanted, so she could open up again. So they could get deeper and rekindle that intimacy he craved.

So she could see where she fit.

If she felt tethered here, she might think about staying. Staying with him. His heart beat hard at the recognition of how very much he wanted that.

Addie looked around, as if remembering where they were. "We should get back to it."

"I'll work on a list of destinations," he said. And he would. Soon.

But while Addie opened her computer, Logan pulled up her mum's picture and searched all the Munro mountains he knew.

The pyramid-shaped peak behind Heather was familiar, but Logan wasn't big on mountaineering.

After exhausting the list in his head, he searched the famous peaks in Scotland. From what he knew of Heather, there was a good chance she'd been in a remote place, but it was worth a shot.

The drone crashed into the side of Logan's desk. "Dammit, Big Mac."

With sheepish eyes under the flop of red hair, he came to retrieve the drone and glanced at Logan's screen. "Ah, the bonnie Kintails."

His heart leaped. On Macrae lands. *Of course.*

"Good man." He clapped Big Mac on the shoulder, forgetting his earlier annoyance.

Logan could take Addie there. Drive up to Eilean Donan Castle. Show her the land of her people since her first attempt had been a bust.

He started researching Macrae history and points of interest. Fell down a rabbit hole of legends and old clan alliances. One site described the clan's *warlike reputation*, and Logan smirked, thinking of Addie's fighting stance when she first arrived.

He'd love to spend his office time like this—learning about places they didn't guide, finding ways to show people his land in the most impactful way possible—instead of hunched over the books.

Custom tours weren't financially feasible. There was too much up-front cost to designing them. He wasn't suggesting it to Addie or testing out a concept here. This was a one-off thing only for her.

By the end of the day, he couldn't rein in his excitement any longer. He glared Big Mac out of the room after the rest of the employees had gone.

With the office empty, Logan crossed to the conference room. Addie sat on the far side, white papers spread out across the chestnut table, inky darkness coming through the windows behind her.

But her face lit like sunshine when she noticed him, casting out the gloom and uncertainty that had built up in him all day. Swiveling in her chair when he reached her, that twinkle reentered her eye, her posture loosening.

Logan's heart thudded. She was dropping her walls, returning to him.

He gripped the curved edge of the table and leaned down to kiss her. "I missed you today."

"I've been here the whole time," she said with a laugh.

But she hadn't been. Their connection had been ephemeral like the clouds, coming and going, evaporating without notice. Her office facade had remained intact, and he needed to know he was still allowed to slip behind it.

The rumbling sounds of traffic outside faded as she ran the backs of her fingers along his jawline. He leaned into her touch. "I missed you like *this*," he said, tugging the pencil from her bun. Her hair cascaded around her shoulders, the light from the lamp in the corner dancing across her golden waves.

She slipped her fingers into his hair and drew him to her, licking into his mouth. He tossed the pencil on the table with a clatter and kissed her hard, lips crushing, tongues tangling.

Christ, he wanted her. Wanted the reassurance of her attention and touch. Her quiet moan sparked fire in his blood.

Logan pulled her to stand and backed her against the side of the table, kicking the rolling chair out of the way.

She settled between his legs and fisted his sweater while he trailed kisses up her neck, breathing in lavender and the sea.

He slid his hands over her hips and down the black fabric covering her thighs, hooking his fingers under the hem of her skirt. She made a sound of agreement and rocked her hips against him, encouraging.

Little by little, he hiked up her skirt, dragging it over her impossibly soft skin. His pulse echoed down to his fingertips. He brushed a strip of silky material, but before he could investigate further, a car door slammed outside, and they both froze. The sound of their heavy breathing mingled in the air.

"Do you want to come to my place?" he asked, his voice gravelly.

"Or we could stay here." Addie lifted herself onto the table, her skirt ruched around her hips, a slip of lilac fabric visible between her legs. Lust shot through his veins with an urgency he struggled to deny.

He couldn't stop himself from stepping between her legs. Couldn't stop touching her. He trailed his thumbs along the inside of her thighs, goose bumps popping up in their wake. The idea of taking Addie in his office... He nearly expired on the spot.

He dragged his mind back to the reality of where they were. "What if someone comes back tonight?" he asked. Even though they'd worked enough late nights to know no one would, she had boundaries about the office, and getting caught in a compromising position was a clear violation. He needed to know for sure.

She glanced over her shoulder at the fluorescent-lit hallway as if imagining someone walking in and seeing them like this. But her eyes held fire when they returned to his. Like the possibility of getting caught excited her. Like it wouldn't be so terrible if people knew about them.

"And sees me sitting on your conference-room table, thighs spread for you?" she said, leaning back on her hands and parting her legs farther. "Your flat is too far away. I can't wait that long."

It was all the confirmation he needed. His whole body shook from the effort to hold himself back, to play this game, instead of devouring her. He ran one knuckle over the satiny fabric between her legs. Addie's whimper nearly undid him, his knees turning soft and altogether unsteady.

Her fingers moved to the V of her blouse. Logan clenched his hands at his sides, his cock throbbing with need. Undoing the buttons one by one, her selkie eyes dark and seductive, she revealed purple lace with excruciating slowness.

He loved the way she teased him, challenged him. The constant push and pull between them. But he was drowning in desire and couldn't hold back from touching her any longer.

When Addie opened her white shirt, Logan's hands were

there, sliding it from her shoulders, his mouth sinking against the curve of her breast. Wanting more of the breathy sounds she made, he licked along the edge of lace before sucking her nipple into his mouth through the thin material. He wrapped his arms tighter around her waist, and Addie arched into him with a moan. "Lass," he growled out, his pulse insistent, needy.

Logan pressed kisses along her stomach. "If someone did come in, we could say I dropped something." He knocked her pens and highlighters to the floor, where they landed with a dull clatter on the carpet.

He held her gaze as he sank to his knees.

Addie's belly pulled in with her startled breath, but her fingers wound into his hair and tightened. "Good idea," she said, her voice husky.

He nipped against the smooth warmth of her inner thigh before hooking a finger inside her panties and pulling them to the side.

"Oh, fuck," Addie breathed out.

He licked and sucked until she was panting. She braced her hands on the table behind her, head thrown back in pleasure, white shirt tangled around her wrists, black skirt hitched around her waist. Like Office Addie was completely unraveled and back to being *his*. He felt delirious from the sight of her spread out before him. Simultaneously light-headed and heavy in his body.

When she moaned like she was close, he slid a finger into her, stroking until she bucked against his mouth, until her cries echoed in the quiet of the office. He skimmed his hands along her calves, kissed the smooth skin of her thigh, watched her come back to earth as her dreamy eyes refocused on him like he was all that mattered.

"Logan, I need you," she said in a breathy whisper, and his heart seized on the words, desperate for her to mean more than his body. He wanted her to need him back, to love him, to stay.

He tugged off his clothes while she slipped out of her panties, and he grabbed a condom from his wallet and rolled it on. He considered swiping the papers from the table and laying her down but had a vision of her panicking over the disorganization and the moment derailing.

Besides, he wanted to hold her close. Wanted the overwhelming sense of rightness when there was nothing between them.

He wrapped his arms around her and burned where her breasts pressed against his chest, where their stomachs touched, where her legs hooked around his hips, even as the chill in the air clung to his skin. Needing to be inside her, to feel her all around him, he pushed into her heat, stealing her gasp with his kiss.

Their tongues tangled, and her arms locked around his shoulders while his hands roamed over her curves. He cupped her bonnie backside, and her legs tightened around his waist, pulling him in.

Trying to show her with his mouth and his hands and his body the feelings he knew were too risky to share, he rocked against her. But the words he wanted to say bottled up in his mouth, fighting to spill out in a kaleidoscope of hopes and dreams for a future together. "I need you, too, lass."

Addie's movements slowed. She nuzzled against his temple. Pressed her forehead against his, her hands on either side of his face, her breath soft against his lips. The gesture was so tender, so unlike the way she usually burned him up, that he pulled back to see her.

Her cheeks were flushed, her lips swollen and pink from his kisses. And her eyes. Her mossy eyes were unguarded and locked on his like a lifeline. Something flickered in their depths that called to his heart, that evoked the peace of coming home.

In his mind, he'd danced around the name for the way he felt about Addie, but her eyes held a matching hope, and the word hit him with the force of a comet, the feeling just as rare and beautiful.

He loved her.

Brushing her hair away from her face, he held her tight against him, one hand splayed across her lower back. She rolled her hips to meet his thrusts and need swelled deep in his belly.

Her eyelashes fluttered, and he moved faster, gripped her hip tighter, kissed her deeper, until he felt her tremble around him and there was no holding back anymore. He chased her orgasm with his own until he was wrung-out and depleted.

All that existed was the warmth of Addie's embrace, the pounding of his heart, the smell of flowers and salt. He rested his head on her shoulder, trying to bring his breath back under control. She stroked his hair, and when he pressed kisses into her neck she let out a contented little hum.

Being with her like this—limbs tangled, hearts joined—felt so simple. And he never wanted it to stop. Wanted to get as far away from days like today.

His earlier plan came back to him, and he wanted it with a renewed vigor. They could disappear into the Highlands where they could stay this close and work through all the complications swirling around them.

He kissed her lips before pulling away, tying off the condom and throwing it in the trash. "I'll take that out when we go."

Addie laughed as she slid off the table and adjusted her skirt before stepping back into her panties. She slipped her shirt over her shoulders.

After tugging his jeans back on, Logan reached for her, doing up her buttons. She tilted her face up, a gleam in her eyes, an indulgent smile on her lips.

"Let me take you on a heritage trip."

"You know I can't get enough of Tour Guide Logan," she said with a wicked grin.

"Just you and me. A Macrae tour."

Addie covered his hands where they worked on her shirt buttons, stilling his movement, her eyes going wide and wary.

27

Addie stepped out of Logan's embrace, bumping into the wooden edge of the table, and finished buttoning up her blouse.

A weekend trip.

That was a big step. A couple-y step. A we-kiss-in-front-of-other-people step.

A flutter took over her belly, either panic or excitement—she couldn't decipher which.

"I've got the university tour this week—"

"The college girls will eat you up." Addie tried to smirk but found a tiny kernel of jealousy lodged in the way. He shrugged like he truly couldn't care less.

Logan's hands slipped to the curve of her waist, and he tilted his head with a soft look in his eyes. "I found the Munro in your mum's photo."

Her pulse sped up in a dangerous race. "You did?"

Logan nodded. "It's up on Macrae lands."

"That makes sense." Giddiness skipped through Addie's stomach. "I found a couple of castles that might have the kind of cannon in the third picture. We could check them out, too." She'd spent an eye-straining number of hours on Google Images searching for *Scottish cannons*. Turned out, there were a shit ton of castles with cannons in this country.

Her online sleuthing talents were nowhere near her spreadsheet skills, and Google seemed uninterested in her additional search term of *battery* and mocked her by returning pages of camera chargers.

But if they were already driving out that way, they could check. "Do you want to go at the weekend?"

She did want to go. She could drive up right now and not have to wait for him. Or rely on him. Or continue to get pulled into the fairy tale he wove, counteracting the warnings in her mind about how hard it would be to walk away from him.

But after her call with Marc, there was no way she could. "We have too much work to do." She didn't even want to imagine Marc's and Devika's reaction if they heard she went on vacation with the owner's hot son when they were off sprinting a marathon.

Logan lips pressed together and he nodded. "True. But we're at a bit of an impasse. We'll take a little break. Get out of the office."

"We just got back."

Logan shrugged. "Maybe it'll spark an idea."

They weren't finding a lot of inspiration here with that menace of a drone buzzing around and Logan nixing all her ideas. Maybe, like the last tour, a change of scenery *would* help.

"We could make it a work trip." If there was a flicker of disappointment in Logan's eye, she ignored it. "Let's see if we can borrow Big Mac's drone. Take some video for the website. Visit some attractions." Stirling Castle was the only place she'd heard of that showed up in her cannon results—probably because it was one of the most popular destinations in all of Scotland—

but it was worth a try. And Logan could give a destination he'd written off a second chance.

Logan pouted, and she patted his cheek. He leaned into her hand, and she couldn't resist running her thumb along his bottom lip. "Come on. It could be fun to explore Scotland again. To feel that first-time wonder you create for your guests."

"Aye. That does sound nice."

"We could get some good pictures. Ooh, you know what would really sell? You, in your kilt, telling the masses to come join you in the craggy mountains of the Highlands... Logan's love letter to Scotland."

He pulled her back into his arms. "You're losing me. But we can visit Eilean Donan, stay in a cozy B and B..." he said, nuzzling her neck.

They could go and have a good time. It didn't have to be a romantic getaway. And she did want to find the places in Heather's Polaroids. The appeal of Logan showing her around the Highlands and keeping her warm through the long winter nights was too hard to deny. It felt good being with him.

And she wasn't leaving yet.

They might as well make the most of the time she did have.

"I'd love that," she said, pushing his hair out of his face. "But I'm driving."

Logan smirked. "Of course you are." He leaned into her, capturing her lips, and blocked out all the tangles of reality with his broad shoulders and skilled tongue.

28

Addie dragged Logan through the arched entrance of
Stirling Castle. Despite the chill of the morning, she was toasty
warm snuggled into Logan's Heart of the Highlands hoodie
under her raincoat.

Hope buoyed her up the ramp. Even if the cannon wasn't
here, she had a list of four other castles that might be the one.

"This feels like a trick," Logan grumbled, shuffling behind her.

"I did warn you there'd be *some* work this weekend. Tell me
some history to console yourself."

He only grunted.

"Fine. Have it your way." Addie dug into her shoulder bag
and pulled out a guidebook.

"That is *not* a Rick Steves book." He yanked the paperback
from her fingers and growled, stuffing it under his arm and out
of her reach. In a monotone voice, he recited, "Mary, Queen
of Scots, was forced to abdicate the throne, and her son, James
VI, was crowned King of Scotland at Stirling Castle at only
thirteen months old."

Addie bit back a smile. She was constantly impressed by his depth of knowledge, that he could remember so many tiny details and give them wings.

She liked it when he remembered her details, too.

Logan pointed to a tan building that almost looked like it belonged in New Mexico with its stair-stepping peaked roof and rim of horizontal posts. "That is The Great Hall, built in the early 1500s. The building was controversially limewashed to make it look much as it would in James IV's time." He rubbed a hand over his face and across his jaw. "I'll take you through the Royal Palace when it's not so bloody crowded."

Addie wrapped her arms around Logan and squeezed. "See? You could totally make this work."

At the top of the battlement, a row of cannons stuck through rectangular cutouts in the stone wall and pointed over the city. Addie knew zero things about what distinguished cannons from one another, but they *looked* like the one in the photo. Her breath swirled in her lungs.

She pulled a Polaroid from her bag, holding it out to Logan. "What do you think?"

Same glossy black finish, same cannonballs stacked inside wire pyramids.

"Aye, look at the brick pattern in the wall, it's definitely here."

Addie's heart soared like the blackbirds overhead.

Around them, kids climbed on the cannons and made booming noises. Logan nudged her lower back with his fingertips. "Go on, then."

She looked back at him, but he was serious, encouraging. Feeling silly and childish, she glanced around at all the people who might see her stepping onto the locked wheels of the cannon and climbing up sidesaddle. No one was paying her any attention.

Heather would not have cared who watched her. For reasons still unclear to Addie, her mom bit the bottom of the cone to suck out ice cream. She wrote notes from the tooth fairy in loopy handwriting on sparkly paper. She was on a constant quest for the perfect skipping stone. She'd been playful and adventurous.

Addie could see why her dad took a snapshot here, capturing Heather's spirit.

The chill of the metal seeped through her jeans as she ran her hand over the shiny black paint. The cool wind blew strands of hair across her face and toyed with the ends of her navy scarf, lifting them up toward the gray sky before suddenly letting go.

It wasn't a ghost, but a lightness settled around her, a contentment she couldn't remember ever being so solid.

"Off the cannons, aye?" an exasperated voice called. Addie turned to find a burly security guard headed their way. He gave her extra stink eye, probably for being over the age of seven.

She slid down, picturing her mom getting told off. Heather would've given him the finger or at the very least made moose antlers with her hands behind his back. Addie tucked her smile into her scarf.

She leaned against the battery wall, pressed up tight against Logan, taking in the view. The land seemed to go on forever, dappled in shades of yellows and greens, the gray hills blending with the sky in the distance.

She dug through her shoulder bag again and pulled out the worn pictures of her mom and the cannon. Happiness danced in her veins. "It's pretty cool to be where she's been."

"Aye, lass." Logan wrapped his arm around her.

She'd been afraid of finding the places in the pictures and feeling nothing, but it was powerful and comforting to stand where her mom had stood. The closest thing Addie had to handwritten recipes.

What she hadn't expected to find were new places to visit the memory of her mother besides a graveyard in the desert.

Places that felt like bright life, like a beginning instead of an end.

Addie flipped to the picture on the moor. The vibrant green of summer stretched across the valley and crept its way up to the tops of the mountains, capped in misty clouds. Of course Heather was down by the stream.

"She could find endless wonder near a river."

Logan slid his arm up her back and into her hair, and she relaxed against the gentle movement of his fingers.

In one of Addie's surly teenage moments, as her mom had basked on the banks of the Rio Grande, her dad had gone on and on about rapids and currents and the bridled power of the water.

"It takes the path of least resistance," Addie said with an eye roll.

Heather had gazed out at the river, sunlight dancing in tiny bursts across the ripples. "But look what a long way she's come."

Addie had come such a long way, too.

Churning and tumbling but finally ending up here. She'd avoided the memories and reminders—hell, this entire country—hoping to stifle the pain of remembering, but it didn't hurt so much now.

Her heart no longer felt crushed. Fragile, certainly, but hopeful.

Like she was starting to heal after all.

Logan took the fourth picture from Addie, gently holding the worn edge of the photo. "This one's pretty washed-out." The sun spots blurred everything in the background except a moss-covered stone wall. "We may not be able to find it."

Addie's stomach dropped, dots sprinkling across her vision, the ground suddenly unsteady.

He was right. It would be impossible. She'd been counting on more pictures, more time. She felt closer to Heather's memory than ever before. But she still hadn't *found* her.

The moor was the last stop. They would go today, and it would be done.

Fear rooted in her heart like thistles. What if this last place felt like goodbye?

All the small ways she'd had to let go over and over again had nearly crushed her. The dreams were the worst—when she found her mother in the night and woke to a world that no longer held her. How many times had Addie come home to a dark living room and an empty couch? Reached for the phone to tell her mom about a promotion or a terrible flight or the Taj Mahal, like her heart was simply incapable of remembering that she was all alone.

She wasn't sure she could survive another parting.

Suddenly, Logan was crouched in front of Addie. "Talk to me, lass."

She blotted out tears with the heels of her hands, pressing her back against the stone wall she'd slumped against. There was one last chance to feel the spark of a new connection with her mom. After, it would be only memories.

And she knew how easily memories faded.

"I'm not ready for this to be over," she whispered.

"You're so brave, doing this." His hands cupped her hips, and his thumbs stroked soothingly across her jeans pockets, but she shifted away from him, pushing the pictures back into the envelope and sliding them into her bag. She didn't feel brave. She felt petrified.

She wiped her hands across her thighs and stood. "We should get going. Make it to Eilean Donan before we lose the sunlight," she said, heading for the exit. An actionable objective that had nothing to do with her mom. Anything to keep moving.

Logan grabbed her wrist to slow her down. "We don't have to take the drone out, lass. Let's go to the moor."

She twisted her hair out of her face and into a tight ponytail. The competing desires to hightail it back to Edinburgh or speed recklessly to the site of Heather's picture shifted and swirled in her stomach. She wasn't emotionally, physically, or mentally prepared for either option. "Work first, play later, right?"

His eyes were soft but serious. "Addie, we don't have to work at all."

"We do. We really do." She wasn't sure what Logan thought of this tourist attraction, but she'd lost all sight of why they were here. They weren't coming up with new itineraries or website content all wrapped up in this mom quest and she couldn't stomach the idea of trying to sell Logan on the compromise tours she'd sent Marc.

Her anxiety ratcheted up with every passing moment. Maybe she'd pass out, and Logan would drive her home before they could even make it to the moor. One could hope.

"I'll do the video. My love letter to Scotland. Then we don't have to rush."

"You don't have your kilt."

"We'll splice in images from tours back in the office. I'll do a photo shoot if that's what you need." Logan made muscleman arms, posing for her.

"Please never do that again," she said, but she couldn't stop the small laugh that escaped. His face lit with a grin, and she relaxed into the easiness of it. How well he could calm her.

Creating authentic and engaging content for the website would certainly lighten the weight crushing her chest. Jack probably had better footage than what they could get from Big Mac's drone anyway. It wasn't some high-end piece of equipment; it was a present from Big Mac's wife. Addie wouldn't be surprised if it spontaneously combusted.

Letting out a breath, she took the phone from Logan. "Alright, let's hear it."

"Welcome to The Heart of the Highland Tours," he said, looking directly into the camera, the wind toying with his hair. "Join us for an adventure of a lifetime. We'll visit ancient castles and quaint villages, scenery so stunning you won't believe your eyes. Explore the majesty of the Highlands or the hidden gems of our medieval capital. Edinburgh has a way of slowly revealing her secrets." Logan's eyes found hers. Softened in a way that told her he wasn't talking about Edinburgh at all. "She will captivate your imagination, make you want to uncover the depths of her past. You'll fall in love with not just her beauty but also her heart."

Addie's pulse flickered wildly through her limbs. When Logan turned to gesture to the castle behind him, she used the distraction to surreptitiously gulp down cold air.

Convincing herself that she didn't want Logan was getting difficult. Sharing her secrets and her past made her want to tumble headlong into his arms. To accept what he offered in every gentle touch.

His smile seemed to say *I've got you*. Soft and dangerous at the same time.

It was one thing to let him pull her out of the mud or be soothed by his stories, another to rely on him. To not be able to carry on, alone.

Devika was full of shit. This thing between Addie and Logan was always getting too serious, always tangling her up more than she wanted. This was a work trip. With a small amount of exploring and a tentative detour. It was not meant for declarations of love.

Addie ended the video with what would have been sweaty hands if it wasn't so freaking cold. She shoved Logan's phone in his direction. "That was awesome. Nicely done." She moved past him. "But let's go play tourist at Eilean Donan." She needed a distraction, to get lost in exploring for a bit and avoid all these emotions threatening to consume her. "It'll be fun."

29

Eilean Donan was one of the most photographed and revered castles in all of Scotland. For good reason. As if painted onto a storybook page, it sat on its own island in the middle of a murky gray loch, the same color as the gloomy sky.

Logan and Addie passed tourists taking pictures in the cold as they walked along the long bridge leading to the imposing fortress and climbed the steps to the keep door.

"The tidal island was first inhabited in the sixth century, and the first fortified castle was built in the thirteenth. It was partially destroyed in the Jacobite uprising and lay in ruins until its restoration in 1911."

She bit her thumbnail and raked her eyes from his head to his boots. "That's hot. We should record you for self-guided tours."

His chest tightened. He couldn't even tell if she was teasing.

She'd spent the long drive playing I Spy as if he couldn't tell she was doing a piss-poor job of hiding behind a happy face when he could sense her turmoil, the same as the churning tides. They should have gone to the moor first. Her mum was clearly on her mind.

They walked through the castle to the Billeting Room, the part Logan looked forward to most. As much as this site was hugely popular, it was also unique. The Macrae family displayed important heirlooms for public viewing.

The room was made entirely of stone, but a wooden table and chairs situated on a large rug in the middle of the space made it welcoming and homey.

"Look at this, lass." Logan studied the pictures of the Macrae family for some similarity he could point out. A giddiness rose in his chest looking at Addie's extended, albeit distant, family relations. He could see running a tour like this for Macrae groups, turning something touristy personal.

Her gaze skimmed over the photographs.

"Four generations of Macraes are still constables of the castle today," he said, swallowing his disappointment as she breezed past the family portraits, trailing her hand over an exhibit of cannonballs.

"Sounds fancy. Do they take tea with the Sheriff of Nottingham?"

Logan let out a low breath. She was tossing up walls faster than he could break them down. His arms hung heavy at his sides. The constant effort was exhausting. Especially when she gave so little in return.

Addie walked through the kitchens with dated pots and pans and leaned in to inspect one of the waxy mannequins wrapped in dirty period clothing. "Hmm…they look more modern than I would have expected. I had no idea they were so advanced in the Middle Ages."

"It's a diorama of the 1930s, not medieval times."

"Really?" She smirked, catching him in her joke. He crossed his arms.

Addie grabbed his hand and led him through the next room where she bowed to the suits of armor, giggling at herself.

She wasn't even trying to find a connection.

Logan scoured his memory for a fitting story to tell her, hoping, like the time she drove the van back to Edinburgh, it would soothe the anxiety he knew she felt over where they were heading next. He wanted her to give this place a chance to hold her interest and her heart. "Have you heard the story of the Five Sisters of Kintail?"

"Oh, goodie." Addie clasped her hands together, overblown delight on her face.

"Clan Macrae is often referred to as the children of Kintail. Legend has it, during a particularly violent storm, two Irish princes washed onto our shores where they fell madly in love with two daughters of the King of Kintail. Promising to send their brothers to marry the remaining sisters, the two princes returned to Ireland with their new brides. The five sisters anticipated their ship, but the men never came. The Gray Wizard agreed to turn the sisters into mountains to preserve their beauty while they waited."

Addie's eyebrows pinched together. "That's a terrible story."

"It's a story about steadfastly waiting for love."

"Or wasting your life away for some guy who never showed."

Logan felt her absolute dismissal deep in his stomach as she walked away.

It shouldn't have surprised him. No one ran faster than Addie when feelings were involved.

When she realized he wasn't right behind her, she circled back and looped her fingers around his wrists. "Oh, come on, it's just a story. Lighten up."

He didn't want to lighten up. He wanted her to get serious. *With him.*

Addie grabbed the lapels of his jacket and pulled him around a corner, into a window alcove. "I didn't know this about myself, but I *love* castles. So many secret places." She ran her palms down his chest, her eyes hot on his, a seductive tilt to her lips. When Logan didn't react, she stepped up on the shallow stairs. "Don't you want to know why?" she whispered in his ear and slipped her hands into his back pockets.

"Come on, there's more to see," Logan said. Her body wasn't a substitute for the intimacy he craved.

A devious look floated across her face before she pulled him in for a kiss and bit his bottom lip.

"Ow! Ye wee water sprite." He pulled back, pressing on the sore spot.

Addie's brows knit together, and her gaze turned heavy. She cupped his jaw and ran her thumb along his lip. "I'm sorry," she said on a low breath, like she was apologizing for more than the nip. Eyes locked on his, she moved slowly, bringing her mouth to his in a quiet touch, like she was kissing it better.

He melted into the softness of her caress, reaching to tangle his hands in her hair when a loud *Ahem* sounded from behind them.

Logan turned to find the security guard watching them with a severe look on his face. Addie backed away, and Logan couldn't help the wayward thought that while he loved kissing her in dark corners, all he really wanted was to hold her hand in the light.

"We'll be going, then."

30

With every turn closer to the moor, Addie's stomach shoved higher into her throat. Realizing her chest was nearly pressed into the steering wheel, she forced herself to lean back and blew out a long breath.

Logan's hand brushed against her neck and slipped into her hair, massaging small circles there, but the anxious thrumming would not be quelled, egged on by Gigi's cheery directions and the twisty back roads.

Addie had been miserable at the castle, stalling, pretending to have fun, and hated that she was hurting Logan by not taking it seriously. But she'd set foot in that castle and the overwhelming guilt and regret of not getting to experience it with her mom had nearly crushed her.

This was all too much to process. Her ancestors' plights felt like nothing compared to the fairy dust she carried in the form of a thirty-year-old picture. One last ticket to a magical connection. And once it was all used up, it would be over.

"The destination is on your right," Gigi singsonged.

Dread wound through Addie's limbs, leaving her weak. She parked in a small lot on the side of the road and climbed out of the car, clinging tightly to the door handle as she gazed up at the mountains.

Low clouds made the cradle of the valley feel small and desolate, so similar to where she grew up. The raw power of nature. The determination of things to grow in an environment that wasn't lending an ounce of help.

The burden of solitude in a barren landscape.

Addie's heart kicked in an unsteady rhythm. She wasn't ready to see this last place.

She wasn't ready to say goodbye.

Blinking furiously did nothing to clear her vision.

Logan appeared by her side, holding the keys she'd left in the ignition. "I'm here for you, Addie. But if you want to get in the car, I'll drive us straight back to Edinburgh."

A part of her couldn't release the safety of the door handle, but who knew when she'd be back here? When would she have another opportunity like this? She could leave the possibility out in the universe—but then she'd never know.

And she didn't have to do this alone. Logan was here.

"I want to do this."

Logan nudged her with a hand on her lower back, leading her.

Wrapping her arms around herself, she dragged her heels through the gravel, leaving sliding indentations through the parking lot.

As soon as she hit the deer path, she caught sight of the bend in the river.

The spot where her parents had stood. Completely unchanged.

Addie's heart raced ahead like a shooting star. She pushed through waist-high grasses, swaying in the wind, catching on her clothes. Her heels sunk into the frosty moor after each crunching step, as if the earth wanted to slow her down. Along the rocky riverbank, past the lone copse of evergreen trees, she moved until there was nothing between her and the majestic mountains.

Wind tugged at her hair, the smell of peat sharp in her nose.

The vast, empty valley didn't feel empty at all.

The image of Heather's dark hair tumbling down her back, a few rogue strands lifted by the breeze, superimposed in Addie's vision.

Her chest swelled like an incoming tide.

Addie could picture her mom out here, unencumbered by the unsteady footing, swept up by the open land and the striking terrain and the gentle flow of the river, rushing to take it all in at once. She would have called over her shoulder, "Hurry up! Come see this," waving Brian around the densely packed trees and climbing onto the boulder.

Then, his laughter at her impatience, barely noticing the grandeur all around them, only seeing her.

Lifting the camera to capture her joy. To freeze a moment worth remembering. Worth living. A testament to an endless love.

Addie climbed up, stepping into her mother's invisible footprints. A direct line rooting her to this spot. A heavy heartbeat like an echo across time.

Born and raised in the desert, she'd finally come home to this lush and ancient land. Addie's throat tickled, and tears filled her eyes.

She'd been unmoored for so long, this tug was a parachute opening, ripping her back from the free fall.

Heather used to say that life was waiting to surprise you if you went looking for it. She lived with an openhearted exuberance Addie had tried to emulate but confused with wanderlust.

She couldn't bring her mom back, but she could honor her memory by living with the same fearlessness. Open herself up to the people and places that left an imprint on her heart. Heather's courage ran through Addie's veins, too.

Suddenly, she wanted something permanent. Some token to remind her of the whispering wind, full of secrets, the opalescent clouds watching stories unfold beneath them, and the wonder she felt in her bones.

She turned to Logan, the flutter of her heart brushing her breastbone. "Will you take my picture?"

Surprise skittered across his face, quickly smoothed over with a smile. "Of course." He raised his phone camera.

Addie spread out her arms, tipped her head back. Smiled into the swirling gray above her. Pearl, lead, silver, steel. The winter air felt light in her lungs.

Logan drew closer, the pebbled riverbank protesting his footsteps. She hopped down and nudged the rocks aside with her muddy boots, searching for a skipping stone.

Addie reached for the perfect one, like it was left there just for her, and slipped it between her thumb and index finger.

She was tired of outrunning her past.

Tired of punishing herself for the way her father pulled away from her. Of holding so tightly to her grief and anger it all but defined her. She was ready to let it all go, to leave it here on this moor that made her scars feel insignificant in the face of its timeless beauty.

With a flick of her wrist, she sent the rock hopping across the water. "My mom always skipped rocks. She liked the idea of defying the things that would pull us under."

Logan picked up a stone and copied her motion, but his hit the water with a plunking splash before sinking into the river. He frowned, and her chest filled with a swelling warmth she couldn't quite name.

Gratitude? Awe?

Without Logan, she would never have recognized Loch Ness in the picture or found this remote mountain. Even if she had, she might not have worked up the courage to go without him. Might have turned back at the first rogue sheep.

The stream gurgled by their feet, and a bird's cry pierced the air. Addie picked up a smooth oval stone. "My dad says it's all in the curvature of the rock."

Logan's hand curled around hers before slipping the rock from her grasp. He placed a lingering kiss to her temple.

Rolling the stone between his fingers, examining it, he tossed it above the shallow rapids. It went skidding across the water, and he turned that warm smile on her.

Addie didn't want to hold back anymore. At Carbisdale Castle, she'd asked Logan to take a risk, but she hadn't given in to it herself.

She slipped into his embrace and breathed the familiar smell of pine as his hand skimmed up and down her back, soothing as a sunrise.

She burned and shivered at the same time, an unsettling fever of recognition.

Of rightness.

Logan turned her, unzipped his coat, and tucked her inside. She nuzzled against the soft fabric of his sweater, dipped her head under his chin.

She had it. Exactly what her parents had in this same place, across time.

Logan touched her cheek, tilted her face up to his. He looked all the more rugged at ease against the jagged mountains and glacial air. His eyes crinkled with concern.

Because he knew what this would mean to her.

Because he understood.

A shiver crested through her body.

Logan challenged her. Teased her. Made her feel safe and wanted. Today he'd given her a history, marked the exact spot where she could put down roots.

He offered her the one thing she hadn't been brave enough to admit she wanted: belonging.

The fading sun highlighted Logan's face as if the universe was sending out a lighthouse beacon to make sure she was paying attention. Finally she was.

She belonged here.

With Logan.

Addie's stomach flipped over at the admission, but her heart ballooned with hope for a future with this man who was thoughtful and deep, who gave her everything she needed.

She could picture a life here. Picking a destination on a Saturday morning and hopping the next train. Exploring. Taking detours. Watching the wind off the moors ruffle Logan's hair, waking up beside him, holding his hand.

Reaching up on tiptoes, she pressed her lips to his. "Thank you," she said on a whisper. She hoped her eyes expressed the rest. *Thank you for bringing me here, for loving me, for being so easy to love.*

Addie's heart soared, reaching for the deep purple of the gathering darkness.

31

Logan held Addie close as she shivered against him, but he'd stand there until his feet were blue with frostbite if she needed him to. His heart constricted for her loss, for the lonely years, for the wandering.

Discovering the spot in this last picture must've been bittersweet. She finally let herself feel something deep and unexpected, and he needed to know every piece of it so he knew what to do next. Were they grieving? Reminiscing?

"Talk to me, lass."

She squeezed him and stepped back. "This meant a lot to me. I'm glad we came." The smile on her face wiped away any trace of her memories or how she might be feeling. "Let's go before the sun sets."

"We can stay here as long as you want."

"I'm freezing. Let's go, Tour Guide."

A wave of frustration rose up in him. It wasn't that she hadn't engaged with this place, she just wasn't willing to share. He was trying to show her she could trust him. Lean on him. He could help shoulder the weight she'd been carrying for so long.

"Addie, I want to support you."

She tilted her head before flashing another smile. "You already are." She turned her back on him, heading for the car.

The retreat maneuver. *Of course.* He ran his tongue over his teeth.

By now, he should have expected it. How many times did he need to learn that particular lesson? Addie only opened up on her own terms.

He was nearing the end of his patience, his ability to wait around for her to catch up. To keep pretending what she offered was enough.

He'd shown her his favorite bits of Scotland. Invited her into his childhood home. Brought her to the places important enough to her mother to warrant a picture. If all that hadn't moved her, if Addie didn't recognize this as a place to set down roots, to grow with him, if this wasn't enough to convince her to stay…

He had nothing else.

Inside the car, she pulled all the vents toward her and cranked the dial, flooding the space with the dusty smell of heat. As they drove to the hotel, Logan cast furtive glances her way. She didn't say anything about him driving.

She didn't say anything at all.

They checked into the hotel and used a brass key to unlock their door. The curtains were pulled to the sides of the bay window, letting in the starlight, but the room didn't feel like the hideaway he'd imagined.

His pulse grew heavy, like a tug-of-war in his veins. He couldn't know what she'd been through, couldn't understand why she kept to herself, but he'd tried to show her he could be counted on in every way he knew how. If he could carry some of her hurt, give her comfort and a place to call home, he would do it in a heartbeat. It wouldn't be completely selfless. He wanted this woman more than he'd wanted that first tour with his dad.

More than a return to the way things had been.

But it wasn't his choice. She had to choose to let him in.

32

The hotel room was a Highland fantasy getaway. Two cozy chairs flanked an honest-to-god fireplace, wooden mantel and all. Gold-medallioned wallpaper covered the walls, and blue-and-green tartan curtains hung from the window. Wrapped in a tan-plaid blanket, Addie sat cross-legged on the bench at the foot of the ornately carved four-poster bed.

Logan set to work building a fire, crouched on his heels, adding splintered logs to the grate. He slid kindling into the gaps, grabbed the matchbook off the mantelpiece, and struck it, waiting for the wood to catch.

Once a flame flickered in the grate, he stood and brushed his hands off along his jeans. "How are you feeling?"

Addie didn't know. Too many things filled her mind at once. Unraveling the specific threads of her emotions was harder than pulling apart old, tangled, silver chains. "Overwhelmed." She adjusted the blanket over her shoulders. "I'm not sure how to put it all into words."

"Try." His voice rasped over the word, almost desperate, and her eyes snapped up to his. Hurt clung to the edges. Maybe a bit of betrayal.

Her breath left with a whoosh.

Logan connected through stories, and she'd withheld hers.

Her stomach clenched around the truth: she'd put that pain on his face, on his heart.

She couldn't convince a jury she had no idea he needed more from her. She'd never met someone who wanted to know her the way Logan did. But today shed light on another truth: she was stronger than she thought. She could give Logan her stories.

Addie swallowed. "Okay."

Logan knelt in front of her, the breadth of his shoulders blocking out all but the glow of the fire behind him. She leaned forward, tracing the hidden smile lines under his stubble with her thumbs. "When you took me to the Kyle of Sutherland and told me how the land and the water and the sky were in your bones and your blood, I believed you. But I wasn't sure I could feel that strongly anymore. Seeing these places I have some claim to, that I get to call my own because of the people who came before me…it's more powerful than I realized."

Knowing she was part of a chain stretching back to the beginning comforted her, like she could never be all alone again. Like she'd never been alone at all.

"I've seen some of humanity's greatest achievements, all the wonders of the world, but I haven't felt that tires-in-the-driveway feeling."

Sometimes she thought it settled around her when Jack let her have the chair by the window and they read in companionable silence. At the Sutherlands' with holiday music and good food and people who embraced every time they saw each other. And right now, sitting in front of a glowing fireplace with Logan.

"Lass," he said in a low voice, looking up at her with those limitless ocean eyes. He tucked a strand of hair around her ear, and the tenderness of his fingertips along her sensitive skin stole her breath.

"I've explored the whole world but never a place I can claim. Never a place where I wanted to take a picture so I could remember how I felt in that moment."

Logan shifted and slid his phone out of his pocket, pulling up the picture he'd taken today.

The mountains stood proud in the distance, and Addie's hair twisted in the wind, golden against the bright yellow of her coat. With her arms spread out and her head tipped back, she looked...free.

After a minute of tracing the curve of her smile and letting that feeling settle on her heart, she handed the phone back to Logan.

His fingers closed around hers. His lips parted, like he wanted to say something else. Then his gaze fell to the phone, and his thumb swiped. "There are others."

She grinned. He probably had a whole montage of her throwing her arms back and staring up at the sky. He handed the phone back, and she nearly dropped it.

Addie's heart slammed against her rib cage. Not a picture from today.

Older.

Beside a different body of water.

On the screen, she stood with her back to the camera, staring out at the flat, gray water of Loch Ness. A blond replica of her mom's picture.

Addie's eyes watered, and she roughly brushed away tears with the heel of her hand.

Swipe.

Addie choked on a laugh. A panorama of children sitting on cannons, Addie perched in the middle.

Swipe.

A zoomed-in version to match Heather's.

Swipe.

The same brooding mountain from today, the evergreen trees off to the left, a yellow-clad woman turned away, gazing up at nature's dramatic display.

She stared at the image until the colors blurred together into a shimmery gray. The same color as Logan's eyes.

She knew the word she couldn't think of out on the moor, the one to describe how she felt about him.

More than *gratitude* or *awe*.

Love.

Addie brushed the soft waves of Logan's hair off his forehead. "My mom said she always knew my dad loved her, but when she saw those pictures, she realized what they had between them was even bigger." Addie knew exactly how her mom had felt.

She pulled Logan's hand to her mouth, placing a kiss in the middle of his palm. Then she settled his open hand over her heart. It thundered under her skin. "Does your heart feel like mine?"

"Exactly the same," he whispered.

Logan reached for her and moved her onto his lap, chest to chest. Her knees sank into the plush rug on either side of his hips and then his mouth was on hers, hot and urgent, as if he felt the same way she did. Like her chest might break open from the overfull feeling fighting to escape.

A fire sparked between them, and normally she couldn't rein in her impatience, the all-consuming need for more. But this time, she pulled back.

Slowed down.

Touched the tip of her nose to his. Logan's breath skated across her lips, and his eyes held hers like a caress. She kissed him, slow and passionate.

His fingers trailed up her sides and a wave of goose bumps spread in their wake like wind across the water. He lifted off her shirt, placing kisses along her collarbone and the curve of her breast.

This time, she didn't pull him closer, didn't nudge him faster.

She sank into the soft pressure of his lips on her skin, the scrape of his stubble, the heat of his mouth.

Logan tugged off his sweater and rolled them, laying her back on the soft rug. The firelight danced along his skin, kissing the rounded curves of his chest and flickering copper through his hair.

"I can't bear the thought of being without you," she whispered, bringing her hands to either side of Logan's face and pressing her lips to his.

They moved together like this was second nature. Inevitable. Fate.

In the dreamy aftermath, she curled into him. Locked together, their breathing synched.

Their heartbeats did, too.

Logan slipped quietly back into their hotel room and sat on the edge of the bed, rubbing Addie's back. She buried her head under the pillow, blindly swiping at him. "Go away, Logan. It's pitch-black out."

The sun rose late this time of year, but he wasn't complaining about the long nights with Addie in his bed, lighting up the dark and warming his soul with her passion. He couldn't count the number of times he'd woken up, unsure if he'd whispered *I love you* in his sleep or only in his dreams.

He settled the cup of tea with far too much milk on the nightstand. Addie mimed following the wafting smell with her nose like an old cartoon, making him laugh, the glint in her sleepy eyes sparking fire in his chest.

Sitting up in bed, she pushed her bramble hair out of her face and took a big inhale of the rising steam. Saluting him with the teal mug, she sipped the tea and asked, "Where have you been?"

"I didn't want to wake you, so I went exploring and met the

owner. Did you know this structure has been an inn of sorts since the 1750s?"

"Look at you, tourist."

Logan hadn't felt like a tourist in...well, ever. Even growing up, they'd pop into a new place, and the owner Logan couldn't remember would say, "The last time I saw you, you were but a wee bairn."

The new connections were invigorating.

Logan rose and opened the curtains. Sleepy mountains blanketed in a dusting of snow curled around a valley painted in the sepia tones of winter. His heart thumped with the childhood excitement that came with orange plastic binoculars and treasure maps. "Wow."

The river wound through the valley and swept past the hotel, but the jumbled river rocks gave the impression that the building sat in the middle of the water. The views were stunning. He'd love to bring guests through here.

Addie joined him at the window, wrapping her arms around his waist, resting her cheek against his back. "I recognize that wanderlust."

"Aye." Logan was so used to feeling the pleasure in watching other people discover new places, he'd almost forgotten he could experience it, too. He had Addie to thank for that reawakening.

Turning in her arms, he moved her back toward the bed.

Their lovemaking was as soft and dreamy as the morning light. The intimacy of it kept him wrapped around her until they'd nearly missed the hotel's breakfast, but he couldn't part with the feel of her nestled against his heart.

For the rest of the morning, they pulled to the side of twisting roads and explored the wilderness. Held hands. Took pictures to capture a perfect day.

Addie led him through a craft room in Fort William packed to the rafters with wool clothing and scarves, Christmas ornaments, local whisky, and spools of yarn in every color of the rainbow. In the attached tearoom, she slurped soup while Logan chatted with the proprietor whose photography graced every available space on the walls.

At Inverlochy Castle, in ruins since the 1200s, Addie only rolled her eyes twice as he read every placard along the perimeter. He hadn't spent much time on the west coast of Scotland, but the excitement of new discoveries, the reclaimed wanderlust, burned brightly in his chest. Right alongside this love for Addie he finally felt free to embrace.

In the late afternoon, they found themselves in the village of Corpach, walking along the canal, their footsteps muffled on the damp pavement. The gentle winter sun peeked out from behind the clouds to greet them.

"This is perfect. Exactly what I needed today." Gesturing to the man-made waterway system connecting the west and east coasts of Scotland, Addie asked, "Don't you want to tell me all about this?"

"Well, in the early 1800s—"

Addie cut him off with a kiss, slow and tender. He committed to memory exactly the way her lips pressed against his in this moment, the touch of her cold fingers tunneling into the hair at the nape of his neck. An overwhelming sense of rightness enveloped him, arms and hearts looped together like an unbreakable Celtic knot.

The sound of tires on pavement interrupted them, and they moved out of the road. Addie hopped onto his back, wrapping her arms around his shoulders.

He followed the path down to a footbridge, and they stopped on the wooden planks, watching the rushing stream race to meet Loch Linnhe. The leafless trees partially obscured the view of the shoreline and the mountains in the distance.

"So peaceful," Addie said, tucking her nose against his neck, soothing the cold with a kiss. Around the bend in the path, she gasped and squeezed his shoulders. "Wow."

The view before them was breathtaking. Curved mountains towered over the loch, their tops obscured by the low clouds. Washed-up seaweed covered the rocky beach, and an old fishing boat lay shipwrecked by the shore, the black hull tilting away from the water.

"You know the name of that mountain?"

"I have a feeling you're going to tell me."

"It's Ben Nevis."

She snorted. "No, it's not."

"Aye, it is. The highest mountain in Scotland. I haven't seen it from this side of the loch before."

"How could you let me miss the painted-pink sunrise? This is an outrage."

"I had more important things on my mind this morning, lass," he said, setting her on her feet.

She smiled at him, and he placed a kiss on her upturned nose, chilled and rosy from the January air. "We'll have to come back another time."

His chest swelled. *Another time.* That's all he wanted. More time. More days like this.

Addie sighed, a content little hum. "God, I love it here."

His spirits soared, gliding across the open sky. She could stay here, in this place that reminded her of her mum, this place she loved exploring as much as he did.

They could build the most beautiful life together.

Swinging clasped hands between them, they walked along the rocky beach.

"Tell me what you picture for the future. You've been working at The Heart your entire life. You must have had ideas, things you wanted to change." This time, when Addie talked about the company, it felt like asking to understand his heart, not a deflection. "What would it look like if you weren't trying to make your brothers or your dad happy? Or me."

Logan kicked at a clump of blackened seaweed.

Planning a trip for her had been eye-opening. He loved the way she looked when she saw the empty moors and the mist settling over the mountains.

Of course, watching Addie was more impactful than it would be with tourists, but if he felt even a fraction of this exhilaration at work, he could happily do it the rest of his life. There was still so much to explore, so much of his country he could share.

This weekend only added fuel to the torch he carried for the idea of custom tours.

Before taking Addie on this trip, he might have been content to leave the idea tucked away indefinitely, but now he couldn't put it out of his mind.

If she said no, he'd have to give up on the little glimmer of a dream, the one that felt so perfectly right.

At the same time, if anyone could find a solution, it would be her.

"I have an idea I've been kicking around for a while now."

"Hit me."

"It might be terrible."

"Worse than golf trips? Because we're getting close to using my original plans."

The skin on the back of Logan's neck tingled. "Custom tours. Clients come to us with either a list of places they'd like to go or the type of trip they always imagined for their family, and we research where to take them, how to show them the pieces of Scotland that are unique and memorable and personal."

Addie's lips pulled to the side as she thought. Her lack of enthusiasm was a rip cord, killing all his excitement.

He knew it was a bad idea.

"I can see why you'd be interested." She tipped her head back and tapped a drumbeat on her collarbone with her thumb and middle finger. "Custom tours break down in the planning stage, though. You can never tell how serious a potential client is, but you spend countless hours planning a trip. They might take your research and go alone, or end up going with another company, or were never serious in the first place."

An anchor settled in the pit of his stomach. He knew it wouldn't work. He'd researched extensively on how to get around that very problem, with no luck. Maybe he would never hack it being a business owner, making the right calls—he'd thought secret whisky tours were a clever idea at one point.

He should never have let himself dream.

Addie steepled her fingers under her chin. "But I think there's something here. What about heritage tours? It would be semi-custom. You could design tours based on the clans. Every Fraser from Australia to Arizona would be over the moon for a clan tour," she said to the inside of her bag. When she resurfaced, she had a notebook and pen.

"How would it work?" He curled his hand around a skipping stone, trying to keep the desperation from his voice. He couldn't very well inject her ideas into his bloodstream to get them any faster. But if there was a chance for something big, something authentic...

"We could design, let's say, eight new tours for the biggest clans. Let's use Clan Sutherland as an example." She drew out a grid in her notebook. "Here, you add high-profile attractions that are important to any clan. Loch Ness, Stirling Castle..." She looked up with an arched eyebrow. "You didn't think you were getting out of tourist traps, did you?"

He huffed out a laugh.

"Here, you add stops in those areas with businesses you already know, but you'd have the space to negotiate new rates. So you'd include the glassblower or places like the fairy well which are impactful, but also free, which is great for your margins."

Excitement pounded in his veins in time with the lapping waves as a new sense of hope settled around him.

She drew another line separating the sections. "Then you'd add new attractions specific to each clan's history, like Carbisdale Castle."

"The clan seat is Dunrobin, actually."

With a droll look, Addie dramatically Xed out *Carbisdale* and wrote *Dunrobin*. "The mix of spots people wouldn't want to miss on a trip to Scotland and more personal places would set your tours apart."

His pulse raced so fast he was in danger of keeling over.

Addie grabbed his shoulder, shaking him, her pen hooked between her fingers. "Logan, this could really work."

"You think so?"

"Yes, it's unique but has a broad market appeal. It could be perfect." Her eyes shone in the fading daylight. "I love this."

"I do, too." Not just the idea but working with her. Traveling with her. Showing her his favorite places and finding new ones. The way she supported him, gave him the courage to take risks.

"And we know you'd be great at it because this weekend was amazing."

A niggling thought slowed the joyful warmth spreading through his body. "What about your boss? This isn't exactly what you're supposed to be doing, is it?"

Addie bit down on her lip, eyes tracking across the horizon. Then she shrugged. "He'll have to come around. This is so impactful."

Logan's heart was near to bursting out of his chest. They could do anything together.

"Let's head back, and I'll pull demographic data to back it up."

A little chorus in Logan's mind chanted *This could work, this could work*, and it wasn't only singing about The Heart.

"I just need to make a call first."

34

Addie walked along the banks of Loch Linnhe, trying to absorb the peacefulness from the water. The Highland air and Logan's bracketing presence made her brave, some magical combination that made her feel like anything was possible. She could do this.

She calculated the time difference—8:00 a.m. in New Mexico— but her dad had always been an early riser. Finger hovering over his name in her phone app, she opened her email instead. Closed it. Pressed the phone against her forehead.

Just do it.

She took a deep breath and called.

Brian answered on the first ring, when she wasn't at all prepared. "Addie?"

"Hi, Dad… Uh, how's the weather?" Addie dragged a hand over her face. There were weather apps galore if she was dying to know the state of Albuquerque's winter. But for them, *How are you?* was a loaded question to be avoided at all costs in order to keep the very delicate balance between them.

"We had a dusting of snow this morning. How's the weather where you are?"

"Rainy. I'm in Scotland."

"You are?" he said, surprise in his voice, and then he paused like he might say more. Like he might bring it up before she did.

He might remember where that fourth picture was taken since he'd been the man behind the camera and all. Addie switched the phone to the other hand, stuffing the frozen one deep inside her pocket, willing her mouth to ask the question.

This superficial connection wasn't enough anymore, but she didn't want to blow it up, either. And the surefire way to spark a months-long game of phone tag was any mention of Heather. It'd been years since she chanced it.

Addie's ribs cinched down tight against the possibility of his retreat, steeling herself against the sting of rejection if he didn't want to talk about her.

But it was his choice, and she needed to stop taking it personally. And stop taking away any opportunity for them to move forward.

No one would break the cycle but her.

"I, um, wanted to ask you something."

He huffed in amusement. "I thought you might."

"I have the pictures from your honeymoon, the ones that are just Mom—"

"Looking for wonder?"

Addie could hear the smile in his voice.

He hadn't shut down. She nearly tripped on the rocky shore from the mix of excitement and relief.

"Yeah. I've been trying to find where they were taken…" If she was going to invest in this relationship, she had to take some responsibility for the way things had been between them. She had to give a little, too. "I needed to reconnect with her or something."

"I do that, too. The balloon festival, the arch in the desert where we got married. I understand that need to keep her memory alive, to relive those happy moments. Honestly, I'm really glad you're doing that."

Addie's eyes brimmed with tears. They'd both been searching for what they'd lost, all alone.

"I know it's hard for you to talk about her, but I've been filling in the blanks on the stories. Will you tell me about that trip?"

"It's getting easier to talk about her. Could you text me the pictures? I'd love to see them again."

"Sure." Every instinct in Addie told her this was a bad idea. Seeing old photos stirred up the kind of feelings that tipped him over the edge, that made him pull back from her, no different than Post-it Note reminders written in loopy cursive or a rediscovered collection of beach glass.

But she was so hungry for his stories, desperate to know where the last photo was taken, and so damn encouraged by the way he was talking to her that Addie pulled up the pictures in her camera roll, tapped on all four, and sent them.

A scratchiness like a microphone meeting fabric came over the line followed by a completely unnecessary number of frustrated grunts for the task of switching between applications while on a phone call. Addie's breathing quickened, waiting for that stilted cadence to reenter Brian's voice, that first sign of withdrawal.

"That damn cannon." He laughed, and Addie's heart took flight. He wasn't shrinking back. "She did this at every castle we visited. Worked her way up to standing on one like a surfboard by the end."

A grin stretched across Addie's face. She could picture that so clearly.

"God, we were young," he said with a huff of amusement. "The one with the lake is Loch Ness. She insisted we rent a canoe even though it was stormy as hell. We paddled out, the wind pelting us with rain, and sat there shivering while she scanned the water for any sign of the monster with her old binoculars."

Addie's throat tightened. She knew her mom wouldn't have forgotten the binoculars on such an important occasion, but the story was even better than she'd imagined. "That sounds just like her."

"She was sure Nessie was kind and shy, that she must be lonely all on her own and just needed someone to believe in her."

Addie smiled through her tears and glanced over her shoulder at Logan. Maybe that was all she'd needed, too.

"Honestly, I'm shocked we didn't get hypothermia." Brian sniffed. "This one by the river... I got us horribly lost in the Highlands. We fought the entire time. I kept turning and ending up in the wrong lane, and she'd shriek and stab a finger toward the other side of the road." He let out a loud breath like he was relieving the stress Addie could very much relate to. "I knew our marriage could survive anything after driving in Scotland, but it was dicey there for a minute."

"I drove up yesterday and thought I was going to kill us."

Logan had been beyond patient and nurturing. If the Highland roads were some sort of relationship test, he'd passed with flying colors.

"It's not for the faint of heart."

Something warm blossomed between them, a shared experience when, for so long, it had been a strained recounting of separate lives. It didn't undo the past, but the rosy tones of a watercolor picture swirled in Addie's heart and made her feel less alone.

"Heather," he said, sounding far away, clearly looking at the last picture, the one where her gaze held so much love. The longing and hurt in his voice, even muffled in the background, pierced Addie's heart, so all the longing and hurt she still held poured out in tandem. "I miss her so much. Every day."

"I do, too," Addie whispered, her throat thick.

This is what they should have done in the first place, shared their pain, grieved together, leaned on each other. Shared their stories and fears. They should have gotten closer, not closed each other out.

"She was so full of life, of hope, always looking for the beauty in every little thing." His voice turned wistful.

"I loved that most about her."

"Me, too."

Addie breathed into the silence that for once was companionable and safe.

"I don't remember where this was taken, though. I'm sorry."

"That's okay." And it was. Addie's heart was so full hearing his stories, talking to the one person who knew Heather like she did. This first step felt hopeful and promising even as the path was long. "This has been really nice. Thanks for telling me."

"Anytime, Addie." Brian paused, the familiar silence shooting up a flare in her chest. "I know we haven't gotten a chance to talk lately, but I have some news."

Addie's muscles tensed at his serious tone, waiting to hear he was selling the house. She'd often wondered if he would. It was too big, and he was getting older. If he was ready, she could understand. She would fly back, walk through the rooms, cut sprigs of lavender, let herself soak up the memories the walls held.

She could do it now.

She was strong enough.

"I'm getting married."

His words slammed into her, doubling her over.

Married.

Addie's line of vision distilled to a single poppy on her wellies, the sounds of the lake fading until all she could hear was her own uneven breathing.

Married?

They were just talking about how much he missed Heather.

They *bonded* over the strength of his love for her. And now he was telling Addie this?

How could he? What he'd had with her mom was a once-in-a-lifetime love. The kind there was no coming back from. The kind he'd nearly lost his daughter over.

"To who?" Her voice came out a ragged whisper, and she folded an arm across her stomach.

"I'm sorry, Addie. Things between us are always so... I didn't know how to tell you. Her name's Becky. We met in the bowling league."

Becky? Who was this man? Her father would never date. Never remarry. Never *bowl*.

God, she was about to be sick.

"She has two daughters, sixteen and seventeen."

The same age Addie had been when she'd lost her mom, lost Brian to grief. He was starting a new family. Getting a do-over. Two brand-new daughters that would get his full love and attention. They'd replace her *NSYNC posters with Harry Styles and eat SpaghettiOs and Cap'n Crunch at the bistro table by the bay window and get everything she'd lost. Everything she hadn't been able to claw back. Anger slicked through her.

"I think you'd really get along. Olivia especially. You should've seen her all wide-eyed at the Tent Rocks. She reminded me a bit of you at the hot-air balloon festivals."

He'd knocked the wind out of her without a single touch. Replaced her so easily. Built on their traditions with strangers.

No... Addie was the stranger.

"Well, congratulations." She could hear the bite in her tone, but how else was she supposed to feel? She hadn't meant to picture Christmases at home, but her mind had conjured images of digging through boxes of Heather's old things, decorating the tree with ornaments they'd collected on their many travels, and reminiscing about the time Addie drank and promptly threw up an entire carton of eggnog.

But not now.

Once again, he'd managed to push her to the outside of a home she'd only recently started wanting again.

"I'm sorry I didn't tell you sooner, but you haven't been the easiest to get ahold of lately."

The steady thrum of Addie's pulse beat in her fingertips. Maybe that was true, but she wasn't letting him put the blame on her. "I have to go."

"Addie, wait—I want to answer any questions you have. And they really want to meet you. Please don't shut me out."

"Pretty bold ask." She railed against the insinuation that she had a choice to make when her dad had made the choice for them years ago.

Jabbing the End Call button, she sank to a cross-legged seat on the rocky shore. Ran her hands along the rocks. Picked up one after another and tossed them across the glassy lake where they all sank straight to the bottom.

Her throat burned with unshed tears. Tears she'd promised herself she was done with. But the impulsive conversation tore away all the distance between her and her father. Maybe a bigger person would've been happy for him or, at the very least, followed the path of light exposed through the newly cracked door. But she wanted to kick the door closed so hard it shattered and her dad felt the pain of a million splinters lodged in his skin.

His voice, his small apology for a big betrayal, reduced her to the lonely and heartbroken girl she had been. She hated him even more for it. Resented the hell out of the childish longing she had naively assumed would stay safely buried in the face of a rekindled connection.

She'd done everything in her power to avoid feeling this way for so long. She'd opened herself up to this conversation, to this hope, to this version of herself she was becoming with Logan, and her dad had *ruined* it.

Addie took quick breaths until she was light-headed, her mind buckling under the weight.

Logan appeared, worry etched around his eyes, and lifted her into his arms. "I've got you." Trying to shoulder her pain.

But this was too raw to share.

She couldn't feel her fingers. She was too numb to tell if it was even from the cold.

Logan led her back to the car in silence.

The open sky at the lake had been wide enough to contain all Addie's emotions, but inside the stifling car they crammed in around her, pushing and throwing elbows.

The trees opened up as Logan turned back onto the motorway and she stared down the dark lane.

"Want to talk about it?"

Addie studied Logan's profile, a moving picture of concern, lit from the dashboard glow.

She didn't want him to make it worse. And she didn't want him to make it better.

"He doesn't know where the last picture was taken."

Logan reached out and squeezed her knee. "Lass. I'm so sorry."

"It's fine. I don't need it. This weekend was perfect."

And it had been. For a while. But that giddy hopefulness was sucked farther into the fairy realm the closer they got to the city, replaced by a deep sense of foreboding.

This thing with Logan—comfortable, warm, safe—this place that welcomed her with open arms…felt suddenly dangerous. Like it could be snatched away at any moment.

She wanted Edinburgh to be home with a fierce longing. But when had wanting ever been enough?

35

Jack looked up from the TV when Logan opened the door to their flat carrying Addie's suitcase. His eyebrows pinched together. Logan wasn't sure if she'd told him what they were doing this weekend, but Jack could put two and two together.

"Hey, Jack!" Addie sounded unusually chipper, like she was forcing herself into a good mood. Most of the drive back had been in silence. Logan gave her space, holding her hand while she processed the very real possibility that the location of Heather's picture was lost to time.

Surely there were feelings mixed up in there over speaking to her dad. She'd downplayed it, of course, but it took immense courage to embark on a path of forgiveness. Logan was proud of her. And so bloody hopeful that she'd push herself with him, too.

"How was the weekend?"

"Dull." Jack stood up from the couch and stretched. "Yours?"

"We figured out the future of The Heart."

The fact that Addie had called her dad after their trip had kicked Logan's confidence into high gear. This was the right direction for his future. Their tours could inspire, could connect people, not just to his country but to something bigger.

"Clan tours," she said, stretching all the vowels in her terrible accent. "Find your Scottish roots—"

"Is this an Australian accent?" Jack asked, looking at Logan with wide eyes while gesturing to Addie.

As much as Logan wanted to be in on the fun of teasing Addie, he couldn't see why Jack didn't shut this down, why he and Addie were still allowed to discuss the future of the business, but Logan was locked out.

Addie slipped her jacket onto the coat rack. "In all seriousness, we're thinking eight tours with a mix of hot spots and your local connections. I'm about to check demographics, but you know the market. Do you think the big clans have enough pull to make this viable?"

Logan's confidence had stretched and swelled all weekend but at Addie's question, it suddenly deflated. Why was she asking for his input? Maybe Jack had run more of the business, but Logan ran the tours—he met the people who stepped on the coaches, knew their histories. A high percentage of them claimed Scottish heritage.

"That's brilliant. You could add a more general tour for people who don't know their heritage, exactly."

Now Jack wanted to dream up new tours? No. That ship had sailed months ago. He didn't get to intrude when Logan finally had his legs under him again or claim any sort of credit for their success. He couldn't come in here and pick up the part he always played: the leader, the hero, the eldest and wisest.

This didn't belong to Jack anymore.

"That's a great idea. I have to get my computer." She headed down the hall, but Logan's attention remained on Jack.

"I'll be there in a minute." He had a brother to speak to first.

Logan gestured for Jack to lead the way into the kitchen and followed him in, curving his fingers around the wrought iron back of a chair. "I can't for the life of me understand why you two are in cahoots."

"I answered a direct question. Did you want me to ignore her?" Jack asked, filling up a glass of water from the sink.

"You do with me. You won't discuss The Heart, won't consider steering us back to an even keel before you bolt—and for what?—but suddenly Addie's here asking your opinion on something you shouldn't know anything about. You don't get a say anymore. That's what you wanted, isn't it?"

Jack raised his hands in a show of retreat. "I supported her at the beginning because I needed to know you'd be alright and because it looked as if you might stonewall her. Although, that wasn't exactly what happened, was it?" Jack arched an eyebrow and sat at the small table.

"Excuse me, are you chastising *me* about inappropriate relationships?"

Jack's eyes hardened. "Foolish ones. Believe me, watching you fall all over yourself has been the most entertainment I've had in a long while. But a weekend away?" Jack took off his glasses and cleaned them on his shirt. He squinted up at Logan. "She doesn't live here, mate."

Logan traced his teeth with his tongue, the rest of his body going still at the reminder of the future, pushing in and zapping the bubble he'd been floating in. "I'm aware of that fact, thank you. You say you don't want to be involved, but you were giving her counsel as soon as she arrived, and you're meddling now. You can't have it both ways."

"I don't want to be part of the business, so I have to sever all ties with you? Is that it?"

Logan was out of line, he knew it, but he couldn't let it go. "Back off, Jack."

"When she finishes this project and walks out *that* door—"

Jack pointed to the front room and the image of Addie leaving, dragging Frank behind her, imprinted in Logan's brain "—I don't want to see you hurt."

Heat gathered in the pit of Logan's stomach. "What a doting older brother. Making sure I'm alright when people leave me."

Jack ran a hand through his hair, exasperated. "I didn't leave you, Logan."

"Sure felt like it." Logan crossed his arms, as if that would fend off the memories of their last day at The Heart. Of Jack, fingers steepled under his chin, sitting on his desk, and Reid leaned back against his, legs crossed one over the other, both of them examining the floor. The look they shared, the silent communication between brothers that Logan could no longer decipher. The dulled words they used—*so sorry* and *guilt-ridden* and *the best thing for us*—that did nothing to lessen the impact of *you're on your own*. That cloying sense of helplessness to redirect his own future, to understand how something so monumental, so foundational, could be decided without him.

"I know you don't understand my reasons—"

"What reasons?"

Jack pushed away from the table and stood. "I'm not getting in a row about two things at once. I was only trying to help with Addie." With a heavy sigh, he patted Logan on the shoulder on his way out of the kitchen. "Have a care, little brother."

The door to Jack's room clicked closed before Logan dared to breathe. He released the chair, rubbing at the round indentations across his palms.

Addie poked her head into the kitchen, hand curving around the doorframe, with a smile to rival a summer day. "I think this could work."

Logan pushed aside the swirling sea of emotions and gave Addie and her clever ideas all his attention and enthusiasm.

But later that night, when she curled into Logan with her

hand fisted in his shirt, her breathing deep and even in the dark, he replayed his conversation with Jack.

Logan had done a remarkable job staying away from the grand plan concerning Addie, having seen that deep-seated instinct to run, to retreat into herself. But their bond had changed somewhere between here and the hills of Kintail.

His heart was fully invested. He might have qualms about how exactly they would sort out the future, but his feelings for Addie hadn't wavered since the first time he'd kissed her.

He wanted to give her connections. To make her happy.

His family loved her.

He loved her.

But this thing between them felt so fragile. Deep and raw, but it could go up in smoke if he pushed.

Addie hooked her ankle around his leg and sighed in her sleep, burrowing a little deeper into his soul. Logan's whole heart longed to envelop her while he drowned in the fragrance of her hair, her body soft and molded around his.

He'd skipped over her words—*I can't bear the thought of being without you*—wanting to believe they meant the same as *I love you. I'll stay with you. I'll do whatever it takes to make this work.*

The fear of pushing her away held him back from asking her *Will you stay?*

The question tossed in his mind like waves upon the rocks.

He wasn't at all sure of her answer.

36

Logan sat at the conference-room table with Addie, papers spread out all around. She'd made them work the entire week, frantically building out spreadsheets and rapid-firing directions at him.

With a pencil shoved in her hair she looked focused. Determined. But they'd been at this for the better part of five days, and his interest had long since waned. His legs cramped from sitting in the same position for so long.

She chewed on her bottom lip in the way that made him think of other things they could be doing right now. He wanted to hold her, craved the assurance he felt when they were together, but he needed words, too. Plans.

These dreams and hopes for the future bottled up inside him, but it was impossible to share them when she was stressed and shutting down.

The past few days, she'd been more reserved, tense, taking calls at all hours of the day. He knew they had work to do, that this was the most important thing right now, but he wanted to whisk her back to the Highlands where everything felt simple and lovely.

Addie pushed a notebook out of her way. "Where's the print-out with the demographic—"

He handed her the packet she'd highlighted in at least six colors.

"Thanks," she said without looking up. She flipped through the pages and ran a finger down a chart.

"What was that ruined castle...?"

"Tioram. It's quite romantic, out on a tidal island." Logan slid closer, brushing his arm against hers.

"I'm sure." Addie's lips lifted, but he wouldn't have noticed if he hadn't been looking for it. She kept her eyes on the spreadsheet. "Alright. Here's the tab for the Clan Tours. It has spaces for all the costs and prices with the total down here. You don't want this number to turn red," she said, pointing to a high-lighted box at the bottom right.

Logan leaned in, resting his chin on her shoulder and draw-ing light circles around the freckles on her forearm. "Got it. No red numbers."

They'd finally found a rhythm. Working with Addie made him feel confident. She was clever and thorough. Even though he was a bit petrified of breaking the monster of a spreadsheet in front of him, he could handle it. He could take on anything with her by his side.

"Right." She shifted away. "So after you get that finalized, you add the tour to the reservation system." Addie opened the application. They'd been over that workflow at least three times. He agreed he should know the end-to-end process, but the res-ervations sat squarely in Elyse's domain.

"We don't need to look again. I've got it."

Maybe she was *too* focused. Stress wasn't good for a person. Hours ago, she'd complained about the fluorescent light giv-ing her a headache, and he'd turned it off. Now, the lamplight kissed Addie's cheek, turned her golden hair shiny. He ran his hand down her back and up again, sliding under her hair and rubbing her neck. She didn't relax into the pressure of his fingers like he'd hoped.

"Okay." She typed in The Heart's website. "Here's the template for the new tours…"

They'd been working on the website for weeks. He could build a page in his sleep. There were far more interesting things he could think of to fill their time. Logan wrapped his finger around a curl brushing Addie's shoulder.

The office had emptied out. It was just the two of them left. His body heated with thoughts of the last time, hiking her pencil skirt up her hips, his mouth following—

"Logan, are you even listening to me?"

"Hmm? Yes. Spreadsheets, reservation system, website. Got it." His fingertips traveled into the sensitive dip behind her ear.

Addie grabbed his hand and pulled it away. "Please pay attention. You have to be able to do this by yourself."

A stone settled where his stomach used to be and slashed away the desire clouding his mind. "Why are you so worked up today?"

"This has to be perfect to pitch to Marc. And it should have been done by now. I have to wrap this up." The venom in her voice poisoned any lingering fantasies Logan clung to. Addie stood, collecting her papers and stuffing them into a folio.

Her emotional armor that he'd been wrestling with all week—all month, really—snapped back into place, the lock bolting so loudly he could practically hear it.

Here he was, distracted by how great it felt working with her, while she'd jumped ahead to the end.

His stomach swirled with the uncertainty of the next step, but the time for avoiding the reality of her imminent departure had clearly passed.

Straightening his spine, he breathed deeply and then caught

Addie's wrist, forcing her to turn and face him. "What happens when this is done?"

"I write up an official plan with The Heart's next steps and share it with you, Neil, and Marc. But I need to have a conversation with Marc first. I can't blindside him with this."

Logan clenched his eyes shut. He couldn't reconcile Office Addie with how emotional and open she'd been by the side of the loch a week ago. *That* Addie had vanished like the Scottish mists.

This Addie always thought about work, never giving their relationship the gravity it deserved. At this point, it chafed. She constantly fought the pull, the rightness between them. The stale air turned bitter as he sucked it in.

"I meant with us."

She pressed the heels of her hands into her eyes, hiding from him.

Always hiding from him.

"Let's talk at my place," he said.

Time passed with a quiet *tick, tick, tick,* but the sound of Addie slipping through his fingers was a raging forest fire, crackling and burning him down to ash.

37

Addie walked into his room, Logan trailing behind, and turned on the bedside lamp. She breathed through the jitters zipping through her chest. It wasn't like she thought she'd avoid having this conversation, but she wasn't ready for it yet.

She'd meant it when she said she couldn't bear to think about life without him—so she hadn't. It hurt too much.

Logan perched on the side of his mahogany dresser. "Are you walking out of here when this project is finished?"

"Of course not. How could you think that?" It scared her how much she cared. How his easy laughter seeped in through the cracks and seemed to glue her back together.

"Because you're pulling back from me. I can feel it."

"I'm stressed—"

"What do you want, Addie?"

She moved past the bookshelf full of picture frames and knick-knacks, to the window, out of the direct line of his demanding gaze. The cold air seeped through the glass and settled on her skin, dampening the fear. Orange ribbons cast by the streetlight glow rippled over wet cobblestones.

If she gave herself permission to dream, she'd buy plane tickets as far out as the airlines would let her, to know with full certainty when she would be in his arms again. She wanted to sit around his tiny kitchen table eating hearty soup on an extended layover. To snuggle into a reading nook in a bookshop on a dreary Edinburgh morning.

She wanted to sleep in an ice castle. Make love in a humid room with the sound of ocean waves crashing out the window. Dance in the street.

She wanted to take him to the desert.

Their adventures together would be sporadic, but wasn't the possibility, the spontaneity, part of the fun?

Addie moved between Logan's legs and gripped the cut of his biceps. "I want to meet in cities all over the world. I know this little café in Paris and we can eat ourselves sick on pain au chocolat. And I've always wanted to see the sea turtles in Costa Rica. We can find places neither of us have been before and meet new people, try new foods, explore. Just like our Highland trip."

"Aye." Logan's hand cradled the back of her neck, and he pressed a hard kiss into her hair. "But after that... I want more than a holiday. I want a life with you."

The words curled around her heart—but not softly. Sharp and pointed like thorns. It hurt to dream the way Logan did. They had reality to contend with.

"Are you ever in London?" Heathrow's Terminal 5 was basically her vacation home.

"Never. It's nearly six hours each way on the train. How often do you fly through Edinburgh?"

"It's not exactly an international travel hub."

Logan stood up, pushed past her, paced in front of his door.

This was exactly why Addie had wanted to keep it casual. So they both didn't walk away broken.

Long-distance didn't work indefinitely. Especially for two people with erratic work schedules. Addie didn't even know what *country* she'd be in in a handful of weeks.

"What if I was in Boston?"

Addie scoffed. "Doing what? Running the Duck Boats? Logan, your entire life is here. I would never ask you to give that up for me." Where Addie was a tumbleweed, he was an ancient oak tree, roots deep in the soil, bearing witness to the lives that took comfort from his protection. A tree like that couldn't be transplanted.

He would wither and die.

No matter how much she wanted every available minute with him, she wasn't that selfish.

"What if you worked from here, then?"

Addie's heart lunged for that dream.

A home. Here. With Logan.

He leaned back against the door and the latch clicked into place. His stance was so much like the first time they were together—blocking her exit, asking for more than she was ready to give, *wanting her.*

She felt herself slipping past her boundaries, just like that night, willing to do anything for more of this feeling. To attach herself to him and never let go.

It was a dangerous illusion he presented her with—pixie dust meant to turn a fantasy into reality. But what happened when the magic wore off? When they couldn't coordinate their schedules, when they never saw each other?

"You don't have an office in Boston, so it's an option, right?"

"At some point we will. Hopefully. I have no idea what the expectation would be. Or if it's even a possibility." She licked her dry lips.

"But you could find out."

Addie's stomach churned at the idea of asking for something so huge when the company was still so young and she was so wildly off-task with The Heart. "I'm already going way outside the bounds of what Marc wants with these tours. I don't know how I can ask him that right now."

Logan ran his hands through his hair, gripping the roots. "You don't owe him a success story in exchange for a home. You said he cares about you, and if working here makes you happy, why would he have any problem with that?"

Because he might decide she was more trouble than she was worth. "You're asking me to give up my life to fit in with yours."

His hands dropped to his sides, his body going perfectly still. "I thought you'd be gaining some things, too."

Addie shut her eyes against the pain in his voice. A reel played behind her eyelids of a life here. Birthday parties at the Sutherlands'. Bonfire Night and Beltane with Elyse. Tea and scarves and endless exploring in this city. In this beautiful country her mom had loved, that Addie had fallen for, too.

And Logan.

Devika and Marc were in Boston…when they were in town. Which was never. A handful of girlfriends who were less and less interested in drinks with no notice now that husbands and babies had entered the mix. Blackout curtains. No one asking her to make hard choices.

No one asking anything of her at all.

Logan crossed the room and sank down on the edge of his unmade bed, propping his elbows on his knees and catching his head in his open hands. The light from the lamp illuminated his profile and the curls that hung down from his bowed head.

His body practically vibrated, sad and powerful and breakable, like he might shatter into a million little pieces if she got too close.

He lifted his head, his jaw set, his eyes pleading, a swelling mix of hopeful and hopeless that dragged her under and wrung her out. "You push me to take risks. Take a chance on me, Addie. I'm a good bet."

So fucking earnest.

She moved to him, unable to fight the pull. He wrapped his arms around her waist, grabbing fistfuls of her shirt, and settled his ear over her heartbeat. She cradled his head and buried her nose in his hair, the comforting smell of his shampoo choking her.

She closed her eyes, sinking into the way his body told her things that were too big for words, but felt like *I need you.*

Despite every last attempt she'd made to not rely on him, she needed him, too.

"What if you change your mind?" she whispered.

Logan tipped his face up and shook his head, his jaw tight. "I will never change my mind about us." He kissed her roughly, the pressure of his lips, the slide of his tongue full of possession and hurt. His hand twisted into her hair to the point of pain. She could feel his need to claim her, to push her, to prove she felt it, too.

"Tell me we'll figure something out." His voice broke.

Addie stared into his stormy ocean-gray eyes, the raw need, the swirling uncertainty. She had once thought Logan predictable. But that wasn't right. He was steady, his love unchanging and enduring.

She nodded. "I'll talk to Marc." *About a whole slew of things.*

38

Addie sat in the pub while Logan and Jack hurled insults at the football match on TV. Elyse sipped her Cider and Black, the pinkish hue matching her nail polish. She quirked an eyebrow at Addie over the rim of her pint glass.

Clearly, Addie wasn't doing a great job pretending to have a good time. She tried to smile, shoving a cheese-drenched chip in her mouth.

Everything felt out of control, like she was making decisions about her future in the middle of a storm surge. And it was only going to get worse.

Dread had coiled around her stomach last night and wouldn't let go. She needed to talk to Marc and hope for the best.

Like the time she'd gotten back from Armenia with Devika. In a department-wide meeting, Marc had called Addie *brilliant*. She could still feel the blush spreading across her cheeks and the pride in her chest.

The hope that Marc would react the same way this time was

self-deception at its finest. They could take risks at an established company, but not now.

Visions of his reaction hadn't stopped playing in her head. A cold stare, a rough voice, a stiff spine. *I trusted you to get this done.*

She couldn't put off this call forever. She'd give herself an ulcer. If she didn't call with an update soon, he certainly would.

Addie picked up her phone, and after checking her world clock to make sure it was an acceptable hour in Greece, she texted him.

Addie: Will you call me when you have a free minute?

Her phone lit up on the table. *Marc Dawsey.*

She flinched, then scrambled to silence the buzzing, her phone shooting across the slick tabletop. Logan caught it, his face awash with hope as he read the name. Addie tried not to grimace when he handed it back to her.

It vibrated against her palm, but she felt the disturbance through her whole body. "I'm going to take this."

"Buzzkill," Elyse said, but Addie was already pushing through the bar line on her way to the door. She'd never make it outside before the call went to voice mail. She answered in the echoing entryway.

"Bad time?" Marc asked with a smile in his voice.

She winced and cupped the bottom of the phone as if that would help dim the noise. "No. Let me just get outside."

"You know, you're entitled to a personal life. I'm glad to see you taking a break. Let's catch up later."

"No, now's good." Addie pushed open the heavy wooden door and gulped in the cold night air.

She fought the instinct to chitchat, to ask which toiletry he ran out of on this trip just to stall for the length of a tirade about spray deodorant. *Suck it up, Macrae.*

"Okay, keep an open mind."

"Uh-oh. Did you learn this trick from my husband?"

"I did, actually. Damien could write a book on you."

Marc chuckled. "Alright, tell me this thing I won't like."

"But that you *could* like," Addie reminded him, curling her fingers around the poky branch of a potted pine tree.

"Let's hear it."

"So, The Heart of the Highlands—"

"I'm familiar."

"Right." She sucked in a deep breath and powered on. "When it came down to it, they weren't excited to push some of the bigger attractions. We've spent a lot of time—" Addie winced at her choice of words "—brainstorming amenable solutions and came up with heritage tours."

"Which is different from the tours you already sent?"

Her hands and arms prickled and not from the icy air. She never should have sent those itineraries to Marc. She'd wanted to make sure The Heart had options in case a new project started, but he was sure to latch onto the work that was nearly complete. "Right. Logan and Neil haven't seen those yet. I just need a little more time to finish designing these heritage tours. We'll build out eight for the biggest clans—"

Marc's harsh exhale crackled ominously through the phone. She pictured him rubbing his hand over his face. "We can't use clan tours in our portfolio. We've got to keep these projects moving quickly to turn a profit this year. You need to steer them back to the original vision. Implement the tours you showed me."

Addie's racing heart battered her chest. She'd failed Marc, jeopardized their future, but she couldn't just abandon Logan's idea. His passion. He'd be destroyed. "I know this isn't ideal. But at this point, it seems like we should complete what the client wants."

They weren't going about this in the right way. Addie wanted to make a shift to custom work, bucket-list trips, to work with clients creating once-in-a-lifetime experiences for the people who passed through their countries.

"Neil wants the company to be profitable so he can retire in good faith and leave this business to his kids. He'll sign off on what you've proposed."

"I just need a little more time."

"There is no more time. Amsterdam City Tours signed on for round two. I need you there by Wednesday."

Wednesday.

The word was a game-ending buzzer rattling her skull. *Time's up.*

A wave of nausea rolled through her. She knew there was going to be a next project and that it would be soon. All their forward progress had brought them closer to this point.

But she wasn't ready to leave.

This was the moment she'd been fighting against, shoving to the back of her mind, and here it was, somehow still catching her completely unprepared. Staring her down at the end of an alley, while she stood there helpless, with ringing ears and wobbly heels.

Wednesday.

She pushed her fingers into her eyes, swallowing back the bile in her throat.

"I need to know you're on my team, that you've got my back. That we're all working toward the same goal."

"I am. Of course I am." Addie's head swam with the spiraling fear that everything she cared about could be ripped away in an instant. "This is going to be a surprise. Give me some time to talk to them about it, alright?"

"Will do. I've got your back, too, you know."

Did he? It didn't feel like it right now.

"Anything else while we're on the phone?"

Here was the perfect segue to ask about working out of Edinburgh, but she couldn't take it. Couldn't risk her position any more than she already had. And if he said no…she wasn't ready to give up on this dream yet.

Her breath came out in white puffs, the cold air like a numbing blanket. "That's all."

Addie hung up and slumped against the black metal window shutters behind her.

She could take a few more days to finalize the compromise tours, then she could present everything to Logan, show him that she had a plan that would save his company, keep his connections to the people and places that held his heart, and allow him to keep doing what he loved, even if it wasn't perfect.

So far from perfect.

"You okay?"

Addie startled at the voice and dropped her fist from her lips. The sight of Elyse brought on a wave of prickling tears. Addie shook her head. "My boss wants me in Amsterdam next week."

Elyse wrapped her up in a hug. "Shit."

Not even a *dagnabbit*. Addie pinched her eyes closed, leaning into the embrace, trying to siphon some of her strength. But all she felt was a gaping nothingness swallowing up everything she'd found here.

Over Elyse's shoulder, the buildings disappeared into the fog above the lamplight glow, transforming the streets of Edinburgh into a rat maze with no way out.

And Addie was the rat.

39

Logan looked up when Neil appeared, drumming knuck-les on his and Addie's shared desk. The caterpillar was happy today. "Can we all meet in the conference room?"

Addie had been heads-down working all afternoon, not even looking up when he flicked a paper clip her way. She gave Logan a questioning look, but he shrugged. Neil probably wanted to discuss which poem to read on Burns Night.

Settling into the leather chair, he clasped his hands over his stomach. "I just got off the phone with Marc, and I can't wait. Can you walk us through the new itineraries?"

"We've only finished building out half the tours so far…" Logan's assurance that they were talking about the heritage itin-eraries diminished with each word he said as Addie's face went shock-white, her lip turning the same shade where she bit down hard.

Neil waved off Logan's comment. "No, the new tours."

New tours? Logan's shoulders tensed as wariness swarmed around him like midges in the summer. "What are you on about?"

Addie sat up straighter. "Oh, I don't have everything polished to present—"

"I'm not fussy. Whatever you have now will do."

She shifted in her seat, twisting her necklace as if it was choking her, and Logan's heart rate kicked up a notch. There wasn't anything to present yet, polished or otherwise. She'd been keeping something from him—something everyone else was in on.

"Neil, I'm sorry. Can I speak to Logan privately for a minute?"

Adrenaline pumped through his veins. He didn't want to hear her explanation. He wanted to know exactly what was going on. Right the fuck now. "No. By all means, I'm also impatient to see this."

Addie held his gaze a moment longer, that pleading in her eyes that brought him right back to this room when she'd hoped he wouldn't reveal she'd snuck onto his tour and completely beguiled him.

His breath left him at the reminder of what she would do to get ahead in her job. "Come on, then."

Neil's brows drew together, and he shot Logan a look meant to bring him in line. But he wasn't the one double-crossing anyone here.

Addie closed her eyes for a long moment before pasting a half smile on her face. She shuffled papers and fiddled with her computer's connection to the projector before pulling her hair back into a bun.

She stood and gestured to the screen. "We've already gotten positive feedback on the reservation system. It accomplishes the needs of guests for a smooth booking experience and for the guides to have easily accessible personal information to tailor trips on the go."

She couldn't look more corporate and distant if she'd dug out a red laser pointer.

Neil smiled up at her. "And if Elyse is happy, we're happy."

"Speaking of Elyse—she's one of your greatest assets. It would benefit you to give her more responsibility and autonomy as part of this transition."

An interesting thought to be pondered at literally any other time than now. "Were you showing us the website next?"

She looked at Logan with desperation in her eyes, hesitating like she was giving him an opportunity to call this off.

He leaned back in his seat and crossed his arms.

"The website is much cleaner and easier to navigate. We'll build out a landing page to book for next year when we're ready to add the new tours." Pursing her lips, she clicked into a draft folder of the website. "Marc…and I…think these itineraries will give you the broadest market appeal and the best chance of success. I tried my very best to keep as much of your current itineraries as possible and add more recognizable destinations with your hidden gems to balance out the margins," she said, rubbing at the side of her neck.

He could feel her eyes on him, but he didn't look away from the screen as she pulled up web page after web page. Itineraries she hadn't talked to him about.

Destinations he'd never guided.

Not so much as a footnote about the clan tours.

The only thing he recognized was a Hogmanay itinerary—an exact replica of the tour she'd brought him on.

His stomach hardened, his pulse heavy. "You've sold yourself short. This looks quite polished, indeed."

Addie winced.

Oblivious to Logan's sarcasm, Neil reclined in his seat, a grin splitting his face. "It's brilliant."

Logan might have thought so, too, when he'd wanted something safe. If they had simply looked for a compromise. But she'd urged him to name what he wanted. Pushed him to recognize a dream he'd been happy to leave banked but now burned in his chest.

And she was here to douse it.

Her boss and his dad were committed. Apparently Addie was, too. There would be no changing course now.

She'd made an irrevocable decision about his business that affected his entire future, without him. Just like his brothers.

Jack had been meddling from the sidelines, and his dad would never retire. Addie made Logan feel supported and confident, like his dream mattered, but clearly she never believed it could work.

Just like them, she didn't believe he could do this on his own.

"This way, you still keep your relationships with current vendors, although some will need to have renegotiated terms. Neil, you haven't even adjusted for inflation," she said with a tip of her head and a smile to reassure him she was only gently scolding.

Logan's blood simmered that she could be lighthearted when his world was collapsing. He ran his fingers through his hair, trying to pull some sense from this conversation.

"And you have financials for all these?" Neil asked.

Addie watched Logan, a deep groove between her brows. "Yes." She clicked through detailed financial plans and the marketing changes that would come along with this shift. Neil rambled about his delight in the tours, but the words sounded far away and distorted.

When he stood, he gripped Logan's shoulders and said to Addie, "Thank you. Truly. We're indebted to you."

She watched him leave the room and turned to Logan. "I'm sorry—"

"What the fuck was that?"

40

Logan gripped the armrests of his chair, blood pounding like the Royal Military Tattoo.

"I asked Marc to give me time. That was not how I planned to tell you." Addie shifted her weight back and forth, her hands pushed together in a gesture of pleading, pressing against her lips. "I'm so sorry."

"Sorry you didn't warn me or sorry you've pushed through an entirely new proposal behind my back?"

Addie folded her arms over stomach. "It wasn't like that. I didn't know when my next project would come up, and I didn't want to leave you with nothing. Worse than nothing. I was supposed to recommend golf trips, Logan, so while we were figuring out what we wanted to do, I've been building out these tours. They're a compromise."

Or a half life. A concession. A surrender.

Logan tipped his head back and closed his eyes against the flickering fluorescent light. "I never wanted a compromise. I wanted it all." He let the double meaning linger in the air.

With a heavy breath, she braced herself against the table, as if it was the only thing keeping her on her feet. "All the things I know you love about the itineraries are in there. I added some touristy spots, but you've seen that they're not that bad."

Logan didn't give a flying fuck about the merits of tourist traps. He stood, bracing his hands on the table. "Were you just humoring me with the heritage tours? Trying to distract me while you did your real job?"

"Of course not. I believe in those tours."

"Then, why won't you stand by them?" he roared.

"What am I supposed to do? Defy my boss? Turn down work my company needs? You of all people should understand the sacrifices that go into building a business. Dawsey needs a fighting chance at stability, too." She rubbed at her collarbone, her eyes dropping. "There's no time left. I have to be in Amsterdam next week."

Logan sank back into his seat.

She was leaving.

She was always leaving.

"Bags packed already? Need a lift to the airport, or were you planning to sneak out in the night?"

"Logan."

"Let me guess. You didn't get a chance to talk to Marc about working from here."

Her eyes shuttered. The silence quaked through him.

"I want to build a life with you, but you make all your plans, all your decisions, alone. Were you going to ask him? Or was that just a line to appease me, too?"

"I would never do that."

"How do I know? You give me table scraps of yourself, Addie. You keep everything else to yourself." All the yearning in the world couldn't change that. "I'm not chasing you around the globe."

Someone else could play Where in the World Is Addie Macrae? but he wouldn't put himself through it.

"You said you wouldn't change your mind about us," she reminded him, seal eyes brimming.

"About a fantasy of what we were. But that was clearly never real."

"It *is* real." Her breath came in short gasps.

Logan shook his head and gripped his hair until the pain stung. "It's not real if you won't share your life with me. Christ, Addie, you've fought this the entire time. Things are always on your terms. I've walked on eggshells, unable to tell you how I feel because you bolt at the first sign of real emotion. You have people in your life who want a relationship with you but you're too afraid to let yourself feel anything. You think this life is freedom—this constant traveling, never connecting—but it's a fortress. And it's of your own doing. You're no different from your dad."

Addie gasped and pulled back. "How dare you."

"Tell me I'm wrong. You got hurt so you shut people out. I try and try to prove to you that I will stand by you, to show you how much I care, but you shut me out, too. I'm done. I can't spend another day trying to force you to be someone you're not." He had to get out of there before he imploded. "I hope you find what you're looking for."

Grabbing his jacket, he smashed down the stairs, leaving Addie slumped in a chair, her hand over her mouth.

He closed his heart to her.

The street was empty and drizzly. Logan shoved his hands in his pockets and wandered aimlessly in the cold. He couldn't go to his flat where his sheets smelled like flowers. He couldn't even go to the shore. The Firth would only remind him of the plunge they'd taken where Addie stuck a toe in the water and he misjudged and threw himself into the sea.

Maybe that was an idea.

41

The steaming shower only exacerbated the balloons under Addie's eyes, heavy from holding in tears. And the lavender soap did nothing to soothe her—she couldn't even smell it through her stuffed-up nose. She tied her wet hair into a topknot and slapped on undereye masks before heading to the kitchen.

Jack's eyes widened in terror as she thundered into the room. His mouth opened, but she was having none of it.

She held up a hand to stop any conversation. "Don't even look at me." If he asked if she was okay, she'd start crying. And if he told her she looked like shit, she'd cry, too. And she wasn't crying anymore. She'd gotten it all out of her system.

Addie swiped an entire bottle of whisky from the counter and grabbed a flowery teacup and a bag of Pink Panther Wafers that didn't belong to her before slamming the cabinet door. Jack threw his hands up in self-defense, not saying a word, as she stormed back to her room.

She poured herself a cupful of whisky, taking an extra swig in the process, and set the teacup on her nightstand. The scent of pine, infused into her blankets, wafted to her—thankfully before she made the perilous mistake of climbing into her bed and wrapping herself up in Logan's smell. Holding her breath, she balled up the comforter and flung it into the corner of the room.

Her mom's black-and-white plaid blanket wasn't up to combating the chill of the Scottish night—or the desert for that matter—but the whisky would take care of that. And hopefully dull the ache in her chest.

Addie turned off all the lights except the small lamp and climbed into bed, pulling the knit blanket up to her armpits and pinning it in place with her chin. It smelled like wool, which only reminded her of those godforsaken sheep she'd nearly crashed into.

They were lucky they weren't meeting her now. She could go *off* on a snooty-ass sheep.

Yanking her computer onto her stomach, she tapped on the mouse pad seven times before it turned on and typed in *Flights to Amsterdam*, stuffing vanilla wafers into her mouth like they were made of air.

She booked the next flight out of Edinburgh, which, unfortunately, didn't leave for another twelve hours. If she wasn't creeped out by airports at night, and if Logan hadn't accused her of sneaking out in the dark, she absolutely would sneak out in the dark. She'd sit in the airport, trying every British candy on the snack wall of the souvenir shop because she was never coming back here.

After saving a copy of her boarding pass, she texted Elyse, whose phone was always on Silent.

Addie: Broken heart. Airplane. 6am. Heart U

Full sentences were too hard.

All that mattered now was finishing her report for Marc. She finalized color-coded spreadsheets, spell-checked the new website, and wrote detailed instructions for everything else she could think of.

Addie couldn't go back to The Heart's office. The team would have to get by on the training she'd done and iron out the hiccups over Zoom.

Even through the computer screen, seeing Logan would be devastating. But as long as she couldn't smell him, reach out and touch him, or watch him turn from her again, she would manage.

She always did.

By three in the morning, her eyeballs burned, and she rubbed out the grittiness. Only, when she blinked to clear them, she made the mistake of looking up at the picture above the dresser. Her heart clenched. The heather fields. Which made her glance over at the castle with dark corners.

Between that and the lingering smell of pine which Addie had been resolutely ignoring, this place was a shrine to everything she'd lost.

Slamming her laptop shut, she crossed the room and yanked the picture off the wall. The string snagged on the nail, pulling it out and sending it clattering behind the dresser. Addie let out a frustrated growl before getting down on hands and knees to retrieve it.

Her movements swiping for the nail stirred up a commotion on the floor, and she inhaled an entire dust bunny, bumping her head in her haste to retreat.

Coughing, she rubbed at the sore spot and brushed off her arms, blinking back a wave of complete hopelessness at the inability for one single thing to go right.

She absolutely was not going to pieces over this.

The other pictures came off the walls without protest and she stuffed them into the closet. The slamming door probably woke Jack, but it couldn't be helped. They had to go.

She had to go.

Addie pulled her suitcase from under the bed and opened it against the headboard. Grabbing handfuls of clothes, she balled them up, chucking them across the room with all the power and none of the finesse of a professional baseball pitcher. It felt good to be impulsive and violent. Or, as violent as one could be wielding a blouse.

When she was through, the absolute mess towering above Frank's zipping capacity zapped her glorious rage. Cramming it all back inside would be an insurmountable feat, same as fitting all the feelings she'd spilled back inside their original packaging.

Addie dumped the contents on the floor and started the monotonous job of folding. No matter how fast she went, the process took too long.

Sitting on the stuffed suitcase, she finally managed to zip it. The streetlight shone into Addie's room, lighting up the emptiness. Adrift, with nothing to do and nowhere to go, her nausea matched the swirling of the dust mites drifting lazily in the air.

Cleaning. That was exactly what she needed.

Addie found some supplies under the bathroom sink and got to work. None of this was Jack's fault, and the least she could do was clean the flat.

She scrubbed every available surface until her fingers were raw and her body was completely drained of any more bullshit thoughts about Logan and *home*.

While she finished eating a bowl of cereal, Jack came into the kitchen wearing a gray T-shirt and sweatpants, dragging his hands through his unruly hair. He kept his mouth shut and went about making breakfast.

He slid into the chair across from her and slurped spoonfuls of Weetabix, the disgustingly hearty shredded wheat. When he finished chewing, he asked, "Did we have a burglar last night? Your room appears to be utterly cleared out." The look he gave her stung.

"I've had a change of plans." Her voice came out as a croak.

"Heading to Amsterdam this morning. I wanted to clean up for you."

The penetrating stare made Addie shift in her seat, but no amount of big-brother intimidation was going to make her open her mouth and tell him one thing about how Logan Fucking Sutherland had broken her heart.

Jack went to his room, and she thought he might stay there until she left, making this easier on all of them, but he returned and handed her a book. "It's the next one in the series. I haven't finished it, but it looks like you need it more than I do."

Addie half laughed, half sniffled and took the Iain Banks book from him. "That obvious?"

He gave her a guilty smile.

After she called a car, she perched on Frank by the front door. Jack tilted the pillow on the couch and ran his finger along the top of the TV, finding it immaculate, Addie knew. He grunted.

She held every part of her body as stiffly as possible to keep her shit together and not give in to the temptation of telling Jack everything or, worse, asking him to intervene. He'd probably only yell at her for hurting Logan.

Addie's app buzzed announcing her ride, and Jack moved toward her and her bags. She waved him off. "I've got it."

"Don't be ridiculous. I complain about my mum plenty, but you know she raised me right." He took Frank and tipped his chin for her to get moving.

Addie followed him down the stairs, but he turned at the bottom and set her suitcase down, effectively blocking her path.

"Does Logan know you're leaving?"

She'd never once noticed the elaborate light fixture in the atrium with tarnished, intricate silver loops.

"I'll take that as a *no*, then."

Startled by the derision in his voice, Addie's eyes snapped to Jack's. "I don't think he'll be too surprised." Tears blurred out Jack's face, but she could tell his combative stance softened.

He let out a heavy sigh before opening his arms. She shook her head, frantic to get in that car and onto a plane, to get as far away from here as fast as she could.

Jack mumbled, "What a bawbag," under his breath before stepping forward and putting his arms around her. "You two will figure it out."

All the years of practice to keep her emotions inside crumbled in the safety of Jack's hug. His certainty was all the more crushing. Addie burst into heaving sobs, too broken to even be embarrassed. She clung to him, her shoulders shaking and his cotton shirt absorbing the torrential flood of her tears.

"He doesn't want me," she whispered. Jack's arms tightened around her before the horn of the car blared.

She pulled back and wiped her tears with the heel of her hand, like that was all it took to keep back further hysterics.

Jack stared at her for a long moment before he gave her a resigned nod, picked up Frank, and headed into the early morning darkness.

Footsteps caught her attention, and for one wild second, she thought they were Logan's, here to take it all back, to keep her from going.

Elyse walked down the street in pink-striped pajama pants and a wool coat. Addie had to be out of tears by now, but her eyes filled again with a crushing disappointment and a heart-stopping appreciation for her friend.

"Gee whillikers. You can't leave without saying goodbye."

Addie made a gurgling sound as Elyse looped an arm around her neck and pulled her in for a hug. Addie squeezed her back.

"It'll all work out."

Addie nodded, even though she'd never be okay again. Even though she wasn't sure how she could come back here. She was afraid Logan had broken the part of her that could dream.

She got in the car and waved out the back window, watching Jack and Elyse until they faded from sight.

"You've got some class friends who'll see you off so early," the driver commented.

"Yeah, I do." And she was leaving them behind.

The driver wanted to talk, as they always did when it was still dark and you had a foreign accent. Addie shut down as much of the conversation as she could and let the tears track down her face, distorting the buildings passing outside into the miserable gray of a Death Cab for Cutie song.

When she'd left New Mexico all those years ago, sitting on a Greyhound with everything she owned under her feet, she'd expected to feel the buzzing of freedom and possibilities opening up in front of her. Instead, a hollowness had spread through her with every passing mile.

Addie swallowed past the tingly sensation at the back of her throat as the echo of that old ache settled in her chest.

The future rolled out in front of her like a sparse desert.

But she had gotten over it once. She could do it again.

42

Addie never dreaded leaving. The excitement of the next destination always called to her, tugging her forward. On to the next discovery. She never had anything to leave behind.

But panic threaded through her veins the second she stepped foot on the plane, finally slowing somewhere over the North Sea. None too soon, either. She'd been minutes away from using the barf bag to keep from hyperventilating.

She checked into a hotel near her client's office, so tired she couldn't see straight, and popped melatonin. The dark and anonymous room didn't smell like anything besides commercial laundry detergent and the faint trace of cleaning solution. And for that, she was profoundly grateful.

She woke to the late afternoon sun streaking through the unavoidable gap in the hotel curtains, unsettled from fragments of dreams stitched together. Logan at her childhood house. Running her fingers through the lavender. The growth chart in the pantry, and Logan's smile warming her as much as the sun setting over the pink Sandia Mountains.

Shoving the white pillow against her eyes did little to dim the perfect, imaginary images.

Even sleep wasn't an escape. Her mind constantly returned to Logan, to the feel of his body, the way his stormy eyes sought hers. His voice held a promise of the laugh she always turned to for the happiness it brought out in her.

And now it was gone.

Addie's heart beat too quickly, and her lungs weren't taking in oxygen fast enough. Maybe a bit like drowning.

She stared at a modern painting with a lopsided red circle and a golden *X*, completely sick of her own company, ate something from the lobby grab-and-go, and prowled the musty hallways.

By the time the night stretched into Wednesday morning, she'd never been so excited for a project to start.

At least she could throw herself into work and feel like a human again.

She went through the motions of getting ready. Shower. Blow-dry. Curl. Makeup. Suit.

When she stepped into the conference room, she took her first full breath since Edinburgh.

She was in control here. *This* was where she belonged.

Large windows overlooked the canal and bathed the room in a welcoming glow. Not to mention the smiles from around the table.

Amsterdam City Tours was one of Addie's favorite clients. Talk about firm handshakes all around.

"Welcome back, Addie. Glad you could make it," Hanna said, her cheekbones rising in a smile, accentuated by her blond bob.

The previous summer, their small team had been open to Addie's changes, encouraged by her suggestions, and ready to get to work. They gave her their sales data, their cost break-downs, and their competitive analysis the minute she walked in the door. And Hanna was amazing to work with. She really listened to her people. Like Neil, she included Addie in the team. Treated her like she made important contributions to their future—not an outsider imposing their will or a figurehead to blame for unpopular choices.

"Alright, everyone, let's get started." Hanna turned on a projector. Financial statements appeared on the screen and everyone leaned forward. A smile spread across Addie's face.

The numbers were better than she'd hoped. She couldn't wait to get started on the next phase of this project. It was going to be just as exciting as figuring out a direction for The Heart.

Addie encouraged clients to choose which type of traveler they catered to: ones who wanted to see as much of the country as they could, or ones who wanted to immerse themselves in one place to live like a local. The Heart wasn't the only company who managed to pull both together. Amsterdam City Tours could do it, too.

Based on these financials, they did it very well.

The group broke out into side conversations, congratulating each other.

The teams were similar, too. They were included in the decision-making process. Consulted. Cared about.

Addie had simply fallen under the magical spell Neil and Logan cast with their stories and enthusiasm. She only needed a bit of space to remember it wasn't unique to The Heart. There were other teams and businesses like them.

And there would be others in the future.

"Thank you all for your contributions. And thank you, Addie, for joining us in person. We're always happy to see you. Now, let's get to work." Hanna turned the meeting over to Addie, and she stood at the front of the room fielding ideas. She wrote on the board with dry-erase markers, their stinging scent clinging to her fingers, and basked in the collaborative energy of the group.

She put up with the appalling hours and schedule of this profession for the chance to explore the world, but she loved her job for moments like this, too.

Which was a good thing, because it was all she had left.

When the meeting was finished, Hanna shut her leather-bound folio, and the room filled with the sound of closing laptops and shuffling papers. The team filed out, and Hanna shook Addie's hand. "Good to see you again."

"You, too. Hey, do you want to grab a drink tonight?"

Hanna's face pinched. "I'm sorry. I can't. I have a friend's birthday tonight."

Addie's eyes pricked. She'd been counting on a breather, a distraction. Not more alone time with her thoughts. Elyse would have dropped everything to get a drink with Addie.

That wasn't fair. Hanna wasn't Elyse.

"Maybe another time."

It was fine. Addie loved this city.

Outside, the wind bit into her ankles, wrists, and neck. She pulled her jacket tighter around her. Strolling along the canal, she made her way through the city center, as ice-skaters zipped by on the frozen water below. The streets were lit with golden lights.

Edinburgh wasn't the only place that made her all goo-goo eyed. Amsterdam had the same old-world charm. Both small cities had interesting histories and beautiful architecture and… were really fucking cold.

Addie buried her nose in her scarf and stuffed her hands deeper into her pockets, rounding her shoulders against the sudden gust of wind.

Amsterdam shone in the summer. She didn't remember it being quite so gray or the humidity being quite so close to one hundred percent. She stopped in a restaurant for warmth and sustenance and found a table by the window. The waitress asked her something in Dutch.

"Sorry. Do you speak English?"

"Of course. Are you dining alone?"

The pang in her chest annoyed her, and she pushed it away.

"Yes." She was perfectly capable of sitting at a table by herself. She had years of experience.

While she waited for her steak and fries, Addie checked emails on her phone. The prickly awareness that had taken so long to shake returned. Heat washed over the back of her neck and she looked up, catching a woman in a red sweater and graying hair watching her with pity in her eyes. Addie straightened her spine.

She hadn't eaten many meals alone the whole time she'd been in Edinburgh. It was ridiculous to get used to the company in such a short amount of time.

Resentment toward everyone affiliated with The Heart and everyone in the restaurant settled under her sternum. How dare they make her miss them? How dare they make her feel lonely? She didn't get lonely.

She'd made the right choice leaving Edinburgh. She was getting too dependent on everyone there, anyway.

As she sat alone, doubt seeped in through the edges of her convictions. To amp herself up, she tried to picture offices in faraway places, the unique destinations she could see, and the people she'd meet. Except…she'd be passing through their lives. Without meaning to, she pictured empty holidays and a constant, inescapable loneliness.

Her life would be filled with airports and takeout and not enough time off to visit Devika or Elyse. She knew what this life looked like.

Addie took a drink of the well whisky and spit it back in the glass with a grimace. Tears burned her eyes. It was ridiculous to cry over a poor-quality drink. There was probably a law of nature that whisky never tasted as good as it did in Scotland. But it was just another thing she loved that she had to walk away from.

The heart palpitations were back with a missed-the-flight hopelessness that made the world daunting and sometimes insurmountable.

She texted Devika.

Addie: When's your project finished?

Devika: Two weeks-ish?

Addie: Want to visit? My room has two beds.

Her distress call was the equivalent of a camper calling her parents to pick her up on night one, and Addie pressed the heels of her hands into her eyes. She was a grown-up, dammit.

But there was nothing wrong with needing a friend. And she *did* need her friend.

Devika: Yes! Will you still be in Edinburgh?

Addie: Amsterdam

She couldn't string any more words together. Couldn't talk about it.

Boss Babe lit up her phone, and she silenced the call.

Addie: Can't yet.

Devika's text came in a second later.

Devika: I'll be there.

Addie simply needed to get back out there. Get back to exploring. Get back to work.

All this reverse culture shock would wear off eventually.

Everything would go back to how it used to be.

43

The frigid streets of Edinburgh, shrouded in mist and si-lence, became Logan's only refuge. He prowled through the city in the early mornings when he'd given up any hope of sleeping. He almost wished for someone to jump out and knife him, to make the pain inside match something he could grapple with, but no one so much as looked at him sideways.

The deranged laughter must have been inside his head. He'd actually believed in a future with Addie.

Logan spent the day on the beach, even though he'd told himself not to. He sat on the frozen ground, the cold sand spreading between his fingers, knowing what it would do to him and wallowing in it anyway. The words she'd said clanged around and drowned out everything else.

I've never wanted anything more than I want this.

Does your heart feel like mine?

When she'd said them, it felt like a declaration, a promise, and a future.

But now he could see how she'd hedged those words, and

he cursed himself for being so naive. For hearing what he wanted to.

The intimacy of meeting new people on trips, of getting to know their hearts and their openness if only for a few days, must have watered down what he knew of human nature.

People were self-serving. Always.

The universe seemed intent on making sure he didn't forget.

He ran his fingers through the stiff sand, flipping a bottle cap he found over his fingers. Out in the water, a shiny gray dome bobbed at the surface before slipping away with a quiet splash.

A selkie.

Logan's heart slid underwater like the seal, sinking to the bottom. He'd known from the very first moment.

A selkie always returns to the sea.

She leaves her lover crushed for the rest of his days, combing the beaches for any sign of her. What a fool Logan had been to hope she'd stay.

Standing and brushing off his jeans, he moved to a bench on the promenade to empty the sand from his shoes. He wasn't getting anywhere, freezing his arse off, waiting to catch another glimpse of her.

She was gone.

Logan pressed his fingers into his eyes. He needed the steady assurance of an older brother's company. And probably a drink. Logan had picked a fight because he couldn't face the possibility that Addie might leave, but Jack had been right all along. Logan swallowed his pride, grabbing his phone and dialing.

"Hi, ye wee bawbag." Jack's greeting sounded cautious, lacking the usual humor, but maybe that was just Logan.

"Want to go to the pub?"

"Aye. I'll meet you there."

Head bowed against the wind, Logan almost missed the entrance. He pulled open the door, and the familiar smell of stale beer and mildewed carpet hit him. The band set up in the corner, and the tellies were all on this afternoon. He gave a half-hearted wave to the old men gathered round the table where he and Addie had sat that first day.

She was gone, but she was still *everywhere*.

He found Jack at their usual seats at the bar next to the kitchen window, tugging off his coat and scarf in the humid room. Jack pulled Logan in for a quick hug, the unusual affection cushioning the jagged pieces of his shattered heart, a comforting assurance that things would be alright between them. It wasn't the first time Logan had been a dick and Jack forgave him. Or vice versa.

Jack's overaggressive backslap sent Logan staggering—a step in the right direction.

He hung his coat on the hooks under the bar top while Jack stared at one of the many TVs littering the walls. "I ordered for you. This round's on me," Jack said with a wink—Gavin always let them drink for free—and pushed a tumbler across the wooden bar.

Logan took a sip, settling onto the high-backed stool. The comforting sounds of the pub washed over him. This place wasn't trying to be cutting-edge, wasn't always evolving. People loved it the way it was, with sticky menus, and overplayed footie matches, and dusty books skirting the perimeter of the ceiling.

He shifted in his seat to face Jack. "I'm sorry I snapped at you before. I know you were only trying to help," Logan said.

"I think I had that conversation with the wrong person."

Logan studied the live-sports schedule written out in multi-colored chalk. Everything Jack had said was true: he was simply too late with his warning. "No, you were right. I truly believed there was some way to have a future with her." But he couldn't build a life with someone who didn't believe in him, who left him to fend for himself, who would always put work first. He took a tentative breath and tried to regain some composure. To not let Jack see he was suffocating.

"She seemed fairly destroyed when she left. In fact, you owe me nachos for the horrible night's sleep I got with her smashing around and packing at three in the morning. You should see the state of the flat. Mum has nothing on Addie's cleaning abilities."

Logan had pictured her angrily rolling Frank down the uneven pavement, a wheel breaking off and stubbing her toe when she kicked the hardside.

Surely crying always accompanied a midnight cleaning bender for Addie, but that image didn't track with the way things ended. It left too much space in his heart for hope. He scrubbed his hand over his face, trying to wipe away that doubt.

Jack fiddled with his coaster. "She thinks you don't want her, and I don't know if I'm the one to blame for seeding this—"

"That wasn't the problem." Logan wanted her.

"Then, why aren't you on a plane right now?"

"I'd like to wallow in self-pity a while longer, if you don't mind."

Jack quirked an eyebrow, and a swell of anger rose up in Logan. Why was Jack always so intent on *pushing* him?

"Are you listening to anything I'm saying? She cleared out of your flat. She got on an airplane. She's *gone*." Logan yanked his bracelet like loosening the leather could free him from the tightening in his chest, cinching down and cutting off his oxygen supply. "Once again, I pictured a life with people who weren't interested and left me to fail on my own." He always did like learning his lessons the hard way.

Jack winced. "Logan. We didn't leave you to fail—"

"Didn't you?" The whisky burned down Logan's throat. This wasn't a fight he should be starting. He was here to fix things with Jack, not pick at old wounds. But everything *hurt* so much, it clawed to get out by whatever means necessary.

"Alright, let's have this out, then." Jack crossed his arms. "Do you think I don't feel guilty for leaving? Like I let you and Dad down? I do. But I wasn't happy. Can you try to understand? It was preordained that I take over the family business with my brothers. This life was made for you, but I forced myself into it because no one gave me any other choice."

Logan never considered how many of those expectations Jack fought against. The pained look on his face doused the fire burning in Logan's belly.

Jack ran a hand through his hair. "I wanted so badly to feel that exhilaration you two had, to throw myself into guiding, but being on the road made me feel unsettled and distant. Like I was missing out on my life back home every time I stepped on the coach. You don't know how many times I thought, *Something must be wrong with me. Look at them and how much they love this.*"

Back when Addie told Logan how hard it was for her to maintain relationships, he'd understood it was the same for Jack. Logan had forgiven him back then but still held fast to this disappointment. It was time to set all those complications down. "I'm sorry we made you feel that way. I didn't know."

"I couldn't very well blame you on the way out, could I?" Jack's cheeky grin softened any of the sting in his words. "We didn't abandon you. I've always believed you could do this on your own. Look what you've come up with. Heritage tours are brilliant. And you throw Addie's business sense behind this idea—you're going to do great."

Jack didn't know about the change in plan, but his confidence muted the siren song of implementing Addie's official recommendations.

Logan wanted a successful company where he didn't lose sleep over layoffs or severing relationships with people he'd known his whole life. Her tours would give him that. Safety. Predictability. Everything he'd thought he wanted.

But mixed in with this deep sadness over Addie's leaving was grief over losing the chance to take on the heritage tours. They felt too daunting without her here.

He could show up to the office tomorrow, check in with vendors, push the website pages live, take reservations for trips that were special and left a lasting impression on their guests. But knowing the trips could be *more*, knowing he had the chance to give someone a meaningful and personal connection and he chose not to because—what? He was afraid to go it alone?

That wasn't acceptable anymore.

His heart thundered in his ears as if he stood on the edge of a cliff, staring at the icy waters below.

It would be so easy to simply turn back.

And possibly regret it his entire life.

Guiding was in his blood.

Logan wanted to build something his dad would be proud of—to protect what they'd built at all costs.

But he also wanted to build something *he* was proud of. A legacy, all his own.

"You think I can do it?"

Jack clasped Logan's shoulder. "Of course I do. You're passionate and creative and goddamn stubborn enough, that's for sure." He gave Logan a shove that seemed to shake free the fear and betrayal he'd been carrying around since Jack and Reid left.

Hope swelled in Logan's chest like an ocean wave, gathering strength. "Thank you. I think I needed to hear that."

Jack ruffled Logan's hair like he was a kid. "Bawbag."

Logan smoothed it back down with a flat palm, but the glower he sent Jack's way morphed into a smile. "I do want you to be happy." Even if they couldn't work together. Even if he missed working alongside his brothers every day, he hadn't lost them. They were still family.

"Likewise. The faster you can forgive her—and yourself—" Jack tipped his head to catch Logan's eye "—the easier it will get."

Logan rolled his eyes at Jack's impression of their dad. "Are you about done?"

An unrepentant grin tugged at Jack's mouth. "Don't fuck about forever."

He wouldn't. He'd build out the rest of the heritage tours. He'd save The Heart.

Tomorrow.

Tomorrow, he could be inspired and driven and brave. But tonight wasn't for any of those things.

He raised his drink to Jack, clinking the glass so hard it sloshed over, the liquid trickling over Logan's wrist. "Let's get pissed."

44

Bundled into an oatmeal-colored hotel robe, Addie opened the door and launched herself into Devika's arms. "I missed you."

It must have been a lack of sleep making her emotional, but Addie blinked rapidly behind Devika's shoulder, trying to get ahold of herself.

"Babe." Devika pulled back from the rib-crunching hug, pursing her lips while she cupped Addie's face in her hands. "You look like shit."

"That certainly makes me feel better."

Especially when Devika somehow made jet lag look chic with her curly black hair pulled into an effortless half-pony. She dug in her purse and pulled out an oversize bag of Lindt peppermint truffles which were, unsurprisingly, already opened.

"You know what happens when we eat these."

Devika waved a hand through the air to encompass all of Addie. "Warranted."

She looked down at her general dishevelment and couldn't disagree. At least she'd passed the raccoon-eyes stage last week and settled firmly into morose territory. She climbed into the middle of the mattress, sitting cross-legged, while Devika dropped her coat and bag on the second bed.

She tossed Addie a chocolate. "Talk to me."

Who knew what would come out of her mouth if she uttered the name Logan Sutherland. *Better not.*

"Picture this. Stroll-and-sketch tours of Amsterdam, led by a real-life Dutch artist." Addie untwisted the wrapper and popped the entire truffle in her mouth, letting the minty chocolate melt over her tongue.

Devika sank into the squeaky red leather chair in the corner and tipped her head with a thoughtful downturn of her lips. "Would've gone with an edibles tour myself."

Addie couldn't summon the panic at the thought of Marc's reaction. She should be falling back in line. But she didn't have the heart to tell the client to get into canal cruises or dispensary tours. The tourists would remember struggling through customs more than the actual trip if they were literally high the whole time.

Devika's look turned serious as her gaze swung back. "But I don't mean about work, Ads."

Addie pulled in a slow breath through her nose. Her stomach buzzed like it was full of bees. She should have known she couldn't call in an international SOS and expect to avoid the subject. If the roles were reversed, the rules would be the same.

"Tell me about Edinburgh."

"Umm." She worried her bottom lip. Scotland had always been a minefield of dangerous reminders of her mother that Logan had helped her navigate. And along the way, the whisky and castles, the kilt shops on High Street and the purple hue of the sky in the gloaming, had become hopelessly intertwined with Logan's smile, the way his eyes narrowed when she teased him, the feel of his hand as it slipped into hers. And she found she couldn't talk about one without the other. *Goddammit.*

Addie rubbed at her eye like there was an eyelash caught in it. "It's a beautiful country" was all she managed to say.

What she needed to focus on instead was the piercing look in Logan's eyes when he said he couldn't do this anymore. The way he pulled his collar up and hunched his shoulders. The sight of his back turned on her.

The look of pity on Devika's face made Addie cringe, as did the extra chocolate that came flying through the air.

"Have you heard from him?"

"No." Addie rubbed her bottom lip, blinking against those overactive tear ducts. She didn't expect Logan to reach out.

Even though she picked up the phone at least once a day, she hadn't called him, either. "This is your fault, you know. You told me there wasn't enough time for this to get serious."

"What happened?"

"He said I was just like my dad. That I don't connect with anyone. That I push people away."

"Oof."

But Addie had tried. She'd tried so fucking hard to open up to him, to show him parts of her that no one knew. To trust him with her stories. And in the end, it wasn't enough.

He didn't want her.

She puffed out her cheeks and blew out a breath.

"That's attractive."

"Go away, Devika."

She clasped her hands under her chin. "I thought it was *Please, Devika. Come to Amsterdam, Devika. I'm so lonely and sad.*"

Addie pouted. "I am lonely and sad." The two things she'd fought against for the last thirteen years. Look where she'd ended up. She crinkled up a chocolate wrapper and tossed it in the trash.

She was doing everything right: she'd taken a canal cruise, walked through a large quantity of museums, tried new foods, shopped in the boutiques, biked the city. But nothing set off the spark that used to come so easily.

She dropped her head into her hands. "Why isn't it working?" Tears leaked out of her eyes, spilling on the waffle-weave robe and splashing onto the bare skin of her legs.

Devika climbed onto the bed and pulled Addie's head against her shoulder. She snuggled into the embrace like a toddler while Devika smoothed her hair back. "What's not?"

"It's like the wanderlust dried up. I don't want to explore. I don't want to eat airport food. I don't want to live out of hotels with only Frank and Gigi for company." The little pub beckoned to her, and Gemma's kitchen, and the bay window. She couldn't even think the words *Logan's arms*.

Devika let out a heavy breath and shifted away. "Brace yourself, Ads."

Addie wiped her eyes on the robe and pulled the collar up against her cheeks. "You're going to say something mean, aren't you?"

"Not mean. Honest. I travel because it keeps Samir's love alive for me. Doing something we did together honors his memory, and I keep a connection to him. I took a chance on a big love. Even though I didn't get to keep it forever, I'm grateful I didn't wait around. We didn't waste the time we had." Devika rested a hand on Addie's knee. "You, on the other hand, have your big love right in front of your face, and you're running away from it. Because giving someone the power to hurt you is scary." Devika held up her hand when Addie tried to object.

Addie crossed her arms over her middle. It *was* terrifying.

Running was what she did best. Only, she hadn't gotten as far from those old wounds as she'd thought. She yanked on the terry-cloth belt, cinching it tighter like it could help hold her together.

Running wasn't the same as locking yourself away from everyone who cared, but maybe the distance it created was the same.

Addie could admit to herself that she deserved some of the blame for the distance between her and her dad. Brian had pulled away, so she pulled right back, walling herself off. And the reflex had permeated into every other relationship she had, until the only people who truly knew her were Devika and Marc. Addie didn't want to be like that anymore, didn't want to push people away, didn't want to guard her heart.

"I support you in whatever you decide to do. But just know, I think you're fucking it all up right now."

Addie let out a pained laugh. She felt like she might be, too.

45

"Morning, lad." Neil waved him in, and Logan sank into the leather chair under the oversize map of Scotland stuck full of fly-fishing hooks. Pictures and postcards plastered the remaining walls. "Alright?"

Logan shrugged. *Alright* was a stretch. The status quo of surviving was Logan's only aspiration. The joy over the new direction of the business was overshadowed by the Addie-size hole in his heart.

Sometimes, he woke in the night with a fierce longing. Sometimes, an unexpected jab pierced his side when he smelled lavender or black tea. It was hard to escape the memories they'd made.

Three weeks wasn't close to enough time to make peace with her leaving, with the future they wouldn't have.

"Getting by." His dad already knew the whole story from a night sitting in their kitchen talking over six or seven cups of tea. "But feeling hopeful. I want to talk about the future."

Neil moved his chair to the other side of the desk so nothing was between them and gestured for Logan to continue.

"With all these changes going on around me, I've fought to get back to our roots, to what I think of as our legacy. These tours bring our guests joy, and they bring me joy, too. Addie designed something that keeps the heart of them intact." As much as her name felt like a blow to the ribs, he would always be grateful that she'd pushed him to dream. "I've been so afraid to change, so afraid that I would muck this all up, that I hadn't taken the steps to figure out what I want *my* legacy to be."

"I take it you have now?"

"The heritage tours. Can I show you?" Logan had barely slept since she'd gone, but the work was a welcome relief. Spending his nights in the office was a vast improvement over his empty flat, knowing he was working toward turning the company around. He showed Neil the itineraries and the cost spreadsheets, the sales projections and marketing plans.

"I can make this work. I know you haven't always believed I could do this on my own—"

Neil's eyebrows crumpled and the caterpillar bunched up. "I've always had faith in you, lad."

Logan gave him a dubious look. "You hired a consultant I didn't want."

"I built a family business, but you are the only one who inherited my love for the stories and connections we make on those coaches. With Jack and Reid leaving, I worried you'd retreat to what was comfortable, when I knew you had ideas and so much of yourself to give this place. I wanted you to embrace this fully, to have the freedom to start over if that was your aim. And… I didn't want to leave you with an utter mess to clean up alone."

"It was my fault—"

"Things were in a state long before the whisky tours. My reasons for sticking around have been purely selfish. I love this place and the people out there." He gestured to the rest of the office. "I've loved working alongside my sons."

"I assumed you thought I wasn't ready."

"You'll understand this when you're a father, but the instinct to step in, to fight your child's battles for them, it never goes away, no matter how much they've proven they can make their way in the world without you."

Neil's eyes turned misty, and Logan's heart swelled in his chest at the unexpected emotion he saw there—a mix of pride and pain. The conflicting feelings of wanting to keep someone forever but knowing you can't keep them fenced in. He could relate.

Or he was projecting.

"Besides, what's a father's job but to nudge their son every once in a while?" With the way Neil tipped his head, the same as when Logan had scuffed a knee as a child, he got the feeling they were talking about two things at once. "You know as well as anyone how hard it can be to leave the safety of a routine that has become more like a ritual with time. I'm proud of you for taking a chance and finding your own way."

Logan nodded. "I will throw you a very large retirement party, but I'm ready to do this on my own."

A cheeky smile settled over his dad's face. "You know this isn't a one-person job?"

"Yes. Not all on my own. I'd like Elyse to head up operations."

"I can't think of a better replacement."

Neil stood, opening his arms, and Logan stepped into the embrace that had sustained him through every triumph and setback in his life. He didn't need to work with his dad and his brothers to be happy, as much as he'd loved those years together. He only needed their support, and he knew now that he had it.

Back at his desk, Logan wrote a newsletter, an announcement for the changes at The Heart. As much as the excitement of making this official buzzed through him, he couldn't shake the thought that Addie had been supporting him all along. That just like Jack and his dad, he'd failed to understand her intentions.

46

The flyer in the elevator had lured Addie to the hotel
lobby with promises of fresh afternoon cookies, but she would
have come for herring sandwiches. While Addie admired the
work-life balance that saw Amsterdam City Tours empty by five
thirty every day, it meant she spent long stretches of the evenings
in her hotel room. Alone.

The quiet—usually the most important feature of an accommodation—was wearing her down, like that old, oppressive silence returned to pay an unwelcome visit.

With the cookies gone, the upscale lounge cleared out quickly,
and Addie was left with the *click, click, click* of the receptionist's
keyboard and the smell of burnt chocolate. Addie sat in a stiff
leather chair, her computer in her lap, sipping black tea in front
of a sleek gas fireplace.

Usually, she would jump for joy over an empty lobby, but
she was used to Jack shuffling around, the kettle whistling and
video games dinging, or Logan and Elyse bickering, sitting
around the conference-room table late at night.

After all the years spent wandering the globe, loving the adventure but locking away the part of herself that died a little from every night spent alone in a nondescript hotel room, she couldn't lie anymore.

This wasn't what she wanted.

Logan once said, in his deep, lilting brogue, *It's not about how many places you've been but how they make you feel.*

She'd been offended at the time, but now she wished she could tell him she understood. Getting to know a place—learning its secrets and quirks, its history, the shiny facades, and the gloomy and twisting streets—was entirely different than skimming the surface of the high points only to move on before learning anything of substance. Before connecting.

Her heart pinched, missing that connection.

Marc and Devika understood her in a way most people didn't, down to their shared hobbies of collecting passport stamps and tiny shampoo bottles with names like Roam and Float. Their impeccable work ethic pushed her to be better at her job. They were the community she depended on to keep her sane in the shifting world of time-zone roulette.

While she could reach one of them at any hour of the day or night, they weren't family.

They weren't *home.*

Addie's computer dinged with a new message alert. She rubbed her eyes and pulled up her email.

From: Heart of the Highlands Tours
Subject: Come back to Scotland

Addie's heartbeat ricocheted down her arms, into her fingertips, and back.

Her hands shook as she clicked on the message and then the embedded video.

The one she'd taken.

Logan stood in front of the picturesque castle, unapologetically earnest. Steadfast. Hopeful.

It brought Addie right back to that moment—the wind tangling in her hair, the heavy scent of damp air, the leaden hue of the sky, and the feeling that the ridge of the vista cradled her soul because Logan stood next to her.

"Edinburgh has a way of slowly revealing her secrets. She'll captivate your imagination, make you want to uncover the depths of her past."

Addie's breath tripped at the words meant just for her. Not the first moment Logan tried to share his heart, but the first time Addie felt brave enough to reach for it.

The video faded into a montage of pictures. Castles, cairns, Keith the driver with puffed-out cheeks playing the bagpipes. Logan in a kilt in front of the tour bus with a sly smile that threatened to undo all the lovely work of Addie's eye masks. His wide shoulders intent on bursting his sweater seams with a group of starstruck tourists gathered around him.

"You'll fall in love with not just her beauty but also her heart," Logan said, right into the camera. Right to her.

She loved him so much.

Addie hit the Replay button another three times.

Below the video was a note: *I miss you! I'm writing with important news about the future, and I want you to be a part of it!*

Her breathing stopped and started like traffic on the freeway. That future tugged on her heart more than her mom's pictures had and promised a connection that would go on forever.

Join us for heritage tours and discover your place in the fabric of Scotland. Bookings open now!

Her heart came to a screeching stop.

Oh, fuck.

This was a business communication.

Addie covered her eyes with her freezing fingers and practiced a shaky version of yoga breathing. The raging desire for those words to be a sign of Logan's outstretched hand coursed through her like a flash flood.

Memories flickered in her mind. His dimpled grin. The way he cupped her head when he held her tight. His low voice that slowed the rushing world.

There was no convincing herself she'd made the right choice getting on that plane. And no assurance he would forgive her and offer her a place to set down roots a second time.

She was the worst kind of coward.

She should have supported him, shouldn't have made him doubt. Shouldn't have left him to do it alone.

More than that, she should have shared her past, her dreams for the future.

Her heart.

He'd hurt her with his surrender and dismissal, and she'd pretended he failed her. But he'd always wanted all of her, always pushed her to give in to the love between them, and she'd always kept part of herself back.

She *was* like her dad. She'd clung to her resentment, freezing Brian out, and anyone else who tried to get close. Pretended random sparks of connection with the woman in seat 24B or the elderly man on a tour of Athens were enough to sustain her.

Out on the moor, she'd resolved to live fearlessly and then retreated at the first sign of trouble.

She proved she was a flight risk in the moment when staying meant the most.

Logan was taking a big chance on something he loved. Pride blossomed in her chest for his courage. He wasn't the same as the person she'd first met, so staunchly opposed to risk and change.

She wasn't the same, either.

She was stronger and braver. Because of him.

For the chance to love Logan fully, she could risk her heart. It was absolutely worth it.

The clicking sound of high heels on tiled floors snagged Addie's attention, and she glanced around the stark lobby. The hearth at the center was supposed to look fancy and a bit aspirational—to inspire the same feeling in weary travelers—but in reality, it was devoid of love or community or family.

What the hell was she still doing here?

Addie grabbed her phone and called Marc, reciting the words *I want to work out of Edinburgh* like a mantra.

"I was just going to call you. Art tours? I feel like I'm living *Groundhog Day* over here."

She pressed her fingertips against the cold brass upholstery tacks on the arm of the leather chair, steeling herself. It was about time for her to stick up for the things that mattered. "This company has ties to local galleries and the Dutch art community. They're excited, and I think it's the best solution for them—"

"You're the consultant. You tell them the tours to run to turn a profit. I need to be able to trust you."

Addie swallowed against the dryness in her throat, at the disappointment in Marc's voice, but seeking his approval was no longer her highest priority.

She wanted to build this business with Marc and Devika, but she didn't want to *be* like them anymore. Untethered and focused on work, on the bottom line, on the quick flip, to the detriment of everything else.

If there was no space for her here, she could find something new. They would always be in her life. She knew that now. "I've done the research. With the right targeted marketing, there absolutely is demand for this. Not everyone who visits Amsterdam wants to go to the Red Light District."

Providing custom work on a short timeline wasn't impossible. So many companies already knew exactly what would be successful and fulfilling. They just needed a little encouragement to embrace it—and a dash of Addie's experience with market research and tour development.

"We've worked together for a long time, Marc. I respect you, but I need you to be on *my* team, too. You undercut my expertise and my client relationships when you go behind my back."

Marc let out a thoughtful sigh. "I'm sorry I talked to Neil before you did. That wasn't right."

"When you hired me, you said I'd have a seat at the table. Was that lip service?"

"No, of course not. I'm honored to have you on my team. I've always said that."

"Then trust me to make the right choices for our clients. If they have connections to their community and unique experiences to share, let me build out custom tours. Sometimes we won't have a portfolio to show prospective clients the carbon copy we can build for them, but there are people out there looking for wonder, for extraordinary encounters to check off their bucket list. I want to be a part of the businesses steeped in knowledge and tradition, who invite people to explore their slice of the world and leave with their hearts changed for the better."

She knew firsthand how profound it could be.

When Marc didn't immediately respond, she pushed on to the thing that mattered most. "And I want to work out of Edinburgh."

Hopefully she wasn't too late.

47

Logan found Elyse in the kitchen while she waited for the kettle to boil. She poured hot water and splashed in enough milk for Santa to have with his cookies.

"Can you even taste the tea?" he asked.

Elyse narrowed her eyes.

It was exactly how Addie drank hers. Which was a ridiculous thought, because Elyse was the one who'd converted her. Logan dragged a hand over his face.

Elyse tossed the tea bag in the bin and made to leave when Big Mac crested the stairs.

"Bide a second," Logan said.

She turned to see where Logan was looking, and a mischievous expression crossed her face. He couldn't fight his answering grin.

That felt like a nice change.

Jack and Reid had always brought a lighthearted cheerfulness to the office with their jokes and pranks. But Logan and Elyse had an entire history of shenanigans at their disposal.

They could bring levity to the office, too.

And new ideas.

And success.

They stood shoulder to shoulder at the entrance of the kitchen as Big Mac deposited his grimy bag on the floor and rolled out his chair. In the middle of his movement to sit down, he braced his hands on the desk and the entire thing collapsed. The pine top took a nose dive to the ground while the legs clattered to the floor.

Pens, Rubik's Cubes, clips, papers, and a full-size umbrella flooded into Brandon's space but for a few papers sifting through the air, graceful counterparts to the crash.

Big Mac nearly fell over in alarm. "The fuck?"

Elyse whispered, "Should we call this one the House of Cards?"

Logan laughed through the tightness in his chest. If that wasn't the best description of his life, he didn't know what was. With Addie gone, the entire farce crumbled. But he was rebuilding from the foundation. Slowly but surely.

He grabbed a shoebox-shaped ice cube from the freezer and brought it to Big Mac like he was bestowing a trophy. "We must have missed something when we built your desk. I found this in the freezer."

Elyse stood beside him, grinning at the frozen nuts and bolts suspended in the ice. "Don't microwave it, you ken. It's got metal in there."

Big Mac's ruddy face split into a grin as he pointed *I'm watching you* fingers at Elyse and clapped Logan on the back. "Cheeky bastard. Better watch yourself." He faked Logan out with a pretend gut punch.

As the laughter in the office faded away, Elyse nudged Logan's arm with her elbow. "I can feel the hope in the air, can't you?"

"Aye." The prank helped take the gloom out of the days. Helped Logan feel like himself again. More importantly, it helped him feel connected to the people who had bought into the vision he had for The Heart.

Logan took a back-slapping victory lap of the office, before settling down to work. Big Mac sat on the floor where his desk used to be as if he planned to spend the day watching ice melt.

Logan didn't have that luxury. New requests had been flying in faster than they could keep up with.

He kept his eyes resolutely off Addie's forgotten fern on the other side of his desk. The fern he and Elyse kept watering in an unspoken agreement to keep it there for Addie…just in case.

He logged into the reservation system and started at the top. On the first reservation, the guest had selected the Clan Sutherland Tour, the one he felt most comfortable leading. The comments section of the request was near to bursting. He made a note to add a character limit to the box, even though he loved customizing the tours based on clients' interests. Just not *all* their interests.

Looking for adventure and romance.

Obsessed with castles and heard Carbisdale is worth it for the White Lady alone.

Logan's lips pulled down in thought. Surprising that a tourist would know about the ghost. But he took every opportunity to support Craig and catch up over a dram.

Also interested in Ben Nevis and Corpach.

Logan's heart seized at the memory of holding Addie on the banks of Loch Linnhe, of the moment it all locked into place, when it felt like forever for him.

He scrubbed at his eyes, trying to dislodge the images of her hair blowing in the wind and the way her green eyes had filled with a love for him that hadn't been enough.

Might like to try golfing.

Logan groaned. Thankfully, he hadn't pushed forward with fully custom tours. Clearly, clients could not be responsible for planning their own tours.

Feel like I missed out on Aberdeen last time I was in Scotland.

It would take weeks to cover the distance they suggested. They were dreaming. They should move here if they wanted to explore every inch of the country.

Benromach Distillery.

Logan squashed the little voice reminding him Benromach was Addie's favorite whisky. He dropped his head on the keyboard, the keys pressing into his forehead.

Dammit. He'd been trying to get her out of his head with a distinct lack of success. She'd somehow managed to wind her way into every corner of Scotland. Every time he took a step forward into the light, some reminder pushed him right back.

Special request that the guide wear a kilt.

He groaned and shoved away from his desk. Someone else was going to have to take this project on. He couldn't handle it. Between the outrageous plan and all the memories of Addie rattling around in his brain, he needed to get out of there.

Logan grabbed his coat and gave Elyse a brief wave on the way out. "I'm off for a bit."

"Perfect timing." Her face lit up like the Fringe was coming to town.

Logan shot her a confused look but didn't have the energy to dive into her antics at the moment. He held his breath as he passed the conference room as if he could fend off the memories that way. Taking the stairs two at a time, he pushed open the door and sucked in the cool air, trying to force some calm into his body.

A familiar voice reached him. "Where's the kilt? I specifically requested a kilt."

His heart battered his rib cage in recognition, and he pinched his eyes shut against an overwhelming surge of longing.

It couldn't be her.

His mind was simply oversaturated with sunshine smiles and stolen kisses.

He turned, afraid to look. Afraid not to.

Addie.

48

Logan's heart and feet came to a complete stop. Addie leaned against the side of the blue bus.

A gull flew past, interrupting the still frame of Addie in his oversize Heart of the Highlands hoodie, her seal eyes wide and questioning. Her hair was twisted in a braid, but the curls around her temples fluttered in the cool breeze.

Just like that first day.

Spots littered his vision, and he was afraid he was imagining her—that he'd conjured her simply from wishing so hard.

The magnetic pull between them was stronger than his uncertainty, and he drifted toward her over the glistening pavement. Not trusting himself to go any farther, he stopped just out of reach.

There was only one reason for someone to fly back to Scotland and show up at his door. Hope fluttered in his belly, but he needed to tamp it down. This was Addie. She could just as easily be here on business.

A stopover.

A tingle that was both parts dread and exhilaration crept over his skin. "What are you doing here?"

She moved toward him only to pull herself back.

He still hadn't taken any oxygen into his lungs. Suspended between her words, he needed to know their impact before he could fall one way or the other.

Toying with the sleeve of her hoodie—his hoodie—she said, "I shouldn't have left in the first place."

Logan's heart leaped, and his body strained to touch her, but it wasn't that easy. She *had* left. And she'd put him through hell.

"When you said you didn't want me, I reacted without thinking. I ran—"

He took a step closer. "It was never about not wanting you, lass. Please tell me you know that."

When she didn't immediately answer, when hurt still clung to the corners of her eyes, Logan cupped her face. "I wanted you from that first minute you turned up on my tour—lost and a wee bit late. I haven't changed my mind. Not for a second. The things I said… Christ, I was a complete bawbag. I wish I could take back the way I talked to you."

"I should have supported you."

"It's alright. I landed on my feet." If possible, he would have liked to avoid the past weeks of torture, but he'd made a choice for himself and his future, and he wouldn't take that back.

"I saw the newsletter. I'm proud of you. And it inspired me to ask for what I want." She stepped back with open arms and wide hands. "You're looking at the newest senior partner at Dawsey Travel Consulting."

"Congratulations." He wasn't sure what that meant for her—for them—but she looked happy.

"The best part—new management will let me work from anywhere in the world. I'd really like that to be Edinburgh. Me and Frank here—" she patted her green suitcase "—we're all in, if you'll have us." Her look, that mix of hopeful and scared, pulled him in.

Logan reached for her hand, slipping his fingers between hers. Words piled up in his mouth trying to get out, wanting to say he wanted her, he needed her, he loved her.

But it wasn't that easy. He couldn't enter the I'll-take-a-risk-if-you-do arrangement again. Their intentions had been so murky and left him indefinitely questioning where they stood and how she felt. He wouldn't go through it again.

"Lass, I want that more than anything, but I'm not trying to clip your wings. It's not about where you live, it's about letting me in. You kept so much from me. I want to be a team. I want to understand how you feel. I want to know when your next project starts. So I have to ask… What exactly does that mean to you?"

As much as he wanted her, as much as he might literally disintegrate into the pavement if she walked away again, he couldn't be the man waiting for her in this port. He had to protect the little slice of his life he'd managed to get back since she left.

"Can I tell you a story? It's not one I've told many people."

"You can trust me with it."

She nodded. "In days gone by," her lips tipped up at the edges, teasing him, "a father showed his daughter how to be curious, to notice things other people overlooked, and turned their life into an adventure. Her mother taught her about the stars and the sandhill crane migration and—standing over a garden—that things only grow in the desert with a lot of love. One day, everything that girl knew was gone and she ran, never really knowing if she was running away or toward something better. Either way, the adventure eased the pain, and maybe, without realizing it, it helped keep her father's spirit alive, too."

Hands braced behind her on the bus, Addie rocked on her heels over the edge of the curb. Logan wanted to pull her into his arms.

But he needed her words.

"Years later, that girl got on an airplane like every other time before. And she stepped into an old city that captured her imagination like a lot of cities around the world. But this one was different. Because her mom had told her stories, and her heart recognized this place. And then she met a man." Tears leaked out of Addie's eyes, and she blinked them back. "A man who really wanted her to understand the difference between a fjord and an estuary and looked inexcusably sexy in a kilt." Logan reached for her then, but she held up a hand to stop him.

"We're getting to the good part now." Addie swallowed and took a deep breath and Logan matched her, willing away his impatience, giving her the space she needed. "She met a friend who barged into her life and demanded her secrets—"

"Aye, she does have that way about her." Elyse had done the same to him.

"And a roommate who shared his books." Addie's mouth tipped down into a frown, and her voice cracked, struggling to get out the next words. "And a family who welcomed her for no other reason than their kind hearts."

"And because I was making an absolute fool of myself over you. Come here," Logan said, tugging her into his embrace. She sniffled and burrowed into his arms. Her body melted into his, and he sank into the sensation. He would never push her away again. Couldn't survive her absence from his life.

He tipped his nose into the crook of her neck, breathing in the smell of flowers, the smell of forever, and ran his hand over her hair.

"That's not the end," she said on a hiccup.

"No, I should hope not."

Addie pulled back, giving him a watery smile and wiping away tears with the back of her hand. "I've spun so many stories for myself about what life could look like in every city I visit, I didn't immediately recognize that home for me was in a potato shop and a bay window and a kitchen at Hogmanay."

He stroked Addie's cheek, following the path of her freckles.

"My life stopped when my mom died. And it restarted somewhere on the banks of Loch Ness. It might have even started that time you stepped back to reveal the skyline in the gloaming, and I recognized that feeling of in-between. You brought my heart back to life."

"Lass," he said on a quiet breath.

"I mean it. I wouldn't have been brave enough without you. I know I pushed you away, that I shut people out. I'm sorry I hurt you. Not just by leaving but by keeping my stories to myself. But I was right there, feeling all the same things."

He placed a kiss against her palm before folding it into his and tucking it against his heart.

"You gave me back pieces of my mom and that sense of belonging I've been searching for since I lost it. I will always want to explore new places, but I want to come home when I'm done. And for me, that's not out on the moor or anywhere else she went." Addie skimmed her hands down the lapels of his coat. "It's with you." When she looked back up, her eyes were as wide and alluring as the first time he saw her. "I love you, Logan."

Happiness radiated out of every nerve ending in his body. The words he'd needed to hear for so long filled in the cracks between all the broken pieces of his shattered heart. His forehead bowed down to meet hers and he closed his eyes. With his lips nearly touching hers, he whispered, "I love you, too, lass."

He wrapped his arms around her and lifted her from the ground. He kissed her with eyes open, unable to look away. The needy sounds she made and the way she tugged at his hair to deepen their kiss convinced him she was real. She was here.

She was staying.

After so many false starts and painful hopes, she'd come back to him.

He ran his thumb along her jaw. "That tour you planned… it's going to take a long time to get to all those places."

She smiled against his lips. "I'm counting on it," she said, before her mouth molded against his and her tongue slipped inside.

He wasn't sure how long he held her in the street, but long enough he could barely remember life before that kiss.

What started out sweet slowly turned heated and demanding. He backed her against the blue tour bus and sank his fingers into her soft hair. Despite the chilly wind, his body temperature spiked. Like they should get out of all these clothes.

Addie must have felt it, too, because she grabbed both his hands and pulled back. The smile she gave him could power the bus all the way to Skye.

"Take me home, Logan."

✦ EPILOGUE ✦

1 Year Later...

Addie cracked her eyes open to Logan rummaging around in his nightstand, odds and ends rolling and scraping. His hair fell over his forehead, and the light from the hallway played over the muscles of his bare chest as he slowly searched for something. There was a sight she wanted to wake up to every morning.

Propping herself up on an elbow, she pushed hair out of her face. "Morning."

Logan snapped the drawer shut, and she would have been curious if the smile he gave her wasn't blinding. He sat on the side of the bed and helped her tame her unruly hair, tucking it behind her ears. "You've been sleeping forever," he murmured as he kissed her.

"I'm jet-lagged. It's the middle of the night in Boston."

"It's 5:00 a.m. at the earliest." He trailed his fingers up and down her arm, creating a riot of goose bumps across her skin.

"Exactly," Addie said with wide eyes. At least her blackout curtains fit over Logan's window. "How long have you been up?"

"About an hour."

"Oh, so you're one to talk."

"You tuckered me out, lass." He nuzzled against her shoulder and nipped her neck while she squirmed and giggled. "I have somewhere I want to take you today."

"You can take me any way you'd like." She shot him a sultry look.

"Uh-uh. Go get dressed. You'll spoil the surprise."

She kissed along his jawline. "I thought this *was* the surprise," she said, her words muffled against his shoulder.

"Come on."

"I'm so tired," Addie whined.

"I'll get you a sugary breakfast on the way."

Never one to turn down an éclair, she reluctantly got up, propelled out of bed by Logan slapping her ass. He hurried her through getting ready, hustled her through breakfast, and rushed her to the Royal Mile.

On the way, she spotted a bright red postbox and pulled a postcard from her bag with the Edinburgh skyline that had first captured her heart.

Dad,
In case you're sending out wedding invitations, here's my new address. We'd be honored to be a part of your day.

Heather would've wanted them to heal, to keep living, to surround themselves with people who lit them up. Addie was done shutting people out, done turning down love where it was offered. Maybe they wouldn't be one big happy family down the road, but she wouldn't stand in the way of that possibility. She was okay with small steps in the right direction.

She slipped the card into the slot, her other hand wrapped tightly around Logan's, and basked in the warmth of his smile.

Addie gazed up at Edinburgh Castle towering above the city.

Emerald green reclaimed the land, and full-leaved trees flanked the rise of the hill. "Where's the gondola?"

"That's enough out of you," he scolded and tugged at her hand.

Addie grinned. They'd fallen right back into their easy playfulness. Freer, now that there were no more questions and complications between them. She felt light and happy—all the more noticeable for how miserable she'd been without him.

Logan walked as if he was trying to lose her. Addie took off in front of him, speed walking with her elbows pinned to her sides. She flashed him a grin over her shoulder.

Taking it as a challenge, Logan easily matched her pace. She flung an arm out to smack him. "Seriously, Logan, slow down. No one thinks I'd beat you in a 5K, alright?"

By the time they made it to the entry gate, Addie was sweating, and Logan was buzzing with nervous energy. He couldn't possibly be *this* excited about exploring Edinburgh Castle. Historical, yes, but it was unquestionably touristy.

Logan strained to see the front of the line. He stepped to the side like he was trying to count how many people were in front of them. It was April. They basically had the place to themselves.

"What has you so impatient today? You're not suddenly caring about timetables, are you?"

He scoffed. "I hate queueing."

"Someone should make an app for buying tickets in advance…" She mumbled under her breath before looking up at him. He crossed his arms and ignored her needling. After they got their tickets and headed in, she said, "Come on, tell me all about it, Tour Guide."

"Did you know Edinburgh Castle is one of the oldest fortified structures in all of Europe?"

Addie stopped in her tracks and raised her arms in a *What the hell?* gesture. "Now I'm staying and you're just letting yourself go? That accent is a four out of ten. *Max.*" He wasn't even trying.

His lips tugged up at the corners, but he kept an otherwise straight face. "Och, lass. Edinbrrra is a verra, verra important fortress. I'll call yer attention to her presence on the high vista." He leaned in conspiratorially. "Ye'll be wantin' to see the incoming armies well before they reach ye."

That deep Scottish burr and his eyelashes and his sexy smirk… The butterflies were back in action. "God, it gets me every time." She pushed Logan toward an alcove off the main entrance. All her attention was consumed by the way his eyes darkened as he walked backward, letting her manhandle him.

She pressed him against the stone arc, gripped his jacket, and kissed him like she would never make the mistake of running away again. He kissed her back as if to say he had a lifetime of passion and love in store for her.

He grinned against her lips, but she was more interested in his hand slipping underneath her raincoat, his warm fingers sending chills up her spine.

"Careful. I might get used to kissing you in castles," she said.

"I know a lot of them, if you need any recommendations."

"That's okay. I've got Rick Steves in my bag."

Logan shook his head as his hand cupped the back of her neck. "That mouth on you." He tugged on her hair and proceeded to render her speechless. She wasn't even embarrassed they were making out in the middle of the courtyard of a medieval castle. Nothing was making her let go of this man now that she had him back.

Logan pulled back to smile at her, and she burrowed into his embrace, warmth radiating through her body.

His contented sigh matched her feelings exactly as he nuzzled against her shoulder. "You know, when I first invited you on a tour, I thought, 'I can't take this woman to any castles. I can't trust myself alone with her.'" He placed kisses along her neck.

"You've always had a strong intuition," she said, before his mouth moved to her earlobe, and her eyes rolled back.

"I've never had a near-kiss work me up so much I couldn't sleep," he whispered in her ear.

"I can't relate." She grabbed his lapels like she could shake him down and raised her eyebrows in mock annoyance. "I was dueling a ghost all night and was far too terrified to be thinking about you, except to be raining curses down on your head."

"I regret nothing," he said with a smile. Logan took her hand and led her farther into the castle.

Addie slowed down as they approached the jagged guillotine-like portcullis, but Logan pulled her underneath before she could refuse to go through. Like so many other things, he challenged her to be braver. And it was always worth it.

On the other side, she came to a complete stop and pulled his hand so he'd face her. "Hey, Logan?" She reached up on tiptoes to kiss him gently. "I love you."

"I love you, too, lass." He brushed the hair behind her ear in a lingering caress. "Come on. I have something I want you to see."

He picked up speed, and Addie tripped over the uneven cobblestones, no idea why they were moving so fast. Probably to find where Mary, Queen of Scots, was born or something.

Logan brought her to the rim of the Argyle Battery. "Do you recognize this place?"

She gave him a dubious look. "Seeing as how I've never been here before…no."

He widened his eyes like she should have figured out the punch line by now.

She took in the mottled stone wall, the thin film of moss turning the top layer green, and the blue sliver of the Firth of Forth in the distance. Addie pressed her hand against her chest to keep her heart from busting out. "Wait, is this the place in the last picture?"

Logan nodded, a soft smile on his lips.

She swallowed past the tingly feeling in the back of her throat.

Her eyes went all shimmery as she scanned the area, trying to commit this last place in Heather's pictures to memory. Although, she didn't have to. She could come back here anytime.

Addie released a slow breath and ran her fingertips back and forth along the worn stone the way her mom rubbed her back when she was a child. The city snuggled against the water in the distance, and she took in the unchanging landscape her parents had seen, too.

This place that had been right under her nose all along.

"You said you couldn't figure out where this was."

"I couldn't. I even sent your picture to a few guides, but no one had any guesses. The picture was too washed-out." The image was all the more stunning for the bleached-out sky. Heather's face was so full of love that the rest of the backdrop would have faded anyway. But it made it damn hard to locate where she'd been standing.

"But?" Addie prompted.

"But I was guiding last weekend and trying to get a break from an overperfumed woman, and I tripped over a rock and knocked into the wall. This wall. And that's when I recognized the rocks—"

"Please tell me you know where they were quarried." She was obsessed with every last thing about this amazing man.

"Well, lass, in 1503…" he said with an eye-crinkling smile that melted her heart. It was a great, big puddle on the rampart floor.

She smoothed his hair away from his forehead. She was lucky to know him. And damn lucky he forgave her. And never in a million years could she get so lucky again that he loved her back.

She hadn't needed this last piece of her mom. Addie would have been more than content with what they'd already discovered. But the gesture made her feel cherished. It said he wanted her to have every bit of love he could give her. She would've floated away if Logan wasn't holding on to her.

After a life of wandering, she was finally home.

"Thank you for giving me a piece of my family back."

Logan brushed across her bottom lip with the pad of his thumb before kissing her sweetly. "Go on up there a bit, and I'll take your picture. We have to get the angle right."

She rolled her eyes at him for being so indulgent, but secretly loved that everything Logan did was thoughtful and authentic. Addie turned with a huge smile on her face. "Cheee—"

Logan knelt in front of her, a ring in his hand. Her heart stopped only to batter against her ribs to make up for the pause. Her vision swam, and she blinked to clear it, not wanting to miss a single detail of the picture in front of her.

"You've turned my world upside down since the first minute you barged onto my tour. You've challenged me at every turn and pushed me to do things I wouldn't have done without you. You helped me recapture that spark of curiosity, that yearning for discovery. Go explore the far reaches of the earth. I hope to join you. But when you're done, come home to me, lass." His eyes shone up into hers. "Addison Grace Macrae, will you marry me?"

Her breathing resumed in a gasp, and she sank to her knees in front of Logan, kissing him through the teardrops tracking down her face.

He took her face in his hands, drying her cheeks with his thumbs. "Is that a *yes*?"

Addie nodded with a watery smile. "Yes. Of course."

She kissed him again before he slipped the ring on her finger, both their hands shaking. She tilted the diamond to catch the light and see it sparkle. "It's beautiful." The setting was simple and timeless. Everything she wanted in a ring and love.

"My mum gave it to me. It was her mum's, and she wanted you to have it. She plans to tell you every last detail, I'm sure."

Addie tried to talk, but her voice came out as a croak. Pressing her fingers to her lips, she tried to stop their trembling and swallowed past the lump in her throat. "Really?"

Logan helped her to her feet. "No, I got it in the gift shop while you were in the loo."

She shoved him, but he didn't even budge, instead gathering her up into his arms. "Yes, really. I want you to be a part of my family. And they want you, too."

He hadn't just given her pieces of her family back, he'd given her his, as well. She couldn't ask to belong to more welcoming and loving people. The crisp air was no match for the warmth in her chest.

Logan pulled his camera out of his bag and crouched down. With the angle, the sun behind her would surely wash out the background.

"Alright, I'm ready now." He tilted his head to meet her eyes. "Look at me like you'll love me your whole life through."

★ ★ ★ ★ ★

ACKNOWLEDGMENTS

Kilt Trip is my love letter to Scotland, and if you'll bear with me for a little more gushing, I have another love letter for all the wonderful people I've met on this writing journey. This book wouldn't be what it is without your support and encouragement.

I'm still pinching myself that I get to work with my wonderful agent, Jill Marr. From day one, I have been so grateful that you connected with this story. I've never been prouder than when you told me you cried on a plane because of my characters. You have been the best advocate I could've hoped for and your belief in this story has carried me through.

Thank you to my brilliant editor, Lynn Raposo. You saw straight to the heart of this book and knew exactly how to make it stronger. Thank you for your thoroughness and thoughtfulness and for loving Logan and Addie as much as I do. I am so happy to be working with you.

A massive thank you to the Canary Street Press team: Vanessa Wells for your impeccable attention to detail; Monique Aimee for bringing my characters to life with this gorgeous cover; Alexandra

McCabe, Diane Lavoie, and Ciara Loader for your marketing wisdom and creativy; and Leah Morse and Kamille Carreras Pereira for your enthusiasm and expertise.

Sarah Brenton and Maggie North, please know how much effort it took to refrain from listing your official group chat titles here. I could never do an adequate job describing how important you both are to me. Thank you for reading my messy first drafts, screaming in the margins, loving my characters, and challenging me to dig deeper. I know you will always be there with a combination of wise words, wisecracks, and humor that can pull me from even the darkest places. You make me a better writer, but more importantly, you brighten my life.

Livy Hart, Jessica Joyce, Sarah Adler, Jen Devon, and the Bananas, I am so lucky to call you my friends, to learn from you, to read your early drafts, and to live in the multiverse of your stories.

A huge shout-out to my Pitch Wars community. Amanda Elliot, thank you for choosing this book and helping me reimagine the perfect ending for Addie and Logan. I learned so much from you and will be forever grateful for your friendship, your wisdom, and your limitless patience reminding me not to stress.

Tauri Cox, I truly believe I wouldn't have made it through without our writing sprints, brainstorms, and wine Zoom calls!

Aurora Palit, thank you for always challenging me to show more, for helping me see the big picture when I cannot, and for all the times your humor has bolstered me.

Hannah Olsen, Gabriella Buba, Elle Everhart, Susan Crispell, and Piper Vossy, thank you for grounding me, encouraging me, and being there through all the ups and downs. I'm so lucky to be a part of this community.

Thank you to Becca Allen, Adrian, Ruth, and Suzanne Junered who endured countless hours of stories about fictional people and still wanted to be friends.

To my mom and dad, who have inspired me to build a life and a family like the one they raised me in, full of laughter and love. And to my in-laws. Thank you all for your endless support and faith in me. I couldn't have asked for a more loving family to be a part of.

Kara and Riley, I don't know how I got so lucky to be your mom, but I am thankful every day for the honor. You bring us so much joy. I love you more than the moon and the stars and Jupiter.

Although embarrassing to admit, I chose to study abroad in Scotland primarily in hopes of meeting a modern-day Jamie Fraser. Little did I know, I would meet him (sans Scottish accent) days before I left and marry him five years later. Dan, thank you for always being my biggest supporter, my safe harbor, and an amazingly selfless partner. I love you. I wouldn't want a happily-ever-after with anyone but you.

And to my readers. I wrote this book never knowing if my words would make it into the world. Sharing this story with you has been the greatest gift.